The Dedalus lists, offers
fantasy. It is the genre of
realism, surrealism, the occult, decadence, the grotesque and
the fantastic merge; a European genre especially suited to the
1990s.

Literary fantasy is reflected in every aspect of the Dedalus list,
from contemporary fiction to its classic programme, but above
all in its anthologies. Dedalus began its series of European
literary fantasy anthologies with *British Fantasy: the nineteenth
century* – editor Brian Stableford (1991) and *Austrian Fantasy:
the Meyrink Yers 1890–1930* – editor Mike Mitchell (1992) and
continues the series with *Polish Fantasy* – editor Wiesiek
Powagà and *Portuguese Fantasy* – editors Eugenio Lisboa and
Helder Macedo in 1994 with *French Fantasy* – editor Christine
Donougher; *Belgian Fantasy* – editor Richard Huijing; and
Germany Fantasy: the Romantics and Beyond – editor Maurice
Raraty following in 1995.

In making his selection for *The Dedalus Book of Dutch Fantasy*
Richard Huijing has given a wide definition to what literary
fantasy is so as as to be able to include the most important
Dutch writers of the last hundred years.

The Dedalus Book of Dutch Fantasy

Edited and translated by
Richard Huijing

Dedalus

Supported by the Eastern Arts Board

Dedalus would like to thank The Dutch Translation Fund in Amsterdam and Eastern Arts in Cambridge for their assistance in producing this book.

Published in the UK by Dedalus Ltd, Langford Lodge, St Judith's Lane, Sawtry, Cambs, PE17 5XE

ISBN 0 946626 69 3

Distributed in Australia & New Zealand by Peribo Pty Ltd, 26, Tepko Road, Terrey Hill, N.S.W. 2084

Distributed in Canada by Marginal Distribution, Unit 103, 277, George Street North, Peterborough, Ontario, KJ9 3G9

The Dedalus Book of Dutch Fantasy copyright © Richard Huijing 1993
Translation copyright © Richard Huijing

For copyright of the individual stories see acknowledgement page

Typeset by Datix International Limited, Bungay, Suffolk
Printed in England by Loader Jackson, Arlesey, Beds.

A C.I.P. listing is available on request.

Acknowledgements

With a project as large as this one, many individuals have contributed suggestions, ideas and criticism. They know who they are and I hereby offer them all my heartfelt thanks.

Special thanks must go to George Barrington of Dedalus Ltd, for the trust he placed in me and my work; to Maarten Asscher, Editorial Director of Uitgeverij J.W. Meulenhoff and a very dear friend, whose tremendous efforts on my behalf went way beyond the call of duty and appeared to exceed the bounds of the possible on many occasions; to Eva Cossee of Uitgeverij Contact, Jacques Dohmen of Erven Em. Querido's Uitgeverij, Jos and Franc Knipscheer of Uitgeverij In de Knipscheer, Erik Menkveld of Uitgeverij De Bezige Bij, Wouter van Oorschot of Uitgeverij Van Oorschot and Nans Spieksma of Uitgeverij Nijgh & Van Ditmar, all of whom generously provided me with copious materials from their lists as well as doing me many other kindnesses.

Maurits Verhoeff, that fine literary 'snifferdog', made all the difference many a time with his enthusiasm and, especially, his cheering words and quiet good humour when times were hard and my spirits low. Theo de Groot, IT colleague and fine friend, performed logistical feats bordering on the miraculous, channelling the tidal wave of electronic mail between our two countries. I owe you!

Without the eagle eye of Ron Mooser, my trusty word-for-word checker and researcher of bibliographical data, and of Louise Jakobsen, a fine and sensitive copy editor if ever there was, many a gaff and infelicity would have found its way into print. Any that now remain — and, alas, there always will be some that slip the net — are my responsibility, and mine alone.

Finally, my profound thanks to all the authors and other copyright holders concerned: without your co-operation and generosity this book could never have been.

I should like to thank the following for permission to use copyright material:

Uitgeverij De Bezige Bij: for Jan Arends *Het Ontbijt* (1972);

Remco Campert *De verdwijning van Bertje S.* (1954, 1971); Fritzi Harmsen van Beek *Het Taxivarken* (1968); Frans Kusters *De Volledige Diagnose* (1991); Harry Mulisch *De Versierde Mens* (1975).

Uitgeverij Contact: for Maarten Asscher *Het Geheim van Dr Raoul Sarrazin* (1992).

Uitgeverij J.W. Meulenhoff: for Huub Beurskens *Hoogste Onderscheiding* (1992); J.M.A. Biesheuvel *Brommer op Zee* (1972); Frans Kellendonk *Dood en Leven van Thomas Chatterton* (1983); Arthur van Schendel *De Witte Vrouw* (1936, 1976); Jan Siebelink *Genegenheid* (1978); Jan Wolkers *Gevederde Vrienden* (1959).

Uitgeverij G.A. van Oorschot: for Anton Koolhaas *Balder D. Quorg, spin* (1958).

Uitgeverij Erven Em. Querido: for Belcampo *Uitvaart* (1959); Willem Brakman *Het Evangelie naar Chabot* (1984); Inez van Dullemen *Na de Orkaan* (1983); A.F.Th. van der Heijden *Pompeii Funebri* (1984); Hélène Nolthenius *Omzien als Wapen* (1981); P.F. Thomése *Leviathan* (1991).

Menno Heeresma Esq.: for Marcus Heeresma *Stortplaats* (1984).
Gerard Reve Esq.: for Gerard Reve *Werther Nieland* (1949, 1990).
Mrs Mieke Vestdijk: for Simon Vestdijk Het Stenen Gezicht (1935, 1974).

It has proved impossible properly to identify the copyright holders for one or two of the works included in this volume. Anyone concerned is invited to contact the publishers, Dedalus Ltd., at their offices in Sawtry, Cambridgeshire, with regard to the matter.

List of Contents

THE EDITOR

Richard Huijing is a classical musician, a writer and literary translator, and an IT consultant specialising in multi-tasking operating systems architectures.

His translations include *Parents Worry* and *Collected Poetry* by Gerard Reve, *The Body Mystic* by Frans Kellendonk and *The Laws* by Connie Palmen.

He is currently engaged on editing and translating *The Dedalus Book of Belgian Fantasy* and translating Louis Couperus's *The Chronicles of Small Souls* and *The Tattooed Lorelei* by Jaap Harten.

Introduction

Fancy that . . .

Those words may well cross many a reader's mind on lifting this volume from the shelf for the first time and comparing its girth with the reader's own estimation of the size of the corpus of Dutch literature known to the general book buying public, not only in this country but worldwide as well. It's an everlasting problem for a big language with a comparatively small flock of native speakers: how to make it and its wealth of literature travel beyond national borders and the borders of countries from its colonial past where (variants of) the language are still spoken today. Add to that a prevailing image of the Dutch as a people of sober habit, cleanliness, order and an almost unlimited capacity to speak languages other than their own, and the task of compiling an overview of Dutch literature as a whole, while concentrating on the fantastic within it, would seem to be a task so daunting as to be an almost impossible one. And so it has turned out to be, but for reasons quite different from those I might have expected: such was the wealth of material at my disposal that a second volume of similar size could have been filled with ease without any compromises as regards quality or suitable subject matter. My turn to say: 'Fancy that!' And *fancy* is the word that rules the contents of *The Dedalus Book of Dutch Fantasy*, that old and trusted expression denoting the entire range of products of the imagination in fiction, in Art as a whole, from the weirdly improbable to the macabre, from fairy tales to pipe dreams, from darkest perversion to religious ecstasy: the Dutch literary imagination in as many guises as could be found.

The Netherlands being a small nation as regards its physical size, and having been a trading nation for centuries, it is not surprising that foreign influences, fashions and trends have played a decisive part in the development of Dutch and therefore its fiction too. Add to that a strong scholarly tradition, rooted in ancient universities like Leiden in the North, and Leuven in the Southern Netherlands (now Belgium), where the exchange of views and cultural values were part of general discourse, and it is not difficult to see how the Netherlands, as a hub of European and world trade through the centuries, should by rights have become in similar fashion a hub for world culture, with a rich and vibrant national literature, renowned worldwide.

The fly in the ointment proved to be the predominant influence throughout the Northern Netherlands of Calvinism, a Protestant doctrine not really known for its enthusiasm for Art as a whole and Literature and Drama in particular — what could be worse to the censorious than a form of human endeavour based on freedom of spirit and boundless imagination? — which in many ways has shaped not only its adherents in the country over the ages, but the fabric of Dutch national life and the very language itself. Dogmatic in its approach and condemnatory, both by conviction and inclination, of most of man's natural actions, desires and dispositions, Calvinist morality or elements and residues of it, at the very least, have crept into every nook and cranny of Dutch consciousness and are now part and parcel of 'being Dutch', to such an extent that, at a guess, most Dutch people living in the Netherlands today would not notice their presence in their lives and language, even when pointed out to them. Not long ago, I heard a good Dutch friend of mine — a devout atheist and (in his own words) a 'paid-up member of the damned' — explain his inability to go out one Saturday evening by saying 'Ik moet mezelf nog klaarmaken voor de Zondag' ('I've still got to get myself ready for Sunday'). Questioned about it, he had no real explanation as to what precisely he meant but, even so, it certainly meant *something* to him, enough indeed to put off a good night on the tiles!

Let it be no surprise then that a good number of the fantasies here touch upon and deal with religion, both directly and indirectly. Whereas *The Sacred Butterfly* by Johan Andreas Dèr Mouw treads the floating paths of ecstasy, *The Gospel According to Chabot* by Willem Brakman revisits the crucifixion, taking in trade monopolies, rural courtship and cross dressing *en passant*, while Jacob Israël de Haan's *Concerning the Experiences of Hélénus Marie Golesco* gives an extraordinary and penetrating perspective, from a Jewish background, on Christ, the Devil and true devotion.

As important in Dutch life is the notion of the *burger* and its concomitant *burgerlijkheid* (a notion perhaps best, but oh, so inadequately 'translated' by a cross between 'middle class' and 'petit bourgeois'), frequently portrayed in Dutch literature as the source of much misery, stifling the individual, while at the same time being the butt of derision and scorn. From here it is but a short step to the morbid, the province of Arnold Aletrino in his *In the Dark*, of Jan Hofker in his little gem *Rustler*, a hauntingly economical evocation of a man's last steps to the gallows, and of Marcus Heeresma who, in *Dumping Ground*, succeeds in combining all the sensuality of voyeurism and lust on a garbage tip with incisive criticism of our Western attitudes to the native peoples of South America.

So where's the fun, the fizz, the wit of Dutch fantasy? Whimsy of a high order is at the heart of the two fancies by the classic master of Dutch fiction, Louis Couperus. His *The Daughter of Bluebeard* and *The Son of Don Juan* are splendid examples of his style, his sly humour and his notably 'modern' thoughts on men and particularly women, given the date of their writing: 1915. Darker in hue is the humour of Fritzi Harmsen van Beek in *The Taxi Pig* while, in *Looking back: the Weapon*, Hélène Nolthenius sets the trials of Orpheus in a completely new light, and Huub Beursken's *Highest Honours* shows bullish good humour from the generation of younger writers born in the fifties, an extraordinarily talented and fruitful bunch, a good number of whom I have been fortunate enough to be able to include.

To mention each and every one of the thirty or more authors whose work has been included in this collection would surely be perverse: exploration of the unknown is half the fun, after all. However, I cannot allow myself to conclude this bird's eye view of *The Dedalus Book of Dutch Fantasy* without addressing a very particular, special form of fantasy fiction: the tale in which all is hidden, suggested, where the menace and brooding is implicit rather than explicit, where the perspective slithers about and warps and distorts while the reader's not looking, as it were. To be able to publish just one such tale would already be a pleasure, to be able to include two, one an undisputed masterpiece of Dutch literature as a whole, *Werther Nieland* by Gerard Reve, the other the debut of a young writer of exceptional quality, P.F. Thomése's *Leviathan*, has to be my own, personal highlight in presenting this volume.

Omissions from a collection such as this are inevitable and, alas, unavoidable: space is not inexhaustible, rights cannot always be agreed, demands from one quarter or another enter the realm of fiction concerned and become quite fantastic. To have had to

exclude anything for any such reason is as good a ground for
sadness as any I can think of. The only subjects absent by design
in this collection are clogs, windmills and tulips — cheese, however,
put up a tougher fight than I had bargained for . . .

Richard Huijing   *London, June 1993*

Note

For a general discussion of Literary Fantasy, see the introduction
by Brian Stableford to *The Dedalus Book of British Fantasy*.

For David F., David P., Maureen D. and Mieke M.
Friends beyond compare.

In the Dark

Arnold Aletrino

It has already been almost a fortnight that I have been perpetually in the dark. My eye ailment does not heal. My spirit is becoming ill through all the solitude.

Today, I got up, a painful pressure above my sick eye and a head as heavy as lead, for I had not slept last night.

Now that, as I do every day, I have come into my dark sitting room, I feel, right through the double curtains, that it is cold, wet and miserable outside.

Again and again, the wind howls in gusts through the cracks in the window frames and blows with melancholy tones down the chimney and the flue. With each gust, the rain is driven against the windows with a clatter.

I attempt to rouse my cat to a cheerfulness which I myself lack and I lure her with a scrap of paper crunched into a ball on the end of a string, but she crawls into her basket close to the fire. She is cold and sad, like me.

Whether it is the fault of my irritability, I do not know, but it seems to me as if the reading aloud of the newspaper is interrupted more often than usual by domestic issues.

At last, the reading is finished and I do again what I have done so frequently: I walk back and forth like a bear in his cage, from the wall to the door and back again. Always the same: the wall, the little table, the sofa, the door . . . the door, the sofa, the little table, the wall.

And during this monotonous progress, it is as if the clock ticks clearly: *una ex his, hora mortis, una ex his, hora mortis.*

The portraits on the wall, bored, stare down at me wherever I go: from the wall to the door, from the door to the wall. My own portrait, which was made in my sixteenth year, in particular.

Dozing along to my regular tread, I see how matters will turn out, later on, when my old folks are dead and the entire family has dissolved. Then I will take the portrait and hang it in my study, and when I am dead, it will be sold together with a house coat, a few old books and an easy chair – to a Jew. A few days later, and it will take pride of place on the bridge with an old stove and a few flat-irons, a pillar of mahogany footwarmers[1] and a few paintings by unknown masters, in sight of all and sundry and spattered with mud by passers-by. One rainy day, it will be sold for its frame, and my image, torn to shreds, blown into the canal and across the street.

Or, otherwise, a married brother or sister will keep it and hang it in the living room, but when they, too, are dead, it will be carried up to the loft, out of piety, by nephews and nieces who still have a vague recollection of me. For a while it stands peacefully among packing cases and dirty-linen baskets, next to a rungless ladder and a basket full of old, mouldy shoes. One day, it is soaked from its frame as this has to be used for something else. Afterwards, it then gets lost in a large, dusty portfolio, filled with old drawings, cardboard and papers of no value. One Sunday afternoon, when children are visiting and they do not know what to do any more, they go up to the loft to play, for here there are heaps of old toys and there are airing rods which they can use for gymnastics. When this, too, bores them, they drag out the big portfolio from its quiet corner. I see myself lying flat on the dusty floor. The little children's faces bend over me and I hear them ask: 'Who's that?' And one of the eldest answers: 'A great-uncle of father or mother, I believe, when he was still very young.'

I continue to walk from the wall to the door, from the door to the wall with an even, sleepy tread, for ages at a stretch.

Sometimes I sit staring in a book for a long time, nodding off. When I look up, it surprises me that nothing has changed. Why this should be, I do not know. All is still the same. The cat's toy hangs, motionless as ever, against the leg of the chair, the lamp shade is still as squiffy as ever, my portrait looks just as bored, and the clock ticks the same, continually.

I resume my walk, and wait, and listen to every sounding bell as a sign of someone coming – but in vain.

Gradually it becomes dead quiet in the house. Now and then,

[1] These pieces of furniture amounted to (often ornately carved) wooden boxes, inside of which glowing coal could be stored, the resulting heat rising through holes in the top upon which the feet would be placed to warm. *Tr.*

the silence is disturbed by the slamming of a door or the rattling of a bucket in the kitchen.

The maid begins a melancholy, tremulous song about a seaman or soldier, accompanying herself with the sound of chopping vegetables, the strokes of which sound harsher and duller in turn, according to whether the cleaver strikes the wood or the vegetables.

I walk up and down all the while, listening to the mournful singing and the ticking of the clock, and I wait.

Would no one come today?!

Dreaming because of my regular tread, my thoughts stray into the future and I rebuild castles in the air from the past.

A large room with books, cloaked mysteriously in dusk, a stove that crackles cosily and casts its shine on to the floor, a tea kettle with soft-singing clouds, lulling a tabby cat to sleep who is pondering a cabbalistic problem. The tea-service on the table, upon which clear light-spots shimmer from the soft, subdued lamp light, and over me, in the big circle of light from the lamp a black-locked woman's head that busily bends over needlework but now and again casts up the long-lashed eyelids to regard me with serious, dark eyes.

It is as if suddenly the light of the lamp is intercepted by a vague shadow and I see a bony hand, stripped of its flesh, descend on that black hair. The head falls over backwards, the dark eyes, devoid of sheen, dull, stare into space; the quiet, soft features are wiped out, the colour disappears, the mouth is half opened. The hand stretches out to me, too, and I hear the warning *una ex his* sound more loudly.

I wake from my drowsing with a start; the maid has stopped singing and chopping, the clock ticks more loudly.

For a moment, I stand staring, devoid of thought, in front of a picture on the wall, then for a moment after that in front of the mirror and I walk on again, my identical walk, always awaiting someone's coming.

Again my mind wanders and I see a summer's day, a bourn sleeping quietly between tall reed curtains beneath a burning sun, upon which yellow and white lilies form large islands with their flat, pale-green leaves. A few tall trees on the banks, and in the shade these provide, in the dense, soft grass, I see myself lying down, playing with clover flowers which I try to thread into the seam of her gown while she lies staring into the deep, clear blue of

17

the sky where humming insects now hover motionless in the sun and then swoop about at wild speed. All of this is a long time ago.

Suddenly, it is as if I have been transported to an anatomy theatre where shapes, vague in outline, lie under dirty sheets on black tables. With trembling hand I raise each sheet and, one by one, I see the features, contorted and drab, of those who were with me that day — that one in particular, the one with the wax-pale head bent over the edge at the back, and the long, black hair that hangs down, lustreless, in a tangled mass. I feel that I myself am one of those shapes, dead and cold, and I shudder-crumple because of the warning *una ex his*.

I start because of the cheering and braying of the children in the street who are coming from school. I see them with my mind's eye as they run after their caps which the wind rolls along down the muddy street and I hear the little girls scream in fun and fear when, their skirts stuck flat to their legs, they are being propelled on ahead by a powerful gust of wind.

It must be nigh on four o'clock now.

In my room it is already becoming night, the glimpse of light beneath the curtain is turning from white into grey and from grey into black. I can no longer see anything and I am tired.

The cat who has been lying in her basket all this time, does not feel happy any longer in this nocturnal environment and she seeks my proximity. I go and sit down on a corner of the sofa and listen to the ticking of the clock, and to the wind, howling more powerfully and more mournfully through the cracks in the window frame. The rain drips continually against the window in a monotonous *tic-toc*. The cat jumps on to my lap, rolls herself into a ball, begins to purr and, purring, spins me a yarn about a strange country, warm in colour and sun-glow, a country with strange buildings and statues, silent and mysterious as Fate. She tells of priests in long robes and tall hats, priests who sing strange-sounding canticles in front of a white bull whose mournful lowing is muffled by colourful tapestries embroidered in gold.

Of a river, a broad, great river, now foaming and wild, now muddy and sluggish again like thick oil, a river rolling on between banks covered in tall greenery where ibises thrust their curved beaks into the grubby silt; of lakes where brilliant white flowers softly bob up and down when the clear water is set in motion by a pink-hued flamingo.

The purring grows more mysterious when it tells of a big city

18

which is quiet and gloomy, and where, in dark caverns, stiff, motionless mummies stare with painted gazes into unfathomable darkness and are kept asleep by the rushing flutter of grey bats. It tells of an idol with old eyes that, motionless in a corner, keeps watch over the dimly visible objects and that remained motionless even when she touched its round eye with her soft little paw.

But gradually the purring, too, grows silent. The cat falls asleep and I am left alone, listening to the ticking: *una ex his*, necropolis, *una ex his*, necropolis.

Thus I continue to doze and it is as though, aboard a fast-moving boat, I am being borne along by splashing waves.

Beneath a dark vaulted expanse that hangs low and oppressive, I feel myself to be taken along in a wild rush. Far ahead of me shines a spot of light in which an old skeleton with a leering grin shakes its bony limbs and, full of rage, shakes a woman's head known to me, shakes it to and fro by its long, black hair.

Fast and noiselessly I slip towards it and gradually I feel myself floating away . . .

Then I fall in a deep slumber and I continue to sleep until the lamps are lit and I am called to dine.

Boring and sad, it passes by. I still feel oppressed by the visions of this afternoon. Afterwards, the same silence again, even more gloomy because of the light, half turned down.

I go out to take a walk and to forget my visions.

The fierce gusts of rain have made way for a cold, misty drizzle that falls fine and penetrating. The wind has abated. Slowly, I walk along the muddy streets and loaf about the backstreets because the main thoroughfares are too busy and too full of light.

Black and dirty these old houses are, and the few people I meet look pale like ghosts in the dancing light of the gas lamps that, because of the wet glass, only shine down on a small radius of the street.

On the corner of a square stands a trader with his barrow upon which there are gleaming cheeses, displaying their greasy cut in the ruddy light of a candle enveloped in a piece of old newspaper. With a long knife, glinting blue in the light, he pricks small, hard pieces from a brown-rinded cumin cheese and offers them on the tip of his knife to bystanders. These, mainly women, look thread-bare in their dirty, faded white or purple jackets and their black, ravelled skirts, soiled with mud spatters both fresh and old. Time and again, the trader lets out a raucous cry that dies away in the dark street and lures no buyers, and that still reaches me when I am already so far away that I only see the yellow-red gleam of his lantern. I walk beside a dark, narrow canal. The warehouses standing here and there among the well-kept houses stand out black against the lighted windows surrounding them.

I pause in front of a big house. A slow, plunky little tune with a melancholy three-four time in the left hand is being played on a piano. The hoarse, muffled cry of the shady, winter radish trader who makes his progress, almost invisible, along the water's edge, commending his sombre wares in a sepulchral voice, makes me start. The ting-tonging of the piano and that cry of winter radish reminds me of my youth, of evenings, long gone by, in a spacious room, warm and cosily lit, with grave, old furniture. We children are sitting around the table opposite my mother who reads stories aloud to us from a book. I hear again the tale of the dog who was shot by his master because he was faithful, and I see myself weeping with childish sorrow again, suddenly to change to laughter because of the cries of the winter-radish man which resound gloomily in the hallway through the little open hatch in the door.

I walk on, through the narrow, winding, filthy little alleys and along different, narrow canals. I walk past turbulent, black factories whose chimneys angrily store smoke and flames in the misty air.

I reach a vastly long, broad street with tall houses, old and dilapidated. I meet hardly anyone except, now and again, for small gangs of workmen returning from work who stomp through puddles and mud, talking loudly, suddenly to disappear into a little drinking parlour, the open door of which casts a bright strip of light across the wet paving stones. Mournfully, the smoking paraffin lamps in the little shops light up the gleaming stripes and the black, rotting fascia boards.

I walk down this sad street for a long time before I reach the end. I cross a bridge and sit myself down on a pile of planks at the water's edge, to rest.

The rain has ceased and slowly the mist hanging over the canal disperses.

Repeatedly, the moon emerges from among the clouds that break apart and close again, and all is still, quiet and lacklustre.

Before me, I see the dark water restlessly rattling its black little waves on towards the darkness beyond the city.

When I have been sitting a while I hear a quiet rustling and I see a thin, wet little dog sniffing about in the load of shavings on which I have put my feet. 'What's the matter, little one?' And I pick up the little dog and put it down beside me. It lies down on my coat and I hear a hard, heavy little tail wagging against the planks. The little dog presses itself tightly against me to get warm and, stroking him, I feel his ribs through his skin that hangs limp from the protruding bones. The wagging abates and I hear by the quietening breathing that he is gradually falling asleep, and while I continue to stroke him, involuntarily, I stare ahead of me along the road I have travelled, on the one side, and the great, dark expanse on the other side of the bridge. In the long, gloomy street, a flickering light here and there, I see my life as I have lived it, without variety and without joy. My youth at a great distance, as far away as the factory with its rising flames that disappear into the darkness; from there on not a single bright spot, nothing but monotonous darkness with here and there a shadowy glimpse; and on the other side of the bridge I see my future, darker still than my past and my present, one huge dark expanse, impenetrably black, on to which a pale moon tries to shed some light, in vain.

The water rattles on continually in restless waves and disappears into the black expanse.

I stare at my future for a long time. Timorously, a shaft of light falls through the rending clouds and lights a stretch of the water with a blue-green sheen. It is not large, the part I see lit up — it disappears and comes again.

Suddenly I see an ill-defined shape loom up from the dark and move slowly up and down in the light-green dusk.

Softly bobbing up and down, it remains on the shadowy spot and I see further shapes join it, vague in outline like the first. When I look properly, I recognise those who were with me and who have been gone a long time now.

They disappear and make way for others, more sharply drawn and more clearly recognisable.

I see those who are with me, compliant and motionless, one with calm features, the other with distorted ones. They are dead; along with them, others arise from the dark waters and float across the clear spot, and beyond it they disappear into the black future.

They come from all sides, thronging together, corpse to corpse, pressed closely together — ever more.

Gradually, the spot becomes deserted as before and I am still staring down, motionless as ever, on the water rattling by.

Again something rises up from the dark water towards the

gleaming shine. A head, a single head, the same one I saw today, with the thick, black hair hanging sodden and tangled around the temples and with the long, dark lashes that cast a shadow on the wax-matt cheeks. And suddenly again I see the old, grinning skeleton grasp with his rough claw the big, black shock of hair and shake the head with its pall of suffering, to and fro, in wild fury, so that the eyes are opened and stare at me with a silent, pleading, fear-filled gaze.

I am startled by the dog that begins to whine as I grasp hold of it roughly, and the vision disappears.

Still the water rattles on with its restless black waves. The little dog drops off to sleep once more, and again I stare down on the dark waters. But now the luminous spot has gone and there is nothing but darkness and black around me.

I see myself lying blue and contorted beneath the water where I am sucked into the mud, soiled and battered, and I follow my own corpse that bloats and rises to the surface. It snags on a barge which drags it along over mud and stones; I see how it comes loose and floats along on the current and how, finally, it is fished out by a passing boatman. I see the little yellow cart, pushed along by an indifferent drudge and accompanied by a single police officer; I see how it rolls along past quiet backwaters where everyone moves out of the way, revolted, as it passes, how it continues on its lengthy way one evening and reaches the church-yard.

The rain that slowly has begun to fall shakes me from my reverie. I take shelter tight against the planks and continue to drowse.

I see the churchyard, a sunny, warm corner, green with tall grass sprouting up luxuriantly among which rough thistles and yellow dandelions grow, quietly rained on by the white petals the may is sprinkling down. Warm and clear, the glow of the sun radiates from the crisp blue sky and scorches the leaves of a copper beech casting a deep shadow over this quiet spot. Humming flies dance around it, a few white butterflies sway gently to and fro on a tall ear of grass-seed that, spindly, sticks out above the rest. Repeatedly, a mild wind rustles through the leaves of the surrounding woods and makes the little spots of shade dance and intertwine on the soft, gleaming, green turf. Now and then, a bird perches on the grey tombstones, hops to and fro for a while on the warm stones and disappears among the quiet twigs. The air trembles, straight from the soil up to the deep blue of the heavens above.

The rain falls more heavily. The wind blows more strongly across the dark water.

This has to be the end — and when I get up, for a moment I still feel the warm breath of the little dog which I have startled from its sleep and I see all the visions of that entire day pass before me one more time, the pale head of a woman with the black hair, the dense throng of corpses; and when they have passed, everything dissolves into the same grinning old skeleton who, like today, stretches out his scrawny hand to me.

While I am ready to do that to which everything propels me, while I already feel the scrawny hand with irresistible grip urge me toward the dark pool glugging forth wildly in the direction of the great, black water, whipped up by the wind, while the gloomy cry of the winter-radish man sounds from the opposite side of the water, I suddenly see in the sunny spot of the churchyard a woman, wrinkled with sorrow, who is staring at a raised spot under which I myself am lying, and I recognise in her my mother . . .

I return home, sadder and gloomier than ever, followed by the skinny dog who stays close to me and trots along beside me with a drooping tail.

Breakfast

Jan Arends

It's not just any old day. It's the first of September. What is more, it's Sunday. And Mr Koopman's birthday. The other gentlemen have already been up for many hours. The night-duty assistant began washing at five o'clock this morning. Now, in as far as they are up and about, they are all wearing their Sunday-best suits and have already had their breakfast.

Most of them are sitting in the sunlounge. They're smoking or chewing tobacco. They're quarrelling or looking outside. Not much to see out there. A dusty patch of lawn. A large horse-chestnut that blocks out a lot of light and will be chopped down this winter. A black-tarred fence.

It's September the first, 1968. But Mr Koopman is still asleep. He's seventy-nine years old now. It is true that Mr Koopman is the most difficult gentleman in the home. He's a little senile. But that doesn't alter the fact that he is contrary in general. He's bad at obeying and cannot stay in bed at night. When the other gentlemen are already asleep, he's still scuttling about the ward, turning over ashtrays still standing there and wastepaper baskets. For he's addicted to chewing tobacco and this way he sometimes finds an old chew that has been spat out by one of the other gentlemen. Four, five times of an evening he has to be tucked back in bed again.

'Mind you stay in bed, Mr Koopman. Or else it'll be off to the asylum for you.'

It makes no difference at all.

The moment the ward orderly – who has a further fifty-nine other gentlemen to bother her head about, after all – has gone to a different part of the ward, he gets out of bed again. Such trouble you then have to get the man back in again! And he won't wake up in the morning. Not with sweet words. Not with threats. Perhaps a good clout would help. But no slapping is allowed in this establishment. Barring exceptions, they keep to that here.

But this morning Mr Koopman does not have to wake up early.

It's his birthday. On their birthdays the gentlemen are spoilt. All of them. Mr Koopman too, therefore. And there is no finer day to have your birthday than Sunday! And September the first, to boot. And all of nature is festive. To celebrate summer's farewell. There's dear, sweet sunshine and there's gold in the leaves of the chestnut tree which will be chopped down this winter.

But now it's a quarter past nine already. It really is high time that Mr Koopman woke up. 'I'll lay his table. I'll fetch his breakfast from the kitchen. I'll wake him up. Then he's sure to know it's party time and that it's his birthday. He's not as potty as all that,' gabbles the fat, kindly orderly. She has the habit of talking to herself.

'Then he'll wake up alright. There's an egg with it, too, after all.'

She comes out of the kitchen carrying a large tray with everything on it. Four slices of bread. A slice of ham (not at all thin-cut). Two slices of cheese. A little glass dish of red jam. Oh, yes. Real cherry jam. And REAL butter. Sugar, coffee, milk. An orange on top of all that as well. And the egg, of course.

Solicitously, she sets everything down on the little table, already laid. She walks over to Mr Koopman's bed. He has woken up at last. But he doesn't seem to be quite as good as usual today. He is sitting half-upright in bed and his eyes do look odd. A bit wild. He might be ill. Then he must stay in bed and the entire breakfast thing is off. Then she has laid the table for nothing. And all that work. You often get disappointments with these old folks, you do. Yet, the good old orderly decides to encourage him to leave his bed. There's always something doing with the gentlemen, after all. Of a temporary nature, in the main.

'Come on, out of bed, Dirk. Then I'll get you dressed.'

Mr Koopman's Christian name is Dirk.

The orderly is standing at his bedside now and in a motherly way she pinches the calf of the leg sticking out from underneath the blankets.

She can't have hurt him with that!

But Mr Koopman is making some of those funny noises that aren't human at all, and ones you wouldn't expect from senile gentlemen either. Not squeaking. Not groaning. Not growling. They're creepy.

'I think he's having me on,' the orderly says.

'There's no gratitude in the man. Never been any either.'

And she starts to get angry.

She walks back to the little table.

'If you don't get out of bed now and come and eat, I'll take the lot away again. Then you won't be having a thing. Then I'll tie you down to your bed. Then I'll teach you to stay in bed. Then you won't be getting out all week. Then you won't be allowed to chew your baccy either.'

With senile gents you never can tell what arguments they're susceptible to. And Mr Koopman is highly addicted to his baccy. Now indeed he does get out of bed. There's something not quite right, all the same. Mr Koopman is still quite nimble on his pins. Yet never bouncy. And now he's suddenly making all those little hops. Like a pierrot loosening up his muscles with jumps, and exercising. It doesn't suit his age, and it isn't human at all, for that matter. With a few of those hops he has reached the sunlounge. Now he looks outside with an expression on his face as if everything to be seen in that garden is perfectly new to him.

'Come over here, Dirk,' the orderly calls out. Her voice is tender now. She is truly worried. There's also something the matter with Mr Koopman's pyjamas. They're blue, aren't they? But all of a sudden they seem a bit brownish. A bit hairy, for that matter. The coat of a monkey. The orderly doesn't even want to look at Mr Koopman's feet. Those aren't feet any more. They're paws.

Now the orderly is sure that it's ingratitude, that Mr Koopman's not satisfied with his breakfast. And she is very hurt. It's pure devilment of the old bugger. He has turned round in the sunlounge now. And he looks at the breakfast. But what a mug he's got: enough to give you the willies. Those small, vicious, beady little eyes. That's not the gaze of an old gentleman whose birthday it is. And certainly not when a festive breakfast is standing ready for him. Those old gents are not accustomed to that much, though the home isn't bad either.

That's it. She has taken her decision. She assumes a dignified attitude and wags her index finger. This she only will do when she means it very seriously indeed.

'But I won't have the mickey taken. To bed with you. You'll never get out of it again.' (Her voice has turned shrill and it cracks occasionally.) 'You'll be leaving this place. To an asylum, that's where you'll go. Then you'll be singing a different tune.' And meanwhile, she has walked over to the sunlounge to grab Mr Koopman by the scruff of his neck and put him back in his bed. As a punishment. But it's already too late for this. Mr Koopman has already turned into a monkey. He has already acquired a tail.

With a few big leaps, Mr Koopman disappears through the sunlounge door into the garden. It's surprising to see the way old gentlemen are able to climb trees when they change into monkeys.

In no time, Mr Koopman is sitting on the lowest branch of the chestnut tree. It's still the first of September. A most splendid day indeed. A day for miracles to happen. A day to make people jolly. And Mr Koopman seems to be happy as well. Though it is an odd way of celebrating your birthday. He sits on his branch of the tree and has his tail in his little monkey-fist. He's got a pondering expression in his eyes as if he's very struck and moved by something happening far away and outside of the world. And now his reflectiveness has changed to jollity. He points his finger at the other gentlemen in the sunlounge and roars with laughter. And yet there's nothing extraordinary to be seen about the gentlemen of the home. Certainly not something that's odd or ridiculous.

The good old orderly has burst into tears. There is no one to comfort her. The gentlemen of the home haven't noticed anything of what's going on yet. That is why she has gone and sat down on a chair and she laments into her own lap.

'There's nothing wrong with that damned breakfast is there? There's an egg with it, no less. The other gentlemen don't even get that when it's their birthday. Just jam. But *he* does. Because you want to make him look happy. Because he always looks so disgruntled. Alright. Perhaps the ham is a little bit discoloured. But what do you expect with so many people in just one house. For that's what it is, all said. Just a house. Even if they do call it a home for the elderly. And then that business of our gentlemen's poo, too. It all wafts over the food. It does make for smells, that does. And so the stuff discolours. There's no keeping the ham fresh then.'

Her sorrow acquires an ever more loquacious character.

' 'Cause it stinks here, after all. Standing here out on the doorstep, the smell coming from the letter box already makes me retch. It's a little warehouse. And just one set of facilities and not a scrap of ventilation. But I eat here too, you know, myself. What the gentlemen eat, I eat as well. Alright, the ham's a bit discoloured. But no way has it gone off.'

Meanwhile, the doctor has entered the home. He is a quiet, placid man who is no trouble to others. He is most outstandingly a doctor. He hangs his raincoat (for his wife didn't trust the look of the sky) on the hallstand. A perfectly ordinary raincoat. And yet so decidedly a doctor's coat that now it almost seems as if the doctor himself is hanging on the hallstand with his coat.

He tears off a leaf from the calendar which is still showing August 31. He smiles, a touch nostalgically.

'Ah, yes. Tearing them off. Amputating days from a man's life.' So the doctor has a reflective nature. Good intuition, too. He knows already that there's something not quite right in the home, though, of course, he doesn't know yet that Mr Koopman is sitting in the chestnut tree.

Before he goes on to the ward, he must just wash his hands first, at the basin in the toilet. There's always a clean towel hanging there. For the doctor, specially, to dry his hands once he has washed them. But there's no towel hanging there now.

'That's really annoying,' the doctor says. 'That's negligence. Such small things as these are the ones that prevent a doctor from doing his work properly and which then begin to play a part in decisions about life and death.'

He isn't in such a good mood at all. He had wanted to do a spot of gardening in his little garden, but he had to go to the home because one of the gentlemen had mild symptoms yesterday. So it's not at all such a festive morning for the doctor.

He goes on to the ward. He's almost sure by now that there are things going on there and that nothing will come any more of raking his garden today.

And the orderly is still sitting there lamenting about the breakfast that Dirk hasn't wished to partake of and about the grotty life she really has.

The gentlemen of the home have taken advantage of her slackened attention by making a bit of a party of things, in their own way.

One of the gentlemen has undressed himself completely and is walking naked across the ward in macabre sexual display. Other gents have done naughties on the floor. The stench is such that it gives the doctor a pain in the nose. He quickly walks over to the sunlounge to open the garden door. There! Now some fresh air can come in, at least.

That's how it comes to pass that the doctor sees Mr Koopman sitting in the chestnut tree.

He's unnerved.

*

'Heavens,' he says. 'That's Mr Koopman up in the tree.'

So he's no doctor who'll begin to suffer from delusions because of minor semblances. He's sure not to take Mr Koopman for a monkey even if he does think the old gentleman looks peculiar. And so thin. Eerily thin, in fact.

He will check him over thoroughly tomorrow.

That's as may be. So there's the rub: Mr Koopman is sitting in the tree and that's why the entire home is all of a doodah. Ah, well; the situation is an unusual one. But from a qualified orderly you may demand that she can keep control of uncommon situations, too.

He takes a few steps forward so he can get a good view of Mr Koopman sitting on his branch.

Malevolently, he looks with his fierce, beady little eyes at the doctor.

However, the doctor is used to much in the field of care for the elderly.

In a friendly tone, and very calmly, especially, he says: 'Why not come out of that tree, Mr Koopman. It's your birthday today, after all, isn't it?' (For the doctor knows all those little, everyday things about the gentlemen.) 'I've got a packet of chewing tobacco for you here.'

Quite true, too. He takes out a packet of chewing tobacco from his pocket which he holds up so Mr Koopman can take a good look at it.

Quite a festive little lure, really, for a gentleman who's addicted to chewing tobacco.

But Mr Koopman sticks his little head down, which looks unusually small, and you would say that he was gathering saliva to spit on to the pack.

'Don't do that, Mr Koopman,' says the doctor. 'Don't do that. This tobacco is far too precious for that.'

And he stretches his arm out a little further still to bring the packet somewhat closer to Mr Koopman's attention so the latter can see that it really is good tobacco. Of the brand he likes to chew so much. But Mr Koopman has returned to his previous position. Quite at ease there among the leaves, and by the look of things, not in friendly mood. 'Oh, do come down, Mr Koopman. There's a lovely smell of coffee in the sunlounge. A man of your age doesn't belong in a tree, surely. You ought to know better.'

By and by, the doctor's voice has become a little more severe.

One's approach towards the elderly is a delicate affair. It's of great importance to find the right tone. This prevents sudden bouts of aggression and the suffering that in turn is the consequence of those bouts of aggression.

Meanwhile, the orderly has appeared in the garden with an old broom stick. Her tears have dried. Her face is now set hard with angry decisiveness.

'Might as well go,' she says to the doctor and she tries to push him in the direction of the sunlounge. 'I'll see to this. My patience has run out. D'you hear, Dirk,' she shouts upwards. 'My patience has run out. Finished!' Her anger seems to amuse Mr Koopman highly. He dances up and down on his branch as if possessed, like monkeys can do when they're having fun they would put into words if only they were human beings.

'You rotten, sodding little monkey. You're taking the mickey out of me as well.' And she begins to poke about in the leaves of the tree. But it doesn't touch Dirk. He only goes and sits one branch higher up and his amusement becomes even more mobile.

'Sodding monkey. Get out of that tree.'

The doctor takes the stick away from her.

'That's not the way, Mrs Wolf. Our gentlemen aren't monkeys. Though they ought not to climb in trees, of course. But what d'you expect? Mr Koopman just happens to be slightly senile. Less usual behaviour is to be expected then. But 'slightly senile' doesn't mean to say no longer human. So 'monkey' is quite uncalled for. On the contrary, we must reinforce his still plentifully present humanity yet further. We must bring that to the fore. This really does not include calling him a monkey.'

'Slightly senile,' sneers the good orderly. 'That bloke's as senile as makes no difference. He lets his shit and piss run free like no tomorrow. The biggest crapmonger in the house. Slightly senile. No, that's a good one, that is. And then climb the tree too. Because the ham is a little bit off. Sodding monkey.' All the hullabaloo surrounding Dirk is now beginning to awaken the interest of the other gentlemen as well. In the main, the elderly don't live within the realm of every day. They are too preoccupied with matters of yesterday about which they tell the most incomprehensible things without ever thinking of stopping. But what's happening now is most exceptional. Even the gentlemen of the home notice this. And so the little lawn, hardly blessed with square metres as it is, slowly runs full of old codgers who really shouldn't be outside at all any more on this no longer radiant September Sunday morning. It has gone chillier and there's black ink in the sky, boding rain.

One of the old codgers has begun to remember his long-gone years of boyhood. He has picked up a stone and a nasty sneer has appeared around the toothless hole that is his mouth. His arm is already drawn back, its purpose to take aim. Fortunately, the doctor sees this just in time.

'Don't do that, Mr Willems. No throwing. We're going to tackle this quite differently.'

He draws up his figure and calls out in a voice full of yielding kindheartedness: 'Come on down out of that tree, Mr Koopman, please. You know your chair's in the sunlounge – course you do. That chair's yours by right. You're entitled to it after a life of hard work. You have a cosy home here, you do, together with the other gentlemen, haven't you?'

This seems to fill Dirk with mirth once more. He's sprawled out on his branch and he roars with laughter. Though he makes do with gestures, these convey the insults well, nevertheless. In a calculated mime he brings his paw to his nose, pinches it shut and pulls a very disgusted face. Perhaps Mr Koopman wants to indicate by this that it always stinks so in the home. And he begins to scratch himself at length too. From time to time, he also holds up something as if he wants to look at it as closely as possible in the best light and this could well be a louse or a flea. That's nonsense, of course. Malevolent insinuations – quite preposterous. There are no infestations in the home. The ladies who collectively bear responsibility for proper order in the home watch over this.

'Come out of that tree, Mr Koopman.'

The doctor's voice is a little more severe again. And he's really put out. Gratitude's out of fashion, apparently. All old hat. It is quite simply the duty of society to give proper care to people who, because of their advanced age, are not capable of taking care of themselves. Mr Koopman there on that branch is taking the Michael a bit. It is of course nice that, his senile condition notwithstanding, he develops so much initiative still, but there are indeed limits. Mr Koopman is still quite capable of having a grasp of his own behaviour and knowing what is allowed and what isn't. Small naughtiness is part of things in the home. But this is not just naughty any more.

And yet the doctor decides to leave things at the word naughty, for this is quite current in the home. Highly functional when the gents need to be called to order.

'You're being a little bit naughty, Mr Koopman. You know, don't you, that in that case we have to do things in your own interest which are not pleasant for any of us. You are very naughty if you continue to sit in that tree. And honestly there's no nasty smell in the home. As for creepie-crawlies, that's just plain nonsense. Now you come quickly out of that tree and you'll have a lovely cup of coffee. It's your birthday, after all!'

Now Mr Koopman roars with laughter very exaggeratedly indeed. He lays it on thick, unsavourily so. It's not nice of him to make the doctor's good intentions look so ridiculous. And now he's tapping his fingers against his forehead to make even plainer what's wrong with the doctor.

The good old orderly, meanwhile, has tried to drive the other gentlemen back to the sunlounge.

'Now just you go back inside then. No good will come of Dirk. You wait and see. He'll be off to an asylum.'

But it doesn't do much good. Understandably so, too. It's very nice in the home; that's not the point. But it is very dull, too. And even though old people no longer have such a need for excitement, when the opportunity does present itself to really relish things like in the old days, it's very nice indeed.

So the gents continue to stand around the tree and the orderly ends up picking up the broom stick from the ground again.

'We're not getting anywhere like this,' the doctor says. 'The best thing is for me to ring the proper authorities. Then they can fetch him out of that tree. It would be too dangerous, too, for him to come down under his own steam. He might break a leg, or worse. He's a great age, after all.'

In desperation, the good old orderly begins to poke about in the tree once more. It doesn't help a jot, of course. Dirk doesn't even take any notice of it. He has climbed up one branch higher and makes the craziest gestures to his fellow inhabitants. Dirty gestures too. Ones as if he's got hold of his sex and is masturbating passionately. Then he points at Mrs Wolf, looking exceptionally lewdly as he does so.

The doctor comes back into the garden. Because it has begun to rain lightly, he has put on his coat.

'The fire brigade has been called. The gentlemen are coming as soon as possible.' But the good old orderly shows no joy.

'He can stay in that tree till his death, as far as I'm concerned. Filthy old goat. That man's nothing but trouble. Contrary. Always. Never co-operates when he has to be washed and dressed. Keeps himself rigid, he does. Effing and blinding and wants to bite you on top of it all. If they were all like that! His pestering drives you round the twist. Last week he took a turd from a potty and plastered the stairs with it. Just imagine the work you're left with to get that clean again. And you won't get a char here. Not on their nelly, thank you. They think it's too dirty here. They're far too much a lady for that, nowadays.'

For the umpteenth time, she begins to poke about in the tree, quite out of control. Nerves all frazzled. And talk? All the time!

'D'you hear me, you old scumbag? You're not pestering me into an early grave. Two women he's pestered to their graves. And his five children went without their nosh. Drank like a fish. And work? Not on your life. And now we've got him here, in the home. And now it's suddenly *Mr Koopman* – the skunk. *Mister.* Because he's senile, now he's 'Mister'. Well, up yours matey.'

And it's still raining. Not that hard yet, but it gets you wet even so.

The doctor, who remains a medical man in all circumstances and who keeps watch on health matters, says in a fatherly manner: 'The gentlemen had better go inside. This weather's nasty. Bouts of flu on top of all this and we'd be in an even greater pickle.'

He addresses the old gentleman in the tree once more.

'You're not some stroppy brat, Mr Koopman, are you? The fire brigade will be arriving soon and then you'll be taken from the tree like a naughty child. Mrs Wolf doesn't mean what she says, honest. You're still most welcome in the home. Why not come down quietly. See, you can step on to my shoulder just like so. Then you can't fall and injure yourself.'

For a good while now, Mr Koopman has had a chestnut, still in its shell, in his hand. He looks at it intently. As if that chestnut is connected with problems you can solve by taking a good look at them on a Sunday morning while you're sitting in a tree. From time to time, he casts furtive glances at the doctor as if he, too, is involved in the problem. He seems to have quietened down a bit, the way he's sitting there with that chestnut. Maybe he's got hungry and the prospect of a tasty breakfast tempts him a little more now than when he had just got out of bed.

Moreover, it can no longer be pleasant there in that tree. It's beginning to rain harder and harder. What, in that tree, looks a bit like a monkey's coat is, in the end, a pair of common-or-garden pyjamas. Mr Koopman must be soaked through.

'What's to become of you if you fall ill? You'll have to stay in bed all day then, won't you? People of your age just *are* susceptible. There are certain things you can't do.' The doctor has crouched: too late.

Perhaps it was the case that the problem connected with the chestnut had begun to bore Mr Koopman. And does it not speak of wisdom when we cast problems for which we do not know the solution far away from us? Perhaps, too, the old man in the tree was fed up to the back teeth with the doctor's continual chatter. In any case, he has thrown the chestnut with remarkable force. The doctor has been struck full in the face.

Well now: we are and continue to be human beings. And this applies likewise, to a great degree even, to people who have completed medical school.

Moreover, it hurts when you get one of those green chestnuts with those prickly spines in your face. And that's why it's obvious that the doctor has become a little angry. He's quite pale with rage and his calm control has gone. Quite gone. To top it all, Mr Koopman has burst into peals of laughter again. And the old gentlemen, too, are enjoying themselves visibly. The capacity for *Schadenfreude* is one mankind retains to a very great age.

The angry doctor has picked up the same stone Mr Willems had wanted to throw up in to the branches earlier on.

'You rotten little pipsqueak. You bloody well think you can do anything you please.'

Scientifically directed anger has no great span, and the stone with which the doctor had wished to repay Mr Koopman in his own coin fails even to reach the bottom branch of the tree.

And Mr Koopman does nothing but laugh. It surely is clear that he's just needling them all and taking the mickey out of the lot of them on a grand scale. Yet, the doctor's deed has not been without its effect.

The old codgers who have so little already, for that matter, are quite prepared to add some splendour in their own way to this festive, first September morning. There's no one to stop them, as it happens, for the doctor has angrily left the patch of lawn, and the good old orderly, who never forgets her duty, is in the kitchen making a lunchtime pot of tea.

And so the gentlemen go in search of stones and anything else that can be thrown. The stoning of Mr Koopman commences.

An end comes to this (in fact unworthy) performance when the doctor re-appears on the patch of grass. He's in the company of an older gentleman with a briefcase and spectacles with golden frames. He's a government official who has come to take a look at what actually is going on and what might be done. 'So one of your elderly folk is in that tree,' the official says. 'And how, in fact, did he get into that tree? Using a ladder, I bet.'

The doctor has little taste for providing a detailed report. 'It's irrelevant how Mr Koopman got into that tree. The only thing is to make him come out of it again as soon as possible. You do understand me, I hope. It's really a matter of a human life here. The man could catch a cold and this is frequently fatal at that age. Have you come all on your own?'

A pertinent question indeed. Though the official has a large briefcase on him, it doesn't really look like he's sufficiently equipped to bring Mr Koopman back into the home where he belongs. The official takes a step forward and now he's able to take a really good look in the tree.

'I thought this was about an elderly gentleman. But it's about a monkey. That's a monkey sitting in that tree there. An elderly gentleman hasn't got a tail.'

The doctor, who has regained some of his calm, is really somewhat at a loss with the case.

'Mr Koopman does indeed look a bit upset today, but a monkey? Honestly, Sir. He's no monkey. He's Mr Koopman. I know my own people, surely.'

The official, too, is in a bad mood. He, too, would have liked to have spent this Sunday morning in a more congenial manner. Though, in general, officials have much respect for people who have studied, the doctor now found little understanding and no patient ear at all.

'That's a monkey. It stays a monkey. That's the way I'll have it in my report.'

The doctor makes one more feeble attempt. He says in a confidential tone: 'Mr Koopman's condition has indeed deteriorated somewhat of late. And we will keep a closer eye on him from now on. But don't call him a monkey, please. The elderly find little understanding as it is. We must try to understand, with a little love.'

But the official with the briefcase has become angry. Hardly a flexible man. That much is quite clear. He says: 'You can't fool me. Even if you are a doctor a hundred times over. If you want to keep monkeys that's your business but don't bother the authorities with it and certainly not on a Sunday. If that's Mr Koopman sitting there in that tree then, whatever the case, he belongs in the jungle of Africa, or otherwise in *Artis* zoo. I can't set the fire brigade on to this. They don't come out for such murky little affairs. Good day to you, Mr-doctor-sir.'

And with his briefcase pressed very stiffly to his side, he leaves the lawn. The old codgers, too, have left, one by one. And so the doctor is standing under the tree again now, alone. And it rains and rains. It's pouring.

By and by, the doctor is beginning to feel ridiculous out here in this garden. It's already one o'clock, for that matter, and his wife is waiting with lunch. In the end, he goes into the house. The old folk are sitting in the sunlounge there, guzzling the bread fingers with sugar comfits which the good old orderly has prepared with loving hand. She encourages them to eat.

'Come on, Mr Willems, have another bite.'

But she isn't cheerful at all. She's on the verge of tears, if anything.

'It's perhaps better if we simply left Mr Koopman sitting in that tree, Mrs Wolf,' the doctor says. 'We're doing no good by continuing to concern ourselves with him. He's abusing the attention he's getting a bit. It's often the same with the elderly as with children. You shouldn't hold it against them, for it isn't done consciously. But you shouldn't encourage them in it either.'

'He's not coming back here, all the same,' the good old orderly shouts, quite thrown back into a tizzy again.

But the doctor has disappeared in the meantime.

'I won't have the old sod back here any more,' she says, just like that, to no one in particular. Yet, she walks over to the sunlounge door the doctor has closed behind him. She opens it ajar. Why? Because she's all at sixes and sevens. Then you do things and you don't even know you're doing them. For that matter, she hasn't even cleared away the festive breakfast though she never leaves food standing about normally.

And Mr Koopman on his branch in the chestnut tree? Often you can't really tell with the elderly. Frequently they're just like chickens clucking because they've laid an egg. Only their emotional

36

life is so much richer. They go through more. Disappointments impress their effects more deeply. Mr Koopman sighs. He sighs in a way that has some human quality about it once more. He sits there so sorrily. It's raining so wet. And he's so alone. And it's just as if his brown pyjamas are no longer hairy. They're turning blue again and they no longer give any warmth. And it's only wise for him to come out of the tree at last. He doesn't seem so agile any more either. He only just manages to come down via the trunk. Now he's standing on the patch of grass. An elderly gent in blue pyjamas, in the pouring rain. Walking with difficulty and with his head bowed like a wrongdoer, he enters the sunlounge. The good old orderly sees him alright, but she's busy with one of the other gentlemen. She really hasn't the time right now.

The breakfast looks very withered by now. The slice of ham, already gone off as it was, has now got a very nasty colour indeed. The slices of cheese have dried out and there are unappetising beads of perspiration on them. The bread, too, is in no state to stir the appetite. And there are two of those suspect little curly hairs on the butter.

But Mr Koopman is once again the same greedy gourmand as ever. He doesn't even sit down. He grabs what's there as it comes. Stuffs bread, cheese and spice cake inside, just like that. Licks the jam pot clean. Cleans out the butter pot with his finger. Only the egg. He doesn't eat the egg. He picks it up like a thief does a stolen half-crown. His frozen fingers close around it. He walks over to his bed. Slowly. With a bit of a shuffling gait. And that's how he crawls under the blankets in his soaked through pyjamas. But lying under the blankets, head and all, he presses that egg against his belly. He will hatch it into a new conception. The truth for a new life, the lies of which he has learned to get the measure of in his old one.

The Secret of Dr Raoul Sarrazin

Maarten Asscher

There are islands which, in the course of their history, are continually being disputed over by neighbouring states. First they belong to one country and have its language and governance imposed upon them, and later, after a battle won or the decline of a dynasty, they end up under the hegemony of the other state. Thus they are shoved back and forth like the small change of history. In time, after so many twists of fortune, such an island begins to develop its own, hybrid culture, a bastard tongue sprouted from the languages of its conquerors, an impure style of architecture combining the influence of both. One might think of Greek-Turkish Samos or of Pantelleria with its Moorish as well as Sicilian characteristics.

Italian-French Argentera is such an island, tossed to and fro for centuries between two Mediterranean cultures. Situated in the westernmost part of the Gulf of Genoa, it lies almost exactly on the French-Italian border were one to continue this as an imaginary line from the land out to sea. There is, however, one particular difference between Argentera and other islands that have fallen to rival states by turns. For centuries, Argentera was held to be an island of doom, and neither France nor Italy wished to number it among its territories. France, even now, considers it to be foreign soil and since 1919 refers to it consistently by its Italian name. Italy, in its turn, maintains never to have signed the relevant treaty so that this little speck is invariably indicated as Argentère on Italian maps.

Thus has been the fate of this rocky little island, from the late Middle Ages onwards: an abandoned child between haughty powers. There was a short period of prosperity in the sixteenth century, when Argentère was colonised by the Genoese in the expectation of there being silver to be mined on the island. On the basis of obscure maps and speculative indications, much money was invested at the time in the sinking of mineshafts but a powerful earth-tremor put an end to these attempts – and to more than a hundred and fifty human lives. Argentera is still worth a footnote in Napoleonic literature, for at first there was a plan to banish Bonaparte there. But, as is well known, having learned from the escape from Elba, the choice fell on Saint Helena.

All of this was as yet unknown to me when I first caught sight of the island of Argentera. I was aboard the ship from Marseille to Livorno and sharing an inside cabin, a piece of French bread and a bag of tomatoes with a not very talkative fellow traveller. Neither in the booking office in the French port nor on the ticket had I seen any mention of a port-of-call, so I got up, hesitant and curious, when the ship suddenly could be heard and felt to be about to berth though we couldn't possibly be at our destination yet. Upon my question as to the reason for our delay, my travelling companion growled something unintelligible and so I decided to investigate. Having arrived on the upper deck, I saw that loading and unloading was already in full swing: crates of vegetables, wooden chests, small livestock and even a patient on a stretcher. In the midst of all the activity and the frantic shouting from the ship's railing to the edge of the dock and back, someone managed to tell me that this was the weekly call at Argentera. All other days, the scheduled service between Marseille and Livorno sails past, non-stop, but once a week, in both directions, the ferry calls at the island.

What with all the running about on board I was barely given the opportunity, during our already short stop, to take in the island properly. Thinking back to that first impression, what I particularly see again are those steep, narrow little streets, the yellow-brown houses, the pebbly beach at the beginning of the concrete berthing pier, all of this in the waning light of the Mediterranean evening sun. Perhaps fifty or a hundred houses could be seen; beyond that, Argentera seemed on first acquaintance to be a forgotten, parochial island with more rocks and trees than houses and people. I would therefore never have called this flash visit to mind with special attention or have got to know anything at all about the island, let alone that I would ever have set foot there, had not an unfortunate incident taken place during the hasty loading of goods that had to join us for the trip from Argentera to Livorno.

Our crew were being rushed to such a pitch by the captain, who sought to shorten the delay as much as possible, that on taking in

39

a sack with items of mail, part of the contents fluttered down like white birds on to the water. The command to take in the two gangways had already sounded through the megaphone and the ship's engines were already making the extra revolutions necessary for departure, so there could be no question of suffering further delay for a few letters. The unfortunate mail was taken up mercilessly in the maelstrom of our propeller, while the ship loosed itself from the little port. Among the people getting smaller on the pier there was an older man in a sand-coloured suit who was beside himself with excitement about the slight mishap with the consignment of mail. He had to be calmed down by three others and, by the look of it, they were barely able to prevent him from jumping into the water, fully dressed, in order to rescue the papers, indeed, to prevent the ship from leaving, or so his wild gestures seemed to suggest.

The ship's turning obscured this tableau from my view and I returned to my cabin to continue my evening meal there. Passing the mezzanine deck I stepped aside a moment as a member of the crew wished hurriedly to pass, and the moment I walked on, I saw a letter jammed in the metal mount of a life buoy. The chic white envelope was addressed to the Libreria Maccari in Livorno. During the slipping open of the mailbag this letter must have got stuck halfway through its fall. Doubtless, I would have quite properly handed it in to the crew, or posted it in Livorno myself, were it not that I was intrigued by its sender's name. Pre-printed in splendid, dark-blue little letters, bottom-left, on the cream-white cover, it read: *Bibliotheca Sarrazina, Dr R. Sarrazin*. What, for heaven's sake, did such an island as this want with a scholarly library? This was a question I dearly wished to investigate myself, instead of immediately handing over the possible answer to others.

Alas, the lights were out already in my cabin and, presumably, the food was finished. From the upper bunk, satisfied snoring rang out, in any case. Feeling my way, I rolled on to the bottom berth and, before falling asleep, I felt a moment for the letter in my inner pocket.

As soon as we had gone ashore in the port of Livorno, in the early light, walking along the quayside, I tore open the envelope. At first sight, the contents disappointed me a little and I felt regret that I had been unable to restrain my curiosity. In refined, old-fashioned handwriting endorsed by a flamboyant signature, Dr

Raoul Sarrazin was ordering a dozen geological studies and reference books from Maccari and Company. Except for author's names and the titles of the desired works, the letter contained nothing other than polite phrases, references to terms upon which previous orders had been fulfilled and, finally, a word of thanks in advance for rapid despatch. The remarkable thing, however, was that there were three books among them written by Dr R. Sarrazin himself, and on re-reading the titles I did rediscover my curiosity of the previous day: *Recherches minéralogiques dans la région nord-ouest de la Méditerranée, L'isola di Argentère e la sua importanza nella letteratura Napoleonica* and – especially – *Description de la vie quotidienne en Argentera. Tome XXXVI.* I had never heard of the remaining authors, nor of their just as picturesquely entitled works.

Sitting on a bench in the light of the sun that was getting warmer, I wondered what kind of backwater that minute island would have to be, what with that academic *Bibliotheca Sarrazina*. Was there a librarian sitting there, day in, day out, working on historical studies of his island in the Napoleonic era? And, in the meantime, did he take down the daily events in the village as well? And how, from this badly accessible clump of rock, could he undertake mineralogical research in what he called *la région nord-ouest de la Méditerranée?* In short: I really *had* become curious now, and counted myself lucky that I had opened the letter and, moreover, that I had the opportunity to sort out this affair right to the bottom.

Before commencing my immodest sleuthing, I first went and had breakfast and subsequently, in the mounting heat of morning, I looked for a cheap little hotel. I found the *Albergo al Porto* not far from the docks, a small, tall building that had not been painted for a hundred years but which, from my rickety balcony, did indeed give, only just, – almost miraculously so – a bit of a view on the harbour and the Mediterranean that stretched out beyond it.

A problem occurred when, that afternoon, I asked the proprietress of my *Albergo* the way to the *Calle delle XV Settembre* where, according to the address on the envelope, the Libreria Maccari had to be situated. Everybody was dragged into it – brothers-in-law, neighbours, sisters – but no one appeared to know precisely this street or that bookshop, though some had lived for fifty years – all of fifty years, Sir – in this town. All the names of all the bookshops were read out aloud from the telephone directory but there was none called Maccari. Only the old father-in-law, wakened from his afternoon nap by the clamour, was able to solve my simply-meant question. Despite the clear manner in which the letter had been addressed, Maccari turned out not to be a bookshop at all, and the *Calle delle XV Settembre* was not such a long walk away: the old gentleman would show me the way, no trouble at all.

At the time of writing this continuation to my tale, I'm on Argentera, in the garden room of the *Bibliotheca Sarrazina* where I enjoy the greatest hospitality possible. Before, however, passing on to a description of life here and of this extraordinary institute, I must first explain what has happened in the intervening weeks and in what manner I have, you might say, made Dr Sarrazin's existence my own, or rather Raoul's, as he has permitted me to call him.

Once arrived in the unprepossessing *Calle delle XV Settembre*, having thanked my elderly guide and rung the bell at Maccari & Co., the door was presently opened by the proprietor himself. He was visibly delighted by a possible new customer presenting himself and invited me in with many words and gestures. In my best Italian, I lied that I was a close acquaintance of Dr Sarrazin's and that he had asked me a friend's favour to take back a fresh order for twelve books for his library to Argentère in a fortnight's time. Standing among high piles of magazine-copies and series of, on the face of it, scientific and technical bulletins, Mr Maccari frowned. He said, in all innocence, that he believed that the orders were always delivered freight to Dr Sarrazin, weren't they, and that no other persons were required for this. Dr Sarrazin did pay extra for postage as well as for discretion, after all.

Until that moment, I had not, to be honest, fully realised what the mysteriousness of this consignment of books might mean. Put on the spot a little, I looked round until I managed to answer Mr Maccari, in a fortunate bit of improvisation, that not only had I known my good friend Raoul a long time and had even worked for him a while, but that, moreover, I, in my own name, should like to order a few books of similar kind from the firm as well. This made all further doubt evaporate and it was now possible to settle matters of business apace. I ordered some three additional books, all with my own name as being the author's, for which I wrote the titles down on a note which was slipped attentively towards me across the counter: *Anthologica Poetarum Maritima, Descriptions des îles Franco-Italiennes* and – why not – my *Poésies de Circonstances*.

Mr Maccari was convinced of the importance of the commission and no less of my trustworthiness. Payment was not even due until delivery. After all, it was already exceptionally kind that I had declared myself prepared, as an act of kindness between friends, to advance the invoice value for Raoul, too. We parted most cordially and I hurried from the chill little alley towards the warm afternoon sun.

Except for viewing Livorno and its surroundings, I had just three things to do during the next two weeks. The books, fifteen in all, would have to be collected ere long; I had to book my passage to Argentère and – last but not least – a letter would have to be written to the *Bibliotheca Sarrazina* to announce my coming to the island.

My letter, addressed to *M. le Professeur Dr R. Sarrazin* was, though I say it myself, a rather well thought-out piece of work. I wrote to him that I had learned he was an authority in the field of the history of Argentera and that, apparently, he had written a number of indispensable works on the subject which, however, were hard to obtain on the mainland. I myself was a young poet who, on the basis of a historical interest in 'his' island, was considering devoting a long epic poem to Argentera, a task for which his help and documentation would be of the greatest possible value to me. In short, also given the laborious postal communications and the fact that I now happened to be in the neighbourhood, I dared hope that I might come and visit him by the next ship to arrive after his receiving this letter, to request his hospitality and co-operation for a number of days. At the same time, I would have the opportunity to hand him a package which our common acquaintance Guido Maccari wished to give to me to take along, destined for his renowned *Bibliotheca Sarrazina*, rightly famed in all corners of, et cetera, et cetera, and, please, would he be assured of my sentiments of highest esteem and deepest respect. I wrote the letter in French and sent it by the weekly mail packet in the direction of Marseille. I could not possibly expect a reply for, when in just under a fortnight's time the scheduled service Marseille-Livorno would call at Argentera again to collect his possible reply, I would already be on the ship crossing in the opposite direction on its way to the island. Sarrazin could not refuse my request, therefore; he probably *would* be suspicious, though. And rightly so.

A good week and a half after my first visit, I stood once again in the dark workshop of no. 11, *Calle delle XV Settembre*. Mr

Maccari packed all fifteen books very carefully, my own works separate from the pile destined for Sarrazin. He showed each one to me before it disappeared in wrapping paper, proudly displaying the cover-toolings on the smooth linen and the tinted endpapers. Doing so, he could not stop himself each time from lovingly allowing the hundreds and hundreds of blank pages to fan out between thumb and index finger. He visibly relished his own bookbinding work and I, in my turn, relished the perfectly serious comedy brought to light here, the precise and rapt attention that, craftsman-like, had been given to the execution of nothing but a farce. In other words, I was looking forward to conversation, face to face, with the so-learned librarian who collected these pseudo-books around him like a phantom collection of soulless works.

Next day, I bore the heavy packages as well as my suitcase to the harbour, there to take the ship to Argentère. Once again, I was surprised at the almost complete lack of clear instructions for passengers to Argentère and, moreover, it turned out that, as a non-inhabitant of the island, I would have to pay full passage to Marseille. That official obstruction, however, I gladly endured for my surprise voyage. And I was in an exceptionally light-hearted mood. Mindful of my learned host, I'd had myself fitted out in Livorno with a classic, pale-grey suit. In some way or other, I was sure that the old-fashioned gentleman in the sand-coloured suit I had seen two weeks earlier on the berthing pier of Argentera had been none other than Sarrazin, and I wanted to try to gain his confidence the moment we greeted one another.

My surprise was great, therefore, when upon the ship's arrival in Argentera's little harbour there was no Dr Sarrazin to be seen at all to meet me. Instead, I was awaited by two gendarmes. They declared that they had been given instruction to accompany me to the notary of the island who had been charged with the execution of the last will and testament of their most learned fellow citizen, Dr Sarrazin, who had tragically met his death six days ago now. If I wouldn't mind following the two gentlemen? In order to render this easier, they both took a heavy package of books under an arm and thus – I with the shock of the news still in my heart – the three of us walked in the direction of the village, watched by a group of children who had been standing there waving off the ferry which had already departed again. The blank-paged books for the *Bibliotheca Sarrazina*, all guilt and regret, haunted my head.

*

The notary did not know the secret of Dr Raoul Sarrazin; this, at first, I believed I could read from his almost ageless face. We were sitting in his study on either side of a large, old, clerk's desk, and he spoke continually of the tremendous learnedness of Sarrazin, much lamented by all; of the enormous importance of the *Bibliotheca Sarrazina* he had founded for the knowledge of the political and natural history of Argentera; of the occasionally absentminded yet always affable academician himself who, selflessly, had put his talent, indeed his entire life in service of the historiography of the island and its inhabitants. What had the community been able to set against this in reward? Too little, far too little. True, the library was housed in one of the most beautiful villas on the island – the former town hall which had been made available for the purpose – and the librarian had been the guest of the *Pensione Minatore*, the culinary pride of the island, for his hot meals each day and, lastly, he had received a modest monthly stipend from a legacy purposed to that end, in order to be able to carry out his historical and literary work and to fund the necessary purchases of books. But these were trifles; they paled by comparison with the great worth such a unique man as Sarrazin had had to Argentera, the island where he had lived and worked from his fifth to his eighty-second year. Thus, still, the notary, speaking in solemn tones and leaving no space for any interruption. I should, therefore, he continued, pressing his fingertips together, consider it an exceptional honour that Dr Raoul Sarrazin, born, then and then, in Montpellier, unmarried, last residing at 15, Rue Sarrazin, Argentera, deceased, then and then, ditto; that Dr Raoul Sarrazin, that is, by his last will and testament, drawn up the same day upon which his life was broken off so abruptly, had left all his possessions and privileges to none other than me. Though still burdened with the tragic events of the previous week that had led to all this, it was nevertheless a privilege for the notary to be the first to congratulate me now in my new capacity as the custodian of the *Bibliotheca Sarrazina*.

To say that I was perplexed is to put it mildly. I had been expecting all kinds of things, but not this. I had assumed that Sarrazin would be something of an elderly eccentric, with his library of blanks, and I had not really wished to do him any harm. He would have had those three empty books from me as a present, inscribed with a dedication, if need be, in which I would assure him of my great admiration, and afterwards I would have bid farewell again to the island with its extraordinary chronicler. What exactly

45

had my letter brought about in him? And to what extent was this notary acquainted with everything? Or was the library most definitely a serious place of study and documentation and had I brought a cruel misunderstanding into being? Thus I tormented myself with feverish questions. The ship would only be going in a week's time; I had not a clue as to what was in store for me, and an expectant silence was being maintained on the opposite side of the desk.

A little dumbfounded, I stammered that I felt deeply honoured and filled with gratitude, but that at the same time I regarded the prospective post as probably too elevated an assignment. Without heeding the contents of my response, the notary got up energetically, shook my hand at great length, and handed me a sealed envelope originating from my illustrious predecessor. Repeating good wishes and congratulations, he then saw me out — laden with my packages and luggage, as I was — indicating on parting the wooden house situated two hundred metres further on, to which he solemnly handed me the key. *Bibliotheca Sarrazina, Dr R. Sarrazin,* I read the by now familiar imprint on the envelope, as I walked along.

By now, I have been staying some considerable time already as resident and custodian of the late Dr Raoul Sarrazin's house, filled to the rafters with volumes of books. Everywhere I am treated with the greatest respect as one who is so learned and gifted that he has been singled out to be his successor by the founder of the *Bibliotheca Sarrazina* in person. The circumstance that I was already in situ only a few days after old Sarrazin's tragic death, to take over the responsibilities entrusted to me, has only reinforced everybody's esteem and my immediate succession has, moreover, emphasised once more, so it seems, that the work in the library may in no possible way remain unattended.

The letter from Raoul — as he had signed the epistle in friendship — handed to me across the grave, was of such a directness and lucidity one would almost not expect from an eighty-two-year-old. The tone, too, with which he bids me welcome and gives me a few bits of practical advice is one so remote from the fact that, when writing, he was barely separated by a day from the moment of his death, that I harbour some doubts about the entire tale of his sudden demise. According to the official version, confirmed by several inhabitants upon my enquiry, Sarrazin fell from a rock during a walk, probably in search of rare stones, and plunged into the sea. I, for myself, question whether Sarrazin did indeed die or, for instance, whether he is hiding somewhere, hand in glove with the notary who wields control over the means of the *Bibliotheca Sarrazina*. But what relevance have these insinuations now that I have made life and work here so much my own that a return is barely imaginable any longer? My sole, be it luxurious problem, is absolutely not financial in nature – I live, eat and drink for free, and receive my monthly stipend on top of that – but rather one of having practically nothing to do. The entire *Bibliotheca Sarrazina* – consisting, apart from my living accommodation, of four rooms, all walls filled from floor to ceiling with volumes of books – contains nothing but bound, blank paper. All these imposing volumes, in leather, in linen, with tooled gold-leaf, in octavo or god-knows how finely and variedly executed, are locked away behind sturdy little doors with glass or mesh in front, so no one other than myself ever takes one out.

I walk across the island a lot, which gets explained as being 'scientific investigations'; my conversation is attended to most gravely, and everyone wishes to be on the right side of me, for they know that I am at work on a new volume of the *Description de la vie quotidienne en Argentera*. It is barely possible to obtain a newspaper here, let alone a recent one, so that my supposed descriptions of daily life on the island have authority ahead of events. I generally get up quite late in the morning, have some fruit from the garden belonging to the house, and bread that is set out ready for me. In the afternoons I mainly stay inside, away from the hot sun, and in the evening I will take a short walk and subsequently dine in the only restaurant here, *Pensione Minatore*, where I am given friendly but, in awe of my thoughts, silent service. I will then sit smoking till late in the balmy evenings on the veranda of my house which offers a view out to sea.

Honesty compels me to say that I do leaf through one of my thousands of books at times, homing in on a title which stirs my curiosity. Almost without exception, these are sound volumes of splendour, full of creamy white paper. From time to time there are questions to be answered, too: people who drop by about something, or a tourist, once in a blue moon, who wishes to view the *Bibliotheca Sarrazina*. For a small consideration, I will then show them round and without exception they will be astounded by the temple of learning which this teeny-weeny island appears to house.

At a given moment, I will have to write to Maccari in Livorno to have some new books shipped out. It is expected, of course, that I publish something from time to time. With the first three works I already carried with me at the time of my arrival here – years ago, it can seem to me, now and then – I can make do for a while, though. Last month, my *Poésies de Circonstances* were released in public. In *Pensione Minatore*, the notary presented me with the first (and sole) copy and read out (ostensibly) the personal dedication on the title page: *A mon cher maître, Dr Raoul Sarrazin, le bienfaiteur regretté de notre île d'Argentera*. Upon which the proprietress of the *pensione* burst into tears and general applause ensued. That same evening, the book was solemnly given its place in Room IV of the *Bibliotheca Sarrazina*, Case 9, third shelf from the bottom.

On rare occasions, I have tried to actually write something, a poem or a bit of a diary entry, but from sheer awe I do not feel capable, indeed, not even entitled to put all those white pages surrounding me to the test. What I might say flows away at once, as it were, in this sea of blank paper, a sea from which rises, like a minute protuberance, the secret of Dr Raoul Sarrazin.

Funeral Rites

Belcampo

By two men who did not speak his language but who could clasp his arms in an immovable grip, he was chucked down the stone stairs into the darkness. There he lay and bled. With a booming blow the iron hatch slammed shut above him.

By the reverberation he gleaned that he had been cast into a large space. It could be a hall. He was lying on a stone floor; he could feel damp sand here and there. There was nothing he could see; it seemed pitch dark there. He could hear something. Shuffling sounds now and then, other ones too occasionally, as if a paw was being put down, a body turned over. Breathing, too.

He was not alone there. Animals? Would he be eaten later on? Had they already smelled his blood? His teeth chattered with fear; his knees, too, began to tremble and he no longer had the power to subdue them.

Though he did not know yet whether the end of his life was imminent, his fear was already accompanied by the feeling of complete desolation each dying human being experiences in his last moments of consciousness. No one any longer could do anything for him; all of humanity had turned away from him: he was alone. All his past experience appeared to have been deception. To be betrayed by life itself: this is the bitter end of every man.

Yet, the space he was lying in seemed gradually to clear up a bit; perhaps his eyes, blinded at first by the sudden darkness, were slowly getting used to it. He began to discern something, to distinguish between things in the dark. The pale gleam of limbs, it would seem. Dim movement, here and there. He recognised human forms, mainly lying down, a few sitting up. No, he had not ended up in an animal pit but in a human one. It grew ever clearer. The entire floor of the subterranean hall seemed covered with a curious life form, with a layer of the living.

Slowly, the terrible truth penetrated his tortured brain: here, in this bottom most darkness, the warriors of vanquished peoples were left to their own devices.

No one any longer spoke a word; not even the whispers between two of them could be heard; all were completely cast back upon themselves. Language had ceased to exist. Nothing else remained but resignedly to undergo the decline of the body.

A movement seldom came, and extremely slowly even then; movement had become precious, it took away from the only thing that remained to them and upon which their lifespan depended: their reserves of strength.

He had a number of wounds but there was no point in examining them; nothing could be done about them anyway. Just wait and see whether he would still survive the healing of his wounds. It was turning into a contest.

There was nothing to do except cling to life. Escape was out of the question: that which walled them in was the impenetrable rock of the earth itself. And concerted action could never again go forth from this realm of shades: at best, concerted death would. In the feeble dusk which grew no clearer, he distinctly saw attitudes of dull resignation all around him, of surrender to the waiting, the waiting for nothingness.

He, too, settled himself down as comfortably as possible on the warm rock in such a way as to benefit most of its support, closed his eyes and did the only thing he was still capable of doing and which they all did: in his thoughts he returned to the past, to where his freedom lay. He had a sudden urge to re-experience his entire past life, more clearly, more consciously than the first time, to realise, before the end, an inner flowering of the images of his memory the way a tree, too, wastes its last strength in an uncommon flowering.

Particularly the first part of his life, before the start of the war, was what he would remember at leisure: when they were still happy and had feasts, when the world was still a friendly dwelling place to him. The darkness turned out to help him in this; in the dark he could bring those images clearly to mind, and the silence, too, allowed him to hear the sounds of the past more clearly. This, to all, was the only thing that remained.

He managed to lull himself within his memories to such an extent that, occasionally, he would catch himself out smiling. In this pit that seemed like a blasphemy, its negation. It would only happen when he felt little pain. Each time when, as a result of lying for too long in the same position, his wounds began to smart, his thoughts would stray to the war, to his life as a warrior: they became searing.

Besides the fact that the business of war itself is pervaded with deep suffering, there had moreover been the certain realisation of fighting against a superior force in this case, of having to experience the fall of his tribe. To die without issue is already a double death, but to leave a world behind in which your language is being annihilated is the most bitter thing of all. And not because of an inner decline but because of a foreign power.

What splendid people they were! Full of strength and agility, rich in ingenuity in making use of nature. And their women: so elegant and so stubborn at the same time, as good helpmeets in battle as pleasure grounds of passion in times of peace. No, they had not been brought low by better opponents but by more numerous ones.

And how many tribes such as the one he belonged to had gone this way and were still going? During the transport here he had soon not seen a single fellow tribesman any more. They were being mingled in. As regards those who must die, too, did they still conduct their policy: the extermination of the foreign tongue. Gods were preserved but languages were exterminated: thus was the conqueror's will.

On one occasion it did occur to him that there was still *something* he could do: crawl out of reach of the big stairwell above him. Stairwell in two senses of the word: the well of all their empty stares. By touch, he slowly moved himself forwards.

He could easily have gone upright, stepping over the others; though he had indeed been weakened by his injuries, he could still draw on a large quantity of reserves of strength even so. They had been given food during their transport, extras too, occasionally, from women along the way. He still had muscles, he still even had fat. If he preserved his energy as much as possible, he could hold out a good while yet. But why, really? Merely to let his thoughts roam for a week, a month longer. Absurd, was what it was.

When he was out of reach of those to come after him — his descendants, he thought bitterly — he abandoned himself to his memories again. To bring each family member and every friend to mind yourself, and to recall words passed between you, to call up each human image from the past and be in its company. And meanwhile he felt how, slowly, his body disappeared. Down to the bone. To take leave of himself.

He had been lying like that for days on end now. Days? There weren't any, not any more. Time ran on in a straight line. The alternation of day and night was something from his previous life, something of which only now did he realise the splendour.

The trace of murky light continued to prevail; the adjustment of the first hours had soon reached its peak. Perhaps, when the senses themselves were affected in the end, a short period of clarity might come through a last hyper-sensitivity of his eye.

The only thing left to him of the world was the stretch of ground he covered with his body, the one he could feel his way across by touch. That, in a way, was still his. It was still so kind as to bear him. This was really his entire fatherland now. Passing his hands over it, he would sometimes imagine a river valley at each little groove, a mountain at every rise. He felt like caressing this ground because it still bore him.

This was the way they were lying there, together, like a pale fire slowly glowing to extinction. No one any longer knew how long they had been lying there like that. They couldn't care less any more, either. An imprisoned criminal continually counts the days, even though he has got twenty years, scratching long ladders of numbers into the wall of his cell. Time, in fact, becomes all-controlling to him. Here, time had been suspended for ever, nothing was expected from outside any more.

Was that something approaching in the air? Was his gaze struck by growing light? Or were his eyes already being affected? Impossible. That only happened at the very end, and he was still possessed of all his strength. Slowly, a soft dusk spread overhead, the vaults of the cavern began to glint here and there. Dusk burgeoned to light, the inconstant light like that of torches, ever increasing like that of torches being carried in.

This turned out to be the case. Up above, at the base of the vault, corridors seemed to terminate and enemy servants appeared there with big torches which they placed in iron baskets fixed to the rock face.

Now that the entire space was lit up, the prisoners saw one another for the first time: their corrupting bodies, their eyes, and a general revulsion arose. This communal suffering gave no feeling of solidarity, no mutual sympathy; things were too far gone. The dead lay between them, and those who merely breathed, who didn't react to the light from above.

Many, however, still looked round and up above, like he did. What did this mean? Did they want something more of them?

It would soon become clear. The enemy servants who had placed the torches – they wore the clothing of the victor – had disappeared down the corridors through which the fumes of the torches was being sucked away as well, and now they began to go back and forth to a large balcony, shaped by nature or by man, protruding from the rock face. The smell of food pervaded the space.

He saw there was a long table on the rock balcony and people were busy carrying a feast of food to that table: huge tureens, salvers piled high with meat, dishes full of vegetables and bowls laden with fruit. And many buckets of wine. Everything was clearly visible; lamps and candles were being put among the fare all the time.

Was this a vision? Was he dying?

Not yet. It went on. Men with stringed instruments now arrived. They arranged themselves to one side and began to tune up. Because of the resonance in the cellar vaults, this jangle of scrawny sounds acquired a certain fullness.

Were they going to serenade them? The serenade of the dying? But why then all that food?

No, the guests stepped forward. A jolly company of men and women decked out most richly, the women mainly with their own abundance, gathered at the table. In the centre, on the tallest chair, a copious *matrone* sat herself down. She had the allure of supreme power. The wife or mistress of stadtholder or war lord, herself perhaps even an empress, she seemed to be the soul of this revel. She gave the signal to be seated, one more for music, she gave the signal to gorge. And together they gorged themselves at length, bringing meat and wine to their mouths by turn.

And as they drank, their mood became more exuberant. It seemed as though they were not being whipped up by the music and the wine alone, but also by the deep humiliation they wished to inflict on the captured enemy. To have him perish of want in sight of their plenty, to let him die in sight of their joy in life.

If this truly was their intention, then it utterly misfired. The mental state of these prisoners could no longer be fathomed by a healthy, free human being. Deeper humiliation was no longer possible for them. On the contrary, each sound, every glimmer they could still allow to sink in, was welcome. Something was going to happen after all, there was still *something* to come. And that music, the most heavenly thing on earth, resounded then: solace and rapture in one!

Who cared whether it was being played to mock them now; not by the musicians: they simply had to and, who knows, perhaps they were making an extra effort in fact: to do them a last kindness.

By no means everyone experienced it in this manner. Many would only hear it in the distance, as sounds calling them from the other side, singing of their release from their suffering. Others, less far gone, looked up the while, mistaking it for the opening up of heaven to reveal an image of what awaited them there. Some, with their last remaining strength, stretched out their arms towards it.

Only those who were intact discerned the full reality. He, too, who had been cast inside last and was the least dilapidated therefore, who still had command of almost all his strength, for his wounds had much improved. Nothing escaped his notice. After all that time of enforced deafness and blindness, the use of his senses was an intense experience in itself: to assuage the hunger of his eyes, to slake the thirst of his ears.

While everything remained motionless below, as though in a petrified world, he saw how the binge up above became ever more impetuous, the voices rising continually above the music. The guests no longer merely groped for food and drink but one another too. Their movements became wilder, their sounds, even their laughter, more bestial. From time to time, a bone, gnawed clean, would carelessly be tossed down, over the balustrade.

As spirits rose this happened more frequently all the time. Not just bones, but bones with meat still on them too. The musicians were exhorted to louder and faster playing, the guests directing more and more of their attention towards the realm below them. Some were already hanging over the balustrade. One raised his glass in space and then drank to them.

The true meaning of this junket now became clear to him. They sought to amuse themselves with them. Like with animals. To have them fight for the scraps from their table. And possibly then to see them devour each other in consequence. They had first drunk themselves into a conscience-less state so as to be able to play this game with full abandon.

More and ever larger chunks of food they cast down, emitting cries such as those one exhorts dogs with. A large piece of pie came down right beside him; he did not stretch out his hand towards it.

They did not stop at scraps. Entire platters of meat, just brought in, flew down amongst them, leaving an arc of vapour in the air.

But not one of the prisoners moved: they went on being that petrified group. Many were incapable of rousing themselves but the strong, too, it seemed, carefully weighed up the effort a general struggle would cost them against the advantage of capturing a chunk. The only thing he saw, was that they would look round occasionally, at the food and back at each other again, only moving their eyes in doing so. Predatory it was.

No matter what was going to happen, he would never join in with that. He'd done with everything for good. He would calmly undergo the decline of his body. He would give the enemy no power over this decision and in so doing, he would preserve a final independence. Or was he able to decide this because he still had his resistance? And would his will desert him too, before time? So that then he would do things which still shamed him now? He shuddered at this.

They had broken up the symposium. Bar a few, the entire company had openly turned to the arena of death. While the music was silent, one of their number made a long speech to them of which he couldn't understand a word but which had to be very droll for the speaker was always being interrupted by general hilarity. He was probably mocking them for their refusal to show interest in the food they had been thrown, asking ironically whether they were too sated perhaps, or so spoilt that these dishes were not to their taste.

The oration was addressed to them but only intended for the ladies and gentlemen on the balcony who amused themselves, moreover, by taking aim at individual prisoners. A big, ruggedly hairy warrior formed their target more than the others. He did not move a muscle. No one did.

This general rigidity could be interpreted as contempt, and anger began to rise in the company the way anger does in a donkeyman when his beast baulks, its legs stretched out, and it can't be driven on, no matter what.

Then they played their final, trump card. The centre of the balcony was cleared for a moment and as the music speeded up and grew into a pandemonium, a tremendous roast boar, suspended by servants from its spit, was dumped into the arena.

With this the spell was broken. This was too much. Those who were first to reach it might sate themselves for months. The chance of living on beckoned from afar again. A general stampede ensued.

Groaning, the foremost struck their teeth into the mound of roast flesh. Atop and beneath one another, they thronged from all sides now, like piglets to the sow, and the moment they struck lucky they adopted the voracious movements of larvae.

The strong smell pervading the entire vault, the exciting music and the jubilant shouts of encouragement from the balcony left not a soul untouched. The weakest, too, tried to get there; they sacrificed their last remaining strength for this. Only the dead remained behind, as did he, the one still intact. His soundness rendered him as inviolable as the dead.

He wasn't affected but he had changed. In this deluge of events, his attitude of resigned waiting was lost. He had a part in it, a most grievous part. The enemy's scheme of depriving them of all dignity, even of that of suffering, to render them like animals, like the least among animals, had succeeded. To let them murder each other. For this was happening. He saw how gradually a bulwark of fighters and vanquished formed round the boar.

Unhindered, he polished off a few separate chunks of food lying within his reach, the piece of pie, too. These chunks were still lying all around, untouched: once the great trek to the boar had begun, no one had bothered about them any more. Many now fighting themselves to death there could have sated themselves with these without any trouble, but nobody any longer possessed the small amount of reflection necessary for this. As far as he could see, he was the only one to have preserved his independence.

He was also the only one to keep an eye on the balcony, who saw their jubilation, the way they were drinking there, the way they took ever fiercer delight in the meat and blood bath beneath them. It was striking the way they no longer intervened in any way, how the throwing and hollering had ceased immediately once the forces had been unleashed. Seeing how these forces would burn themselves out gave them the greatest satisfaction apparently.

The more deeply the mob gnawed its way into the boar, the wilder things became. Those who felt their powers return now formed a likeminded force of occupation and together they defended the boar against the weaker ones all around. A division arose between those who were gaining more and more strength and the ones who were loosing theirs continually. The swine seemed like a lifeboat, already laden with the shipwrecked, which those in the water are still trying to clamber into from all sides and who have to be prevented from doing this with force. And the more the boar was being eaten away inside, the more it began to resemble a boat, with its rostrum and ribs. Bones were laid bare. One or two from the occupying force broke off a rib and in this they had a weapon to batter away with: at hands clamped round the board, at shoulders rising up from the waves, at faces distorted with craving.

The music was way past having anything to whip up any more: it merely followed. All the sounds together formed the voice of the deity who had created this inferno.

But gradually everything returned to calm again. Many had died, others were sated, the boar was finished, only its skeleton was still being gnawed at. On the balcony, too, passions had abated. The men and women had joined in pairs and silently they conducted their amorous dialogue. The end of the great upheaval seemed nigh and he who had kept himself apart all the time wondered whether, after this deepest of humiliations, there would now be an end of it. He was filled with an intense sadness. That glorious life boiled down to this and that others took delight in such an end, to him this was a dislocation of all coherence. But no: he erred in his view. Life did not begin for the sake of its end. The end is not a final outcome but merely the last thing. The journey was the essence, not the manner in which you disembark; it was a delusion to despise one's entire life because of the way its end was now.

He was suddenly amazed at finding the strength for such thoughts and for such a feeling. Had all these events stirred something within him after all? Or was this simply caused by his having eaten again? Then the others, the ones who had devoured the boar, would have to sense a dawn among the ashes of their sensibilities too. And lo: something happened that appeared to be connected with this.

The music fell silent, the guests on the balcony grew quite mute, a deathly silence set in. The servants who previously had carried in the torches now came with long stakes with which they moved the light baskets that turned out to be fixed to pivoting arms, moving them a good way out from the wall. Because of this, parts of the vaulted rock above them, having remained in darkness until now, were suddenly illuminated. All looked up and kept their gaze trained upwards, for what they saw, they had never expected to be there.

Oval holes had been hacked out at' regular intervals in the vaulting and in each opening, accessible from the outside apparently, arms and legs resting on its edges or possibly supported by cords, was a young woman. The unsteady light of the torches played around as many as twenty such floating bodies. At first sight, they seemed to be statues, ceiling ornaments, but this wasn't Greece and only there could such statues have existed.

The music began, a soft, sweet lingering melody; the suspended women now addressed the world beneath them with movements, like in a dream at first, more emphatically as the music grew, with enticing gestures of arms, head and legs. Everything about them seemed to say: come to us, we are intended for you and there is nothing we would more dearly like to do than to fulfil that purpose.

Meanwhile, the balcony had become a complete pleasure ground.

Dash it all. Not satisfied with the havoc they had wrought, they wished to continue their amusement with those who had survived it, whose drive for food had been assuaged and who through this had regained their strength, to continue it by baiting them as regards their second drive. While they themselves were fornicating freely there, they attempted to whip up their prisoners one more time to acts of fruitless rage. Slavegirls served them to this end. Perhaps they had been promised their freedom for playing this role, for they vied with one another in seductive movements of love. They gyrated, they sang and smiled down at the men, and with their arms they pretended to draw them up to them.

With despair, he saw that this devilish intent succeeded too. His cave-mates kept their eyes riveted on the sirens above. They got up in order to be closer to them; they paced back and forth, restless, as though in a fever. He saw some of them stretch their arms aloft as if to say: let yourselves drop, we'll catch you. But the other ones laughed and beckoned and gyrated their bodies.

One now tried to climb up the steep rock face. It was rough; here and there one could gain a hold. Followed by all eyes, the balcony's too, he went on climbing. Half way up, his strength failed him or a support gave way. He plummeted down and lay there.

Others, too, attempted it, chose the most charming of the women or the roughest ascent and began, encouraged by a chorus of cries, their daring journey. The start to the vault, only a few metres removed from the desired goal, when the hands stretched out from either side almost touched, was nearly always fatal. Each time someone dropped down, the music would suddenly fall silent so the thud could clearly be heard.

Once, he saw a man — wasn't he that big hairy one? — almost succeed. He was already clutching the edges of the oval gap. But the same white arm that first had helped him get as far as this, now thrust him down unexpectedly.

Never before had there been such cheering in the cave as when this happened.

The longer he viewed all this, the more his soul unravelled. He felt himself go quietly mad. He felt regret over the food he had taken, for he wished to die. He stretched himself out on the rock floor, closed his eyes and resolved not to open them ever again. He wept over the sight the world still proffered him now on parting. He would turn away from it for good.

That's the way he lay there a little while, the goings on around him forced back to a distant clamour. Then a droplet fell on his chest. The unexpectedness, the strangeness of this cleared his mind completely and made him abandon his resolve at once. He opened his eyes and looked straight up above. And lo: there was a slavegirl right above him. And regarding her closely, things became clear to him at once. She wept.

Oh, what is it, that powerful thing that suddenly can come into being between two people? A current? A force field? An invisible ladder, in this case? He saw that, among all those women, she was different. No less charming, but dazed and desperate like him. He was the only one who saw this in the midst of the hellish uproar. He could not see that she wept but her tear had reached him there. A second one fell, on his shoulder.

A great desire quivered throughout his being. If ever two people must be united in this wilderness, they were the ones. He jumped up and stretched his muscles, felt his strength return to him as though by magic. Did she see him too? He looked up and thought she did. Was that a smile breaking around her mouth? Was that a gleam in her eye? Was it the case that they only existed for one another now?

With the eye of a hunter, he explored the steep rock face. Every fissure, every ledge he perceived and then he plotted his way accordingly, like in the past, when reaching a nest of young vultures was at stake. He gave a sign she would have to understand if the same fire had been kindled within her. And she did understand, for in reply she crossed her arms in front of her chest, thus indicating that she would pray for him the while.

Now the alliance had been sealed. Who knows, she may already have noticed him much earlier on, and her tears had been a call.

Slowly, and uncertainly at first because of his emotion, he began the ascent. As he rose higher and more perilously, the placement of his hands, of his fingers, the support of his feet, the transfer of his weight demanded all his attention. He was inconspicuous doing this: he was one of the many. Only later on, at the edge of the vaulting, did he attract general notice.

Each time he had found sufficient support, he would rest for a moment and look up, and the more clearly he could see her, the more glorious she seemed to him. Now he could read his own, huge desire in her face. No, it wasn't a game with her like it was with the others, a game of cat and mouse, for beyond the radiance of her love's glow he could see the fear, the fear of failure, of him falling. But the others had to think that she, too, was luring him to his death.

There had been one perilous moment; not when, for the first time, he saw her lips, her teeth, her nostrils, the wave in her hair, not even when he could distinguish the pupils in her eyes, when they switched focus from their faces to their eyes. All this was just glorious.

Dangerous was the moment when, for the first time, they could call out to each other. He began, and when she answered him she did so in his own language. She was one of his tribe!

By a whisker, he avoided toppling right over backwards. His entire body atremble, he clung to the rock and waited like this until he'd calmed down.

His language, his language! His language had not yet died: it was still alive. It revived between the two of them, which was the most important thing, the *only* important thing. Now, she was completely like him.

Who cared the way the others spoke? Nobody existed for him any more, except her. What he had wished to do when he believed to be closing his eyes for ever, to banish all that surrounded him from his thought, that same thing happened to him now. To him, she was all that truly existed.

This was no trembling with fear, but trembling with happiness which was why it could change into strength and control. No more abandoning himself to tenderness now, no more words now except the ones trapeze artists will cry out to each other in the circus: no taking an advance on their happiness as long as it hadn't been captured yet.

The most difficult part of all came at the edge, where he must surmount the incline. He now avoided looking at her on purpose; the sight of her so close by would be as deadly as that of Medusa, would make him fall at once.

Measure for measure, he progressed. He, too, began to incline, over backwards: he had to grip the stone tightly. Softly, almost at a whisper, she gave instructions. 'Bit more to the left – a little further – no, not there, that bit's loose – yes, there's a hollow there – now raise your foot: there's another ledge there – slide along very slowly – let go your left hand and stretch out as far as possible.'

Yes, she gripped him: let go!

Now those who were following him with bated breath from below and from the balcony saw him float through the air but to their amazement, he did not fall, though the music had already ceased.

Quite how it was done, no one could really tell: a few seconds on, they saw the prisoner and the slavegirl in deepest embrace up there.

She had truly drawn him to her.

Now they were together. Now they could behold one another, say sweet nothings in each other's ears, melt their joys and their sorrow into one and entrust one another with their bodies.

Both wept with happiness, but they knew, too, that it would not last, and that all that can be between man and woman must be encompassed in that short time.

The sense of this brevity was the only thing that remained within them of the mayhem in the cave; all other things had been completely obliterated by their mutual possession.

Every word, each gesture proved to them that they were alike to an unfathomable depth.

They hurled themselves into the abyss of one another.

Amazement soon turned to anger in those who beheld this. They began to hurl abuse, to shout, to rant. Rage took all in its grip, the prisoners as much as the others. The empress shrieked. Like a fish-wife.

None of this got through to the loving couple.

It took a long time before the order had been passed down the line and its execution came into effect.

Then the servants reached them with their stakes and pushed them down.

They still remained united in their fall.

On the ground, she was torn to pieces over his broken back.

Highest Honours

Huub Beurskens

We have arrived. I can hear the hubbub. People have come by the carload. There is excited calling and shouting. Cheerful, popular music sounds from loudspeakers, repeatedly interrupted by a voice listing numbers. These will be the numbers of parties allowed to go in, in the order announced. They are trying to make everything run in an orderly fashion and so prevent a crush. I can hear more cars arriving all the time. Particularly those with the heavy droning engines will be bringing in throngs of invited guests. There are so many guests that, right through the stink of exhaust fumes, I can even sniff their presence here. I don't mean anything derogatory by that, of course. On the contrary, the smell has something salutary about it, sweetish . . . Doubtless, all have made themselves look splendid.

I presume that I'll go in last and will stride forwards through the guests to enthusiastic applause. This accounts for one of the reasons why the car I am in has been shuttered off. Had the car been open to view, I would be being sniffed over by entire groups of admirers right now – being stared at in any case. Moreover, I'm no spring chicken any more; I'm easily troubled by light that's too bright. In the back here, I can still stretch myself out for a moment, still savour the peace and quiet a while, and that way prepare myself for all the hullabaloo that will bear down on me any moment now. My driver knows this. I can rely on him.

I am tense though. I have been through much in my life, but I can feel my heart thudding now even so. Just imagine: a heart attack right in front of the entrance, on the threshold! So, keep calm, as calm as possible. Best not to get all of a doodah: that I'm wobbly on my pins and because of this I possibly won't be able to proceed to the front, straight as a ramrod, later on. People will understand.

Odd really: you're on your way to receive highest honours, everyone is full of respect and admiration for your achievements and you yourself are fretting about the way you walk . . .

I'd do better, ahead of time, to wallow a bit in the accolade that will be accorded me. It'll probably be a high dignitary who'll present the insignia. But secretly I entertain the hope that the president himself will think it an honour. After all, I was quite in the dark until this morning. 'Come,' the driver who is also my secretary said, and before I knew it, before I'd had time to ask anything, we were on our way by car. Gradually it dawned on me. Well, yes, of course a thing like that has to be kept a surprise until the very last moment: that's the finest way of all.

'. . . I am deeply honoured, on behalf of the entire government, to be able to award you highest honours for your many years of unremitting endeavour in the field of promoting artificial intelligence . . .' The president will signal me to approach him and applause will resound afresh.

It was clear very early on already that I was what is called a genius. I simply *had* it.

Of late, with an eye to my age, I have begun to round things off and at the moment my productivity is no longer high – I might as well say it's *nil*. I enjoy my old age. At last I'm getting down to activities which previously I could and would not allow myself: sleeping through the night, having a bite to eat, just lolloping something down, then sleeping the day away again: *wonderful*.

That's the way things go. When you're young, you yearn for recognition, but that's not forthcoming and you go on, grinding yourself down even though nobody ever truly seems to show appreciation for what you produce. And then, when you withdraw, tired, when you've done your bit and the sorrow you've had because of all that lack of appreciation barely affects you any more, then, from one day to the next, you're being praised and made into a folk hero. In retrospect it turns out to have to be that way; you realise that that way's the best. Appreciation at too early a stage breeds arrogance and sloth and who would be served by that? But just you try telling that to a young ambitious so-and-so . . .

I can still hear more folk arriving. The noise some of them make! Their gleeful anticipation's enough to shatter your eardrums.

My driver's standing outside with one of his colleagues – judging by the smell – smoking a cigarette, awaiting things to come.

I've never mixed with the common crowd. This too is curious in a way. I have never gone among the people; I had no time and opportunity for it. And now, precisely because of that solitary, celibate life, I, with all my being, will end up the centre of attention. No, I have never been married; I've never asked someone to walk out even ... The toll paid by genius. I never experienced it physically as such, however. No earthly reason to bemoan my fate because of that.

Everything will be colourfully decorated in the main hall. Beaming, the president will be awaiting me on the dais. The lectern has been tittified up with flags and inflated balloons. The ceiling and everything behind him is festooned with garlands in the most wide ranging hues of pink and red. His Excellency is wearing a bright yellow rose on his left lapel. Doubtless, later on, after the official part, he will pin this to me with a grand gesture, as a personal, friendly token of appreciation.

Heavens, I haven't got a coat! I haven't got a coat. I'm not even wearing a shirt or a tie ... See, that's what happens when you're not accustomed to move about in public and then one morning, from one moment to the next, without having been informed about it, you're having to go by car to receive highest honours. To be pleasantly surprised is highly enjoyable – that goes without saying – but the consternation it brings along in its wake can also have its disadvantageous side, too, it seems. It's making me grumpy. *Driver!*

He doesn't hear me of course. Let's give the door a bash. He doesn't heed that either. He's too busy talking, with the president's driver probably – again, that's quite an honour for him personally, too. But there will definitely not be time later on to quickly rustle up a frock coat from somewhere. He will, still having a laugh with the president's driver, open the door and there'll be me, sitting there in the flashlight of scores of photographers, and in all the papers tomorrow: LAUREATE UNFROCKED!

I can't help it: this makes me giggle myself. My whole body begins to judder, all the fat joins in, it even sets my belly atremble; it takes a huge effort not to burst forth; the tears are already running down my cheeks; ohhh, there you have it: I'm roaring with it already. I yelp and let off a right-old fart on top of it all!

The driver strikes the car with the flat of his hand. He's right:

soon everyone will know i'm here after all. And I must keep bearing my health in mind. This has left me quite hot. There's not much ventilation. I'll catch cold, getting out in a moment. My lungs and my heart can't stand just anything any more. I'm portly. Since becoming *emeritus*, my weight has even increased considerably. Should I make too much of an effort, my ticker won't cope, I fear. Ah well, like every stage in life, old age too, besides its pleasures, has its afflictions.

In a kind of way, it's possibly quite fitting, in fact, that I'm not wearing any upper garments. People all too readily like to see the genius as a somewhat absentminded character; one doesn't merely have to look up to him, in that case: it makes him earthly and less unapproachable. Not such a bad idea, therefore, to come to receive highest honours without a shirt, tie and frock coat: as a token of absentmindedness. Understanding, everybody will laugh and I'll be able to garner even more sympathy.

What is it I hear the presidential driver say? 'He'll be getting a blue stamp,' he says. 'No,' my driver replies, 'he'll be having a red one.' 'Blue, purple, perhaps green,' the state driver responds, 'but no way red.' This continues for a while between those two.

A stamp?! All the time I've based things on the premise that I would be allowed to receive a medal or would have a decoration pinned to my frock coat at least. Must be an old fashioned image of mine: apparently I'm no longer up to date. If I've got things straight, it's to be a stamp, I gather. Each area of life thus has its own innovations . . . Ah, that's why the driver at our departure did not draw my attention to the fact that I wasn't wearing upper garments! If one is stamping someone on such an occasion, one doesn't stamp the black frock coat, nor the tie or the spotless shirt, but the chest. This at least I may assume: the bare body, the chest, though the advantage of the stamp is that it can be applied not just to one place but to many.

It's doubtless done with indelible ink. Herein, too, must lie the point of this innovation: a medal can go missing, one can forget to pin on a decoration and in the crush, even at the reception afterwards already, it might drop from the lapel. Such a stamp stays in place once and for all, indelible, so the laureate can move proudly among the people at all times.

For that matter, it's not improbable, now I actually think about it, that such an innovation as this one can be ascribed directly or indirectly to the use of artificial intelligence provided by me. Should this indeed be the case, I owe the highest honours to myself in two ways rather than one. Further reason to be grand, methinks.

So there'll be a reception at the conclusion of the ceremony, an informal gathering with all kinds of snacks: Scotch eggs, sausage rolls, canapés, sausages, possibly even a grill or barbecue, for such are also things of these times, it seems to me. I like a bit of what I fancy. There's not much I'll turn my nose up at. My mouth's watering even now.

Meanwhile the president wants to have a cosy chat with me. On that occasion I'll just ask him how things are with the younger generation, whether there's sufficient new talent, and I'll press him to stimulate that talent and to go on stimulating it. Then I take another bite and a swig.

'How, in your case, did that talent come to develop?' he'll ask.

I suspend breathing for a moment, because of a burp. 'Allow me to tell you, Your Excellency.

'At first, I wasn't at all aware of my gift. I was still immature. You know how it is: I frolicked with the others, I was the rascal but never hurt a fly.

'One day I was separated from the others by the chaperon my mother had hired – the same individual who from today is my driver, for that matter – and I was taken to a completely clean room. I must have been a nuisance again, must have played too wildly, been chasing my screaming and slithering sisters too recklessly. Whatever the reason for my segregation might have been, I was left in that room and, rash and playful as I was, I instantly began to muck about there. There wasn't much by way of excitement in that space. In fact it was bare and uncongenial. At its centre there was an object I had never seen before, but one which, oddly enough, I did – how shall I put it – experience at once as something with which I had been familiar for years, longer than my own little life – that's how it seemed. In hindsight, that was the moment upon which genius awakened in me. My chaperon looked on from a distance. I felt the talent kindle, deep within me, like a fire, only it wasn't yet visible to the outside world.

'You must think of it as in the case of a toddler that has never seen a piano before and with its nanny comes into a strange room where there's a grand piano and instantly clambers on to the stool. So far it's all a splendid sight but no more than that. But then that toddler puts its little fingers on the keys and, without a score, plays Chopin's A-minor Mazurka.'

*

A loudly lowing horde passes by, running and trampling wildly. Please don't let the festive occasion be ruined by a protest action or some such! It likewise seems to be part and parcel of the times of today that groups with slogans and banners will make their way to each government-organised solemn occasion, no matter how venerable its tradition or how innocent its nature. I cannot hear what is being cried, that's how inarticulately such louts apparently will express themselves. Oh, my heart!

What's all this worrying I'm doing again? If, at manifestations like this, protest actions are undertaken, reg'lar as clockwork, then the forces of law and order will be thoroughly prepared for it in consequence. Thus, the booing is already beginning to grow mute, in fact.

But I hope that I'm not boring the president with my tale. Though indeed he has asked for it himself, who knows, he may be doing so purely out of formal politeness. Others, too, will want to have a chat with me in order to give photographers an opportunity to take a snap. It will therefore be little or no trouble for the president to take his leave of me with some phrase or other. Instead, he takes a whole string of sausages from a dish, gestures with his impressive head in my direction and says, only just audible in between the smacking noises he's making: 'Continue . . . my dear fellow . . . do continue . . .'

Two ladies are standing somewhat tucked away behind me, bleating that by now it's their turn to exchange views with me. Happily for me – and them – someone arrives with a salver and they each take a carrot and a few cauliflower florets and they have themselves a bit of a nibble.

'As I was saying,' I went on, 'things went as though of their own accord. To be honest, I have felt unhappy – from guilt – because of this. May one, in all propriety, pride oneself on something with which one has been blessed more than others have, not through one's own doing but by nature?

'Soon I was receiving preferential treatment. Others were forced to seek their fortunes elsewhere. At times they would leave by the truck load. On the other hand, it would've been unforgivable should I not have developed my talent and have withheld its fruits from the nation. I should like to add, moreover, that to have a talent doesn't mean by any means that you also know how to exploit it. Most never stop to consider how much discipline and practice is demanded from a genius in order to reach the zenith of his powers. Someone may have fine, muscled legs – a thing I, in my turn, am jealous of – but to break track records with those legs is another matter . . .'

'Yes, ehm, indeed, dear chap,' His Excellency interrupts me, slightly irritated, 'I can dish up such tittle-tattle too, but . . .' – he closes his windpipe a moment to give precedence to a sizeable burp – '. . . but that room, what *happened* there in that room is what I want to know something about!'

I blush, despite my years, all the way to behind my ears. 'But of course, Your Excellency, that room – in that room stood the apparatus with which for the first time I managed to generate artificial intelligence. You must imagine that apparatus as a primitive-looking construction of four heavy wooden beams which, standing a touch at an angle off the floor, support a heavy wooden block. The block is slightly curved at the top and has rounded corners. It is covered in supple hide and that hide has been smeared with a kind of grease that has a smell which I would almost say is intoxicating, were it not for the fact that it makes a genius wildly energetic. It no longer affects me now. It's true that I still dream of it, from time to time, or that a certain whiff can bring back that feeling, but then it's more a kind of melancholy, like a mood which only still expresses itself in a tearful smile or a smiling tear . . . But, not to slip away once more into reflections which are of no interest to anyone: youthful as I was, I jumped on to the apparatus, that's to say, I jumped it from behind. Yes, the apparatus has a rear which implies it also must have a front, but I never bothered about that end. I grabbed the apparatus from behind, as it were, clenching it firmly while I went on sniffing the leather continuously so that saliva began to run from my mouth in floods. There I stood, clenching and pressing up against the apparatus, gaining a firm footing on the floor. And then a kind of miracle took place.

'Whereas others have a barely noteworthy, even a somewhat unfortunate looking little organ through which, let me put it delicately, they urinate, in my case the talent manifested itself in a selfconscious, growing and boastful shape. For a moment it made me reel; my then already quite heavy body began to rock, and I decided to co-operate with myself and began to ram the apparatus with all I could muster and with massive talent, without realising at that moment what it was I was creating, just like the toddler who allows its fingers to roam the keys without knowing what fantastic music will be the consequence. No mazurka but a gush, a whole series of gushes of artificial intelligence came out in my case! How lucky it was then that the chaperon managed to catch it in a glass beaker.

'That this was a case of artificial intelligence, I didn't know yet at the time. I soon did gain the impression that I'd managed something extraordinary. Lovingly, my chaperon led me to my own, completely furnished room and gave me splendid food. I appointed him secretary-dignitary at once.

'Next morning already, someone presented himself in rubber gloves and dressed in a white coat. He put a spotless white cloth in front of his mouth and nose, and began to examine me at length. I was startled for a moment. Could I have been mistaken? Was my talent not a talent but a disease that had manifested itself? But the noises of utter satisfaction he expressed ever more frequently during the examination calmed me down. And then, too, I saw the letters stitched in blue on the breast pocket of his white tunic: DRAIN. The District and Regional Artificial Intelligence Network. I was proud and above all relieved.

'In a short space of time, I became big and strong: quite a bear. By means of concentrates, knee-bends, wee trotting exercises and, especially, daily meditations that frequently would take up the entire late afternoon, I was able to raise the production of artificial intelligence in a short space of time. I became adult which, among other things, was noticeable by the routine manner in which I reached results and the progressive failure of the childish rush of saliva to materialise.

'The inspector from DRAIN paid his respects regularly and my secretary kept a graph up to date on a wall of my room, a graph which soon resembled a cross section of the Himalayas.

'Each of life's phases has its pleasures and ills. It goes without saying that, even when — statistically speaking — he manages to equal Mount Everest, a genius, too, will be depressed from time to time. I mentioned this earlier on, I believe. Not to have to become even more depressed, I have always refrained from speculations as to what happened with the artificial intelligence. Was it, diluted, added to the feed of common folk, or drunk, mixed with water or milk? And what were the consequences of this? Consciously, I've never wanted to take an interest in what DRAIN did with the substance. Everything a genius gifts to the world can be deployed to both laudable and most objectionable ends, after all. One who, being a supplier of genius, wishes to have influence on this himself, has to invest so much time and energy in it that, as a source of possible positive innovations, he drains himself, as near as no matter, with for a consequence that his talent shrivels into an inner, private crisis which, if observed at all, is of no importance whatsoever in the eyes of the outside world . . .'

'I shouldn't quite wish to maintain that I disagree with you, old chap,' the president grumbles, 'but always, everywhere I go, those politics, that whingeing, *excusez le mot*, about politics and morality, makes me sick as a parrot, as a *parrot*!' And he turns away from me, takes five more slices from a steaming roast and then gestures to his body guards to free a path for him.

There I stand, stamped but with the presidential back having been turned on me.

It's my own fault. Though it's a quality of a genius that, sooner than someone else, he will think through the philosophical, moral and even theological implications of his life, precisely because of this, he must also be considered able to foresee that not everyone is always prepared to follow him in the matter, not even the greatest ruling powers in the land.

Had I been wearing trousers, I would now have filled them a packet. I always shit when I feel happy or satisfied — when I'm feeling at ease, in any case. But now I have the feeling that I've had to shit from fear. Odd: there's no cause to be fearful, after all. On the contrary. Must be nerves.

Back home, I didn't think about putting on upper clothing or not, but I did about donning a pair of trousers. I was just about to slip into a pair of slacks but then I instantly abandoned the intention again. Why are you getting that award? I wondered. Those invited will want to see it, the cameras will want to record it: everyone's entitled to it. A celebrated concert pianist doesn't mount the stage with his hands cloaked in thick mittens, does he? A *heldentenor* doesn't accept a prize with a scarf his mother knitted in front of his mouth, does he?! You can no longer demonstrate the powers and capacities you had when in full flower, but if you want to subject yourself to such an accolade — and who would not? — you owe it to display all that still remains of the very measure of your genius, to turn yourself inside out if need be: you're public property, after all!

Now it turns out to have been doubly sensible to have left the trousers at home. 'Come on, granddad,' my driver said when he saw me halting to ponder them, and he gave me a nudge, into the car. Just imagine, the laureate making his way inside in a minute, the old head held bravely high, but with a big wet patch as consequence of a little something in the seat of his pants . . . I can't help it that, once again, I begin belly laughing about my own fantasies: it's all I'm used to, amusing myself by myself. I pee at the same time — might as well — for when, later on, not a drop of artificial intelligence comes forth, that's as maybe, taking my years into account, but when common old urine begins to flow in its stead, that would be a disgrace; the very thought makes me run cold.

The drivers have ended their conversation. I hear the bang of a car door. It'll be the president being driven up to the entrance. My driver, too, now gets in and starts the engine. Oh, my heart, my lungs, my head . . . Can I already hear the festive march?

I must see to it that people continue to treat me with respect and not, at the end of it all, laugh at me good-naturedly, or even with something of pity in their eyes. My driver's hob-nobbing on departure really went too far for my liking. It would be ill advised, when the president asks how I hope to spend the years remaining, to reply that I want nothing other than to eat, shit and sleep. But too soon by far, when you're elderly, you are treated like a small child, and a small child without genius at that — and pop goes your well-earned respect.

'No, Your Excellency,' I'll reply resolutely, for I know that my reply will startle him, 'from now on, I shall devote myself entirely to the critical investigation and control of the application of artificial intelligence!'

The president gawps at me. I see a big chunk of sausage on his pink tongue. I myself, as though quite unaware of any provocation, stuff down a goodly cob of corn.

'Well,' I then go on, 'I have always been wondering, of course, whether the artificial intelligence set at the state's disposal was indeed being employed properly. Alas, I have never had the time to be able to research the subjects of its application and processing. I could have asked the DRAIN inspector, but what could guarantee me the reliability of his information? No, I have resolved to get to the bottom of the affair now.'

The president looks deathly pale and I have to draw his attention to the piece of sausage in order for it not to go down quite the wrong way.

'You see,' I continue, relishing in fulsome measure that the head of state is standing as though rooted to the ground, listening to me, 'you see, Your Excellency, the artificial intelligence produced, by myself, among others, is of such a quality that it must not be frittered away – I mean, that it can only be intended for distribution to individuals who are truly deserving – to those in government, for instance – so that they might execute their tasks even better: to state lawyers, to leaders of business, to high civil servants. D'you see? It would be a disaster if everyone in the country could take advantage of it with as much right or in equal measure, if the common people, if even *female* individuals were administered it! Chaos would be the result. The hallmark of intelligence, after all, is that not everyone possesses like measure of it and that only the most intelligent know what it's like to handle it – right? I cannot bear the thought that all those beakers of precious intelligence which, in the course of the years, thanks to my genius . . .'

The president gives me a few hard, amiable slaps. He has turned quite red in the face and stands there laughing loudly: 'Ho-ho, my dear fellow, I quite misunderstood you at first! Am I right in understanding you have your eye on a ministerial position?'

We drive along. A little way. Now back a little. Stop. I slam into the rear panel.

We must be right in front of the entrance. The driver switches off the ignition. He's getting out now. Will the guard of honour be standing there? I hear hellish shouting and other mayhem. It's clear people are awaiting me on the edges of their seats with expectation. The music is even more modern than I thought. Oh, my stomach, my bowels, my lungs, my throat, my heart . . . I can't get up. I hear my driver's footsteps. I'm now able to press myself up at the front but I still can't manage the rear. I hear him fidgeting at the door. There comes the light! Oh, my short-sighted eyes and all that flashing! Help me, please, help: I can't get up any more, I'm not getting any air, I can't see anything at all. Support me, up to the threshold: thence applause shall bear me along.

Biker at Sea

J.M.A. Biesheuvel

Isaac had been standing on the afterdeck for hours already. He was a pleasant but slightly strange boy: when working on board he longed for a job ashore and when in an office he longed for the sea. He could not bear the dull monotony of existence ashore, and he did not have money to make sea voyages. But when he was on a ship – in the capacity of random member of the crew (bespecta-cled, hence always a cabin-boy, mess steward or officers' steward, never able seaman let alone mate: his big dream . . .) – he had to deal with the rough bragging rant of the sailors who played cards with knives on the table and bawled out one another and Isaac, no holds barred. Isaac was never truly one of them. Aboard ship he fitted into the community least of all, even less than in the harbour town, the bottling plant or in the factory or office, and each time again he believed he would find true romance precisely on a ship. When the work was done you could always find him on the afterdeck. It was already two hours past midnight now, but Isaac continued to stand there because it was such a moon-clear night; you could clearly see all the familiar stars of the southern hemi-sphere and the wake foaming dangerously white behind the ship (one who has stood on the afterdeck of a ship sailing in open sea knows that at dark of night, by day, in rain or in fog, in polar regions or in the tropics, in grey, green or clear-blue water, always and always she sails along a white road, that road running from the horizon to the propeller: someone drowning who crosses its path a quarter of an hour later no longer sees the road).

There was a lovely balmy breeze. If you looked closely you could indeed see the horizon or, a little closer by, the light-speck of a ship luffing away that, had Isaac arrived an hour earlier, had been sailing straight towards him. But, as will become clear, our senses can deceive us. There are philosophers who maintain that all that is, is imagination, and that the opposite is not to be proved either! Isaac sailed on a tramp steamer and never saw ships at night. He thought of how long it would be before he would be home again. He looked at the winches, the bollards, the ropes, the railing and the easy chair he had set out for himself on the afterdeck. At a given moment Isaac saw the little light in the distance swerve abruptly; it seemed to describe a short turn on the water and then it came straight at him. When it was coming ever closer, Isaac had reached the conclusion that this could hardly be or purport to be a ship as it was so much subject to the 'motion of the waves' and particularly because there was never more than a single light. A ship with only one stern light burning? Dangerous. When the extraordinary conveyance had approached Isaac to a distance of four hundred yards, he saw it was a motorbike. For the first time in his life something happened to Isaac which 'could rightly be said to be extraordinary'. What he saw now, someone else would not dare invent, nor be able to, not in his wildest dreams. At first Isaac was afraid but in the end he could not assume that a new prophet or Messiah would move over the earth in this manner – though Christians maintain that Jesus has walked on water. The motorbike had approached Isaac to within sixteen metres or so. Isaac stood there calling out and waving like no tomorrow but in his excitement he forgot to cast out a rope ladder. This was brought to his attention by the rider of the motorbike. As his accent showed, the stranger turned out to be a fellow countryman of Isaac's. He steered his bike in an extra-ordinary manner and extremely carefully to the rope ladder; seated on his bike he behaved towards the smooth side of the ship like a boxer still probing his opponent in the ring for a moment – a slight shaking of the upper torso, hopping rapidly from one foot to the other and making defensive or on the contrary in fact aggres-sive gestures with the arms and then – upsidaisy! – he jumped bike and all in a single go on to the rope ladder. 'Careful, careful,' he cried continually. The man wore specs which were not a little steamed up, and a cap of which the leather flaps, intended to protect eyes and ears from the seawater, jutted out a long way. The motorbike was an ordinary motorbike. It had no special equipment. Isaac helped the man set the bike down on deck. The man said: 'Give me something to eat.' Isaac went to fetch it. He noticed that the sailors, mates and engine room crew had knocked off already. When Isaac returned he asked the stranger: 'Why do you ride on the water?' The man maintained he wanted to set a record.

'How's it possible that you can ride on water?' asked Isaac, surprised. 'It's a matter of practice,' said the man, 'I began by putting a pin down flat on the water. If you do that very carefully it stays afloat. Over a long period of time, I took ever more heavy objects. My bike was what I was after, of course, and in the end I did make my first measly circuits of the town pond. Now I ride across the entire world. I don't come ashore anywhere but because I must eat from time to time, I'll frequently ride up to a ship. I prefer to go in dark of night best of all. Everyone's asleep then. The first few times I went up to ships in broad daylight but people went all of a doodah then. First they cried out that this was the most beautiful thing they'd experienced in their entire lives and then they began to talk gibberish or they went mad. I intend to do forty-thousand kilometres across the sea — don't mind a few kilometres more here or there, I don't: as long as I'm right round the globe. I want to do something no one's ever been able to do before. That's always been my ideal.' 'Are you never afraid of drowning?' Isaac asked.

'Why no,' said the man. 'It's the way you steer the thing, that's the clue, and carefully adding a touch more acceleration each time, and easing off. A high wave, for instance, you should never take at a great speed otherwise the sides of the tyres get wet and once that's happened, you're up the creek.' 'Yes, I can see that,' said Isaac who was looking at the man, full of admiration. The man was quite simply gorging himself. He drank too: lots of milk and alcohol. Finally he asked for a little bottle of iodine, for he had need of that. Meanwhile an hour had passed and the man slung his bike overboard again and hung it on the rope ladder. Then he took his leave of Isaac. The latter asked whether it wasn't possible for him to join him for the rest of the journey on the motorbike, riding pillion. 'I could show you the way, for I've sailed a lot,' he concluded his question. But the man burst out laughing. 'You'd have to practise for years first,' the man said, 'but if I wanted to as such, I'd take you along. I can steer well enough and I could pump up my tyres so that it'd work, but I don't feel like it. What are you to me? I've been riding at sea for months now and then all of a sudden you'd join me for the final week? What point'd that be? I happen to be after a *single-handed* record. I can't explain to the people at the finish that you only joined at the final stage, can I? Besides, I'd have to do my level best to keep the bike going with two people. And I've never practised with a second. How do I know what unexpected movements you might make? The thing is to dance airily across the water, as it were,' the man went on. 'D'you know about tight-rope walking?' he asked, Isaac who, not quite understanding the point of the question, said 'no'. 'Well,' the man said, 'you've got to keep your balance all the time with the bike and you must keep your tyres as high as possible on the waves.' Then he took his leave and descended the ladder again with his bike. Isaac wanted to adjust the rope ladder a touch but again the man cried 'Careful, careful!' at every turn, very loudly this time. Almost having reached the water, he started the engine, full pelt, so that the wheels whizzed round in the air above the water. Occasionally the man would hold the tyres very carefully against the surface of the water and at a given moment he jumped, in an unexpected movement, from the rope ladder on to the roaring bike which jetted off at breakneck speed. It was already getting light a little. Isaac felt sad. The bike had disappeared over the horizon within a quarter of an hour. So Isaac went to bed for an hour. Next day he told the radiographer what had befallen him that night. The latter shrugged his shoulders and when Isaac kept pressing him he began to laugh. An hour later the entire ship knew that Isaac had seen a man ride over the water at night. Everyone laughed. Once the day had passed Isaac was very sleepy. But before going to bed he walked down to the afterdeck for a moment. The sun had just gone down. It promised to be a fine night again. A little more cloud this time. Involuntarily, Isaac began to search the sea, peering. But of course the man on the motorbike was nowhere to be seen. Isaac was on the verge of tears; he didn't belong ashore, he didn't belong to the crew, he didn't even belong to the man with the motorbike. He looked at the foaming, dangerous wake and at the birds flying along, following the ship. He had the feeling he was a lonely man and gradually he came to the realisation that it would always stay like that. He lit a cigarette and began to hum a psalm but he could barely hear his own voice. It had begun to blow and that's why the propeller would rise from the water now and then, spinning like mad, only to end up back in the water again with a booming blow. Isaac looked at one of the sea birds and wished he was able to fly like that creature and go where he wished. He wanted to fly, following the ships, or far away over the horizon. Without him being aware of it himself, he began to imitate the movements of the wings of the albatrosses in the air. The bosun happened to see it. He giggled, for he saw that Isaac was standing with his feet planted firmly on deck . . .

The Gospel According to Chabot

Willem Brakman

At a time of day when it was very quiet in the village, two men were approaching along the path that descended the rocks and ran close past the shipwreck. By the shuffling of their feet through the shale of the path and the listless dangling of their arms it was easy to see that they were at their last gasp. The larger and elder of them was dressed in a ravelly black suit too big for him on all sides – on second thought, it was little more than a collection of dumped, baggy rags. His was a bony figure; though his head, thin and all-jaw, drooped in a tired manner, his prominent light-grey eyes still stared brightly and distrustfully around him. The nose was not the best part of his face: the nose of a progenitor, a robust foundation, large, hooked and doggedly know-all. His companion was a young man with a small head, his skull tapering a little at the top, the nose full and fleshy, jaws broad and heavy, the mouth large and thick-lipped. This was a primal head; the eyes of indeterminate colour stood close together.

The two men sat down by the side of the path and looked at the village: it simply seemed a quiet village yet there was some-thing apparently bothering the old one. 'It's too quiet for my liking,' he said after a while, 'and strange things happen in a village that's too quiet.' While he was saying this, he took off his hat and revealed a wealth of white, fluffy hair; the gesture was a solemn one, but nevertheless his eyes, prepared for any eventuality, roamed along the windows, along the red-grey roofs and on, towards the sombre profile on top of the hill, probably a castle's or otherwise that of a strongly fortified monastery.

Little sounds, like the ones an over-quiet village can transmit, were reaching him now, after all: the unmistakable sound of a last gasp, the muffled screeching of someone being smothered in a pillow, soft hawking elsewhere again, the snap of a chicken's neck, the agonized flutter of wings. These were the bitter sounds from a quiet village, a chabot village.

'See to it that you get talking to them,' the old man said, 'but not in the street or in a doorway: inside, at a table, a kitchen table's best, in the morning and with a woman. I once showed Moses the word, beautifully carved and chiselled out. 'D'you like my word?' I asked, and I held up the tablets, but he shook his head, for he was as spoilt as he was large. 'Honestly not?' I asked, out of sorts; I took him by the hand and led him into a cool cave. 'Not inside a pretty cave either?' 'Not in a cave either,' said Moses, for he could be as stubborn as a mule. Then I took him high up on to a plain; the wind blew around us and I held up the word, causing a dizzying rush, but his eyes were dark and his lower lip pouted. 'Well?' 'Not here either,' he jeered, and he stuck out his tongue. 'And with a pretty balloon?' I asked, and I showed him one, red and gleaming and without a scratch on it. 'O-o-oh!' I cried, 'What a pretty balloon!' But that pigheaded fool stamped his foot and cried: 'I'll chuck it on to the rocks, to smithereens,' and he ran off, down below. No, no . . . No men . . . You have a thin neck and your ears are on the large side and your eyes are dark and moist: this'll send men up the wall, not women. Tell them at the kitchen table about a splendid city, built alongside a lake of gold across which barques are sailing in a setting sun, lute music everywhere and young men who know all the finer points. If you can explain all that to them, can show them what I have seen and describe the joys I have partaken of . . . They would no longer leave you alone but embrace the very last word from your skinny neck.'

The lad looked at his broken-down, patent leather shoes burrowing back and forth in the coal dust, and he said: 'I'm going to the village.'

'I wouldn't if I were you,' the old one said, 'but if you do, make sure you nick some greasy bacon and bread — not brown: it makes me fart so — and some tobacco, too, if poss.'

The young man got up, laboriously.

'Just one thing more,' the old one said, 'a long time ago a young man arrived at a monastery in a wild, deserted region, looking a bit like that one there on the hill. He looked at the tremendous wall turned to the world like a grumpy, sulking back, and deep inside the stone he heard the grumbling of the monks against their Lord. Those brothers were skinny as tally-sticks, only drank rain water and they ate turnips straight from the soil. They raked and dug all day long, preferably as bent over as possible, never looking up, and at night they dragged themselves to their cells to mutter there, to wring their hands and give a kick against the door now and then, or against the wall. This was all perfectly visible from the outside, and so the man shivered when he knocked at the gate and waited. Night was falling rapidly and on the horizon gleamed the yellow light of bad weather in the offing.

The porter brought him to the guest's cell, chucked a bit of wet peat on the fire there, put out water and bread, laid a blanket on the wooden bed, and during all this to-ing and fro-ing he crossed himself, repeatedly and bitterly. Then he lit a stubby bit of candle and disappeared. The man bit into the piece of black bread but instantly had a mouth full of beetles; he wanted to drink some water but this turned out to be so slimy it would not let itself be poured. He felt the straw on the bed, so wet it squelched, and the blanket was hopping with nits.

Disgruntled by such inhospitality, he stepped into the corridor, but everything was as silent and dark as the grave. In order to wake the monks, he called out all kinds of biblical sayings, but the echoes scattered so strangely back and forth through the corridors that the oddest of commandments now startled the monastery: 'feed the dead, bury the naked, dress the thirsty.'

This, in the end, brought the abbot himself on to the scene; he was accompanied by the porter who held up a mean little oil lamp so that two chabot heads floated threateningly towards the traveller. The abbot's mouth was large and black, his skull small and pointed, his nose large, coarse and heavy. 'In my nocturnal prayers,' he said in a sonorous voice, 'I had just arrived at the cursing of the children, the dancers, the lovers, the bards and the rich, of all who just do as they please, gadding about; to these I shall now add the traveller who simply comes and goes as he pleases, goes about crowing and hollering as it suits him and plods about in sin. Seize him, brothers, that harpy, and bundle him in clink; tomorrow we'll nail him to the cross, with big fat nails and without a bum-rest.' At that moment, some sturdy monks loomed out of the dark who grabbed the man, knotted him down firmly and laid him in his cell on the soggy straw, without saying a word.

Next day, when the weather was beginning to grow dark, they fetched him from his bed, put a heavy cross on his neck and pushed him up the hill.

'Why am I being crucified?' the man asked. 'Is it that you think that my soul's bursting with song, like the robber's or the sailor's?'

'Why no,' said the brother going along beside him, and with his stick he gave a firm blow on the toiling one's knuckles, so hard that the latter heard the pain scream throughout his entire body, something that made him fear the worst about things at the top of the hill.

'Or did I remind you of a soft bed with butter and sugar and fine morning tea?' the man cried plaintively. 'Or of a serving wench with thick hair, a springy middle and warm armpits?'

'Not at all,' laughed the brother who did not stray from his side but this time struck him a goodly wound in his neck with his knout, so that the man reached the top, glowing in wondrous splendour, feeling dizzy and confounded. There, a hole was quickly dug, one the cross would come to stand in.

'One favour before I die,' cried the unfortunate.

'No delay,' said the abbot, 'I simply cannot bear to wait any longer.'

They stripped the man, struck him on the mouth when he wanted to say something, and nailed him down firmly. Then they placed the cross upright in the hole and thoroughly firmed the soil up around it. I remember it well: the man hung there against a wine-red sky, all rolling muscles the way these develop on a cross, the bulging rib-cage sharply defined by the glancing evening light, the stomach nicely sunken, thighs well-formed, hobnails splendidly lit, fingers gnarled round them like roots. The monks went and sat down in a circle on the ground and looked on eagerly and attentively. They pointed out details to one another and whispered things in each other's ears causing smiles and rubbing of hands.

'Some day, this,' cried the abbot. 'Oh, God's glorious Grace,' the brothers joined him in support, 'and this is only nightfall; later, when it has got dark, we will hide ourselves away but we'll continue to watch, for then the dogs that gnaw the bones will come and the birds that peck out the eyes, and that can take hours.'

Full of dismay, the traveller listened to all this. 'But why?' he cried, writhing in despair.

'For our great sins and His redeeming Passion,' the abbot said piously. 'To know of it is one thing, but to realise it is another, and a good deal more too.'

'Beware of the women,' the old man cried rather inconsistently, irately shaking a gnarled index finger, 'they're leech-lizards, particularly when you tell them stories.' Groaning softly, he settled himself down on the ground so that his torso was in the shade and his legs in the sun.

'That's the way' – he sighed with cosy contentment and sought his handkerchief. When he had finally managed to get it out, with difficulty, his head sagged forwards in a sudden bout of sleepiness. 'Dear, dear,' he said to himself, worried, 'how my powers do wane of late.'

Things were quiet around him; the tree casting its shadow over him stood motionless; some birds rustled among the leaves and far in the distance there was the sound of footsteps. That was the young man walking with slow tread through the main street; he held his small and peculiarly shaped head that from the side resembled a tapir's muzzle, to one side and his big ears caught every sound indeed, to the very smallest. Thus he heard how the villagers got up, very carefully, to steal on tiptoe to the window and stand behind the curtains to follow him with their gaze. There's something up, here, they thought, he's come here to poke his nose into other men's business, to steal chickens or to take little girls with him, around the corner. This was why they followed the stranger, with sullen eyes and with great acuity.

In the middle of a large square the man suddenly saw a dog – where it came from all of a sudden he didn't know either, but there it was, with drooping head and panting flanks from the heat. The creature had a thin, miserable carcass and a tail gnawed bare by fleas, crooked paws through abysmal feeding and bald patches because of something else again. With a cocked, dozy head the man absorbed this image of physical misery, the muzzle hanging open, the dried-up tongue, and above the immense square he felt the mercilessly empty and glinting sky. 'Blessed be the fly,' he cried resonantly across the square, 'that drowns in wine, but woe betide the one that sinks in honey or sticks to ointment, or the arms and legs of which are torn off by a playing child and left, forgotten, on the kitchen table. Blessed the dog that dies an easy death, snuffed out with a gentle breath and in a single sigh.

'But woe betide the one that dies in a square, openly, dusted with sand, scorched by the sun.' Saying this, he took out a bowl from nowhere, poured it full of cool, clear water and placed it on the stones.

Soft muttering behind hands went round the village, and the windows of the houses on the square misted over with distrust. The dog looked dully at the dish, whimpered and then trudged off across the cobbles. This was a timid and practised looker-round: the back already arched for stick and stone, watchful down to the last knobbly joint.

Looks don't deceive, the villagers said.

The man with the small and peculiar head crossed the square, turned into a narrow street and there he entered one of the little houses. It was cool and dusky there, for all the curtains had been lowered because of the sun. In a corner of the room a woman was sleeping, a heavy, pale woman, her large hands in her lap, palms up, sagged open in sleep, the turnip-like head resting against the back of the chair.

Carefully, the man went and sat at the table in order to stare out ahead of him there, intently, but he stumbled about so clumsily that the woman awoke with a start and believed for a moment to be eye to eye with her murderer. Then she recovered herself, roused herself painfully and, uneasily because of her large feet, she waddled over to him. 'Is that you, my boy?' she said, embracing him tenderly. 'How lovely, you looking in on us again; have people been good to you?' Her hands felt the man's skinny back for a moment, then she pressed his small, pointed head to her chest and began to stare strangely into the room. Her eyes glazed over and turned upwards too, which made a lot of the white of her eyes visible, and things seemed to indicate strongly that the encounter had all become too much for her. Her hands also had changed: instead of heavy and thick, they were now suddenly long and thin, with curled up banana-fingers.

'Mother,' the man said, his voice smothered because of her bosom.

'Yes, my boy,' said the woman, 'mother's here, for a mother must always be prepared. I've got nothing to reproach myself with, I have.'

At that moment the sparse light in the room was diminished by the appearance of two girls in the doorway; by their smell one could clearly tell how hot it was outside.

The woman revived and said: 'Here're Anna and Maria from next door; they're just dropping by, you know what neighbours are like.'

The young man shook hands with them and said how surprisingly easily he had been able to find the house again in the village, as if he hadn't been away. The girl called Anna took another step into the room so that her face was no longer so indistinct. She had a large, very sensuous mouth and her nose was no tiddler either, but her piggy little eyes looked kindly into the world.

'I, on the contrary,' she said, 'am always afraid of losing my way, particularly in the evening, and I also have a fear of suddenly going blind and then falling into the river.'

The young man laughed. 'Those who follow me shall not stumble in the dark. I do like the water, don't like swimming but like standing in it and going a bit wrinkly.'

The girl Anna blushed, cast down her eyes and whispered: 'Now there's a thing.' Then she turned to the woman and asked: 'Shall I give the room he sleeps in a bit of a going-over, and air and make his bed?'

'Fine,' the woman said, measuredly, 'I know my place.'

That evening, when the young man had already gone upstairs, Anna dropped by a moment, out of interest, but many questions hovered unuttered in the room.

'Would you mind taking him some fresh water?' the woman asked. 'You have young legs and if there's anything else you need, tell me.'

The girl Anna went upstairs, knocked, stepped inside and set down the water on the table. Then she settled on a chair beside the bed. The young man sat on the only other chair, at the table, and he stared at the water in the bowl.

The garret room was in part situated above the stables, the smells from which penetrated with great force through the gaps in the floor. These were the smells of a summer's evening so balmy and full of promise as only exists apocryphally. Purple, the evening dashed against the window, jasmine scent and hay-heat hung heavily upon the air and the grievous snorting and stamping of the bull downstairs was clearly discernible. Brightly gleamed the eye of the mother behind the keyhole and, behind a few gaps further along, those of the neighbour and the lass, Maria. What they saw they slurped in greedily, but there was painfully little. Perhaps both knew they were being watched by glittering eyes behind the wall, but they showed no signs of shame or irritation. The room was neat, its furnishing extremely spartan; the bed, however, had been highly aired and made with care, even more reason to crawl away together for a right old cuddle and let farmers make the hay. But no; the young man spoke: not quite audibly, he told of very sad things, for the girl Anna drooped more and more, with hunched back and shoulders and despondent hands in her lap. The mother, not wishing to let any opportunity pass in order not to have anything to reproach herself with later on, fetched her lute from downstairs and strummed a soft and sloping song. 'I hang my helmet on the brazen knob.'

Both youngsters were well equipped for an hour of cheeky bliss: he possessed the attractiveness of someone who comes from far away, that of the stranger, and she smelled so strongly of fresh honeysuckle, it hurt; moreover, the bull boomed downstairs on the cobbles and steamed like Pan himself. The young man, however, just held forth, a strange light resting on his pointed little skull. He pointed upwards with his knobbly finger as if he was probing the chart of heaven, modelled all kinds of strange things in the air, and meanwhile the little virgin Anna blinked away tear upon tear from her little eyes. The mother even appeared in the room for a moment, jazzing up the lighting with a little red table lamp, setting down a pitcher of red wine on the table and a dish of peppered beef.

In the end, virgin Anna left the loft, sobbing, stumbling down the stairs, squeaking with misery, and she cried: 'To what do I owe this?'

'Who cares!' the mother cried after her, triumphant, 'you can't get used to it soon enough, my girl: children ... nothing but misery.'

It came to pass that a great drought arrived in the land, and to such an extent that even a camel standing stock-still threw up a cloud of dust. The earth around the village had been scorched brown-grey, and when the sun had reached its highest point, tongues of flame flickered in the sky. The struggle for water had of old been part of daily toil. The inhabitants of the village owed their chabot head to it: that little pointed skull, the little eyes close together, their nose the size of a sugar beet, and those coarse-grubbing gobs. The songs in the village were full of shade, milk, the rustle of leaves and glugging water. There was even a man who had made himself perfectly at one with the dryness of the soil; it had become the objective of all his considerations, not God, but the withered, asphyxiating plain of scorched shale and sand. 'This earth does not cease to give,' he hummed on the little market, 'tender meat, fine milk, living water, and moreover she also bears the poet on her back.'

Where there is scarcity, there is also the spiv, the crafty one, the canny devil; no milk anywhere ... he has butter; no oil ... his lamp burns as brightly as the first day; has all water gone ... he still perspires, untroubled, speaks with moist mouth and things gurgle in his stomach, juicily.

In the village there is a narrow, steep, quiet little backwater where the sun always shines, but half way up there is a small side-alley where there is a great to-do. Here the water trade is conducted; the atmosphere is tense but lively, and it is a fascinating sight to hear the turnip-heads from the village and its surroundings shout and bid there with cracked lips and parched voices.

The water trade is a murky business, for how the cool water gets there into the cistern deep underground is incomprehensible to the thirsty nit: this is the spiv's, the canny devil's secret. It was whispered that the water owner had connections with little clouds which only watered his garden, whispers too about a basin, that happened to be underneath his house, to which the water flowed and dripped, unstoppably, from far and wide, and where it stayed just as cool as in winter. Whatever the case, the trader had his house extended and purchased white camels with small, precious carpets in the stirrups and golden knobs on the saddles.

Until the real drought came, the drought within a drought which made the earth crack and snap to its very core. Sudden splits and rifts boomed through the rocky ground and the price of the obligatory wooden bowls which had not cracked rose to unknown heights. But the price of water, of course, rose most of all, indeed, it even rose while being passed from one to the next so that the thirsty had to pass it on, from one to the next, incessantly, and they finally succumbed, as dry as St Nicholas's bottom. The chabot skulls mummified, nose and cheeks withered, all hope drained dry from the eyes.

When their plight was at its worst, the rumours started: there'd been thunder, it was said, in the mountains on the horizon, there was even said to be a waterfall there, free and open in the sky, just like that. This last one was not to the rich water merchant's liking and he would no longer give water to ones who believed such tales. Until he happened to have a visit from a feverish young man with a hollow look in his eyes, who told him about a source out there in the desert from which water bubbled up inexhaustibly, a spot blessed with henna flowers, vine bushes, apple trees and the occasional gazelle. As if by a miracle, the merchant was convinced.

'Show me the way there,' he shouted, chalk-white with greed. He quickly gathered some onions, goat's cheese and a few flasks of *aqua*, and off they went, looking back furtively time and again. For days they made their way through sand and cinder, the landscape, naked and drab, unchanging so that it was as if they were rooted to the same spot, for ever, and yearning. The sun beat down, godless and scorching, on the pointed head of the merchant; camel and companion, crumpling, were left behind. The merchant could no longer speak, for his tongue tapped to and fro in his mouth like a twig; the last drop of urine, squeezed out with much effort, carved through his member like a red-hot knife.

The grotto he reached with his last, faltering steps, and the strange figure he found there did not seem to be bothered by anything at all: he munched some locusts, cheerfully spitting out legs round about and appeared to be in fine fettle. His was the primal posture of the spirit: down, splat, on his bum, the thighs carelessly spread wide, the hands scalloped before the cosmic. With intense compassion he addressed the sly dog, having first refreshed him extensively with cool water from a flask he calmly and generously brought forth from the dark of the grotto.

'I am the source,' the man said, 'mark you, I'm not saying he is the source, or we are the source, or them's the source, no ... I'm saying that *I* am the source. Nor am I saying that I was the source, am it perhaps or once ever will be, none of all those: I say that I *am* the source. And I'm not on about the door or the gate or the fence, no, I'm on about the *source* and then not just any old source, but *the* source. What sayest thou to this?'

The merchant, bewildered, pointed to his mouth which still had sand and dust panting in and out of it, and again he was given water, copiously, without any contribution as regards cost, and then the word goes down a treat, it does.

Thus, to everyone's disappointment, the man returned to the chabot village with a spring in his step and, as all and sundry thought, firmly intent on squeezing out every last drop again. But no, this turned out quite differently: the merchant had become a man of the word. Where previously they had bitten each other's ears off to get to the front during trading, chabotteurs now congregated in all tolerance to listen to the merchant, during which they would be handed a little bowl of water: they just couldn't suspend their disbelief for a moment. 'Blessed be they who quench for free,' said the waterman and he let the words roll in his mouth, round and round, with relish, 'for they shall inherit a kingdom.'

'Aha,' the chabot-tops thought cunningly, 'there you have it,' and their eyes moved a little closer together still. But no matter how distrustful they were and continually bore in mind being hauled back to bone-dry reality, the man appeared to be firmly decided to share out his supply of water, to give away his riches, and in so doing to tell about his encounter in the desert. He went round the village like an uncomfortable presence, greeting everybody, smiling in an unnatural manner, and now and then he laid his hand in blessing upon the head of an old dolt or a playing child, who then would making a quick get-away for that matter.

'What precisely did actually happen?' the elders asked, repeatedly, and one evening he addressed them. 'I will tell you of this in parables,' he said, 'for otherwise it looks just ordinary and this it is not, not at all. Listen: I found the master sitting at the entrance to his grotto, deep in thought, pondering, and I saw that his little, pear-shaped head was stuffed full of choicest thoughts and noble passions. He was sitting on a stool covered in gleaming pink silk, like at court, his nose was nicely ripe in shape and his large, broad lips made a pale oval shape in his black stubbly beard. An art connoisseur, by the looks of him, a man from the East cloaked in cool white silk and with a rosette in his buttonhole. A man who would go far; I saw this in no time at all. In front of him, in a marble courtyard with columns, fat white women rolled about the floor, and from time to time, when he had a refined thought, he would, with an elegant gesture, measure a breast or nipple between his thumb and index finger. Occasionally he would caress their skin which was smooth as silk and gleamed like a mirror because of scented oils, and then he would stare out across the wilderness with eyes like gelatine, moist and dark, and very narcotic in the depths. 'Women,' he then said, 'they are yearning . . . eternity and spirit. Amen, 'n over-and-out, folks.'

'Did I already mention the plaster eagle, his opera hat in his right hand, his youngsters: a tailor, a cook, a gravedigger, a nurse and a few more. I knelt before him in the dust but I had so many things to ask him all at once that I ended up being a little lost. When he went into the grotto to have forty winks during the hot noontime hour, I did see that his legs were a little on the short side.'

'Tell us more,' cried the elders excitedly, 'tell us all.'

'One evening,' the merchant said, cosily contented, and after a thoughtful swig, 'we were sitting together, the lights had been extinguished and everybody felt themselves to be in the safe hands of the others, some way or other. It was a dreadfully stormy night, lightning flashing incessantly and unceasing thunder all round. The trees groaned in the garden and in the distance we heard the sea booming against the rocks and waves rolling in, tall as houses.'

'The sea?' cried the elders, 'where did that suddenly come from, where actually *was* that grotto?'

Refined, the merchant raised an already somewhat pale, thin hand and said: 'These are but parables; books and verses, as it were.'

'Continue,' the elders said.

'All had assembled in the hall.'

'In the hall? Now which hall would this be then?'

'In the hall of parables. The house stood in a forest and in the blue light of the streaks of lightning we were well able to see one another's faces. Though heaven was enraged, we did not fear because we were together and our joy consisted of the fact that otherwise we would have been afraid. I looked at my mother's, my father's sweet face jolting out in the light, for they were all there too.'

'They are dead and buried,' the elders cried.

'In a manner of speaking,' smiled the merchant. 'Next day the weather was splendid, the boat floated through the shadows the trees cast on the water. We saw the fish fanning out, stones distorting in the waves and the swaying of all kinds of sea grass, red, green . . . And the master taught the while. 'Don't you be frightened now,' he said, 'for what is truth, after all.'

'But the message,' cried the elders crotchetily, 'something to cling on to.'

'To one it's this, to another it's the next,' the merchant said, 'but he who hears truly cannot but accept it. To me, the word was 'Refresh those who thirst, and no more whingeing.'

When the water from the cistern began to run out, the skulls became more pointed, the ears more deaf. But then, the chabot village does not care much for the word proclaimed; the village was more one for the whisper, for muttering from behind a hand, speech during which one sees no lips move. There came a time when the merchant was standing alone on his box and, beard peaky and unkempt, was speaking of salvation, cleansing water and all things like that, and soon he was only a babbling greybeard with no possessions at all, and they had plenty like them in the village already. Moreover, a little further along, the water trade had enjoyed a lively rebirth; where the new merchant got the water from was a mystery, but he had the stuff and he was a very severe man who went to extremes.

Thus the army of thirsty ones was reduced by one and augmented by one, and therefore not much had changed. When, with some malicious pleasure, they asked the merchant reduced to beggary who was also waiting in the burning sun for his little drop, what he now thought of the word, he said: 'I was with the master, not you: one cannot crimp those who are absent.'

It came to pass that the youth opened his eyes in his foster parents' house in town. 'Lovely weather,' he thought, 'some day, this,' and while he sat up, half asleep, in his bed, the night birds withdrew into the dark niches of his brain. The floral, predominantly pink pattern of the curtains unfolded itself slowly and slid back together again under the slight pressure of the morning breeze; now and then he would see the sharp sunlight on the window sill for a moment.

In the house scattered noises arose, first signs of life on this splendid summer morning: a scrap of radio, a door slamming, the shower turned on. The youth listened to the wind in the garden for a while, and though no one was watching him or sticking their head round the door, he went to lie down again and meticulously pretended to be asleep. But there were more and more noises, on the street now too, and he decided to sit up on the edge of his bed, after all, where he scratched both armpits and head and looked at his feet. 'Some day, this.'

Thoughtfully, he stood up and then walked across to the wash stand to polish and gurgle away sleep once and for all. Washing and splashing, he was flooded with summery resolutions, so much so he tried to push open the window a little further with wet, foamy hands so as not to prevent anything from flooding in, fully and unhindered. He also stuck his damp head out of the window and, morning drunk, he looked around: everything sparkled with dew. He twisted his sleep-stiff neck as far as possible and let the light plunge down into his eyes so that it hurt, then he slowly went inside again and continued dressing. Or so he thought, that is, but with a sudden start he knew that he had been standing at the window for quite a while, drowsing; in a great feeling of happiness he had healed the sick, taken away pain, advanced money, watered a dog, saved children from a pond, and a tremendous treacle eye, black with gratitude, stared at him so that his own eyes became moist because of it.

'It's all ready,' somebody cried from downstairs and simultaneously the scent of toast and coffee curled its way upstairs. Cups chinked sharply, a giggle struck him painfully, a laugh cracked hard and hoarse. He knew what awaited him downstairs, he already knew the jostling, the punches and jokes, and he knew he did not want to enter this day, but wished to stay alone to preserve himself carefully.

Breakfast was in full spate downstairs, but he had always been a tardy riser and he knew they would not yet make things difficult for him. First, he shaved himself until his jaws gleamed like a dog's dick, then he slowly brought out his newly acquired things and settled down in front of the mirror again. With slow movements he began smearing a cleansing morning cream on to his coarse face; still sleepy, his fingers circled and pushed the white stuff across his skin, a service of love with feeling tips to a face that was becoming ever dearer to him. As elegantly as possible, he cleaned himself up with tissues and threw the crunched up balls in the wash basin with coquettish gestures not observed before. Then he applied the moisturising cream which smoothed and tightened the skin, bleached it just a touch and created a splendid foundation for the eye shadow. Most attentively he brushed on his *Kleine Nachtmusik*, spleen looming up around the little eyes, shadows of nocturnal tossing about and refined suffering. He highlighted the cheekbones a little with blusher but all the while he hugged himself over his coarse mouth with those lips like ones from a joke shop: out of these he would make a pink-glossed and moistly sucking openness to the entire world, a warm and flesh-pink flirting from heart to heart. Finished with this, to his regret, he listened sharply to the house and then on tiptoe fetched the wig from the permanently locked little cabinet. Back in front of the mirror, with shoulders high and angular from tension, he slowly domed the elegant mass over his stubbly pate, relishing the metamorphosis. That moment could not really be executed slowly enough and he regretted that the coiffure was in place. Holding his breath, he leant forward deeply and regarded in a misty gaze his image in which his great, pink lips still languidly massaged one another a little. Now, a touch of perfume, little-fingered wispily, in the dimple at the base of the throat, and away he crept, largest size high-heeled shoes in hand, down the stairs and on to the street.

At a safe distance from the house, he put his shoes on and walked in the morning sun in the direction of the park. He was outside like this for the first time, bursting with promise and safe from humiliating recognition and it was as if he hurled himself on to the entire world. With great intensity he tried to find the right walk for that feeling; he built one up, one with a nice, long hip-line, a slight sway of the buttocks, a well-placed syncopation of the heels and a deep, wide swing of the right arm. His first whistles of praise he harvested near the tennis courts, from the morning-fresh youngsters of good taste, yet people did not recognise him there.

He sought a bench in the shade because of the make-up and, light-headed and absentminded, he awaited the moment when the tolling of bells would roll across the park and the city, and would call away the faithful from behind their coffee tables. The way to church ran through the park; whenever it was at all possible, the entire neighbourhood would take the stroll in order to get in the mood for God's word so clearly present in the raked paths, pruned shrubs, flower beds and mown grass. That was where one greeted one another, with one's hat or just a hand, with that slight but not unpleasant worry the tolling of a church bell evokes.

The youth got many looks; he saw men and women looking round furtively, peering, turning away quickly in shame or sinking into a frown, but he knew himself to be unrecognisable in his confusing conspicuousness. His ear, sharp and having a fine instinct, noticed how much irritation had crept into the previously so cheerful, unforced cries of the children who always stayed behind near the ducks and the swans.

In church he looked for a seat as far to the front as possible, at the heart of all the whisperings, and regarding the statues and frescos with great piety, he showed the churchgoers his elevated profile, the white-powdered nose now in keeping with the weight of hair, the little black eyes wide-wafted in Egyptian mascara, the muscular yet well-filled neck and the pendulous earlobes. Women's mouths carved their way in, men stared sombrely between their knees at the ground in front of them; the youth knew all too well what seething fabric of love, anger and hate bound him to the churchgoers, and a deep feeling of happiness tingled through him from his toupee to the soles of his feet.

The gaze from the little eyes of the preacher rested on him a moment and his voice began, high and strong: 'It so happens, dear friends, that I must catch the train this morning early, but this enforced haste in fact gives me precisely the opportunity to seek your attention for a fundamental matter that just occurred to me. Why, I wondered just now, did the Lord Jesus, who after all is love, tempt mankind to commit the greatest possible sin, the killing of Him – and how! Well, my good people, because He is the Truth, too, and for no other reason. Therefore: have faith in moderation, continue to hope, and love thy neighbour as you please. Furthermore, learn three prayers off by heart, one for breakfast, one the Lord's Prayer, and one for the traveller, for there are a lot of evil folk on the road and I have to travel rather a lot. A blessed morning to you all.'

Thoughtfully, the youth sniffed whiffs of incense and wax candle, slow-moving feastday-scents in which bright white tennis players made broad swings against a claret-red background. Deep inside himself, he studied them while listening to the high, lamenting boys'-voices. Some day, this! ... One full of pure mouths down to the last fibre, serious tennis faces, solemn, thin necks protruding from white lace, and pink throats swaying with godswoe.

Now and then he also cast a benevolent glance upwards for a moment, at the darkness of the arches and the yellowy-white body above the altar. Nasty business that, very nasty ... sure.

And yet, a peerless tennis gesture, too, stretched out broadly as if for cosmic applause. He saw himself hanging there, shatteringly coiffed, in a heavenly trance and with pitiable hands large as breakfast plates. His heart swelled with yearning for suffering, sacrifice, doom and bloom; and suddenly bunching everything together – choirboys, church and heaven – he muttered: 'And now for some coffee, a good strong cup of it.'

And in the evening, after a day to which there seemed to be no end, he walked towards his house in the gathering dusk, roamed around outside it a while, took cover among the shrubs and watched. The lawn was lit by a few standard lamps and by the big windows, a barbecue placed the summer scent of a roast on the wind, on a table decorated with flowers stood snacks, canapés and many bottles of wine. Elegantly dressed, the guests walked to and fro, the women to show off their expensive outfits, the men not to trouble others with their cigars.

In the middle of the lawn, so that everyone could see her clearly, stood the hostess, elegantly wringing her hands, who cried: 'Oh, where might he be, what could he be up to.'

'His stubble's prickling him,' said the host, looking up from a conversation a moment, 'he'll turn up again,' and he continued his discourse.

More guests arrived; they drove up, got out immaculately, exchanged words of greeting and spread out heartily across the lawn. From time to time, however, the hostess would wander to the edge of the circle of light, there where the darkness began, and she would call out worriedly: 'Oohoo . . . ' A few half-full glasses stood round her in the grass; above, heaven domed its balmy curve.

The youth in the shrubs turned round and went off into the summer night, alone . . . but not for long. Not far from the house he was already being addressed by a gentleman who apparently was out on an evening stroll still and who stood out because of his screamingly expensive hat which he had placed elegantly on his turnip pate.

His clothes were immaculate for that time of day: a dress-handkerchief caught the fading light and spread the pleasant scent of *soigné* hotels in distant lands, atop his stick a golden knob gleamed mattly but implacably. Judged by the cut and quality of the suit, the man was successful in business relations and, judging by the whiff of cologne, seasoned in financial transactions too. Yet he was nervous, and indeed, having introduced himself elaborately, he told how the frightful incident of yesteryear made him unhappy still and often robbed him of his nightly rest.

The youth regarded the man before him with great intensity, for he experienced much sympathy for all people who were in difficulty, and he searched for an apt and cheering word.

'You must know,' the man said, while far beyond his head some clouds floated past the moon that had suddenly appeared there, 'that, though my influence is large, I was not able to prevent it at the time. Truly, I put in a good deal of my time, conducted bouts of telephoning right down to far beyond the borders, but it was unpreventable. I can prevent many things, maybe all things even, but this happened as if it had happened already.'

The youth's attitude expressed both great interest as well as concern. 'Best tell the lot, ' he said, 'it eases it all.'

'I built roads and bridges,' the man said, 'deposits everywhere, liquidations of associations, stock meetings, speculations, frauds. I knew my way around everywhere and like a master. But everything suddenly collapsed, people began to ask me convoluted questions, worse, I myself began to ask myself convoluted questions. My business wilted, I left the safe wide open, no longer bolted anything, left briefcases and portfolios behind everywhere, tipped off my enemies by mistake. There seemed to be no end to the collapse; I was taken to one of the most respected asylums where in vain I tried to explain that the fate of the world was connected with mine.

'I once was able to prevent the doom of the world, for instance, by guarding heaven for a whole night; I also saved a harvest by making flocks of migrant birds change direction. That's why I beseech you to.' As the man was saying this, he carefully raised a trouserleg a little by the knee, laid his dress-handkerchief down on the stones, knelt on it and raised the great knobbly hands in the moonlight.

With mounting interest, the youth looked down on the man, on the coarse-featured, excited face, the neat starched collar, the tremendous manicured nails, and he felt great respect for this man of the world.

'Speak,' he said, 'and whatever it may be, my good man, it shall be forgiven thee — bear this in mind.'

The man jumped up, a spring in his movement, dusted down his trousers, and he said, relieved: 'Thank heaven I am still permitted to experience this.'

'What then exactly?' the youth asked, patient and curious.

'That crucifixion business, way back,' the man cried, voice breaking. 'No matter what I did, I couldn't manage. The sacrifices I made: transferring money abroad, talking the hind leg off a donkey; but come hell or high water, they wanted that cross. A right royal mess . . . not short on the writhing and groaning, that was of course — ah, well, we know all about it.'

The youth stepped back with shock and his mouth hung open slightly, but the man was just as quick: with both fists he grabbed the hand of the Saviour, pumped it vigorously and cried: 'I'm so sorry I wasn't able to turn things back again; oh please, I *do* beg your pardon.' Meanwhile, he glanced fleetingly at his watch and said: 'Up early tomorrow, must still try to get a few hours sleep.'

'So must I,' said the Redeemer, suddenly a little weak in the bladder. 'Where am I to go?'

The man pointed upwards with his stick where the dark silhouette of the monastery could be seen on top of the hill. 'To the Chabotins,' he said, 'a decent order that says of itself that they're proud of their virtues and have let go of all vices.' Following this, he adjusted the angle of his hat, little finger raised elegantly, said: 'Good night, and good luck,' and walked off, unmistakably and immaculately a gentleman from the rear as well.

The Disappearance of Bertje S.

Remco Campert

Bertje S. had been missing for weeks. His parents, close acquaintances of mine, had, deep in their hearts, without daring to admit it to one another, given up hope of being able to lock him in their arms ever again. The police had dragged all possible rivers, canals and waterways in the area for a body, with no results whatsoever. His description had appeared in the newspapers and had been broadcast on the radio. Clairvoyants had offered their services but had not succeeded in finding a trace of the blond, six-year-old little boy.

Anton, Bertje's father, who was in the service of one of our biggest weekly magazines as an academic correspondent, sat for most of the day, as if paralysed, in an armchair by the radio which was switched on from morning till night, washing waves of sound over the head of the unhappy man. At times, however, he would jump up and telephone police inspectors whom by turn he would bawl out or, weeping, plead with to continue the search with all available force. Or he would take his car and drive around, with a pale face in which his eyes glinted feverishly, at wild speeds along little back roads, stopping, tyres screeching, at whatever farmer's child he happened to spot.

Sonja, his wife, was in bed in her room, refused to take any food and had surrounded herself with photos of Bertje, toys he enjoyed playing with and drawings he had made. A smile played around her lips which I could only behold with a shudder, for sorrow that induces a smile has assumed dimensions that an outsider can no longer understand. When entering her room, she would always receive me very politely, would offer me a chair and would talk to me about this and that as if she were in bed only to rest for an hour or so from the ordinary fatigue of the day.

Then came the morning that I stepped into my car in order to drive to one of the spots in our country where there are still woods which are seldom marked by human footsteps. Day in, day out, almost, I had spent the past weeks with Anton and Sonja, and witnessing their suffering, combined with my impotence to assuage that suffering, had exhausted me. I wished to be away from all of this for a single day, in surroundings which in no way would remind me of the terrible event which had befallen my friends. At about midday I arrived in the vicinity of the woods. I parked my car in a quiet, leafy avenue. The sun was shining, the sky was cloudless and in the woods where I was walking now, setting down my feet with a sensation of physical well-being in the soft moss growing beneath the trees, it was cool and the air was scented. I felt as if reborn. All the misery I had experienced lately had slid from my shoulders like a drab cloak.

For hours I roamed without stopping until, in the end, I was so tired that I decided to rest a moment. I settled down on the moss, leaned with my back against the mighty trunk of a beech tree and lit a cigarette. I closed my eyes and relished my tiredness which, for the first time in a long while, was a healthy, physical tiredness again. It would not be long before I would return to the inhabited world once more, but this I tried to forget right now and I succeeded remarkably well.

When I had finished my cigarette, I carefully extinguished the stub, mindful of the ordinances which tell us to be careful with fire in forests and heathland. With an expansive swing I tossed the stub away, which ended up in some shrubbery that had managed to nestle here. Barely had I done this when I began to doubt whether the stub had indeed been out when I threw it away. Having been in two minds for a while, I got up with a sigh in order to go and convince myself, one way or another.

I moved the shrubs aside, bent down, and what I then saw made my blood curdle with fright.

In the shrubs was a pile of clothes. Children's clothes. Two little brown shoes, a pair of socks, underpants, a pair of khaki shorts and a vest. On top of the underwear there was a wrist watch which I picked up with trembling fingers in order to take a better look at it, though this was really not necessary as I was already sure that it was Bertje's watch. Not a real watch, but a cheap toy thing with a plastic strap, one that would not run.

Bertje had been given it by his father and he was as proud as a peacock of it. I reversed the little timepiece and saw how Bertje's initials had been scratched into the cheap metal. Sonja had done that, and I myself had been there at the time. Not a shadow of a doubt. This was Bertje's watch and these were Bertje's clothes.

It seemed indisputable to me that his little corpse would have to be here, somewhere in the neighbourhood, who knows how gruesomely abused, for I would not find the child alive again, of this I was convinced. It was my duty to warn the police at once, but it could do no harm, I thought, to hunt around a little myself, first. But where? Unable to decide, I looked around me, the watch still in my hand. I regarded the woods in an entirely different light now. The beauties of nature had just then been a source of joy and new vigour to me; now these same beauties had become a backdrop before which a scene, the gruesomeness of which could only be guessed at, had been enacted which had cost the life of an innocent child.

I looked, but nowhere did I see a trace of Bertje. Then (perhaps by chance, but since that day I do not believe in chance any more) I cast my eyes upward and high in the tree under which I had been sitting (it was not possible, it could not be, but I knew that it was the truth), in a fork formed by two branches, gleaming grey-white in the sunlight trickling down the leaves, I saw a huge cocoon gently being rocked, to and fro, by the wind.

Bluebeard's Daughter

Louis Couperus

Her name was Fatma and she lived at one of her country houses in the environs of Baghdad. She was Bluebeard's daughter from his first marriage and she was a wondrously beautiful woman; around her moon-pale face her blue hair cascaded like a cloak down her slender shoulders . . .

It is not generally known that Bluebeard had a daughter. It is commonly thought that he, childless, was vanquished by the brothers of his last, I believe ninth, wife who was said to have inherited all his riches. When one has searched, as I have, the secret archives of the Lay, one discovers without too much difficulty that Bluebeard, his skull cleft in two, died in his daughter's arms and left *her* all his possessions.

The young orphan, the bewitching Fatma, had loved her father most dearly, as he had loved her, though she had never been able to come to accept the manner in which he freed himself of his many disobedient wives. She thought this manner to be *not* mild, *not* noble, and monotonous in its psychology. She understood too well that, each time, her new stepmother had had to give in to the temptation of her curiosity. She did not gloss over her father's actions, and considered them to be something of an inexcusable expression of sadism.

The azure-tressed Fatma, a youthful orphan, continued lonely among her countless riches and all her servants and slaves who surrounded her like a royal progress as it were. The notable families in Baghdad, at the court of the Caliph, spoke much about the young, rich, blue-haired one but, her immeasurable riches notwithstanding, not one desired her as the bride for a son or a nephew. Her tresses evoked too many memories of terrible things, so the beautiful Fatma remained alone on her onyx terraces which made their progress among date copses and rose gardens to her crystal clear, reflecting ponds . . . And she, likewise lonely, wandered back between the onyx pillars of the galleries to her summer palace which, paved with gold and silver tiles, was also clad with gold and silver roofing.

Until she could bear the loneliness no longer and ignited in virgin love for the foreman of her gardeners. He was a very handsome youth, come from the country, and the rusticity of his occupation gave him in Fatma's eyes, which were a little tired through over-refinement, an irresistible power to enchant. Therefore she married him without concerning herself about what would be said about her among the notable Baghdad families or at the Caliph's court.

Fatma seemed very happy. She displayed herself together with her spouse in full splendour and precious elegance, in town and countryside, in tapestry-adorned gondolas on the ponds, in cushion-filled sedan chairs in the streets, with a train of slaves in the bazaars and even at the court feasts which, because of her rank and wealth, she had entry to. Fatma together with her beloved Emin formed an enchantingly beautiful couple: he, sturdy and young, and glorying in his new wealth – the type did not exist then at all yet – she, glittering with love and priceless jewels which glinted on her gauze turban and weighed down the hems of her robes, while her azure tresses had been woven through with wondrously large pearls. And already the notable Baghdad families sadly regretted not having made any effort to win Bluebeard's daughter for their sons or nephews . . .

Suddenly, however, the rumour spread that Emin had died . . . Only the previous day, all Baghdadians had seen him in the Mosque, and lo: one learnt that . . . that he had died! A shudder passed through the city but still there was no cause for the Grand-Vizir and the Grand Procurator to get involved in the case now that the perfectly credible rumour circulated that Emin, on that warm day, had eaten too much watermelon and had succumbed subsequently to a severe colic.

Eyebrows in Baghdad were raised, however, when it was learned three months later that the young, azure-tressed widow was to remarry, to marry the lieutenant of her bodyguard, to be precise. It seemed that Fatma had too wide a choice from among her staff, servants and subjects even to be bothered with the sons and nephews of the notable families of Baghdad. The wedding took place with magical pomp and Fatma's new spouse gloried, as Emin had done, now he saw himself elevated from such a lowly rank to that of consort of his magically beautiful, magically rich mistress. But the young lieutenant – Fatma had elevated him to General of her life guard – died suddenly, of a fall from his horse, it was said.

The message was unclear: had the young lieutenant or the horse taken a fall? Moreover, no one had seen the young lieutenant-general of Fatma's bodyguard, neither on a horse nor taking a fall . . . indeed, *nobody* had seen him on the day of his death, and fierce emotion coursed through the Baghdad families and pervaded the Court of the Caliph, for they remembered all too well that Fatma was blue-tressed the way once her father had been blue-bearded.

The sorrowing widow Fatma, in her black veils and weeds covered in black diamonds, resembled a Queen of the Night, particularly as her blue hair shimmered through the mourning veils so suggestively that, without applying any stage-paint, she would have been able to appear in Mozart's *Zauberflöte*. However, she did not sing such demanding and difficult *coloratura* and preferred to please herself by taking a third spouse: this time, quite simply, one of her palanquin bearers. That the young Ali was a splendid specimen of a man who, as third spouse, now looked like a young sultan in his damask cymar, this it was not possible to doubt, but what *was* doubted among the notable families at the Court of the Caliph was whether, after three months of married life, he had indeed died a natural death . . . How might such a strong, handsome, healthy man as Fatma's palanquin-bearer-consort have died, of natural causes – following malaria it was said – and been buried quietly, without any ado?! Heads nodded to one another, eyes distorted in horror, mouths contorted with secret suppositions, and the Grand-Vizir and the Grand-Procurator deliberated whether they would not involve themselves with the Fatma-affair, with that dying-and-disappearing-after-three-months-of-marriage of one spouse after the other!

They deliberated so long, however, that Fatma married for the fourth, fifth and sixth times. The fourth time was with a Persian merchant from Teheran for whom a long life had been predicted from the lines in his hand; the fifth was with one of the rowers of her pleasure gondolas; the sixth time with a humble slave who worked in Fatma's emerald mine. Each time, after three months, the ill-fated spouses died. And the widow went about Baghdad like the Queen of the Night . . .

Then the limit seemed to have been reached. The Grand-Vizir and the Grand-Procurator appeared before Fatma's pleasure dome but it seemed that she had moved to another abode. For she had several: the one with the onyx terraces and then the one with the mother-of-pearl ballroom, the one with the chrysolite turrets, not to mention the one with the agate bathroom, the one with the fountains of quicksilver and the one with the secret libraries full of occult knowledge ... Which meant that having trudged from one pleasure dome to the next and drawing a blank everywhere, the Grand-Vizir and the Grand-Procurator finally found Fatma at home in her pleasure dome of knowledge ...

She received them, a little irked. She was *not* as the Queen of the Night: the beautiful, azure-tressed widow of six men looked more like a peri from Paradise, in her transparent, white veils, but a slightly irked peri she was, too ...

'What is your business?' she asked, haughtily.

'To know the cause of death of your sixth spouse?'

'Do you first begin,' asked Fatma, 'your researches with my *sixth* spouse?'

'We will ascend to your first!' the grandees threatened.

'I would rather *de*scend to my last,' said Fatma: 'and I have only this to say to you: that I have little to say to you. My sixth spouse has died ... from a tertian fever ...'

The mighty gentlemen wished to give a nasty reply but at this moment, suddenly, the emerald-worker, Fatma's sixth spouse, appeared, alive and well. He looked healthy, solid and lovely, and under his arm he carried a few folios.

'What is *this*?' the mighty gentlemen cried.

Fatma shrugged her slender shoulders.

'It is nothing,' Fatma deigned to reply: 'other than that the dear boy is *not* dead. He is only a little stupid and that is why, in order to give him a little more colour to his conversation, I brought him to this pleasure dome of the Secret Libraries, that he might read a little at his leisure ...'

'But,' – something suddenly dawned on the Grand-Vizir – 'what about your other five spouses, O blue-bearded, I mean blue-tressed Fatma?'

Again Fatma shrugged those ever-slender shoulders.

'They're alive,' she confessed: 'the way this emerald-worker-spouse is alive. However, I sequestered my gondola-rower-spouse in my pleasure dome of the quicksilver fountains, to teach him to be a little quicker in his occupation as gondolier-husband, for he tarried too often for my taste in rowing the marriage-boat on the ponds of love, and quicksilver, administered in small doses, chases the blood through the veins; my Persian merchant still continues to live out his life, which will be a long one, but in my villa with the agate bathroom, for at times he reeked vilely of his camels; my palanquin-bearer-consort I locked up in my chrysolite tower for he would only play pranks, the miscreant, on my handmaidens and I wished to keep him to myself alone. And then we still have my lieutenant-general; well, gentlemen, with him I dance each night in my mother-of-pearl ballroom; he dances divinely and it is simply not fitting that such an intimate pleasure should unfold in the sight of each and everyone: the dear man therefore waits quietly in the mother-of-pearl ballroom, until I arrive and unlock . . . And actually, you know, my first boy is the dearest to me — remember, my gardener? — and truly he, too, is still alive and he dwells at no greater distance from the onyx terraces than I require to reach him every moment that I long for him . . . You regard me most strangely, mighty gentlemen, but it is not otherwise. Look, I am Bluebeard's daughter, and I take after him in soul and tress. He had need of many women, I have need of many men. He, however, killed his wives, on the pretext that they were disobedient to him; I never killed my spouses; I preferred to lock them up, to civilise them and to be mistress over them. If I am hysterical then, at the same time, I am highly feminist, too; in all respects I am *a woman*. What more do you wish to know?'

And proud Fatma stood tall, upright, confronting the two dignitaries of the Caliph. But these, most unexpectedly, called out for their henchman and ordered:

'Drag this wicked woman along with you, drag her before the Overlord's divan!'

Thus it came to pass. Fatma, Bluebeard's daughter, was dragged along all the streets and across all the squares of Baghdad until she arrived before the divan of the Caliph who condemned her to lay that azure-tressed head on the block.

'It is strange,' Fatma thought while she was being placed into the hands of her executioners: 'my father murdered his wives and people judged him severely for this. I myself objected to his actions . . . I, his daughter, never murdered my husbands: I cared for them lovingly, reared them, civilised them and developed their qualities — in a slightly restricted fashion, it is true — in onyx gardens, chrysolite towers, mother-of-pearl ballrooms and what have you . . . and this view on marriage, no matter how well considered, is disapproved of too . . .'

'It is strange' — Fatma went on weaving her thoughts: 'but I believe, I am almost sure, that it is not possible to influence public opinion favourably with regard to love and marriage . . . when one has a blue beard or azure tresses . . .'

And, melancholy for a moment about this incontrovertible philosophy, she bowed the blue-washed head on to the block . . .

Attempted a moment yet to solve the problem . . .

But failed, for, in a stream of purple, her last thoughts fled her twain-cleft neck . . .

And the azure-tressed head of Bluebeard's daughter lay in blood on the floor of the Court of Justice . . .

Upon which the six men inherited.

The Son of Don Juan

Louis Couperus

Did Bluebeard leave a daughter, then it is likewise a fact that Don Juan left behind a son. You do remember, O reader, the history of Don Juan Tenorio, were it only through Mozart's opera in which, however, the son, Don Juanito Tenorio, was given no part to play . . . ?

When Don Juan was dragged by the powers of Hell beneath the floor of his dining room – where there was not the usual cellar but, it turned out, an infernal place of punishment (I refer you once again to the Opera and its mise-en-scène) – Doña Elvira, Don Juan's a touch boring spouse, was left behind with an only son: Don Juanito. She lived, as you know, in Burgos and as she had been through much with her gloriously faithless husband, she indentured her son to a Jesuit monastery, hoping Juanito would learn to tread more virtuous paths than his father had done. Now I really don't want to speak ill of the Jesuits nor of Don Juanito or anyone else, but I cannot keep it from you that, in the monastery school of the Jesuits, Don Juanito took on that proper-posh, chaste, lips-clenched and sickly-sweet smiling quality which, as a young man, did characterise him. Had his father been a dashing cavalier, a magnificent wrongdoer, a sublime seducer, a superb sinner, a royal concupiscent, his son Don Juanito seemed, no matter what, to be turning into what would seem to be an unctuous hypocrite. Would seem, I said, for in fact Don Juanito did *not* become a hypocrite. Don Juanito, with his pale, fine, Spanish *Greco*-face, his dark but pious eyes, his black but straight, black hair – what a lovely curly head Don Juan's had been! All women loved to stroke it . . . – Don Juanito did not become a hypocrite and did not saint it in public and sin it in private at all. He *was* very pious; he prayed a lot, he prayed boundlessly for his father's soul who, following the banquet with the Stone Guest, had disappeared like that in flames and smoke underneath the floor of the dining room. No, truly: Doña Elvira – now she *had* always been very dull and we ought also to regard Don Juan's case modern-psychologically for once – did achieve her goal in the last years of her life: Don Juanito seemed to be about to do penance, for the duration of his life, for all the crimes of his father who had been dragged into Hell. Then Doña Elvira's spirit rose to heaven – and even there her fellow angels do *not* find her amusing.

Don Juanito, in mourning for his mother, doing penance for his father, walked with measured tread through the streets of Burgos and down his path in life, and then, still young, he married the niece of the *Commendatore* – you know, the papa of Doña Anna, almost seduced by Don Juan as well: I mean Doña Anna, not the *Commendatore*. This marriage was fixed up by relatives and friends to reconcile the two warring families – several differing interests were involved in this – and took place with quiet grandeur in Burgos. Don Juanito's wife was called Doña Sol even though she was no relative of Hernani whose beloved spouse was also called Doña Sol. Doña Sol was an imaginative young woman and her name seemed aptly chosen: her eyes glinted like little black suns, her blonde hair glittered like sunshine, a sunny gleam filled her sweet soul and a sunny glow coursed through her veins. She had heard tell *many* tales about Don Juan and, though she had never betrayed this, she in fact cherished a kind of secret love for her husband's father and this was why she had not made any objection at all when she had had to wed Don Juanito. Now, together with her spouse, she dwelt in Don Juan's palace in Seville and they sat opposite one another at that same table to which Don Juan once had invited the Stone Guest . . . Don Juanito unctuously said the benedicite but Doña Sol looked with curious glances at the parquet floor, the same which on that terrible night – now some twenty years ago – had opened up to devour Don Juan . . . But she said nothing and after supper Don Juanito and Doña Sol soon went to bed.

Doña Sol had actually imagined the nights to be rather different in this sombre room which Don Juanito had caused to be upholstered in black velvet: his was the most sober of tastes. When Doña Sol, in the big, catafalque-like bed, would surreptitiously half-turn her sun-blonde head toward the round back of Don Juanito, peacefully sleeping the sleep of the just, she would continue to muse for an hour at least on the mysteries of married life, before drowsily dropping off, with a sigh. The little light in front of the crucifix and the image of the Mother of God in the black velvet room-night faintly lit the unmoved contour of Don Juanito's back and the other, momentarily distinguishable contour of that of Doña Sol, turned towards him under the covers in the ink-gloomy shadows. Such, that in the daytime, Doña Sol would frequently shake her blonde little head and wonder about thousands of things . . .

She began to worry fretfully about those thousands of things. She had realised that her spouse, Don Juanito, was a most proper and virtuous human being, man and son, doing penance for his father's sins; he was blameless and faithful as no other. Faithful? Most certainly: every night Don Juanito's conjugal back would curve next to hers in the dark velvet half-light. Until Doña Sol's thoughts and feelings became confused, confounded-confused, and one fine day, kneeling on her prié-Dieu, she directed her morning prayer not to the Mother of God but . . . to Don Juan, whom, in secret, she bore such a great devotion.

This was a sacrilege of which this sweetest, now rather fretful little woman did not become aware. But the one who *did* become aware of it was Don Juan himself – his soul, I believe – who after a time of punishment in Hell, through heavenly compassion had been given entrance to Purgatory in order to have the chance to be purified. Don Juan, still by no means turned into a saint in the no longer bright-scarlet but sulphurous yellow flames of Purgatory, heard Doña Sol's prayer and quiet lament, and decided, having consulted the purgatorial authorities, to help his daughter-in-law. Don Juan had probably been too sinful: Don Juanito was probably too virtuous. It's curious, this issue of sin and virtue: on earth, nobody seems to have cracked it; earth, heaven and hell between them don't quite seem to have cracked it either. In any case, that sinful Don Juan was given permission by his purgatorial superiors to go and debauch that virtuous Don Juanito, his son, just a little bit. And one fine evening, when Don Juanito was returning home along the dark streets of Seville after his game of dominoes – it's dark very early in Seville – with the virtuous intention of laying down his back to rest beside that purest contoured little back of Doña Sol, there emerged from the paving stones – the supernatural seemed to shelter quite frequently *below* ground in those days – the ruddy-red spirit of Don Juan.

Son took severe fright from father. Father did look rather scorched and Bengal-fire-surrounded yet he was still the same dashing cavalier, though no longer such a superb sinner . . . Don Juan truly had purged much of his sublime ill-doing already, in order to prepare himself to be received by Saint Peter – some day. Even so, son took severe fright from father, but Don Juan calmed Don Juanito down. After the first, ruddy appearance, he made himself invisible and walked on alongside his son. His phantom arm, however, was curved across Juanito's shoulder. And he was whispering in Juanito's ear . . .

'So you are my father . . . ?' Juanito whispered back, still startled and looking askance.

'I am your father whom you barely knew', said the spirit of Don Juan. 'Dear boy, at last I have appeared to you. Do not be afraid of me: truly, I'm busy reforming . . . Lately I have been as chaste as you on the Sabbath Night, and now, in my new surroundings, there's no such thing as living it up . . . They are all very satisfied with me: all of them. But, you see . . . I *must* have a talk with you. Your mother – God have mercy on her boring soul! – was not the wife for me. However, had I been allowed to have a wife such as my darling daughter-in-law, such as Doña Sol certainly is to you . . .'

Confidentially, Don Juan continued to talk at his son's ear without the occasional passer-by and the Sereno, who cried the hour of the night, seeing anything of the paternal spirit who walked with his living son . . . And gradually it seemed to Don Juanito that his father, whom he had always disapproved of severely, had not been an entirely bad man . . .

'I,' Don Juan entrusted his son; 'never went to a Jesuit school, though I do believe that studies are good there . . . What should I tell you, my boy. I was an unmanageable lad. My first love was my nursemaid and when my good old parents saw *that*, they did not think of the Jesuit school but they locked me up in that same cellar underneath the dining room through which I passed into Hell later on . . . That's *very* good in Mozart's opera; I mean, in the opera which, in a later century, a certain Mozart will write about me. But then there will be another artist who will compose a great poem about me: he shall be called Byron and his verses will excel in their glow . . . Do you hear, my boy? About you no composer will make an opera nor a poet an epic . . .'

'Still, I have been more virtuous than you, O beloved father,' asserted Don Juanito.

'My dear man, what is virtue and what is vice?' the shade of Don Juan asked Don Juanito, and the one philosophised a long while at the other's ear during that evening walk through quiet nighttime Seville.

Don Juanito listened attentively and occasionally would nod his head in agreement with a movement that this indeed might be so ... He asked his father to tell him about his second love now he had already told him about the nursemaid, after all. Don Juan told his son of many loves, though not of *all* which Leporello had once accounted for in the long list. Now, Don Juanito shook his head disapprovingly again the way a sensible and living human being does to an altogether too frivolous spirit who wishes to conjure up all kinds of things for him.

'No,' said Don Juanito, 'so much waste of the vital force is not right, is not proper, and only granted to an epic soul such as you who will later be glorified in rhyme and rhythm and music. Though I might admit to you ...'

What exactly Don Juanito admitted to, I would not be able to give away, just like that; I do believe, however, that Don Juan's opinion on Marriage as being a divine and human, as well as religious and social institution did make Don Juanito think.

'You must not forget, my good fellow,' said Don Juan: 'that I had blown the lot. That last banquet for my Stone Guest ... cost fifty thousand ducats and ... those were my last ... more or less ...'

'My mother, Doña Elvira,' Don Juanito held forth: 'you left her behind almost without a penny.'

'Your wife is rich, is she not?' asked Don Juan.

'We are comfortably off,' Don Juanito confirmed.

'Did you know,' whispered Don Juan: 'that she can petition for divorce? And that she will do this ... when the spirit comes over her?'

Don Juanito gave a start.

'Father!' he cried. 'Father! What was that you said? Truly?! Oh, what good fortune that you warned me, beloved father! That your spirit ... may come over me!'

'Truly?' asked Don Juan.

'I believe so!' cried Don Juanito. 'I'm almost sure!'

'Then home at once, where your wife awaits you!' cried Don Juan and without Don Juanito having to take out his front door key, because of the supernaturalness of the mise-en-scène, the spirit of the father pushed the body of his son through the front door ... Moved, Don Juan remained, alone.

'He will become a good husband,' he thought. 'A faithful husband. An impeccable husband ... There was something of his mother in him: there is also something of his father in him ...'

And he disappeared in a glow of Bengal light through the paving in the street.

That night, that little head, the sun-blonde one belonging to Doña Sol, was slumbering, turned towards the darkly outlined face of Don Juanito, Don Juan's son.

And next day she gained her husband's permission to soft-furnish their bedroom, instead of with black velvet, with pink muslin held up everywhere in soft pleats by gilded, fat-legged cupids. The Rococo period was just beginning at the time.

The Sacred Butterfly

Johan Andreas Dèr Mouw

There was a monastery in the forest and the summer morning lit up in a distant haze.

And a young monk emerged from the monastery, a prayer book in his hand, and he went into the forest.

And a little white bird flew round him that settled on a branch and began to sing, and he listened.

And the little bird sang, and he listened.

And clouds came and clouds went and the little bird sang, and he listened. And the bird flew away, and he went back to the monastery with the prayer book in his hand.

And the monk who opened the gates did not know him and the prior and the other monks did not know him.

And there was an old man who lay dying, for he was very old, and he said that fifty years earlier a young monk with the prayer book in his hand had gone into the woods and had never returned, and in him-whom-no-one-knew he recognised the young monk.

And fifty years had passed since he listened to the little white bird and to him they had been but an instant.

For eternity is a second; time stands still to him who leaves the world of semblances and submerges himself in the Eternal Sea of Beauty and Rationality. Semblances are the many-eyed laughter of the Spring meadow and the weeping of denuded forest.

The earth is but a semblance when, with green leaf-flags and green waving sea-robes, it swerves round the sun.

The stars are semblances, distant fire-flies in the fields of the night. The time shall come when no meadow laughs any longer nor forests weep; when the earth sinks down with fatigue, like a child that has been playing a long time; when the fire-flies die. World-twilight is coming and Space disappears and Time disappears and Sorrow disappears. The World shall fall away like the cocoon round a butterfly, and God shall Think in sorrowless peace. I wish to dive into my soul. Down there, on soft-sanded soil, in blue-green dusk, pale red flowers bloom; the finely scalloped petals are still and they muse. High above them, the waves roll and the storms gambol, and they do not notice; and Summer, with its lilac-purple steeds and its cracking fire-whip, rides past, and they do not notice; and slanting rain-squalls and white-whirling showers – they do not notice. They grow quiet and stand soundless in the peaceful dusk.

Hunger for knowledge for my life-raft, I wish to descend into the dark country. Or do you think you know it because, when staring down, you see a strange reflection there where the green transparency ends?

And when I caress your hair and say to you that I love you – when you hear unspoken words and can feel my thoughts come and go, do you believe that those binoculars will tell you what blooms unfathomably deep? They, who roamed for fifty centuries across the Asiatic plains and saw the silent stars migrate, remembered the returning changeability, the changeable regularity of their trajectory and bethought themselves to know what was their nature. And yawning telescopes sucked the light miracles closer by and mirrors and lenses stared through the universe; and the bundles of light, rarefied obelisks, told of distant worlds, of distant times, in multi-coloured hieroglyphics; like a child making a may-beetle fly in a circle, thus science showed errant comets the path they would follow. But does the child know which co-operating bifurcations of muscle and nerve-tissue make the beetle fly? Likewise, we do not know the power that carries and inspires the long-living light-beetles. Nor dost thou know what miracles grow in the mystical twilight of my soul.

That which I shall find there, down below, I wish to show it to *thee*; reverently shalt thou stroke the tender petals and bend back with gentle finger that which is warped. For not every plant has grown the way its original nature wished and needed it to. There is a Power that lured the sprouting twigs away from the direction first embarked upon and forced them into capriciousness, that made the flowers bend round on their stems and made the calyxes point toward an identical spot. The way sunflowers look, ever look toward their ambulant ideal, the bright Sunflower: from the moment she is lifted above the horizon by the invisible stem until she ends her tremendous circle at the other world's end, thus my mysterious flowers stare at one single miracle image.

For it was not always a quiet-happy field here, full of dreamy stillness and expansive peace; *now* there hangs a calm over the unmoved garden the way still-hovering sanctity mists around a golden autumn-forest; *now* the Hours have unlearned their rushing course and they lie in the calyxes like sleeping butterflies. A forest stood here once, great with heavy trunks; the rich primaeval power of the Being of things had raised them up and bore the weight of their growth; it nourished them all with equal love, the one into a fruit-cascading blessing, the other into an assassinating curse.

For, to Him who is all, there is no Good and no Sin, nor is there day or night; He forces himself to create willing weapons with which to combat Himself; having abandoned eternal-pondering perfection, strifeless peace, he wages war on Himself.

He has chased himself out of a spaceless, timeless paradise and wishes to make the wall, built by thoughtless striving, fall; this is why He took Time into service which slung humming centuries against the endless bastion and powdered it to star-rubble that he further wrenches loose with drilling seconds; and on this his Sacred Master set his triumphant foot, in order, at last, having blossomed into a human soul, to grow and enter the earlier sanctity.

But his own work hampers the Mighty One and forbids Him to be what He wishes, and to attain that which He strives for, for as long as Time already is; it forces the Free to grow into an impediment to themselves and they ensnare themselves in Paradise-closing vines.

Thus He grew into a forest of Hate and Anger and Pride and Love and Sorrow, which was I, and the wrestling trunks destroyed one another in a powerless crowding-in.

And Pride spake:

I wish to remain what I am; Time shall come storming with hurtling Years, but he shall not tame *me*; and his tireless showers, those gnawing hour-drops, shall not soak *me* loose.

And Anger and Hate and Sorrow fumed and wailed in unvanquished rage. Love alone stood timid and still, fearful of the perceptivity of her stronger sisters.

And darkness hung over the battle, blackened by the moon-pale magic glow of the Love-blossoms.

And a butterfly, a Sacred Butterfly, thy Soul, came fluttering by and the darkness did not strike fear into her, nor did the muttering threat of destruction.

She, God had sent, Who sped to His Own aid. And she perched on a Love-blossom and the wings trembled in strange light.

And a rustling such as had never been heard before, hummed

through the battling chaos – thus the evening star shines among the shards of cloud when November storms – And the tree upon which the Butterfly sat, began to grow and branches sprouted on all sides, and the blossom, curious, was coaxed out carefully.

And the Butterfly sat quietly; only its wings trembled in golden light.

And the tree shone with white-gleaming flowers, the Christmas Tree of my soul. For the Messiah had come, the Anointed One, the Christ, who makes blessed. The one who was lost, She sought out; She raised him who wept over the unwilling-willing fall. She was the pure child of God; She was the Law and the Prophets.

But She had not come to bring the sword; She brought peace, for Hate and Anger and Pride could not grow in the white light, and they said:

Who is it who hampers us in our most mighty growth? This is our domain; here our enmity reigns in unity. We tolerate no usurper.

And they resisted and with tough root-joints they clamped themselves fast to their territory and sought to suck power from the soil that had been willing until now. But that which was meant to serve their victory flowed to the young tree. And the calyxes began to ring out: an Alleluia for the Christ, a dead march for the vanquished.

And they cringed and withered, the tremendous ones; they recognised their weakness and their injustice, and their death honoured She Who Rules Alone. And there She stood, my sacred flower, singing light, white-glowing music.

Thou hast saved me. Thy weakness is the strong shepherd who snatches the lost lamb from the jaws of the wolf and returns it to the warm stable.

What dost thou wish to do with my life? The sky was dark and I was standing on a lonely heath; the spruces did not move and there was not a sound; the flowers were gone; November had washed them away and all was grey and drab-brown; and slowly the clouds slid forth across distant-sorrowing forests. And dusk came, and the silence became even quieter when the gloomy colour-music ceased. And the clouds travelled on, ever more new clouds, endless; and the woods vanished; the black absorbed everything into itself. Once upon a time they had been cheerful; the sun's rays had played tag among the tree trunks when July had been their guest, and high up among the crowns had hung a lively net of cheerful insects, marquetry in the blue sky, a living mosaic, buzzing specks of light. And now, all was gone. They no longer wished to live, the cheerless forests, and they dissolved themselves in the heavy void. And I alone still lived. Everything died away around me; Nothingness enticed to flee the sorrow in its endless quiet. For, there again stood she, never ageing Sorrow, the only damsel who stands outside of time's power. I saw her emerge from the mists and she came and stood and stared at me. And I pleaded with her and said: what have I done unto you that you persecute me? Have I not served you above all others, for many years? I was your friend when you were modest but my obedience rebelled against your stringent demands. Why do you desire that I do homage only to you? You are not God's sole daughter and Your greater dominion does not entitle you to exclusive claim on my loyalty. Black is your cloak and black your veil – and I am young.

How can you wish that I devote my soul to dull-mute mourning? Your tread sounds like a dead march and I want wedding music. Let me go free – And Sorrow regarded me and said with a voice that sounded like high winds rushing in indifferent progress over the earth:

You are not free; my Eternal Father gave you to me in perpetual ownership. When he woke me from sleep and sent me abroad into the World, I asked him: how shall I rule, as everyone is hostile to me? Though my power is great, how shall I not be inferior to the hate of all and to gnawing fatigue? And then he spake: People will hate you and struggle against your kingship, but I shall prepare you a resting place in the souls of those who help others in their struggle. He who wages war on you for others, he shall be your property – And therefore I follow you, for you belong to me – Why should you honour my sisters? Beauty is not intended for you; she laughs and you have been in my company too long to join in with her laughter. And Reason? She is too rigid and too cold and cannot satisfy your feeling. Your heart is my home. And I wanted to flee; kindly, Death signalled me with serious-smiling face; he seemed to await me and he looked at me encouragingly. Oh, I longed for peace. I stared back down my life and sought for sun spots, and the road was a long and monotonous one.

Thou know'st not how much I love thee: how could a girl feel the glow of a man? What do you wish that I shall do for you? Shall I pile Switzerland upon the Rocky Mountains and make the ocean flop down from the barely visible peak, a world-rending waterfall so that you say: isn't that charming? Or do you like fireworks? Shall I tie comets to Vesuvius, bright flags for our high day, and the Milky Way, vane of light-gauze? Shall I make green and red and gold suns whirl about in mystic figures, a multi-coloured shower of sparks, as a small tribute to you? Would you like wedding music? Then the storm shall howl an Appassionata and the thunder will roll the drums. Do you want bridal raiments such as no empress has ever worn, raiments befitting you, radiant empress of my radiant soul? Out of the scarlet sun-down I will weave you a cloak and I will hang the Southern Cross upon your breast. But what shall I set around your hair, your dark-smooth hair? Shall I weave the rays of the sun into a bridal crown – no, that is too dull. I will lay my mouth upon your head and I will whisper how much I love you: and flames in whose presence thunderbolts would cast a shadow shall crown you.

What shall be our bridal couch? Come! The cloud-shore is hilly, full of bright valleys there where the sea of moonlight dreams. No, those are not stars; those are golden waterlilies; no, those are not meteors: it is the radiance of the sea –

Behold how I have furnished our bridal apartment, worthy of our love.

The walls I have covered in blue light and pondering sea-roses, and cushions await in twilight, and the sea hums Fingal-melodies and the South Wind – there, in that grotto – plays the harp.

Oh, I love thee, thy hair and thy shoulders and thy breast; I wish to kiss thee unto intoxication and sink away in God. I feel how thou dost tremble with desire; thine eye glitters my festive light to gleamlessness. What flames are those that thou see'st? Those are the flames of thy love which shall shout with joy around thee in sacred glow – And those noises humming in thine ears?

It is the organ-playing in thy soul, it is the hymn singing of thy love. Come – I wish to drink thy soul from thy lips and breathe unconscious sanctity into thee; the fire-flower of bliss shall bloom in us, the wonder-flower which grows in the caressing glow of thine eyes, in the scorching coolness of thy mouth. Thy dark plait shall I wind around my throat, for I wish to be the happy prisoner of thy Beauty; I lay my right arm around thy soft shoulders, my left hand around thy tender breast.

Curious Things on the Plain

Lodewijk van Deyssel

When, at the end of the eighteenth century, the great French monarchy sank, strange things, it is said, happened on the plain. Society turned topsy-turvy and one saw noisy, seditious riff-raff babbling and singing in hordes, screeching, gesturing and dancing stumbling dances in those gracious areas of the city where until then only the well-styled, finely-coloured promenaders had moved, and where the carriages, driven by coachmen who themselves were aristocrats, ran their elegant course.

In the streets of Paris meanwhile, among all kinds of pedestrians, one had also seen many unfortunates and drab figures: hunchbacks, paralytics, squints and twisted-ones, purple noses, longlobes, dwarves, flatfooters, idiots with green-hued faces and folk with large sweatmarks on their backsides, creatures in drab-grey rags from whose nose and red-rimmed, cunning eyes ran sickly gin, and especially no mean number of ordinary, dull dunces – but at the time when it was so bad the monarchy was being mocked in its own dwelling, one saw something extraordinary occur: on the squares which one overlooked from the windows of the Palace, monsters in human shape appeared in the open spaces, right out in the sun, unfortunates and ass-heads whose defects were so garish that, until then, they had never shown themselves outside of the alleys, slums and subterranean pits where only nightfall would see them, together with the mice and the spiders, creep timorously along the walls. So extraordinary were the humps, of such huge dimensions the flat feet, so far advanced the tumours at the back of the head, so wild the twists of the noses combined with the appearance of the eyes, that these catastrophically afflicted ones could not appear without at once attracting the most violent and nigh magnetic interest of all physicians, nurses, students of surgery, proprietors of circus booths, zoo-attendants, while at the same time drawing such unstoppable snorting and careering belly laughs, not just from street urchins, the pale and bored shop assistants in their doorways, the hearty travelling salesmen returning from a free lunch and even from posh professors and bankers, but no less from staff of the Salvation Army – anachronistically, astrally and prophetically present there – from preachers, from zealots, from melancholy-minded ones, from the deeply griefstricken whose loved ones had just passed away, from the sick, from ones in a state of dead-faint, and from all the folk who, for humanitarian reasons, never laughed otherwise, be this out of principle or by nature.

Now, confusion in society was so great, to such an extent did the whole world appear to be standing on its head, that everyone made common cause with these apparitions in the end. An illustrious marquess, noble of face and fine in mien, became familiar with a half-rotten dwarf-monster from a very remotely situated fire-and-water business: an enormously large, Jewish Easterbread-coloured, moth-eaten and bald head on a, because of a grave case of waterbelly and backswelling, egg-shaped short body, green, with innumerable glass bead-encrusted slippers below – and to this the marquess offered a pinch of snuff. A slim duchess in lace and satin, the truffle of a beauty-spot like an aroma of loveliness in the pale white of the face, spoke chummily to a woman-figure surrounded by an invisible cloud of acrid emanations who for thirty years had spent her only sober half hour each day lying about, sucking out the fishheads on the scrapheaps of public eating-houses, and who now stood listening and nodding with a downwardly sagging, purply-red nose from the pores of which greenish worms wriggled up, and from the nostrils of which, besides manifold warts and pink secondary ulcers, greasy spikes of hair pricked down on to the bin-shaped bottom lip – down which eyes like rancid hatpin tips peered – laughing with her mouth which, as regards teeth, sported but a lone fragment of black enamel.

And in the end, the most eminent citizen in the land was surrounded too: he, who himself previously had chased the riff-raff from his marble floors with his own hands, with the knout and the whip for those beggars and thieves whom one does not tackle with sword or floret – and on his great king's head, on those hairs soft as silk, was placed an old fool's cap which housed two colonies of lice.

After the Hurricane

Inez van Dullemen

The sea was where she was meant to be again: behind the white coastline marked by groynes. The tide was low and the sea had withdrawn into herself, her water smooth as oil, perverse, sweetly smooth. I stared at her in disbelief, sitting on the collapsed dune, at my back the grey, defoliated land of doom.

I had always felt on an easy footing with her. As a child I would walk into the water, up to my armpits, and would allow myself, touching the bottom on tiptoe, to be rocked lightly to and fro by her surf. I had never been frightened either, unlike the other children, of her unknown inhabitants; when I felt the touch along my legs of a slippery passer-by, I would pull up my knees and calmly let what was moving in the deep pass by. I caught crabs in shallow coves and played with them by tickling them underneath their armour with a little stick so that they would make big leaps with rage – these were the clowns in my circus. And the grey sea-fog, too, I loved, which so suddenly could come rolling up the coast so that it seemed as if the entire world was being rubbed out with a wet sponge.

Now, I was sitting here on that gnawed lump of dune and looking at my hands, covered in red scars, resting on the sand. I had the feeling that a question needed to be answered, that there needed to be an exposition of views between us. For I was sitting here like something that had been released by her and cast back ashore, quite like all those splinters and ribs of boats and the twisted scrap-iron of Biloxi's amusement park. Shards of china with golden rims or decorated with daisies glinted among the sand. The sea must have gulped down dozens, dozens of tea sets. Tea sets or people: it had made no difference to her.

Already there were children back on the beach again, playing. A little girl ran towards the waves to draw some water with a tea kettle and pour it out over the head of one of those monstrously large fair-ground dogs in orange plush – like those that had stood in the booths of Biloxi – which had apparently been washed up. Its coat was drab with sand but it was still wearing its black plastic specs on its head, and with these it sat staring at that perversely smooth sea, like a tatty professor.

Why had I gone back? You won't find anything, they'd said to me, you won't recognise a thing. But I wanted to gain a hold within that floating irreality; I wanted to see something confirmed, to assay the nightmare against reality. Even when I slept, I could still feel the surge of the water; I would retch, spit my lungs out, feel the black spiders running across my body until I woke up, bathed in sweat. *Not recognise a thing.* Those words had been repeated too often; my thoughts had run aground on them.

You will not recognise him, they had said; they've only been able to recognise him by the ring on his finger: apart from that, he's black and bloated. There's nothing left of his face; he barely resembles a human being any more. But I did not believe them; I thought he would still have to look the way I had known him. I fought with them, I was hysterical. It took three of them, in the end, to press me down on to the bed and give me a jab of some sedative. Eight days after the hurricane, they had found him in the top of a tree with a mattress on top of him – the only corpse still dressed, they said, for he was still wearing his *Levis* and his shoes. Together with the other mortal remains, he was brought to the cold stores of the meat factory, close to the airport, and he had already been put in his coffin and sent to Vancouver when I was discharged from hospital. His parents had claimed him for themselves – even the ring on his finger had not been mine but a signet ring engraved with the family coat of arms – and that's how he had been sent: like a dead, ringed, migrant bird, back to its place of origin.

The entire morning the weather had been clear, without a breath of wind, the water in the Gulf melting-blue, and you could see the inlets lying there in the blindingly white sand; but gradually the sky discoloured to an opaque drab-grey, and sea and sky became one: a dirty-grey wall that rose up behind the blanched beach, motionless and still.

We organised a storm party. For that's what you usually do here on the Gulf coast; you have to sit out the time, indoors, while the severe weather passes over. It was still hanging there, that thick, fish-coloured fog that seemed to have been drawn up like a curtain; it was drizzling, but otherwise the weather was dull and windless. We danced and the water rose steadily and began to run across the terrace tiles. The needle of the barometer sank to its lowest point. Our eyes strayed towards it without us mentioning a thing.

Suddenly, towards evening, the wind pounced and made the entire row of windows quake in their frames, and we saw how the mist was torn to shreds and began to whirl in front of the windows in long trails. We clambered up to the top floor and heard the roar with which the water burst into the house. Because it was a summer house, the walls were only thin; it wasn't that big either. Peering down over the bannisters, I saw how the chairs and the sofa rose up and began to spin. The electricity had failed but we had torches with us, for one who lives on the Gulf is always prepared for calamities. I felt how the whole house began to rock and suddenly a black star shot through the ceiling as chunks of plasterwork dropped down upon our heads.

'I'm getting out,' I said to Fritz.

He tried to prevent me. 'That's madness,' he said.

We looked at one another. 'We're going to die,' I said, 'but then we may as well do it out there.'

I climbed out of the window and clutched a divan cushion that came floating by on that upward surging mass of water. With the beam of my torch, which I was still holding in my hand, I looked for Fritz who was straddling the window sill. He hesitated. He could not swim. I heard him shout as he jumped: 'Help me.'

Then he went under and did not come up again.

I flailed about, searched for him. Now you could no longer see anything but black: black clouds scudding past and occasionally letting through a glimmer of light. I felt a wild, ice-cold rushing about me but my arms mowed through the water of their own accord; my body knew what it wanted: there was an animal in me, an animal captain who had assumed command; it was as if my spirit travelled along as a passenger – it simply didn't have a say in the matter. Between the backs of waves I made out specks of light from other torches, and I heard voices crying out for help. I shouted back but in the tumult my voice was lost – it was also impossible to reach one another. One after the other, I saw the lights go out.

All was movement, eddies, waterspouts, wind that cut off your breath. Furniture, driven insane, panicked into a stampede like animals, shattered everything that got in their way, smashing each other to pieces, to smithereens: all those possessions that had always stood, good as gold and ready to serve, in kitchen-diners or sitting rooms, now rampaged at us, random, in an annihilating attack of rage. We ended up trapped in between, our bodies ripped open like squishy melons. More people were done in by furniture than by the water, I should say. You had to fight cupboards, beds, trapdoors, chairs; all those consumer goods you had cherished now seemed to be out to crush your ribcage, to pile up on top of you and push you under water. I fought to stay on top of them, to keep my mount like on the backs of crazed horses. Uprooted trees gathered the floating household goods in their tops and pushed these out in front of them. I was in danger of getting caught up in the branches. I was continually pulling at something or climbing on top of something; my arms seemed about to be torn off. But I did not give up: within me was that animal that wanted to live. In the end, I managed to get hold of a door on which I could keep myself afloat; I kept the broken-off blade of an oar in front of my mouth to create a lee in which I could breathe. The cry of voices had fallen silent and I believed I had floated out into the Gulf, for nothing stuck out above the water any more, no tree tops or telegraph poles or roofs of houses. There was nothing other than a huge mass of water.

A large dog came swimming towards my door, tried to climb on to it, almost made the whacking thing turn turtle. I kicked his head with my feet: off! You or me, one of us has to cop it: the law of the jungle. But when the wind began to abate a little, I floated to a standstill in the top of a tree; I still had to be over land, therefore. My door was wedged among the branches and I understood that I was safe. I was bleeding heavily. My leg was torn open from my knee down to my ankle and I ripped up my blouse to apply a tourniquet.

Then the spiders came. They did the same as I had done: climb up, out above the water to dryness and air – a few measly cells full of vital force and with claws to grip a hold. I flicked them off me but they were determined and ran with their hairy legs across my body: spiders wishing to reach Noah's ark. (*'Noye's Flood', a picture from my childhood, illustrated bible: naked men and women on a rocky outcrop above the water, a lioness with her cub in her mouth, and sucklings with round tummies, all with the same curves as the waves, everything very fleshly, outrageously sensual. A woman with streaming long hair hung by her fingertips from the outcrop.*)

I must have suffered bouts of unconsciousness. I saw the spiders with lifesized faces, climbing up towards me; their legs snapped, broke off or became entangled: they became one single, dancing mass, teeming above me in the sky. Occasionally, something would drop on to my face with a dry tap; then I would wake with a start. I saw the moon lying, scythe-shaped and thin, on her back in the paling sky. The shine would have to be that of dawn. I threw up the water from my lungs and saw corpses floating by: the miserable rag of a poodle, the corpse of a man – of that fat boy from the Oyster Bar who had always looked so suggestively at my breasts while, tauntingly slowly, he set the cutlery, and who had such flabby hands, quite as flabby as his oysters. A settee floated by with a seagull on top of it for a pilot – or did I dream that? A beam bobbed past with a man who had tied himself to it by his trouser-belt, but he was dead, with his skull half bashed away. As the water dropped ever further, I saw that beneath me in the tree a child's dress was hanging, red with yellow little flowers, the material billowing out a bit. There was still a little body inside it. It hung across a branch with its head in the water while its silky hair fanned out on to the pulsing waves.

With the lull and the drop of the water level, a silence had arisen, simultaneously, one in which you only heard the lapping of the waves. I am the only one left, I thought.

But later on, the enervating yackety-tack of a helicopter passed overhead and voices began to call out in the drowned landscape beneath me. It was the man from the post office in Biloxi who found me. He tried to carry me but he was of slight build and, moreover, so exhausted from wading through the water that after every ten paces he asked: mind if I take a rest for a moment? In the end, he found a floating piece of corrugated board and managed to lay me down on top of it so he could push me the rest of the way across the rapidly falling water and through all the rubbish.

That's the only thing I can still remember.

I now began to climb over the edge of the dune. I knew exactly where I was, for I could get my bearings from the lighthouse and what was left of the marina. The roads inland were covered in a thick, dried-up layer of mud, and barricaded in many places by crashed-down trees, boat hulls, and cars spread around at all angles. Beyond were the woods. But these had been thinned out, had become transparent, and the spring light beamed down sharply among the bare branches. A tree stood beckoning me slowly with a piece of grey net-curtain as if it was beckoning me in, to a landscape of ghosts; clothes dangled from the branches, sleeves without hands, waving.

White sand covered the dead moss and all the wood had been corroded by the salt water; everything had a sheen of silver. You could see exactly how far the sea had run inland, for everywhere in her footsteps barnacles had stayed behind, and oysters, cloaked in their grey-ish lacework, and razor clams, still quite perfect. And, like a cuckoo fledgling in a strange nest, a barge sat grounded among the torn-down pine trees. I passed along underneath her red-leaded keel: I walked along the bottom of a submarine landscape.

Skeletons of houses lurched askew in the ground, grinning with black window openings and fluttering with the last remains of a tattered awning. The bared beams of their attics resembled the bones of fish stripped of their flesh. On top of a roof sat a chubby armchair the springs of which dangled like entrails from the seat. This was all that remained of the little summer palaces, those little temples of luxury. Plaster, glass, chipboard, everything crunched beneath the soles of my feet. Otherwise there wasn't a sound. But perhaps there was, after all: I heard something that was like the tapping of a stick. You could see a long way through that leafless forest and some hundred metres away from me I saw a strange, shady character with a bulky sack over his shoulder, who looked inside the empty window spaces and poked methodically among the objects spread across the ground. Someone's walking over my grave, my grandmother would always say when something gave her the creeps.

I quickly walked the other way, looking round about for identifying marks. Hadn't this been the house of the preacher? In my head, the voice of the radio newscaster sounded: *the preacher had been washed out of the window and had managed to keep himself afloat, but his wife and seven children had drowned.* It was as if I saw him sitting like Job on top of the remains of his house.

The ground was still soft and everywhere hung the salty scent of rot, of slimy organisms, seaweed, sea-snails, dead things. Millions of little dead things. Of larger ones too? Cadavers of pets, of people still? Children? Or had these already been salvaged? (Odd word, really: salvaged.)

The ghosts kept open house. I walked in through open doors,

roamed among the remains of their wild orgy: tipped-up rocking chairs, cracked ceiling-cherubs, Christmas baubles, letters, piles of cheque books, faded photographs, open books – for the ghosts to read in – and telephones, broken adrift. All those certainties, all those networks of people's manipulating, their threads to both the past and the future – all that stuff was lying here like organs that had been rent apart. The sea has taken revenge, I thought, revenge for our arrogance. There were gramophone records: *The Ballad of Bonnie and Clyde* and *When the lights go out*. Here, the lights had indeed gone out. It was as if I was picking up the echoes of lives that had taken place here. In a grey-muddied bath tub, lovers had embraced in an aromatic, scented foambath. The muddied clothes were still hanging in the cupboard. The dead had written in their cashbooks or played a Schubert sonata on the piano. They had taken down the latest stockmarket figures and had poured each other a glass of whisky. Praying, or dead drunk, they had been washed from their houses by the tidal wave.

Somewhere, I happened upon a number of dolls, some of which had the dimensions of a small child. They lay there, dumped down head first, naked, bums up obscenely, or on their backs with windswept hair and mud-soiled porcelain faces in which the glass eyes stared up at the sky. Their degeneration rendered them fearsomely alive, nymphomaniac smiles playing around their rose-bud lips. All that was dead spoke a new language. What was human was dehumanised and called to a different, ghostly life: around me, a Salvador Dali landscape had turned into reality.

Suddenly I recognised the tiles of our own terrace; this was where the camellias must have stood which, in winter, Fritz had always carefully packed in straw against the chill sea wind. The moss-covered terrace-lion was still standing. But of the house itself, no trace; only the foundations still lay there like a huge, square tombstone in the soil. I went and sat on the edge of the terrace and looked at the little stone lion. It sucked my gaze in towards it. Everything around that object became unimportant, shadowy, like in a dream where an insignificant thing can suddenly assume other proportions, as if it lights up from within and conveys a signal – though you cannot translate its meaning, cannot unravel it. The meaning remains just outside the border of your capacity to comprehend, and you struggle and struggle to understand it, and when you wake up nothing remains but a feeling of oppression. That's what befell me with that lion. It was of vital importance that I should understand something but I could not grasp it.

I stared at the scar on my leg – which would turn white, the doctor had said; my skin would become perfect again; I would be able to begin a new life. As if a new skin and a new life were one and the same. And of course he had said that to all those washed up who still had a breath of air in their lungs. What else could the man do.

A question forced itself upon me, a question I'd still managed to keep at a distance: *now what?* I could walk up the road, go somewhere, in this dress I had borrowed from my sister. But how could you escape from a house of air? A man without a face? For that was the most horrific: that I could not bring Fritz's face to mind; I always saw it before me without a mouth and without eyes, and flattened so decadently into an egg-shape, like a head in a nylon stocking.

I walked back into the woods. The sun was shining more fiercely. It had to be afternoon already; my sister's dress stuck to my back with sweat. Where the road veered off, I came across the railway line. It was still lying there, intact, though the rails looked very rusty and unused. The overhead wiring hadn't been repaired yet. I could follow the railway line: you would always end up somewhere, in that case.

Still, there were already signs of life in the woods, here and there. People were sitting on steps in the first spring sunshine, were scooping mud from their houses or running up a flag [*we're back*]; a man tipped out a bucket of water near the only tree still alive.

Suddenly standing there, an old woman in a dressing gown who had come crawling up from a black hole. She stood there in front of her subsided house with behind her that forest, bleached white, full of splintered tree stumps, and she seemed to beckon me. I heard her voice like a rarefied hum. She held a tin can in her hand and in the other a paint brush with which she appeared to be making signals.

'Have you come to help me?' she cried.

Paint dripped down her lower arm but she did not seem to notice. She spoke monotonously without waiting for an answer, just as if something was unfolding within her, a meagre musical ditty.

'Have you come to help me? Everything hurts – that's because of the damp in my bones. They took me somewhere, inside a big store. They put me in a room on my own. I was so hot and again

127

so cold, too, that I went and lay between two mattresses, 'cause there were mattresses everywhere in that store – I set out on a recce later on. The elevators were crammed full of people, but I found some stairs down. I wanted to get back to my house. A captain wants to go down with his ship . . .'

She stirred her can of paint.

'You've got to speak up,' she said, 'I've gone deaf with the water.'

She was treating the teetering door post, blobs of dried paint lying on the ground.

A ga-ga old woman wielding a brush, one who was tackling chaos with a brush and wanted to bring the entire apocalyptic world back to life with thick strokes of hard-green paint. The shards of existence had dropped to earth in a muddle: dead lovers embraced in a muddied bath tub, a barge was grounded in the middle of some woods, my house had walls of air – nothing added up even remotely any more.

'This house was once my grandmother's,' she said. 'I used to come here when I was still a child. Sometimes we'd go along the railway track, collecting seeds which we put in a little can.' She pointed at hers.

The spring sunshine, the minute paint splatters on her grey skin between the glistening hairs on her chin, a tatty sunhat on the straggly strands of white hair – nice one for a photo in *Life International*, it suddenly coursed through me in a flash.

'When I've lots of courage I put on my boots,' she said, 'and I go and take a look at the seedlings. Yes, there are those that come back, that take a chance, the bulbs living in the lowlands. They, too – they've got the courage, too.'

On her pyjama legs, and cloaked in her mucky dressing gown, hanging open, she was walking out ahead of me when one of her slippers got stuck in the mud.

'That dirt's only good for breeding snails and worms to fish with,' she said, disdainfully. She bent down to pick up her slipper. And as she straightened herself, groaning, a hand pressed to her side, she cast up her eyes at me. For the first time she seemed to see me, consciously. Her errant gaze focused on my face and she nodded her head several times, as if she saw something confirmed to herself.

'Yes, I know,' she said, 'you'd rather be dead. But as long as you've still got this,' – and she tapped against her skull with the handle of the brush – 'all's not yet lost.'

Then she shoved her brush and tin can into my hands and went and sat herself down in a broken armchair standing in the mud-stained garden. A moment later I heard her snore.

Concerning the Experiences of Hélénus Marie Golesco

Jacob Israel de Haan

Dedicated to Georges Eekhoud: there is nothing in the world more inhuman than to be a burgher and of all burgherdom that of Holland is the most inhuman possible. It would quite definitely sell itself were it not so unrespectable and were a bidder only to come forward. However, as I have grown progressively stronger in human living and the business of Art, I have hated this country as purely as can be. My solace is this, that these respectable little burgher-folk surely will go to their doom prematurely because of Christianity,

Schiedam gin and Marxism. One of my sorrows is that I am a Dutch artist. Master Eekhoud, let us not be two burghers.

> *Oh, the poor head, all wounds and blood,*
> *How heavy it hangs, glow-gleaming in the night,*
> *The black petrified sorrow-lovely splendour*
> *Of red Roses round a Cap of Thorns*

1

When the Devil did visit me last, he said, before the restless departure: 'Helenus, do not forget this: think of me often, for I love you, and think so strongly of me until you have the feeling that your body is black, without communion with the outside world. Wherever I may be, I shall then know that you do not forget me and know where you reside, and what your condition is. Will you do this?'

'Yes,' I had said, trembling, 'I shall think of you always ... I cannot live without you.'

2

It was upon a late afternoon and I was sitting beside a bordered lawn, all red roses, in the sun and the scent, while I thought of myself. Then a boy in white came from the house bringing me a letter from France. Oh, it was from the Devil. I recognised this immediately by the finely formed manuscriptum and by the pentagram that sealed the letter red. The Devil wrote:

'Dear boy, for a considerable time I have not become aware that you have thought strongly of me, perhaps perchance on occasion, yes, but such thoughts do not reach me. I do so regret this, for now I do not know how you are and where you live. In Amsterdam, I hope, and that you will receive this letter in good order. I must call upon your friendship, for I have made a wager with one of my enemies – alas, one only needs to be the Devil to have many of those – a wager that, with loving words, it would not be possible to lead my best friend among men astray from me. I should dearly wish to win that wager, more for the intimate pleasure of it than for the gain. I have indicated you as being my best friend. Should you accept this indication, then write to me to that effect immediately and come, tomorrow if possible, to the Bradford Hotel, 17, Rue d'Arcade. Ask for the Viscount of Chelsea, the name I am travelling under. In that hotel you will also find the enemy to whose loving temptation you will be exposed. Be warned and do not trust in your loyalty to me, and do not think lightly of the enemy. He is someone of middling, easy capacities and therefore has great influence on people. You shall have to be strong and steadfast in order to withstand him. Do not pain me to my soul by succumbing, for I love you so dearly.

Totus in me tuus,
SÓTÒN'

3

Shivering with emotion I wrote back at once, though I kept a firm grip on my handwriting of strong, stark, fine shapes.

'Great Lord and Friend, indeed I have not often enough thought strongly and purposefully of thee. Forgive me this for the sake of your affection for me. Yes, happily I am still in Amsterdam and I shall leave for Paris by the night train. How happy I am that you believe me to be the most steadfast of your friends. I will not renounce you. And may I not think lightly of the enemy? Do you believe this to be the beginning of my defeat? On the contrary, I have felt myself grow stronger the more purely I have contempt for the people who, after all, are my natural enemies.

Good Sire, you ask after my situation in Holland? I live, and this, to these countrymen who do not live, is sufficient to make things awkward for me. Yes, it is said here 'live and let live' though to them it means 'make much money and give another a little, too'. Moreover, most people here are addicted to religion, alcohol and marxism, to such an extent that one does not get to hear an artful word. On the other hand, these people have some national virtues, too. They are fittingly gullible and docile, so that anyone can be the leader of a political party, and thus everyone is. A favourite proverb is 'where one sheep goes, more will follow' and after genever, the Good Shepherd is the one most worshipped here. Indeed, there are regions where strong drink comes after the Shepherd as regards esteem. Thus, it is still bearable over here.

From the money you gifted me I bought a diamond of pure kind.

Until tomorrow. Be convinced of my steadfast affection.

Totus in te tuus,
HELENUS MARIE'

4

While writing this, I thought: now I'll try to think of him so strongly that he can feel this and then he will know that I will remain true to him in the face of all. Fearful of loss, I brought my missive to the post myself. Afterwards, I did not enter our spacious garden again, the bordered lawn full of ruddy roses dripping dark, like blood, into the green. Loosely attired, lying on my back on my bed, I, overwrought, thought of the Devil. As though I were leaving my dwelling, ready for travel . . . passed along some streets . . . Oh, and crossed the shade-splendid canals . . . the station . . . the railwayline through Holland and Brabant . . . other countries . . . Paris . . . the Bradford Hotel, familiar to me – thus I considered, loyal and attentively, the paths of travel that separated us. My head was being tired out to a point beyond thought . . . it tingled behind my eyes, soft and pleasantly . . . my body felt engulfed in black . . . without communion with the outside world. My last known thought was: would he now feel that I thought of him sufficiently?

5

That next day, it rained over the wide city of Paris, dust-fine rain from a low sky without sun. Afraid of hostile influences, I had arrived at the hotel, trembling with fear. I kept my thoughts trained exactly on the Devil in order to be faithful to him, no matter what. Sharp-shy, erring in some of my words, I asked for the Viscount of Chelsea.

'Are you from Holland?' the doorman said, quietly distinguished.

'Yes . . . yes . . . I'm expected.'

The man had a boy come along to show me the way; I was so unsteady in my gait that this quick child kept an eye on me. My face was stretched to its deepest grain, it grimaced with snarkling pain. The boy-child looked at me and I thought: what a beauty that boy is. Oh, startled immediately afterwards, the way I was, I chased that thought away and I thought solely of Him.

The Devil was sitting in the chamber writing thoughtful scriptures, for he did not look up at me. I said: 'Sire . . .' He shivered . . . He approached me, and he did not touch me.

'What's the matter . . . is something wrong? I came at once, did I not?'

He was dull in his eyes.

'I am going into town, my child . . . no, we say nothing to one another now . . . then I would influence you unfairly . . . I've received your letter . . . thank you . . . and I have felt, too, that you did think of me, yesterday . . . do not leave me.'

'Must I wait here?'

'Oh, no . . . next door . . . this one . . . think as strongly as possible of me and do not succumb . . . you know the enemy, indeed you do.'

6

I did not dare enter the other chamber, but later I did, thinking urgent-strongly of the Devil. Having entered, I saw the hostile man. It was Jesus-Christ, whom I knew at once. He sat, dressed agile in white, in front of an oak lectern. A broad book lay upon it, open, its pages white-pale without lettering. He had read in it by means of strenuous attention. Attentive were his dark-purposed eyes when he looked up at me. 'Baruch haba', he said. Thoughtless, without knowledge or resistance, I left Sótòn's fealty.

Jesus had me sit opposite him and I became full of love and reverence, free from thoughts of the Devil. He spoke for my benefit and his conversation was like rippling spring water, simple in its insight, and strong. This I so enjoyed, and new verses trembled on my soul in the metre and manner of the old, splendid sonnets through which, in the past, I had sung of his love and suffering. While speaking, he moved his hands, all simplicity; in the main they lay for all to see on the arms of his chair. I saw that they were white without blemish, free from red punctures, like the letterless pages of the book in which he had been reading attentively. Reverently, I asked after the kind and value of that book. Lovingly, he put his hand on it: 'It's such an extraordinary book . . . you think the pages only white? When you learn to read it with great attention then you will discover differently . . . and the better you yourself become, the better you read the things in the book.'

'Might I learn to read in it . . . would You teach me?'

'I cannot teach you . . . you must do that yourself . . . you must have patience and love.'

The tone of his voice turned asper, hostile: 'There is also a red book, without letters like this white one . . . it is in the possession of someone who wishes to deceive you . . . and I tell you this, once you have begun to learn to read that red book, then this white one is lost to you . . . eternally.'

Then, sharply shocked, I thought of Sótòn whom I had abandoned so.

7

I felt that, present in the wide city of Paris, with me, in this room, he had continued in communion with me, and his suffering over my easy faithlessness touched me sorely. It had happened as, in his pain and knowledge of the world, he had predicted. I had abandoned his tenets for the easy persuasions of his enemy. His enemy, who spoke so unremarkably of humility and love of mankind. Oh, and Sótòn had so appreciated it in me that mine was a rockhard pride, without any sign of humiliating meekness, while I had never loved anyone to my own disadvantage. And wilfully I resisted the pernicious influences of Jesus. He had now taken the white book

134

and, his attention strong, he read aloud from the clean, letter-free pages. But I did not listen to him any longer. On, and on, I thought of the Devil, hopefully so strongly that he could feel it.

The reading voice that I felt to be hateful, became remote, lost, heard. Behind my eyes it tingled pleasantly and soft. My body felt black, without communion with the outside world and I desired so much that the Devil might feel my regained loyalty. While I hated the humane Jesus.

8

He stopped reading, and this I heard, likewise that he said:

'You have not listened . . .'

'No . . . indeed I haven't . . .'

'You have thought of Sótòn . . . he is your doom . . .'

'Shameful enough that I have forgotten him for a single instant because of your unremarkable philanthropy.'

'I have suffered so much abuse for the sake of mankind, as you know . . . and I have forgiven everything . . .'

'Because it's your nature and your profession . . . yes, indeed.'

'I forgive you these words of contempt . . . like I forgive everything . . . of all things, love is the best . . . I had wished to lead you to that understanding . . . you are so sorely lost . . . roaming, quite errant through selfishness and lovelessness . . . and you do not wish to return to the right path . . .'

'Don't reproach me with being loveless and selfish . . . with as much reason I might reproach You with being humane and loving, those are two characteristics antipathetic to me.'

'You are so far from the straight and narrow . . .'

'It is so immoral of You to try to influence me . . . don't You know that . . . why do You wish to push me down a path that is not mine . . . do You still not know that for everyone his own path is the right one . . . at Your age one either knows or one never will . . .'

'I see that I cannot help you . . . in a moment Sótòn returns and then I will go . . . I suffer so because of your erring . . . do not think that I only suffered on the cross . . . daily, I suffer for the suffering of every human being, and for everyone's erring . . . just look.'

9

From his white-folded clothes he showed me his hands and they now contained heavy-burgeoning red, bleeding stigmata. Recoiling from him, horror struck, all shock, I saw them.

The torpid, tepid blood dripped down broadly. He said: 'Because I suffer intensely for your errant badness, my painful wounds of the cross have bled open again ... and never will they close for ever until no man errs and suffers.'

I looked behind me, believing I heard the sound of Sótòn's fine-sweet laugh, but he was not yet back in the chamber. I, calm with shock, said cruelly to the bleeding one: 'Show your splendid wounds of the cross to whomever you wish ... but do not demand belief from me, belief that you have suffered on the cross. You enjoyed it so, a fine, nervous enjoyment ... don't you know that torment is the finest pleasure? Don't you know that?'

'*That* is my fiercest suffering ... such blind erring ... there is no remedy for it ... my hands bleed for it.'

'That, too, gives you joyous pain ... and the nuns who in white cloisters kneel around those red images of you, they enjoy it in their own way ... don't you know anything then, about the connection between love and cruelty ... and between religion and cruelty?'

'I only know the suffering of mankind ... and I suffer because of it.'

'Then Sótòn was right after all, that yours is a charming mediocrity ... and that because of this so many people venerate you.'

He did not answer this discourse and I lashed him further with my mock-making words: 'And the poets who sing of your so-called suffering: do you think that they feel anything other than pleasure at your finely-coloured death? I know one ... in Amster-dam ... he has made many very admiring verses about you ... and he has the walls in his dwelling hung full with images of you ... this gives his body sufficient sating. And I assure you that in this manner you are being used by quite a few more people ... this is apparently not in conflict with any of the three vows ...'

'Not those words ... but your foolish erring pains me ... I forgive you ...'

'Of course you forgive me ... that's your job ... better not to make so much of it, I should say ... do I make much of the fact that I do not forgive, not ever ... though the latter is surely the better disposition ...'

10

He got up and he said: 'I must make haste now, and alas I cannot do anything for you ... I give you my forgiveness and my sincerest blessing.'

He approached me ... he stretched out his hands, the bleeding ones, above my head. I hated his loving humaneness, while I feared most terribly that he would soil my dark-tressed head I loved so well with his tepid blood. Dizzy with hatred my fingers gripped his wrists and I wildly wrenched his red hands downwards so the joints crunched. He moaned with pain but I did not spare him. In tepid streams his stigmata bled more rapidly under the cramped grip of my fingers.

'I forgive you ... it is not this blood that flows away that pains me ... but your erring does so ... how is Our Father to forgive you this ...'

Rage over his forgiveness turned my eyes red, the blood was raging in my ears. Then, wildly, I broke his stance ... twisting his arms, pushing him over backwards so that he sank down, miserable in the dripping blood. I mated him with the rage of my lithe body that jerked over his and humiliated him. And thus I violated him, with hands that flailed; with feet that trod down; with tremulous mouth full of fine-marauding little teeth that tugged at flesh beneath thin-white clothing. He did not defend himself.

Then sadness and tiredness came over me from this wild, furious union. My overwrought body lay on his, powerless. My eyes touched upon the still-deep gaze of his own, dark and benevolent. And I hated him for his love of humanity.

11

After I had regained consciousness, I saw the dark-deep eyes of the Devil gleam down in mine. He had laid down my body close to his so that I heard the blood-beat of his heart. Timidly I looked around the chamber. 'No,' said Sótòn, 'he has gone and his filthy blood has been cleared up ... be calm.'

'Do I never have to see him again? I don't ever want to see him again . . . I hate him so much.'

'No, Heleen, now he will leave you in peace . . . not because you have beaten him so and bitten him . . . his profession is to be tortured in public really . . . but in private like that, this he quite likes too . . . but he does see that you remain loyal to me, no matter what . . . I am so pleased about that.'

'At first I didn't . . . I was faithless . . . do you actually know that?'

'Yes, my boy, I know . . . I stayed in communion with the two of you . . . and at first I was indeed afraid . . . he is so easy and so unremarkable, and with that he has so much influence . . .'

'I did love him in the past . . .'

'You see, Heleen, people live and think in tribes . . . they have fatherlands . . . you have to stay out of all those . . . only live and think . . . despise all fatherlands . . . don't be meek in life and don't be charitable . . . then you'll see what beauty you will find . . . do you know, my boy, that you must be everything yourself?'

I looked into his eyes and listened to the ecstasy of his voice. He laughed. Trembling, sobbing, I knew that my happiness was approaching.

The Devil bent forward, his mouth down to my mouth . . . he kissed me, and he called me: 'darling'.

The Taxi Pig

Fritzi Harmsen van Beek

As we were getting in, we hadn't noticed that there was a taxi-pig in the car, along for the ride as well. And it's questionable whether we would have said anything about it, had we noticed.

Not very likely, to be honest.

For a start, it's not really advisable, before placing one's life in another's hands, to embark on comments which the driver of such a vehicle might take to be unpleasant. Such a taxi-pig might easily be his friend or, even worse, his little lady wife he had been forced to drag along everywhere from sheer necessity. But even the one who is prepared to take such a risk is left with another difficulty, is left sitting there, gob shut, often until death follows – or else maimed for life, in any case. For how, for god's sake, does one recognise a taxi-pig before the driver has started the car?

Am I right, or am I right? An impossibility: as long as no driving is being done, it is not to be recognised, and as long as it cannot be recognised one can hardly come trotting out with objections. There's the rub.

Imagine you said, – Hold on, mate, slowly does it, please. Before we set off, what's that pink little animal down there in the front; not a taxi-pig by any chance, is it? – and the chap says how COULD you say such a thing, that's my own . . . (you name it) and if you don't like it, you'd better take the bus, – so that, from a feeling of self-worth, you're obliged to get out and make the journey by public transport in the random company of eighty-five other pigs, and later on you then hear from others who were less prone to flying off the handle that it WASN'T even a taxi-pig: it was quite simply the peasant's brother! There's you looking goggle-eyed when you're just returning, right brainwashed and almost beyond repair, from the local transport corporations. Such things, too, are irreparable.

But the taxi-pig I'm talking about right now: we hadn't noticed it. The notion that it was simply sitting in, somewhere in the front, of course, this had not entered our heads because we were far too busy with ourselves and with the beavers.

Those beavers: having to set out on a journey with them is no joke. It had been for their sakes, more or less, that we had conceived the plan of going IN COGNITO, so there we were, all four in the back: the two of them together, clearly recognisable, and we, as if nothing was up, in our shoddy disguises. And the driver did look old-fashioned for a moment, but even if he did cotton on, he never showed that at all.

– And that's how it should be, we even thought, with that stupid smugness which, on the whole, leads you to sail, eyes skinned, head-on into disasteration.

Our wayfaring began at once. Bawled out by preposterous crows, we travelled in stately slow-motion down the garden path, crunching the sparse gravel festively beneath our huge wheels, triumphantly leaving behind a clear and meaningful little chain of deadly exhaust-fume-clouds in our knife-sharp wake. The day was wintry. And of a similar colour – that colour of gravely isolated, insufferable, stale bread – were heaven and earth that day: skies snow-blending with fields, their differences only feebly shored up by some black stick-and-branch-work.

There we were, travelling quite busily from the word go, really: leering, refined and brain-dead by turns, sideways at the not particularly varied perspective behind the car-door windows, and then again staring, wam-bam, narrowly past the back of the remarkably detailed head of the driver, on to the road ahead of us, at the vanishing point ever-running out ahead of us: that head start in the snow, never to be caught up with, and at the vague whiteness of the stretch still to be covered which, meanwhile, passing immediately beneath us, was already being covered in elegant gulleys of sludge and muck.

So ambiguous, so elevated and yet vulgar at the same time, so full of mysterious contradictions, shifting inconspicuously – when all goes well and everything happens without accidents – that's travel.

It's quite certain we had already gained speed alarmingly when, in the first bend to the right, sliding like greased lightning across the imitation leather, we were slammed into the car door on the left and we began to shout – Hey, you; and the taxi-pig suddenly said – Yeah, sure. No more than that. Just this: yeah, sure. In a neutral tone of voice, it is true, but incontrovertibly pig-like.

From fright, we forgot we had those beavers and were IN COGNITO and had to keep our traps shut if we were not to have fingers pointing at us, in all the villages and God-knows-where-else, throughout the entire region even, as being debauched half-wits; for, once a rumour like that spreads then there's no stopping it – and we burst forth in unholy ranting and raving.

And then that cunning, incomparable taxi-pig!

It sat there, motionless, and kept on driving, even gave proceedings an extra dose of the accelerator, and kept its gob shut until we'd shot our bolts and, unpleasant and delicate, went and sat in silence and already began to worry about what the catastrophic consequences of that gasket-blowing might be, and even began to feel like saying – Ah, well; and – Come, come; and more of the like, not so much out of shame or regret, but only to salvage the salvageable.

Then it went and sat staring out ahead of itself, inscrutable, mumbling so we couldn't make out a thing and we finally ended up saying – Hey; – What; and then, at last, it could point out its specially prepared party-piece to us: mounted, clearly visible, on the dashboard, a nameplate which in white little capitals read BACKSEATDRIVING?NOTHANKS! – that hurtful, hurtful pig.

There, now: it finally had us where it wanted us.

Dumping Ground

Marcus Heeresma

Thudding and jarring on its shock absorbers, the man in the immaculate, off-white, three-piece suit steers the large car through a gradually narrowing network of unlit, unmetalled streets with open sewers and crooked, tumbledown hovels. The man appears immune to the penetrating stench of garbage and excrement. And yet it must be here, he thinks. It had been explained to him, more or less, at the club, after all. Again: respectable people, all of them. Here too, in Perú, things were going to suit him just fine.

The man in off-white works for a European government which flogs all kinds of things for which no market can be found elsewhere any more: for lack of parts, because of faulty materials or defects in an even broader sense, but for which an application can be found even now, here or in other so-called third-world countries, or for which applications can be created and such 'creations' must simply be endured. They're quite simply forced to, the man thinks, smiling. On pain of being denied the monies set at their disposal by the delivering country, monies, gathered in by the taxpayers of those countries and earmarked in principle for all kinds of idealistic purposes often viewed by others, however, as being impractical. And these monies are often used largely to finance those 'creations' therefore, and to finance the people on the spot who have to keep the markets open a bit. Ah yes, indeed: business. Many Latin-American countries, once a year, for goodwill too, sell a war criminal from stock and for a great deal of money. That's the way it should be, too, all this.

The man has been here some seven months by now, and trips such as these have already obliged him a few times to replace the shock absorbers on his car. But it's worth it no end. And money no object, of course. At the club, somebody had called him 'one of the dump-mongers' but, well, the man had been tiddly and, roaring with laughter, had declared to be dealing in waste himself, too. 'These countries are dumping grounds, after all.' And yet, you need to be careful where you shout such things about the place.

'Garbage,' the man in off-white mumbles. A glass and a bottle stand in a holder fixed to the dashboard and the man pours himself a drink.

Rats, children, pets, the prematurely elderly, people with drab dog-skin shoot away in the dancing floodlight of the heaving car manoeuvring its way round the deepest potholes. Hours of driving through darkness and stench in the damp, hot Lima night have strung themselves into one until finally the network of stinking mayhem runs into a dead-end on one of the many garbage tips of the Peruvian capital — in the night, according to the man, that trembles sultrily with heat and impending manslaughter.

He shivers and smiles. The car has been fitted with armoured glass. Circumspectly, the man in off-white drives the jolting car along the edge of the rubbish-tip tillage and stops. Only with a tank or some such, on caterpillar tracks, might you be able to go any further, or on tow or pushed by something similar. The strong beam from the searchlight, operated from inside, on the roof of the car, sweeps in all directions across the immense plain of filth. This excites the man. It's a form of malicious pleasure, one that strikes him as erotic: one he is entitled to. Malicious pleasure is quality pleasure and he works hard enough for it in South America: has been doing so for years now. It's made him grow up — and made him important. This, too, is again a *beautiful* South American country, but hard, gruesomely hard and cruel. However, one has to adapt if one wishes to survive and amuse oneself a little. Malicious pleasure indeed. Why not? If they're too lazy to work, they're good enough to be used.

The man in off-white has taken good care not to come to a halt in a pothole. Not on the edge of that rubbish tip either. No police come here. They are powerless, for the people do not mind being shot dead. People live so close to death here, continually . . . And a revolver and an automatic pistol make for excellent sources of income to desperados. A comfortable old age. A kingdom. Were he to get stranded here, no one would ever hear of him again. 'Anarchist rabble.' But then, they belong on a rubbish tip. Garbage.

It's the same as with all those other garbage tips where, particularly at night, he has spent so much time. Dumping grounds as far as the light — and, so he presumes, the horizon — will reach: filth, garbage. Exciting. It continues to enchant him. Here, too, it's busy again. Day and night, thousands are at it there. The man in white switches off the searchlight. For a moment it is pitch black.

Then his eyes have got used to the rather light night. Like a leering cayman, the car stands on the shore's edge of the immense sea of garbage.

The man winds up the windows tight shut against the asphyxiating stench and the dangerous gasses that develop spontaneously deep down in that garbage and are forced up to the surface by the pressure. But still the car slowly fills with that stench, that gas and that heat. On the car's bodywork rattle the index-finger long, fat, armour-plated *cucarachas*, the cockroaches. The tough, excreta-sucking, bacteria-carrying spreaders of disease that also can fly. They wrench their way in through the holes in the bottom of the car, next to the pedals.

The man − carefully, with an eye to the crease in his trousers − draws up his legs on to the seat. He has brought along a hammer for those creeps, to protect his white, bespoke, fine-meshed tropical shoes. A hammer with a fist-size head. Such an instrument can always come in handy in these regions, for that matter. The creatures' wing-cases snap, hard, like mica, when he smashes them beneath a hammer blow. The man resolves not to forget to have the girl or the gardener clean the car on the inside as well, tomorrow. They've been lucky with staff, as it happens. But then, they're well looked after. At times, to everyone's satisfaction, they are paid in kind, the gardener in jeans the man in white can no longer wear and T-shirts with, to the gardener, foreign-language inscriptions which he walks around in, peacock-proud. The girl receives all kinds of garments from the woman: garden robes, slacks, and the girl is especially pleased with the European underwear which only needs to be taken in a bit for the little, fifteen-year-old Cholo girl the man regularly relaxes with. The man thinks it rather exciting and *piquant*, actually, to have the little one in his bed in the reduced underwear of his spouse.

All of a sudden, he shivers. Like a child belonging to him, a cucaracha has attached itself to his upper leg. With the hammer, he shoves the creature from his leg on to the floor where he bashes it to death. The heat and the stench are almost unbearable and the rattling of the cucarachas on the paintwork, the floor and the leather upholstery of the car's seats make him itch everywhere. He takes a deodorant spray from the glove compartment. The spraying does not help much. Many in Perú, the man knows, believe that the enormous clouds of poison gas that form deep down in the dumping grounds probably constitute the greatest disaster threatening the inhabited areas. The cities in particular, of course. Lima most of all, the capital with a population numbering eight million, the one to which all paupers, bereft, swarm as a last resort, the *serranos* in particular, the farmers from the mountains, to pauperise in an even shabbier fashion after having served as voting fodder. On, towards an even quicker death, for it is said that the *serranos* are not resistant to Lima's damp climate which, moreover, is poisonous in the places where they dwell. The man in off-white shrugs his shoulders. Stupid to come here, in that case.

If it's all actually *true*, that is, and not propaganda from one group or another. You never could tell, over here. The drier, healthily inhabitable parts of Lima, situated closely against the surrounding mountains, are lived in by the rich. Lucratively operating *gringos*, *extranjeros*, foreigners, in the main. But, in the man's opinion, they had tasty garbage, in any case. And were one to make the tips disappear, something politically unwise, for the people have a vote in Perú, then one would be 'taking the bread from the mouths' of innumerable people, wouldn't one . . .

Like a dispersed people, thousands on the tip are busily at it, spread in among the dirt. Silently. And seriously, as is the case with heavy, complicated handicraft that demands attention. Here and there stand the roofless reed huts of families who have established themselves on the only viable bread-source: the garbage dump. All are in search of something. Of something edible, of bits of wood, tin or cardboard which might be employed, if not in reinforcement, then in any case as an adornment for their hovels on or near the tip. Here too, the man knows, no difference reigns between race, faith, culture, man, beast, large or small. Between male and female only just, perhaps.

Upon the approach of a number of filthy, ragged Indians or some such, the man locks the door in a reflex, absentmindedly pulls the handbrake on and firms up his grip around the handle of the heavy hammer. What have we here now? He wants to watch *safely*, quietly: the world belongs to us all. He smiles again and pours himself another one. He comes across a German language station on the radio. The Vienna Boys' Choir sings through the stench in the darkened car and through the vapour forcing its way in, but it does not drown out the rattle of the cucarachas. The silent, barefoot and almost undressed Indians or whatever, lean in their rags against the car and press their broad, mongoloid faces against the windows. They look like grey, blind eyes, blocked up with dust, trying to discern something. The man in off-white, inside, has moved away a bit from the door. Outside he now also hears the squeaking of the cat-sized rats, innumerable ones which scuttle about here. The Boys' Choir sings of skies so high, of peace, of *Wälder* and the hunter pacing along cheerfully, and about the birds, so free, so free.

The rag-wearers try the doors. 'Locked,' the man says softly. He laughs nervously and shivers. They are too frightened or too weak or too lonely to break open the car or to smash such an armoured glass window with the great force of iron bars. 'Not a heroic people, no.' The men press themselves up against the windows again. A primitive life-form, the man thinks. A barely viable variant of shit, dung and garbage creepers and gorgers, of dumpground-shuffling rustlers, that has raised itself up on its hind legs. The only solution, even so, would be, never mind the politics: wire netting round the plain and set the flame throwers on them.

The narrow, grey mouths of the life-form in the sand and dust-covered faces form the words *'limosna, patron; propina'*: 'alms, please, boss; a tip'. With a heart beating more rapidly with the excitement that has something so enchanting about it, the man winds down the window a touch. That hurts: he has strained a muscle 'at golf'. A narrow slit appears, no wider than that of those tight-pinched collection boxes designed for cosily folded banknotes the man recalls from the churches of the latitudinarian protestants in the country of his birth; boxes with a pinched stripe of a slit with which latitudinarian little boys also would try to indicate something situated down there in the wife of the preacher or the deacon.

The man in off-white forces his loose change through the slit. Outside the car it drops into the garbage: a stream of ever devaluing coins, greedily picked up from the filth, for the total value of which, the man thinks to himself, one might be able, somewhere on the opposite side of one of the oceans, to buy half a bar of chocolate of an unknown brand, second-hand. 'And without a wrapper,' the man mutters, smiling. 'Loose, in a strip of news-paper, should one ask for it *politely*.'

He has gone and sat a little closer to the window again. His forehead rests against the glass while he watches how the soiled life-form outside bends down laboriously in the dust, with probably arthritic limbs, and languidly tries to push one another away from the coins that have dropped into the waste, coins the man in off-white slips into the slit above his head. 'Just like an action slot-machine,' the man says, and he shivers for a moment. 'But then in slow-motion.' It reminds him of the train between Cuzno and Puno. There he — and tourists too — always holds out bananas from the window when the train stops somewhere, or biscuits, sweets or a little coin. Men, women, children and the elderly will then jump up high against the train together, at the goodies or the coin. His wife has taken highly amusing photos of this.

The coins have gone and the man again slides away from the window a little. Then the man in off-white in the posh car makes the slit close. Slowly. In order not to anger or frighten the men. Maybe these life-forms enjoy solidarity among one another, all of them, there on the tip. And yonder, life-forms with more developed muscles are crawling about, too. Ah well, it's a case of starting the engine, accelerating and off we go. The thought of danger, whether imagined or not, from the putrefaction of the dumping ground, flickeringly lit by fires, stimulates him in a pleasing manner: things are getting light in his underbelly. They stand there, impotent, after all. 'Impotent and indolent,' the man says quietly. 'He who does not work, neither shall he eat. Thus spake the Almighty. As revealed to us by a reliable Spokesman.'

The life-form outside the car presses itself up against the windows again. '*Limosna, patron, propina.*' The man laughs while he pants slightly. This makes a curious, squeaking sound. Then, in the dark, slowly and emphatically, he gravely shakes his head at the men. Likewise, too, he wags the raised index-finger, slowly and in a contrary direction to the head. 'Party's over.' He is reminded of his father for a moment, dead immediately after he had moved with Mother into the house in the suburbs Mother had lived her whole life towards achieving. Fifty-eight: still young. Worn-out, the doctor had said, and he had muttered something that he ought not to have moved, not from his house on a canal. But *had* he lived, he would have been the age of these men outside. A strange jump in his thinking suddenly. Father would have been *proud*. Proud of his son. Waste products . . .

The man in off-white shakes his head. The men retreat, warily it seems, and their silhouettes dissolve in the darkness of the plain of filth. Now and then they are lit up a moment when something explodes spontaneously in the rubbish and, just like New Year's Eve and its fireworks, is slung up high into the air: thousands of sparks falling back in a languid arch to earth's reality: the dumping ground, the tip. Dogs bolt, howling, or are those people there, on all fours? Spread across the entire plain, a province, fires burn, giving off greasy smoke.

The people busy here on the tip, the man knows, are not the first in the chain of filth-sifters. The domestic waste daily filling the streets in open boxes, tins, bags and oil drums, first gets sifted by the ones operating the streets, before the waste is collected by the 'City Cleansing Department', frequently in open trucks which the waste is then dumped into, loose, thus forming little mobile garbage tips in which shaking people scrabble about. The garbage trucks, in the end, dump the waste of the metropolis, having been sorted by staff, on to ever fresh dumping grounds around which new shanty towns then arise, for Lima continues to grow explosively. Lima, with paupers on the one side and wealthy entrepreneurs on the other. 'With precious waste,' the man in off-white mumbles. 'And that way everyone is happy and satisfied as long as the life-form casts its vote for the right man. How could it ever be capable of casting its vote independently? The vote must be prescribed, firmly.'

Intently, he peers at the silhouettes on the tip. Curious people, he thinks. But they make beautiful music. The *Serranos* in particular, the mountain Indians. So beautifully tragic. He is in regular contact with relatives and friends on the other side of the Atlantic, where – in cassette cases in the cassette caddy with the tuner and the tapedeck on top – the professionally performed music of the South American underworld piles up relentlessly; mountains like spermiform, nourishing-skincream-packaged cries of despair of the *Criollos* and the *Serranos*, the *Cholos*, the Indians. Of the Indians, especially the *Huanas* and the *Huaylas*, whose cries in primal form once resounded in the thin air between the slopes and precipitous rock faces of the high Andes and which now, distorted in deepest despair, are being absorbed into the rubble and the reeking garbage of the dumping ground, with the shrill, high-wailing, shouted singing of the women. At times, many will sing along, with broken voices, in those unbelievably high voices of the women who once lived in the healthy air of the *Cordilleros de los Andes* – a distressed, screeching *a-cappella* choir of lost, dying garbage grubbers, rooting in the poison gas, the heat: at their wits' end and capable of anything. 'Beast-man', as all are called in the healthily inhabitable parts of Lima, all who do not live up against the mountains where breathing is done freely; and they keep themselves firmly apart and fear, one day, a 'unification in attack' by beast-man. One knows the army to be on one's side, however.

Again, an interesting country, is the man-in-off-white's opinion. Fine climate, too, in every respect. Intently he regards the ragged crap-creepers. Some are professionally equipped with gloves or have bars to turn over the filth, again others wield pitch-forks, rakes, children, shovels, and plastic bags and newspapers to wrap something up in, and here and there people are even busy with a wheelbarrow. 'Small businessmen,' the man mutters, smiling again. He shivers, and he grabs and rummages, flirtatious, at his crotch.

The Indians and Creoles and whatever else there might be of bastardised races that make the man puke, vary in all ages; often entire families scuttle about, touched by the soft wind which, shroud-like, wraps them slowly but surely in the clouds of smoke and gas from the spontaneously combusted fires and smouldering spots. Regularly, enormously tall fires flare up: fed by nourishing waste or waste gas, yellowy-orange flames wheel up high to heaven. And taken by surprise, the silhouettes then stumble off, away. Occasionally, such an explosion will come about in a place where they are busy: hands, sticks or bars providing oxygen to something below the tip; then their rags, too, catch fire, which they attempt to quench by rolling themselves in the filth, thus frequently causing fresh fires from which they then must take to their heels again. It's exciting, according to the man in off-white and, fascinated, he follows it all. Regularly the fist of the hammer bangs in the car on the wing-case of one of the smaller excrement-creepers.

In the dim light of a suddenly flaring fire, the man discovers an almost naked Cholo girl, still Indian, primarily. She is sitting, legs wide, in the filth and stares motionless at the thousands of people busy around her, most of them searching resignedly in the night in the garbage. From a velvet case the man takes out a pair of opera glasses on an extendible handle. The girl is little more than thirteen, fourteen years of age. She has small breasts and a wondrously fine figure. Splendid legs, too, he thinks. He takes the handle of the opera glasses in his left hand and, having undone his trousers, he allows his right hand to disappear inside these. He hears shuffling round the car. Furtively, he looks around him. Nothing. Probably the mild wind is playing tag with the garbage. He grasps himself with his right hand and begins to give himself relief, now staring through the glasses at the girl, then at the rooting paupers and quickly back to the girl again, postponing the climax each time. He pants and pushes his trousers down further. Ah, so what: nobody can see him anyway. Like a small, pale fish the colour of his suit, his member sticks out at the steering wheel. Cucarachas are now crawling into his trousers, attaching themselves to his jerking, bare legs, but he doesn't notice.

Not far from the car, a young negro approaches. He is pushing a laden, sturdy, two-wheeled handcart. He is a large, agile and strong negro. He would have to be. Otherwise he wouldn't have been able to steal a handcart. The negro feels himself to be the king of the tip and he takes fire along with him: wherever he goes, small fires erupt in the stinking tip, oddly enough. The man, off-white in part, is irked: something of his hardness disappears, from fear, and he stares quickly at the innumerable rooters and then at the Cholo girl, and moving rapidly with his hand, he makes himself rise again towards the gleaming steering wheel. The game of wind and filth around the car, coming to him like a kind of whispering and shuffling, banging softly against the bumpers and the wings, excites him; he sees the waste before him, raised up by the wind, half a metre off the ground, bumping softly, caressingly against his car, against him. His shirt and jacket become soaked with perspiration. For a moment, he lets go of himself and the glasses, tears his jacket off, his waistcoat, undoes his tie and quickly unbuttons his shirt, panting. Then he lets the back of his seat go back, grabs the opera glasses, aims, and then he grabs hold of himself again, firmly. Now he rises in front of the wheel, like a big compass-needle of firm, throbbing flesh. 'Garbage,' he mutters, and he smiles. Sweat runs down his face and body in rivulets. He slips about in all the sweat on the leather of his seat. He looks at the negro. The man senses danger in the air about him, danger, revulsion and garbage; he growls and groans softly, his mouth half-open, and he moves, rhythmically and more rapidly.

That the negro is proud can be seen by his bearing, and he makes the two-wheeled cart with garbage bob rhythmically up and down with his relaxed, dancing gait. He grins, baring some snow-white teeth in the night, but primarily black gaps, though. He is only wearing a pair of dirty shorts, very off-white. Near the beautiful, almost naked girl, still sitting wide-legged in the garbage, the negro stops. Their dark skin is lit by a bright-orange kind of Easter fire nearby, sicking up black soot like a kind of grim redemption. The negro tips up his cart and begins to dump his garbage, slowly. Over the girl. She laughs, abandonedly, all of a sudden a toothless old woman, and she puts up her hands to the stream of garbage.

The man in the car groans and has to contain himself severely. It throbs and thuds and tenses and trembles against the smooth steering wheel. The girl catches a bottle in her hands, one that got overlooked. She wipes the dirt from it and clasps the smooth bottle between her breasts: suddenly she is fearful and grim-faced. A few pennies deposit. The cheerful, muscular negro tosses his cart aside and upside down with force, lets himself drop onto his belly and digs up arms full of waste which he tries to pile on top of the head and shoulders of the girl. After a cautious look at the negro, the girl sets the bottle down beside her and, now effusive again, clasps her arms round the negro. All of a sudden, the negro gets himself upright again and stretches. The girl pulls the last few remaining rags off her body and tugs down the negro's trousers. Proud, his sword rises up above the garbage; pointing in the stench and the flickering night the negro stands above the girl sitting on her knees. She takes the Creole into her mouth and the negro looks down on her, laughing. Then he lets himself drop on top of her and together they gambol about, round and round, like the squeaking, still turning wheels of the handcart lying upside down. 'It's the wind,' says the man in the cream-coloured shirt that hangs open, 'or me.' Dirt or whatever surges against the car which shakes gently and seems to rise up at times. 'It's starting to blow.'

Suddenly he lets go of himself and the glasses again, takes the hammer and bangs away at random on the floor of the car which seems to be moving in itself because of the innumerable cucarachas scuttling over and across one another thus forming a kind of brownish blanket underneath which there is wild movement going on. He sees the creatures on his legs, on his thighs, his underbelly, but this only gets through to him obliquely. The sight of the creatures seems to intensify his excitement. He becomes very excited indeed and grasps hold of himself again. The opera glasses are trained on the negro and the Cholo girl. All of a sudden, he tears away his trousers and underpants from his ankles, over his shoes. The cayman no longer sleeps but moves, or is being moved, jerkily. The wind wails softly together with the men and women and children, writhing and singing in the filth. The *Huaylas* of the rubble, the waste, the stench, the gas, the heat, the threat, the excrement, of flight and despair.

Flames, shooting up high, suddenly light up two silhouettes also nearby, ones the man in white had held to be bent and battered oil drums. They turn out to be two men in innumerable torn rags being worn one over the other. They are sitting not far from each other, their under-rags down, on their haunches in the dirt, relieving themselves. 'Where on earth did they get *that* idea from?' mutters the man in the cream-coloured shirt that hangs open. There is a sound of indignation in his voice. He allows the hand around his member to rest a moment. He directs the opera glasses and peers. Nothing doing with one of them. Or he has done it already and lingers a little longer in the aftermath, unhurried. But he is grabbing wildly around him, up to his elbows in the filth. The other man produces but a child's-finger-thick but uncommonly long, ochre-coloured trail. Some time is involved in this. The leering, almost naked man, covered only by the shirt hanging open and those numerous creatures, scuttling about or attaching themselves, pants and he moves his hand again, ever more wildly. When the trail has been completed, the man half gets up and languidly wipes his lower torso with some dirt. He straightens out further, slowly pulls up the rags and disappears, shaking in a sudden bout of coughing, into the dark across the tip.

On the radio, the foreigner now rules with a polka; something from the Danube or the Moldau or a probing tributary. The other man sits motionless. He is eating something now which he holds to his lips in both hands like a mouth organ. The negro and the Indian girl have found one another satisfying. The man sees how they move ever more slowly and how, slowly, the negro frees himself from the girl. For a moment then they lie next to one another, motionless, their gleaming faces turned up to the dark sky, at one with the tip. Then the negro rises, agilely, and disappears rapidly into the dark, into a multitude of more and more shades moving about not far from the car.

There's constant singing now: soft, shrill and sad. Furthermore, sounds are being formed by the wind, the crackle of spark-spitting fires, dull rumblings, deep inside the dumping ground at times, and by the explosions. And by the soft shuffling of humans and animals around and among these, and around the car. And, of course, by the rattling of the creatures with which the almost naked man now appears to be merging. Countless numbers of such creatures are now crawling over his perspiring body: in his armpits, on his sweating belly and chest, in his pubic hair, his neck, on his arms, on his hands, around his throbbing member. Through the glasses, the man keeps his gaze trained intently on the girl lying asleep, legs wide, in the filth. The fires conjure up a moving sheen on her body and then the man's body arches, jerkily. Off-white drips down the wheel, covers the cucarachas on his thighs, his right hand, and the heavily perspiring, sodden man leans back. In the car that stinks like the immense garbage tip.

Slowly the car with the panting, somewhat dazed man begins to move, half driving, sliding, occasionally borne by a multitude of grey, dusty, scrubby shades: a barely viable life-form, but of a size in which the car is barely noticeable. At first the man with the cucarachas does not notice anything. Then he raises himself up with a jolt and looks around him, wildly. Suddenly it gets through to him that he is covered in those sticky waste and excrement eaters. He screams and then he sees the compact mass of dusty, soiled figures in front of all the windows.

That the car has already been pushed, dragged, hoisted a good way up the tip, this he has not yet noticed. His view outside has been taken from him. He steps on the brake but this makes no difference. The heavy car moves from left to right like a sedan chair, banging down on the waste at times and then being lifted up again.

All of a sudden, the man relaxes. 'Calm down,' he mutters, 'we've been in worse pickles.' He laughs for a moment and then he draws himself further upright by the dripping steering wheel and he starts the engine. He accelerates, but the car has been lifted up, rear wheels and all, and the wheels spin in vain in the stinking gas and fetid air.

After a few booming blows, a heavy steel bar forces its way in through the shattered windscreen. The door is opened and a muscular, black gleaming arm switches off the engine and pulls the key from the ignition. The hammer is taken from him. Simultaneously, grabbing arms have pulled away the trousers and the underpants, the waistcoat and the jacket, the bottle and the glass, and in two tugs the shirt is ripped from his body.

The door is closed again and the car is pushed further along up the dumping ground. People are no longer walking alongside the doors so that the man with the cucarachas has something of a view. He sees how progress is being made across the boundless garbage plain; he now sees the fires at close quarters, sees those dying in rags.

Ahead of him, when the mass shuffling the car forwards allows him an opportunity, the man sees how, in the rather bright night, the plain of filth stretches out as far as the horizon will reach. The stench, the heat grow thicker inside the car disappearing slowly but surely ever further away from the barely inhabitable world near the dumping ground.

The man screams. He switches on the lights, but without the keys only the parking lights will work. In a panic, the man puts the car into gear. The car stops. At the rear, people, or life-forms, bang into it. The door is opened again and a blow to the temple almost throws the man from his seat. A hand shifts the gears back in neutral. The lights go out. The door closes again.

People are shuffling towards them from all sides now. Knives are being drawn. Inside the car, the man screams, muffled and futile. They let the car run down under its own steam, down one of the sloping garbage-sides of a deep, black-scorched pit. In a moment or two, the car is covered with a slow, insect-like layer of crawling people. The four doors are pulled open. Almost simultaneously. The car fills up.

Pompeii Funebri

A.F.Th. van der Heijden

'Sight . . . hearing . . . taste and speech . . .' With both index-fingers
Lex Patijn described tiny little circles, fast as lightning, a little way
away from his eyes, ears and mouth. 'When these fall away, you've
. . . you've got absolute loneliness. Panic, fear and absolute loneliness. Take my word for it. Only the sense of smell remains. And
not even that, for you can only smell the plaster.'

He was saying it for the fifth or sixth time already, in a voice
getting more drunk by the minute and without remembering that
he had brought up the matter earlier on. 'No, honestly: hearing,
sight, speech, taste . . .' He couldn't dismiss it from his mind. His
words were being dictated by his cowardice. One could smell his
sweat in the little dressing room. 'Loneliness, absolute, but I mean
absolute . . . loneliness.'

Being a sculptor, Patijn had worked on the conversion of an old
monastery into an 'educational theme park' for youngsters. He
himself had modelled for a number of characters from mythology
(crouching as Atlas, for instance, with a big ball on his neck) which
had meant that he had been wrapped in plaster-of-Paris bandages,
head to toe, after which the plaster cast had been cut into
segments in order to be welded into a single entity again and
finally painted. The panic and fear and loneliness he had undergone
each time, prior to being cut open, had given him an idea. Here he
was being handed the possibility, as a sculptor, of giving shape to
his idea of 'realism' . . .

That evening, we celebrated the first night of a play (a free
adaptation of *The Chinese Wall* by Frisch) in which Lex's lover,
Jody Katan, was playing the lead. Before drunkenness had struck,
Lex told me about his bursary for Naples.

'Not exactly a centre of modern art,' I pointed out to him.

'I've rented a studio in Naples, that's all. Pompeii's the point for
me. I'm going to make sculptures like ones that exist there.'

'Has Lex Patijn converted to classical art?'

'I'm not talking about those three, four sculptures they've hauled out from underneath the ashes, no: I mean the *corpses*. The petrified bodies of Pompeii's inhabitants. They are the true statues ... Not shaped by the limp mitts of some artist but by a malevolent quirk of nature. I'm going to apprentice myself to Mount Vesuvius, if you get my drift. I want to change into a rain of ashes.'

I asked about his materials, his new working method.

'Together with a chemistry student, I'm busy perfecting plaster bandages. We're a good way there already ... but I'd like it to be even more pliable, even more elastic ... so the model can impress his last convulsions upon my material. Without it tearing. I have my models assume a death-pose ... as naturalistically as possible ... They must die in the harness I apply. The moment the stuff begins to set, I'll cut that plaster suit into pieces I weld together again into hollow dolls. I'll give them a wooden skeleton, if need be.'

'Hm. The hand of the artist isn't lacking ...'

'Not entirely. Not *yet*. *My* hand – the hand of the one who applies the bandages and cuts open the harness, the artisan's hand, that is – that's the one that may be discernible in it. But the hand of the artist I am must be kept from it as far as possible. Through direct contact with my material the model transforms himself into a work of art. That's the creed of my realism. Look ... that wireless transmission of model to material, that's what I want to be shot of. That's how it's always been, hasn't it: the model stands and poses *there* – and *here*, at five metres' distance, I stand at my easel and dip my brush, functioning as an aerial, in the paint on my palette, and my transmission to my white paper or canvas is *wireless*. The artist as telegraphist. My pursuit now is to carry my paper, my canvas, my white sheet to the model and ... and drape it around him, cutting his suit according to my cloth, so that the model, like Christ with Veronica's cheese cloth, can imprint himself directly on my material.'

When alcohol had begun to heat our feelings and I no longer kept my criticism of Patijn's realism to myself, he began calling me names, making me out to be an 'idealist', by which he probably won't have meant that I entertained such things as ideals.

'You, you see everything through the rose-tinted spectacles of ... of ...' he shouted. The deal that had been struck was not to utter the word.

'*You*, Lex, are a drinker. Alcohol eats away your liver, your heart and your muscles. It'll give you tits and your balls will

156

dissolve in it. What you think is a theory, is nothing other than your own jadedness.'

Jody, in his white overall of 'Nowling' or 'Presentman', kept himself to himself and didn't take sides.

2

In order radically to divest myself of the horseflies that had latched on to me in Amsterdam, I accompanied Lex Patijn in late November 1978 on his study trip to Naples. Jody would be following him midway through December when the little theatre on the Nes was to close for a week and a half.

The slightly built Katan, who had only just enough time before curtain-up, took us to Central Station in a taxi. He was wearing his white costume and was already in full make-up. With him between us, we drew a lot of attention, lending something public and theatrical to our goodbyes. The troth my two friends pledged in all haste had perhaps no eternal value, but it would be sufficient until Christmas, in any case.

Our reserved seats were in the rearmost carriage which was otherwise empty – and remained so even when the train was about to leave. I was very chirpy. At the beginning of the evening I had let all poison I still possessed go up in smoke and had inhaled it. For this, I used the coloured little pipes from the 'Blow Football' game – grudgingly, for it was the most revolting of family games from my childhood days: the slimy saliva dripping jelly-like from the tubes on to the plate ... But, now I was an adult, I no longer needed to blow on them, just suck. And moreover ... any inconvenience and all roundabout ways were preferable to me than intravenous or subcutaneous applications.

When, at almost midnight (six hours after my last game of blow football), the train approached Cologne, I noticed that the large dose was beginning to lose its effect – however, this was without my mood suffering in consequence. I was even able to resolve with perfect equanimity never to take anything again. A precious oath, hysterically sworn, wasn't even necessary. Later on, between Bonn and Koblenz, it had left me completely. The chains fell away from me. A solemn moment: here was where my freedom began. Not a trace of the weariness I knew so well ...

The great restlessness only came towards morning, on reaching the Swiss border. Listening meekly to Lex ('Art will only have reached its completion when, in its attempt to depict reality, it coincides with reality itself and thus becomes superfluous. It's art's ultimate task *to render itself superfluous*, that's to say . . . that is . . . to approximate that state of superfluity as closely as possible. In other words: art must attempt to destroy itself . . . it must attempt suicide, incessantly. In any case, art must strive to make itself *as superfluous as possible*. To create, in the no-man's-land between traditional art and reality – until the frontier between this no-man's-land and reality has been approximated as closely as possible, bar the crossing of it . . .') I began to yawn. It seemed perfectly normal after a night awake like that, but this was a kind of yawning that provided no relief though it did give you cramp in your jaws.

'Fine, sure: if you're not interested . . .' Lex said, irritated, and he took another swig of *Joseph Guy*.

'I can't help it. I'm not yawning from hunger or sleep or boredom . . . I've never known it like this.'

As I yawned, tears began to flow from my eyes, copiously. A little later a runny nose joined in. In order to dispel my disquiet, I went and walked up and down the corridor. But weakness in my legs which no longer knew how to brace themselves against the train's jolting, soon forced me to sit down again. Severe shivering started. At the same time, I was perspiring from head to toe. The yawning became so bad I was barely able to get my mouth shut at all. I produced gorging noises during this.

Lex, suddenly quite bewildered, fiddled with the heating regulator. We moved to another compartment where it was warmer but the shivering only got worse. Ceaselessly, moisture poured from my eyes and nose and pores. Face, neck, shirt – all wet.

In Basle, the train was given a different composition. Shunting to and fro for almost an hour, which only made me even more ill. *I* was the one being pulled apart and put together again – carelessly, no body part was in its right place any more. Forwards . . . backwards . . . a bang in front, a bang at the rear. Again and again, the deck was being shuffled. It was no longer the train we had boarded the previous evening, not by a long chalk. Things would never come right again. When, without interruption, the new train had been running along – almost soundlessly – in the same direction for a few minutes, I fell asleep.

I dreamed of the game of 'blow football'. On the strip of aluminium foil with which I had clad the inside of a tea-strainer I was holding above the flame of a candle, the fine grit began to turn into vapour. This was the moment to inhale, but I could not make a choice from the coloured little pipes. Red, green, blue, yellow . . . I didn't know which one to take. My free hand hung above, undecided. And meanwhile the precious substance evaporated . . .

No they weren't goosepimples that covered me from head to toe on waking up. Worse: on every square centimetre of my skin, chilled through and through, the little hairs were standing on end. I felt myself to be a hairy caterpillar waiting desperately for the breaking of the cocoon – to be a butterfly again.

Between Rome and Naples I never left the toilet. In my belly the gut was behaving like strands of wrung-out laundry: I could see them wriggling beneath the skin. I sat on the bog like a cowboy on a young bull. The train – shaking me about, tossing me up and hurling me down, quartering me – was pulling me down to the lowest point rather than toward a final destination.

All the way down there, at that lowest point, Lex lugged our suitcases to a luggage depot. On our way to the nearest boarding house, I was forced to let my juices, my slaverings, my crap run freely – twice, no less . . .

That the room had no windows didn't strike one immediately. In one of the walls pasted over with floral paper, there was a square opening which offered a view on to the corridor wall, the wallpaper of which was also floral . . . The room amounted to a perfect simile for my condition.

'Keep calm,' Lex said. 'I'll rustle something up. Back in an hour.'

And he left me alone with the fears which came to keep my physical terrors company. I tapped the walls: cardboard. The boarding house was on the fifth floor, which could only be reached via a narrow stairwell. Were fire to break out, I would be surrounded by a labyrinth of floral-papered walls, corridors and blank walls . . . Hobbling up and down between bed and toilet I waited for Lex's return. Four times, no less, without having touched myself, I'd had an involuntary orgasm. Searing ejaculations devoid of any pleasure. Hellish pain rather than satisfaction.

Late at night, Lex returned with four innocent-looking cigarettes. He had got them for little money from a member of the crew of an American aircraft carrier permanently lying at anchor in the bay.

Lex helped me smoke one, my tremors preventing me from holding the cigarette myself. After this, my hands had calmed down to such an extent that I was able to light the second one myself.

'There're special bars here for American servicemen,' Lex explained. 'So-called piano bars. All of them in the neighbourhood of that big fort on the waterfront. They drink Heineken there from little disposable bottles. And there's quite a bit of opium-popping going on there, if you ask me. Even though there's a kind of military police hanging out there. Two of those guys per bar at least. They've got 'SP' marked on their sleeves . . . I'll take you along there tomorrow.'

In a quarter of an hour, I had perked up completely. Lex just couldn't understand how that stuff could do such wonders . . .

Lex's studio (he had not seen it yet: the rental agreement had been reached by telephone and by post) was high up above the centre of town and the harbour, of which it had a splendid view. It was on the third floor of a house on a corner, painted red, situated on a square which was used as a car park on the top of *Monte Echia*. As dusk fell, small cars congregated there, their windows pasted shut on the inside with newspaper. A number of the shuttered vehicles would rock gently on their springs . . .

Thirty years ago, Patijn's father, together with a friend, had taken up employment in an Eindhoven car factory. At first, they had both worked there in the paint shop but soon the friend had gone on to higher things within the same company. His promotion had gone over Lex's father's head, more or less; reason why the friends became enemies. Years later – Lex was ten – the paintshop worker had hurled himself from the highest storey of the factory building, on top of his rival's car. That evening, the boss drove home, bowed under the imprint of his subordinate's body.

Lex showed me the photo in an American magazine of a woman who had landed on top of a parked car after jumping from a skyscraper. The roof of the vehicle had moulded itself, elegantly almost, to her shape. 'D'you see? Like a spoon in blancmange.' He was shouting himself down with that joke. I knew that, with all his indigestible theorising about 'realism in art', he was solely in search of the shape his father had left behind in the tin roof.

I helped the sculptor weld a frame, comparable with the frame of a small bungalow tent. Within that set of tubes, the model would be tied down by his arms or legs in order not to tear the plaster bandages while still soft.

As his first model in Naples, I had to shave my body as smooth as that of an Apollo. Over the hair on my head I wore a tight bathing cap. Lex would dip each strip of plaster bandage, before attaching it to my naked body, in a bucket of warm water. On contact with my skin, the bandage turned icy cold within half a second.

Work was done from bottom to top, my head coming last. Lex ordered me to close my eyes: he put felt patches on the eyelids. My ears he filled with soft wax and began to plaster them shut with bandages. My jaws and lips, too, ended up rock solid. In the end, I was only able to breathe via my nostrils — but very gingerly, in tiny draughts, for my chest, too, was pinned down . . .

Never before had I been sealed off from the world more radically. A deaf-mute, blind man can *move*, at least; I was frozen solid in the ice. Not to see, not to hear, not to speak, not to move a muscle . . . only maintaining contact with the atmosphere through tiny gasps of air through one's nose . . . How long did I keep up this absolute isolation? Two minutes? They seemed like two hours. Hours during which I learned to be amazed that I could still hear something like *the rustling of silence*. A little patch of skin had been left bare underneath my right heel. It was there that Lex scratched me with his nail as a sign that I was to perform my Pompeiian death scene. I could not feel that my arms were being freed. In the panic that suddenly seized me, the stiff suit became as pliant and elastic as pyjamas.

When Lex took the mask from my face and looked at me, grinning because he could see the fear in my eyes, I hated him deeply. Once, but never again.

One day early on, of an afternoon, we were standing on the boulevard, looking out to sea, when a rowing boat appeared from behind *Castel dell'Ovo*. Inside, a multicoloured clutch of flapping dresses and hats with ribbons and parasols. High laughs and squeals reached us on the wind. One of the women rowed the boat ashore, skilfully and with powerful strokes. Only when the company grouped together on the quayside did we notice that it consisted of dressed-up men. The transvestites posed in Lex's studio for nothing or for almost nothing. They did it for fun, or rather: to exhibit themselves. A negative kind of exhibitionism, for they would hide their sex between their legs. Most of the transvestites weren't as finely tarted up as the company in the boat. The *femmenielli* – as they were called in dialect – from the *Quartieri* especially turned out to be a sorry sight. Their so-called femininity was suggested more than it was depicted: a hairpin, the smallest of pigtails imaginable, a fuzzy jumper, high-heels worn down to one side, those sad little humps of bras filled with stale bread . . . Stolen goods from ever-full washing lines! They begged the sculptor to be allowed to keep their bras on in order to have a feminine *cast* of themselves, at least . . .

Lex turned them into sexless snowmen.

Early in December, I travelled on some more, to the South, on my own. In complete solitude in Sicily, I wanted to try one more time to get my blood back to purity again. Two weeks would have to be enough to restore my metabolism, in my opinion.

Though I lost some four kilos in a few days through dehydration, the withdrawal symptoms proved less serious than during my journey to hell, *Transalpino*-style. My body recovered quickly but the worst was still to come. I got involved with number 90 of the *tombolella*, the Neapolitan game of lotto: *la paura*, the fear, which in the end drove me, in those godforsaken Christmas specials of Italian Railways, back to Naples and Lex Patijn's studio.

3

On New Year's Eve I finally found the door to the red house on *Monte Echia* open.

Lex was working in his studio as if, during the past few days, he had been doing nothing but. Upon my entering, he looked fleetingly, almost gruffly, at the door without allowing his concentration to be disturbed: the plaster, now setting, gave him no respite. A greeting was barely forthcoming; Lex treated me like someone who had dropped in only an hour previously . . .

He was putting the final touches to plastering his model – no transvestite clenching its sex between the thighs, this time – one that looked like a ballet dancer in tights. A dancer caught in the jump . . . that's how the man – legs wide, arms raised to heaven –

had been tied to the frame with thin bits of string. Only a part of his right heel was still uncovered. I heard him breathing, snortingly, and immediately I felt the suffocation like a vice round my chest. The model played the death scene.

'Yes, sorry about this,' growled Patijn. 'You see . . . I just have to . . .' In his hand glinted the knee-shears. 'Did you get my telegram?' Telegram . . . stupid git. A *letter* was what we'd agreed on. Telegrams were a separate department of *poste restante*. But Lex wasn't even listening, so much was his attention being taken up by the meticulous cutting open of the bandage, set almost solid. Behind the model's ears, the blades of the shears cut smoothly through the plaster, across the skull and under the chin. The sculptor put the implement in his pocket and with both hands, very carefully, wrenched the white mask free. I could breathe again. The felt patches fell from the eyes of the model . . . and there was Jody Katan's face.

Jody had to blink a few times before he could see me. There was mild panic in his little laugh. We could not even embrace one another. He reeked of the olive oil his body had been covered in so as not to allow the plaster bandages to stick to him.

Lex's workspace was populated with poor imitations of Pompeiian dead: the cocoons of the transvestites, left behind. What was striking was the cramped attitude of most of the dolls.

During one of our first walks through the city I had had to translate POMPE FUNEBRI on the window of an undertaker's for the sculptor. Now it read on the walls of the studio, in his scrawl:

POMPEII FUNEBRI - LEX PATIJN'S ONE THOUSAND DEAD
This was the title for his forthcoming exhibition.

Though time and again I almost choked hearing Jody's panicky breathing, his death scenes were still too posed for Lex.

'Splendid! Terrific! But . . . *much* too beautiful. You're a dying swan . . . a kneeling ballerina . . .! *Die like a dog* is what you must do . . . not like a swan, but like a dog, dammit! Think of your old ma copping it.'

But Jody, packed head to toe in plaster bandages, did not hear him and continued, as Lex sneeringly put it, 'to audition for RADA.'

The fireworks being set off ever more frequently in the course of New Year's Eve, began to agitate Lex. His hands were shaking.

At a loud bang on the square in front of the house, the shears slipped and wounded Jody's upper arm. The scratch wasn't that deep but the drop of blood sucked up by the plaster had an effect on Lex like that on a pack of hungry wolves: it drove his fanaticism to extremes. A band-aid, some hurried comforting, and the sculptor went on with his work, fast and practised, cringing and cursing now and then after the explosion of a jumping jack . . .

It was eleven o'clock, and once again —'for the last time, honest, I swear,' Lex had said — Jody was being covered in plaster, layer by layer. Patijn's nerves, though tensed to the utmost, had meanwhile become prepared for the bangs, now coming in shattering series. When he was done, quicker than ever before, the plaster turned out to be damp and elastic in all places.

'Perfect . . . *perfect.*'

Quickly, Lex freed his model's wrists, and for the eleventh or twelfth time that day, Jody — deaf-mute and blind — began his convulsions. The bandages were still so supple that the actor was able to let himself fall on to his knees without the white crust tearing. The upper torso snapped forwards, supported by a wood-enly moved arm . . . Imagined suffocation drew a knife through my chest, but Lex thought Katan's pose still too theatrical.

'He doesn't get it. He *just* doesn't get it, but only just . . .' The voice of the sculptor had acquired a whining quality about it. I saw him take a few strips of plaster bandage and dip them in the bucket, after which he stuck them together. It was possible he had seen a crack appear in the harness after all . . . Because of the growing noise outside, I had mounting difficulty in translating myself into the rustling silence in which Jody was performing his little play. Just the rapid breathing through his nose was capable of squeezing shut my windpipe.

Lex walked up to Jody with the dripping strip of bandage. He approached him from behind.

'Lex . . .! What're you doing?'

'Just leave me be a moment . . . I only want to put the wind up him . . . let him stew for a moment. Nothing more. I'll pull it off in a minute.'

And he knelt behind his lover and pushed the strip of plaster bandage under his nose. With a few light kneading actions of Lex's fingertips the substance was fixed down. I now no longer heard snorting, only a kind of hum from the depths of the white suit.

With a jolt, Jody came up out of his pose as a dying swan. The sculptor got a bash under his chin and moved backwards on his knees. The plaster round Jody's arms (I could hear it crack under the force of his effort) had meanwhile become so hard that he could not get them up high enough to free his nostrils himself with his fingers. Emitting muffled groans, he stood in the middle of the studio, underneath the blotchy light from the chandelier. I strode over to him – but Lex stopped me.

'A little longer . . . two seconds. He's doing splendidly. This . . . this is *real*. Those wrinkles . . . He won't choke that quickly. He's getting plenty of air; I could feel his breath coming through the goo . . . I'll pull it loose in a minute, honest.'

His hand was clenched round my arm like a vice and I told myself that there was no point in trying to resist him. Yes, he'd pull that strip of bandage loose any time now and then I, too, would be able to breathe again.

We watched the clumsy dance of a polar bear making attempts to jump out of its skin and in so doing kicking over the bucket with warm water. Vapour rose from the floor around its stiff paws . . . Without realising what it was doing, it stormed right at us. Lex pulled me aside and with a crack the bear ran up against the wall, after which it fell on its back, hard, without being able to break the fall. And that never ending growling tone, close and yet far off, at times drowned out by the bangs outside . . . I was surprised at the strength the slightly built Jody still managed to make apparent through the hardened armour.

Finally, Patijn let go of me and I fled outside to give my constricted ribcage some air.

There were only a few shuttered cars on the square. Here and there one stood wobbling about beneath a starry sky almost as clear as that above Agrigento when the town lighting had failed. On the traffic-control tower of the aircraft carrier, deep down below me in the bay, the date *1979* could be made out in luminescent figures. Right now we were still marking '78.

A quarter to midnight and the city, full of unrest, was on the point of exploding. Now already, the bangs were incomparably more numerous and loud than in Amsterdam at the stroke of twelve precisely. A haze of gunpowder fumes began to rise up from the streets. On the top floors of the houses, children held a kind of torch out of the windows which let down waterfalls of liquid light.

Round midnight, the paroxysm reached its climax. The aircraft carrier lit two searchlights trained on the city. They drilled into the curtain of smoke growing rapidly denser, and began to swing about like two mighty arms wishing to sweep this Naples-gone-mad into the sea. Out above the tumultuous crackle sounded the wailing sirens of ambulances and fire engines. The bells of all the churches were tolling. Within ten minutes the city had vanished. Wiped out completely. Crawled away into a smog which could not have been denser had it been in London. Above me, there wasn't a star to be seen any more.

I left the square with its gently rocking cars behind and walked up the *Via Nunziatella*. The gunpowder fumes which by now had also penetrated to the *Monte Echia*, began to irritate my lungs. To escape from it I wanted to go up *Monte di Dio*, the Mountain of God, where I believed I could vaguely discern, like an asymmetrical cross, the stand pipe used for work being done to the battlements there.

In the *Chiaia* quarter I began to mount the steep stairs, but here too the poisonous fumes managed to catch up with me in order to take my breath away ... I gave up in the end and returned — to where there was no longer a city. I descended in the direction of the *Quartieri*. Down the mountain, the little streets became narrower; they lay there packed ever more closely together. Just as if that entire district had slid down the steep hill: an avalanche of houses that had halted deferentially in front of the posh *Via Roma*. Entire streets had truncated themselves, harmonica-wise, into stairs.

The back streets were full of stinking, smoking fires around which children clustered. As I approached the *Via Roma*, I saw more and more people with shawls in front of their faces against the gunpowder fumes. I did not even have a handkerchief on me.

The *Boston Blackies' American Bar* turned out to be full to the gunnels with drunken servicemen. A marine was trying to bash the head of a mate he was holding by the hair against the wall. But the hair was too short: it slipped from his hand every time.

'You son of a bitch ... You dirty motherfucker ... I'm not leaving until that fucking face of yours has seen that fucking wall a thousand fucking times ...'

Near the two combatants stood two SP-s who saw to it that the short-cropped head did not actually get bashed into the wall. One of the policemen was punched in the shoulder by a drunken spectator.

'Hey you, Mr Motherfucker . . .! This motherfucker says he just killed his friend. How about that? He's trying to tell you something, *something important*, but you won't even listen!'

The person who wasn't being listened to was Lex Patijn. He was standing there with his back towards me, apparently unmoved, a bored spectator of the row. What was it that sozzled American had said? *'This motherfucker says he just killed his friend.'*

I put a hand on Patijn's shoulder. He turned round and I looked into eyes I did not know even though they were in Lex's face.

'I only wanted to put the wind up him a bit . . . I only wanted to let him get in a bit of a lather . . .' He went on repeating these little sentences in a trance. 'I only wanted to leave him stew for a bit . . . put the wind up him a bit . . .'

He also looked repeatedly at his fingertips, maybe because with these he had felt Jody's hot breath, 'right through the goo'.

A little later, as if something just occurred to him, Lex said with an idiotic grin on his face: 'Yes, well, I came here in the end. I thought . . . I thought: those Yanks will understand me better than those Eyeties.'

Now the row between the two marines had been settled, those Yanks were prepared to listen to Lex. But he seemed to want to retract. 'I only wanted to depict . . . to *depict* his death.'

The SP-s shrugged their shoulders and called the *Carabinieri*, who in their turn were a long time in coming, possibly because of the New Year's rush. For the time being, the world did not seem to be inclined to take Lex's deed seriously.

Perhaps it was because of the plaster bandaging that it did not affect me to see my friend Jody Katan lying there motionless. He was lying in a corner of the studio like a parody of a crashed wintersport reveller, a joke-figure from a variety show . . . But at the same time I was struck by the similarity to the Pompeiian displayed in the bathhouse in a glass sarcophagus: lying on his back, head inclined to the left, raised left lower arm with snapped, drooping hand, right hand in right-hand groin, fingers at the ready to raise the too narrow trouserleg by half a centimetre . . . The scissors, with round eyes from which Lex's fingers had hastily freed themselves, stuck in Katan's side. Jody's bandaged arms reminded me of bedsheets, wrung out by hand; the hands little propellers, they might whirr back into their original position any moment now. The breast plate had burst and crumpled; it hung round his body this way and that: a harness of jumbled pack-ice.

At the *Carabinieri*'s request, a doctor cut open Jody's suit. Each piece freed was numbered. The helmet, the felt patches ... No death struggle could be read from Katan's face. Its expression was as neutral as that of a tailor's dummy. He had closed his eyes in life already.

By means of the passport, the body was identified and taken off by ambulance in the end. Patijn and I were taken along in separate cars to the station.

When the *Carabinieri* let me go after the laborious interrogation, in the early morning, the city's cleansing department was already busy clearing the New Year's Eve ravages. Slowly, a clear sky appeared over Naples. All gunpowder fumes seemed to have dissolved — yet still Jody's suffocation seemed to seek to tear my chest apart. I gave myself some heart: before I choked, I would have reached the street where the American bars were.

Rustler

Jan Hofker

Now, the townsfolk have pressed in from all sides. They occupy all windows, all roofs are black with them. Humming life, warm-stuffy life, working like a great machine of destruction. It is a continuous oppression. Like a nightmare, truly, in clear light of day. Oh, Air . . . air. If only it could flee the throat, the entire body . . . if only it were gone, that living human mass, reacting in one's head.

That, now, is the End. That, now, is the end of life. That, now, is life, seen through to the very end. Life entire. Including youth – and the village – and the heavy servitude – and the peasant-talk. And all the calculations. All the hope. All the glossing-over. And all the miserable trudging beneath great burdens. That, now, is the end.

Now It comes. Can you still hear? Can you still see? How the legs throb; such tiredness in old legs. Oh, tired, tired – oh dear, oh dear.

How the crowd hums. Such a *crowd*. What a mass of people. That is destruction. That is total destruction. That is the destruction of the person right-now before death. Do you not feel that you have now become the least of all men? Irrevocably? For all eternity? Now you are timid. Now you are afraid.

Afraid of each and everyone. All can now command you. A small child might now command you. You move out of the way for a child. Away, gone; you are gone completely already.

You thought Death so terrible. You were not yet paralysed then, paralysed by the machine of formality, by the ceremonial. Now you *are* paralysed. Do you hear how you do not cry out? You, who thought to crawl and groan? Do you see how Necessity works as does Superior Force? Death is nothing.

Oh, that humming crowd and those quiet whisper-men, at their task of the noose. You no longer cry, you no longer ask for mercy. They would have to spell it out for you now: mer . . . cy; mer . . . cy. Now, only the masses and the quiet-busy men. You are now docile who never were docile. You are now obliging, ready to help. You do what is wanted. Go where you are wanted to go. You go the way you are wanted to go. You are now feeble, too feeble to will the contrary. All is mood. Most-serious mood. You are to die.

It's coming closer now. Now It will happen. How the crowd does hum. The black-mass crowd in the daytime sun. This, now, is the Universe, eternity. Eternal pitilessness. Lost, lost. This, now, is Death.

That man will do It. That man whose breath you can already smell. That man seen close-by. With the blue eyes. With the sweating forehead in the hot daylight. And coarse-blond hair. Do you hear his voice? He utters sounds. That man close-by will do it. That tiredness the worst.

Oh, that tiredness. That tiredness and that humming crowd. The heart is feeble. The will is weak. Fear past. That tiredness the worst.

And that they are close around you. And that they are so quiet. Quiet—busy around you. Doing *thus* in quiet haste. It hurts, their taking trouble for you; it embarrasses you, all those men, the work you cause them. All those men and hands. You wish *their* will.

Only the ascent still. With the tired legs. And that narrow rope that forces a going-up, a going-up backwards behind the man ascending first. Humming, oh, humming — black, black is the fullness — terrible humming. Do not go mad, poor fellow.

Do they not weep? That ladder wobbles. We both shall fall. Oh God, how heavy with these throbbing legs, this ascending back-wards, and a ladder that wobbles. We both shall fall. Hear now the drums rolling close-by. That stomach-searing roll. Hear, hear.

Hear the terrible townsfolk,
mounting the tide of High Pleasure.

Death and Life of Thomas Chatterton

Frans Kellendonk

'No, I won't get up for you. I no longer get up. When I was young, I don't know how long ago, long ago, if there were visitors, I would hide behind a door. Then I would trip, knees bent and on tiptoe, into the room. Not this room. A different room. Everybody was charmed. I'd better not bother with such pranks nowadays. My ankles would collapse. Even with two servants supporting me, my ankles would collapse. Can you see what gout has done to my hands? They lay chalk stones nowadays. I can no longer run along like a chicken, but twice a year my hands lay a little chalk egg. I keep them in that urn there, to have a gravel plot laid out with them on my grave.

If you're afraid of *le catch-cold*, as they say in your ravaged fatherland, then I'd be happy to ring for my gruff Swiss manservant. However, I would advise you rather to close the window yourself. Philippe is on the booze and he keeps his ears quite deaf to me. I myself no longer catch any colds, not since I abandoned wearing hats.

Meet Tonton. Shake paws with the young man, Tonton. Tonton is too fat to shake paws with the young man. He was left to me by your much lamented countrywoman Madame du Deffant. *'Je suis tombée dans le néant . . . je retombe dans le néant,'* she used to say, and now I repeat her words. Tonton can't move because he's too fat and I can't because of my gout. We have been condemned to each other's company and to this settee. One lives and lives and then, one day, one wakes up dead.

Were Philippe not so ill-tempered then I might have asked him to show you round this gingerbread castle of mine. Alas, Philippe is always ill-tempered nowadays. But I shall tell you what you must see. Something that certainly will interest you is my collection of armour and weaponry. Oh yes, I have noticed that you are a martial young man: I gleaned it from your build, your thighs in particular. That collection's housed in the stairwell. Shields of rhinoceros skin, hand-bows, arrows and quivers, all having come from – that is what's said, at least, and I genuinely believe it – all having come from my distant forebear, the renowned Sir Terry Robsart!

Sir Terry Robsart. The English crusader. Knight of the Garter . . .

François Premier, does the name mean anything to you? Your art-loving monarch, indeed. As a Frenchman, you are sure to be interested in *his* suit of armour. Inlaid with gold. You will find it in the entrance to the library. Should you then walk on, into the library, you'll come face to face with another prize exhibit, the painting depicting the uniting in holy matrimony of our Henry the Sixth and your Margaret of Anjou. Two highly talented people but an unhappy marriage. Our countries were at war then, just as they are now. Would you mind also looking up a moment then, up at the painted ceiling? Designed it myself. At the centre, pride of place, my family escutcheon. Do this for me, please. I have not seen it for months.

And then I have another request. Would you mind not looking with your fingers, not under any circumstance? Last week a vicar's wife from Birmingham broke one of the pipes which Admiral Tromp smoked during his last sea battle. A few days later it turned out that my Roman eagle had lost its beak. It's a miracle that *I* still have all my teeth. I just sit here all day like an antique. The flesh withers on my bones. An old bunch of faggots is what I am, only fit for the fire. I'll be eighty this coming year. Recently, I heard a visitor say: 'Just take a look at this, Annabel, see that mummy there? That's what the fops looked like in grandfather's day.' Soon they'll be fiddling with me, too. Ah, just look: he's bald underneath his switch. An ear breaks off, and an eye runs across the floor. Better put it in your pocket, Annabel, quick, then no one'll notice.

You do have a ticket, don't you? You know that tickets for admission must be requested in advance – in writing. I'm sorry to have had to institute this rule, but as this edifice consists merely of breadcrust, wallpaper and stained glass, I cannot receive more than four visitors a day. And definitely no children.

You do *not* have a ticket.

You have *not* come to see the exhibits.

Have I ever met you before?

Do you play faro? D'you play loo? Would you like a cup of tea? Or ice-water, perhaps? I only drink ice-water, because of my complaint. No? Take some snuff? I do enjoy taking some snuff, be it from my finger tip, for I have been obliged to sacrifice my *tabatière anatomique* to the gout. Finest tobacco, from Fribourg's. No? Again no.

Then I will tell you a charming story. It's about Madame de Choiseul, in more youthful days, when she had two lovers, Prince Joseph of Monaco and Monsieur de Coigny. As if that wasn't enough, she fervently wished to possess a parrot as well, one which would be a miracle of eloquence. Macaws, parrots, cockatoos and what have you, Paris has these a-plenty, as you know, and the Prince rapidly managed to lay his hands on a Jaco which was appointed her secretary by the grateful nymph. Not to put Monsieur de Coigny at a disadvantage, she also acquired a fierce longing for a monkey. Strangely enough, monkeys *were* a rare commodity in Paris in those days – not so now, I believe – but, with great difficulty, the other paladin managed to find one in a restaurant, where the creature was working as a kitchen boy. Madame de Choiseul was delighted and appointed the monkey her chamberlain. Monsieur de Coigny, however, had neglected to mention – on purpose or out of forgetfulness, it's not for me to say – in any case, he had not mentioned to her that the chamberlain, in his previous place of employment, had gained great dexterity in the plucking of birds and when Madame, one evil day, returned from making a visit . . .

Ah, you already know the tale? You do not care for tittle-tattle. You are a *serious* young man. Oh.

I have known marchionesses as old as the hills who were more amusing than you. Of course they didn't look like the Apollo Belvedere. I have been able to admire your thighs from all sides now. They are divine but not for sale, no doubt, so don't lead this old rag-and-bone man into temptation and please sit down, on one of those hundreds of chairs here. There. And now tell me frankly to what I *do* owe the honour of your visit.

Chatterton?

Chatterton.

Our countries are at war. No ship can cross the Channel. Letters are being intercepted and copied out by your *cabinet noir* or whatever it's called in these bloody times. Chit-chat, on the contrary, is still as free as the wind. Chatterton – tsk-tsk-tsk. A jungle full of monkeys is what you hear gabbling in that name. You disappoint me. Moreover, you're not *au courant* at all. Here in England, we ran out of things to say about Chatterton ten years ago.

But you haven't . . .

Not by a long chalk . . .

Well, well: you don't half know how to use your tongue! Go on, sock it to me! My my, a chiasmus, just like that: *'le martyre perpétuel et la perpétuelle immolation'* – that's a chiasmus: anyone else would first have to chew down an entire pen for that. And those antitheses of yours, just like flints: sparks fly. Go on, bawl me out. Your rhetoric is amazing: Madame de Choiseul couldn't have wished for a more talented parrot. It's as if you're reading it all out loud to me. Such irony! Brilliant, razor-sharp, just like that guillotine of yours. Beg pardon: guillotine of *theirs*. I first thought you were an officer but words are what you set a-marching – you are a poet. There: an alexandrine escapes you, just like that – take care that you don't begin to rhyme spontaneously. Went to school at the Jesuits', did you? Pity it's such tosh you put into words so splendidly.

No, just put that back where it came from, that dress-sword. Tosh: I hold to that. A scorpion is what you just called him, the former boy? Imprisoned in a circle of fiery coals heaped upon him by the malevolent bourgeoisie? He seeks a way out, does not find it, and in despair he stabs himself to death. An affecting image of the imperilled poet-of-genius, I admit. Except that scorpions cannot sting themselves to death: that's superstition. Hallowed by being copied out and parroted for centuries, but no less superstition for that. It can do no harm to delve in the Great Book of Nature from time to time – for a poet, too, this can do no harm.

Ah, your scorpion comes from a *poetic* bestiary. A creature of fable, just like the basilisk and the griffon. In that case, I'm sure you will forgive me that I won't take that Chatterton of yours quite literally either.

A tale of monkeys and parrots after all! For, heavens above, how they have patched up that little urchin in the Valhalla of tittle-tattle. Changed beyond recognition is what he is. You were on about his *'profil d'un jeune Lacédémonien'*. Ever seen him? A portrait? Certainly, there are portraits of him, as there are of the unicorn and of the archangel Gabriel. I myself have never been allowed to behold him, but those who did know him, this I do know, *they* are agreed that here on earth he had a round, childish forehead and a pug-nose. His eyes weren't *'noirs'*, they were grey, and as to the *'très grands, fixes'* and, what was it you said again? – ah, yes, *'perçants'*, that's quite a nice description of his right eye, but not of his left. To put it mildly, his face had something unbalanced about it. Then you ascribe to this lad of seventeen an appearance you call *'militaire et ecclésiastique'*. What must I imagine at that? Are you saying that he looked like an almoner? He walked hunched over and went dressed in tatters, in rags that had known broader backs and stronger legs. A dressed-up monkey is what he was, nothing else.

Best not feed a songster too much? Ho-ho! Who said that — did *I* say that? Poverty as the poet's capital? Again those wingèd words are mine? Truly it gives me great satisfaction that, via the recycling process of gibberish, something witty comes flowing back to me for once. Harsh it may be, but witty too! That I might be granted to make myself laugh even in my dotage, imagine . . .! The fruits of my ill repute are not all bitter, after all. Permit me . . .

I will have you sent away by my Swiss manservant if you won't allow me to tell you what precisely my involvement was in this phantasmagoria. Yes, do start stalking the room, by all means. Make the floor boom beneath your Werther boots, do. The porcelain quivers before you. As you're walking about anyway, perhaps you might take down those four volumes from the bookcase for me, second shelf from the top? The ones stamped with *Chattertoniana*, of course. Thank you. As you can see, I have collected all the hogwash. And annotated it. Not that my finicky scrawl can effect much against such bold print. But a monkey is not complete without its fleas.

Chatter-chatter-Chatterton. That I would have driven this joke-figure of yours, this toddler-on-stilts, to suicide through my neglect, no, through my haughtiness — haughtiness is what you said — that's not just an invention, it is a libel. That's a lie which, for more than twenty-five years, has marred my life, me, an innocent. In you, already the second generation of pen-maulers announces itself to venerate this pitiable mite as its martyr and patron saint, and ascribes a gruesome act to me which I have never committed. Never *could* have committed. As I said earlier: I never met the wonderboy. I can only feel involved in this affair with great difficulty, and only very obliquely at that. If I have been the angel of death to him, then he has allowed himself to be cut down by . . .

By a loose feather. Now listen carefully. That the boy had taken his own life I only learned in '71, at the annual banquet of the Royal Academy in London. This always takes place in April: he had already been dead 6 months, therefore. Oliver Goldsmith . . .

175

Oliver Goldsmith, that glassy Irish potato, that inspired fool, the penman surgeon . . .

Goldsmith tapped the edge of his plate. Important news! And he told with grave aplomb how recently a chest full of old manuscripts had been found in Bristol, in the church of St Mary Redcliffe. Not full of bills or deeds, no, *belles lettres*: chronicles, poems, verse dramas, all written by a fifteenth century monk called Thomas Rowley. We – Reynolds, Johnson, etcetera . . .

Just you imagine the other gentlemen as cauliflowers, turnips, beets – what odds . . .

We laughed at the good doctor to his face. He had to be the last man in London who did not know that these manuscripts were fakes. That, out into the world from within the darkness of Rowley's cowl, it was the snotty nose of Thomas Chatterton that . . .

Don't touch that bell, if you please! It's a real Benvenuto Cellini – that's what I was told when I bought it, in any case. Oh, do sit down, *please*!

So, we laughed scornfully at Goldsmith, to his glassy face, and I recalled, and this I told the company at the time, too, that I could have gladdened the literature-loving world earlier with that particular damp squib. In '69, let me look it up for you – March 27th, 1769, I had received a note from a Thomas Chatterton, in those days an attorney's apprentice in Bristol. He wrote to me that he had old documents in his possession which might interest me. From these, it would become clear that painting in oils was already being practised here in this country in the twelfth century, and this by an Augustinian abbot from his home city. Were I to tell you now that a short while previously I had held forth in print that Jan van Eyck could not be the inventor of that particular art, then you would understand that I was highly delighted with this news. I took the bait, I believed the boy, and that is the only injustice I ever did him. Fraudsters are flatterers, and I was flattered. I wrote him an encouraging reply in return. Only afterwards did I consult experts, my friend William Mason . . .

Mason, an eminent scholar, take it from me, and others, and they made it plain to me that I was dealing with a trickster. The transcripts of a number of documents he had sent me had been couched in a macaronic kind of language quite as mediaeval as this house of mine. The cumbrous spellings, the consistently barbarous idiom: these were the unmistakable hallmarks of falsification, so I was assured, the way the ever-present signature and the never-absent craquelure are on a painting. That was when I terminated the acquaintance. That's all. Nothing more was transacted between us.

I recounted these facts during that banquet as well, and curiously enough only silence emanated from that otherwise so lively company. It was there that, for the first time, I got the feeling I have had ever since when Chatterton is mentioned – that without wishing to do so, I was defending myself, no matter what I said. A dull atmosphere prevailed, one of which I understood nothing at all, until someone remarked: 'And now that poor rascal's dead.' Then it was *my* turn to be the one who was the last man in London, the last one to hear that. Even Goldsmith knew. Thus I heard for the first time, too, of his mad pride and ambition. That, after my letter – nobody said it, but it thundered in my ears – *because of* my letter he had seen all of London lying at his feet. I heard the whole incredible story that would be ludicrous had not death, that great big bully, been haunting it – of the laurel wreaths which failed of fall down from heaven when he had come to London posthaste; of the bread the baker did not want to supply him with at no charge, in awe of his genius; of lifelong disappointment and lack of recognition having driven this seventeen-year-old to suicide.

In each of these defamatory pamphlets, almost a hundred in number, it is painted in the most garish colours what happened that early morning in August, in that slum where I have never set foot but nevertheless turn out to have been to, after all. How the seamstress from whom he had rented an attic room had clambered up the five steep staircases, rasping breath and cursing *sotto voce*. All made up, it is, but right down to my dreams I hear her step, the wheezing of her lungs, I hear her cry: 'Master Chatterton! Master Chatterton!' and bang against the door which shall never be opened by him again. I can even hear her fall silent and, in two minds, hesitate, and I don't need to fetch a locksmith to see that he is lying dead on his bed. His face is ashen but he smiles and indeed, you all are quite right, he is beautiful. The attic window, overlooking the city, is half-open and across his temple and his cheek falls the glancing light of his mendacious glory, already dawning above the roofs of London. His dead hand is clenched around a crumpled piece of paper, on the floor lies a broken ampoule, scraps of paper everywhere, and on the table beside his bed a burning candle stands smoking. *My* wet finger doused that candle prematurely. How dare I deny that?

Only the facts, the poor reviled facts, are the ones whence I derive my audacity. In one of these little volumes you will find my *Letter to the Editor of Chatterton's Miscellanies* where I published them. Chatterton was said to have done himself in with opium, hence the smile playing round his dead lips. Poets very much like to have their corpses smile; they like to smuggle a bit of life into death. I will not maintain that he did not eat opium – remnants of the stuff were prised from his teeth by the coroner, for that matter – but for a *felo-de-se* something more potent is required: arsenic, let's say, or vitriol. I plump for the fact that he drank from the vitriol with which he was trying to cure himself, for this boy of not yet eighteen years had already had such intimate knowledge of so many little seamstresses that he was quite squishy with the pox. I don't wish to deny him his glorified body, but when he was lying there, dead, he had a face like a wrung-out dishcloth – this the seamstress herself has testified to.

And then to think that, with a little bit of luck, this apparition might have been a respected soapmaker. Immediately before his desperate deed he wrote to a school chum in Bristol that he was planning to say farewell to Parnassus. From now on, he wrote, he wished to devote himself to the preparation of 'smegma', which is Greek for soap, so my good friend Mason assures me.

Don't think that the lies of your idolising poetry can do no harm. Suicide is all the rage nowadays. Every messenger boy and attorney's apprentice who has ever managed to rhyme two successive lines and has then not been admitted instantly to the pantheon of the immortals, grabs for poison. They bring it to their lips, at the crack of dawn, sniffed at by the mist, leaning against the pylon of a bridge or lying full-length among the peelings in Covent Garden. And what do these chaps then see approaching them? The alluring appearance of a pale beauty, a young Lacedaemonian. They would have bolted I-don't-know-how-quickly had they seen a prosperous soapmaker in a worsted coat and wearing a palm-wood wig, a tricorn, and with a few glasses of port down him. This little fact alone might have saved scores of lives.

But against such an appetising concoction of lies, the facts are powerless. Years ago, I wrote a book of objections to Shakespeare's depiction of Richard the Third. In my innocence, I believed that my argued evidence might have an effect against the libellous talk of the Bard. Even scholars who knew better did not wish to believe me. To Chattertonians that book is even a half-admission of guilt. Why should I seek to whitewash that child murderer? Because he and I are brothers in crime, of course! Richard is still the same monster. Yet I have no regrets about my investigations. I learned something from them: that is, that the lie can be given to any story granted the necessary keen nose and tenacity. Then I believed that we must respect the facts of history, because they are real and because everything that is real deserves respect. Confabulations like your Chatterton-myth force the facts into a malevolent, subcutaneous existence. Not just the facts of the past, but the recalcitrant ones of the here-and-now, too, ones which refuse to drape themselves in accordance with your myth. These then cause a pain which must be suffered in loneliness, outside of history, by each human being individually. He who falsifies history sets a long repetition of doom and failure in train. I am convinced of this still, but that facts can do something about it, this I no longer believe. In themselves, they mean nothing. They're loose stones, rubble without the cement of the personalities which perpetrated them. When writing my book about Richard the Third, I noticed how each event from the past, each tradition, becomes incomprehensible if only you stare at it for long enough, and also how your objections and doubts become certainties over time and join up to form a new tissue of lies. Faith is stronger than reason. Clio cannot do without myths. They are her suitcases on her journey through time. The straps snap, the locks burst open and the dirty linen tumbles out. Not to worry! She puts everything back and goes and sits with her mighty whatyamacallit on the suitcase until the lid can be closed once again.

No greater Jezebel than Clio. Written history is cobbled together from lies and falsifications. Chatterton falsified Rowley. The angelic poet in whose name you have come to indict me is a falsified Chatterton. But you would not give even a penny to the *historical* wonderboy. Don't you deny it: I am sure of this! The counterfeits of Chatterton and Ossian are read and discussed in every salon: original mediaeval poetry is something for dusty archaeologists. In painting the story is perfectly similar. Most people think copies more real than the original works after which they have been made. Copies flatter contemporary taste. They make a cosy costume drama out of that strange, distant past. And I don't wish to present myself as being better than I am: the little fake castle we now sit chatting in so cosily suits me infinitely better than any authentic mediaeval draught-pit conceivable. We need falsifications to make the past inhabitable.

Let me tell you something: at this very moment, under this same roof, my typographer Kirgate is busy reprinting those expensive books on the sly, the ones published by my *Officina Arbuteana*. He can't even restrain himself until I'm dead, the ungrateful scoundrel. Gray's *Odes* go for five guineas in London at the moment. But I'll have my will changed this very week. I'll soon see to him!

Ah well, I do understand the necessity for that Chatterton myth. Because of a suicide the remaining relatives feel despised and rejected. They appear to have failed, *post hoc* and *propter hoc*, which is why they are all too prepared to point an accusing finger. One, that nameless all-powerful creature *one*, has decided that I am Chatterton's executioner. Not one of all of those who throw stones at me wish to realise that the same goes for them. Or they throw harder than ever because they do realise this. The fools. Suicide, dying as a public gesture – what folly, what vanity! Is it not bluffing on the grandest possible scale, to invest yourself with the authority of the Unknown? But they fall for it, they're affected by it. When now, in my autumn years, I happen to venture forth outside, I am shaken by my reputation. A long, black intangible shadow walks ahead of me and darkens the faces of the people I meet. My history has been written: I am Chatterton's murderer.

All that I have done is as naught compared with that which, in '69, I did not do. All I know is as naught compared with what then I did not know. I didn't know that Chatterton was an insane poet. I believed him to be a vulgar fraudster. Everything else I have meant is no longer of any importance whatsoever. My friendships – my friendships are ones with those deceased who can no longer testify on my behalf. This house I have been building my entire life, these curios I have collected with boundless patience – when later no one knows any longer who were the owners of my Apostle spoons, my snuffboxes, my moth-eaten gloves, then this place will not distinguish itself in any way from a common-or-garden junk-shop. People will laugh at me when they hear that I kissed those silver spurs over there when the dealer came to bring them to me. Go on, laugh! I kissed them, Sir, because King William the Third wore them at the Battle of the Boyne.

My misfortune is that I'm not dead yet. I'm standing in the

lobby to the House of Life. I can see inside how the party goes on without me. I am waiting for Clio and her carriage. A frail little man is still connected to that monstrous reputation of mine. I can still suffer, young man; your rage at my name still strikes at this greybeard, too. In the past, I never hankered after power. Only now I'm a helpless wreck, the desire gnaws at me, the desire to make people quake, to have them fawn and compromise themselves. To see everyone jump to attention as you approach – how wonderful that must be!

When, later on, you leave and you cross the river, you will come past a ruined archway. In the past, the palace of Sheen lay behind it, where our Queen Elizabeth died. She was gone on sugar, a rare delicacy in those days, and suffered hideous toothaches. For fifteen hours she stood dying in that palace, standing rigid and straight, like a post, the knuckles of her hands pushed into her mouth. No one of the court was allowed to sit down as long as the Queen was standing. The entire court stood upright for fifteen hours and when finally her heart gave way and she dropped dead, her entire court fell down with her. I, too, should wish to die like that.

What was it you said? Oh yes, you did say something. 'I, too, cannot resist smuggling a bit of life into death . . .' Yes, you do have a point there, indeed. And do you know why that is? Because death is so utterly uninteresting. There's no scent or glory to it. We cannot speak about it without tittifying it up a bit. But certainly, you are right: I ought not to mirror myself in such false images, not at my age. With the passing of each day I gain more admiration for your Marie Antoinette. When the riff-raff asked her whether she still had anything to say before she lost her head, she merely said: *Rien*. No mean feat, that . . .

Far more stupid, however, is to smuggle boring, sleep-inducing death into life, and this is what you do, with your *dépit* for the world, with your cult of genius. Thus you condemn yourself to loneliness. Loneliness is quite as bad as death, at the very least. To yourself you're nothing. Let me give you a good piece of advice: don't be a scorpion, don't be a Rousseau. That way leads to insanity. You know what happened to Rousseau in the end. Don't take up battlestations against the entire world for in that case the world might well turn its broad back on you. If you absolutely must be subversive, then be so on the sly. Cloak yourself in the garb of hypocrisy and flattery. Jump and gabble even though your ears are revolted by that which comes forth from your mouth. Borrow money from the world, then you won't be from its mind for a moment. Only in its mind do we have our soul. Only by its tongue are we given shape. The bear licks her cubs, the poet his verses, Joe-Public-and-his-mate lick you. Allow yourself to be licked by that great, rugged tongue, no matter whether they speak ill of you or praise you: that warm wet tongue will make you grow, grow so large they can no longer get round you. The name is all. Where one or two be together in your name, there be you. What does your Chatterton have in common with that sot roaming the streets of London but his name? And yet he exists, more so than during his lifetime. And through him, I exist. God grant that one day some softy will get up who shall commit himself to the restoration of my honour, and with more success than the way I have done on Richard the Third's behalf.

There. I have spoken some home truths to you and now I shall bestow on you an exceptional favour. I will show you my house, in person. Where's my cane. No, don't trouble yourself: I've got it already. The last one I did this honour was my old friend Lady Diana Beauclerk. A versatile woman. I named one of the towers on the North side after her. In it there is a cabinet containing seven bistre watercolours she painted. They are illustrations to a tragedy from my pen. My only tragedy. Doubtless you will already have written ten, young as you are. My talent lies more in the comic. As I have said in the past: life is a tragedy to one who feels, a comedy to one who thinks. Now I must get up very carefully. Tha-aa-aa-at's it. Ouch! Alas, there's no escaping from feeling when you are as old as I am. Now lend me your arm. When I am dead, my house, like my body, will fall prey to putrefaction. The junkdealers will wrestle their way down the corridors like maggots and worms, and gnaw my collections to bits. You are privileged. You are just in time for the last glimmer of my light of life. By that light you will be able to see everything for just a moment in its true context and full significance. And we'll take a look at Kirgate, too. Such a fright he'll have! Should be a laugh. Now, don't stand there dawdling like that. Give me your arm. Oh, those darned feet of clay of mine . . .

Your arm! Come, lend me your arm!'

Baldur D. Quorg, Spider

Anton Koolhaas

If I wasn't a spider, I would love to be one, thought spider Baldur
D. Quorg, and he thought this not without reason, for he had just
made his first descent from the top edge of an iron fence to the
first crossbar, half way down. He was now sitting on this crossbar
he had ended up on with a bump. With a very funny feeling in his
hindquarters – because of the speed with which that first thread
had appeared – yet, it has to be said, especially with one of
satisfaction. When he had begun to let himself drop, he had in no
way borne in mind the downward distance he had to cover, for
this was simply a fever: he *had* to descend, *now*.

He had started by walking some way across the ground, until he
had ended up by that fence and, wild and possessed, he had
climbed it. Without pausing for breath, he had then run along, on
to the top edge of the fence, to the point where there was a lump
in the paint with a hair from the brush the painter had used
sticking out from it. Without a moment's thought, he had cast the
first beginnings of his thread round that hair and, hot-headed, had
hurled himself down.

At first, he only dropped seven and a half centimetres, and then
all appearances indicated that no more thread was to hand internally. For a moment, he was taken aback by this, for though
spiders occupy themselves with the future more than other animals
do, and tend to put their trust in it, it did occur to him that these
seven and a half centimetres were possibly all the thread he could
manage to produce, and this was not much, or of much promise.

Nervously, he thought about what it was he must do, should
this meagre length prove to be all, but it was then, without him
making a plan to this effect, as though something had happened to
the apparatus in his hindquarters with which he was then able to
spin. Before setting out to make a thread in proper earnest, he had
practised and wondered at the curious feelings this evoked in him,
but these exercises had really not brought him much more than the
insight that it was truly possible to produce a thread. But something

183

was now happening in that apparatus of his, and suddenly Baldur D. Quorg dropped further at fearsome speed. Quite a relief, for at seven and a half centimetres below the top edge of that fence, he had been made to think for a moment that it was all just nonsense, what he expected from life, and that this would keep him on a far shorter leash than his over-confidence had presumed. Such thoughts had now been wiped out again, however, and Baldur dropped a further sixty centimetres at a stretch. Then a short interruption again, but this passed so quickly that it did not lead to fresh panic — and then the spider landed with a bump on the first crossbar.

Baldur D. looked up along his first thread, being waved very elegantly in a curve by a zephyr. And when he had looked a long time, and not without emotion, at this first piece of handiwork, he spoke the words that indicated that he would gladly have come into the world as a spider should this not have been the case.

Outsiders, had they spotted this terribly measly little thread among those iron bars of the fence, would certainly have smiled, but to Baldur this was a different matter. He was not remotely struck by the difference in dimensions between the bars and his thread, for this was *his* thread and with all its length it had come forth from him, and this made him so extraordinarily proud, rightly so, that he sat back a bit in order to consider his work once again, somewhat more leisurely now. That thread belonged to him and nobody else. 'And,' said Baldur D. Quorg inwardly, with an amount of grim determination, 'I make an issue of this. Never you fear,' he now said out loud, 'it's not lost on me that this thread belongs to me and not to anyone else at all!' At times, when the wind was more powerful, the thread would bend way out beyond the bars of the fence and then it would glisten and twirl a little; and when the wind vanished again, the thread would fall back between the uprights and hang there, quite motionless. Baldur D. would then climb up it a little way and calmly let himself drop again. This went very well.

And when Baldur D. Quorg had done this sixty-odd times, he went and sat even further back to look with even greater satisfaction now at his thread which could quite legitimately be called something colossal.

Having sat there like this for a good while amidst feelings of which quiet pride and a restless urge to act fought for precedence, he suddenly fell asleep.

This was no cause for surprise, for as his first effort, Baldur had delivered a very fine thread with a slight thickening at seven and a half centimetres from the edge, a barely noticeable thickening at sixty-seven and a half centimetres and otherwise as straight and flawless as can be imagined. And that this must have left him dog-tired was clear.

When he woke up, it turned out to be blowing a little more. The thread was continually bending far beyond the bars. It had not turned any colder. The thread still glistened, but no longer as freshly as that morning. If anything, it had gained something mysterious. The thread was his property more than ever, was Baldur's opinion, now it looked somewhat less physical and rather more like something manufactured, a thing made by Baldur, and his forever.

Baldur climbed up and he instantly felt the difference now it was blowing. It'd be bitter if it broke, he thought, for he would not gladly see any possession lost. But when he had progressed halfway to the top edge and had to hold on tight in the wind, the thread, in his own eyes too, became rather flimsy – and everything really turned all fine and dandy, making Baldur highly active. He would like to dash off in all directions to make repairs in the places under threat; he ought to be in charge of overseeing a whole network of threads encompassing a gigantic space. Animals would swarm towards it from all sides and be left dangling in those threads, caught by their silly spiky bits and hairs.

'Ahoy,' shrieked Baldur on just his single little thread, as he already felt that network tense and tremble around him, and now he shouted passionately: 'Shulk the flyzum – snuff the hum; calcium marrow, hook the buzzers!' What a wild triumph this is, Baldur thought, such a poisonous dash towards the threats. How I'll block this blowing, he thought, allowing himself to go with the wind, sitting on the tautly drawn bow his thread had become because of the force of the wind.

'Come on,' he shouted. 'Silent flyers. Let's be having you augurs!' That's how Baldur D. Quorg sat on his first thread and he understood so well that it might snap in a hard wind, that he didn't dare laugh. But he had to do something to give his joy an outlet and that's why he chuckled, most mindful to do this moderately and cuttingly, grinding his jaws together in the process. Ah well, he had just one little thread, and he looked along it from the bottom to the top and from top to bottom, and it wasn't much, that single little thread! He had to have very many of them, and not all loose ones, but ones arranged in such a way that they contained and balanced each other. Then Baldur climbed up rapidly, for he suddenly felt that the wind was not a force to play with on a single, wobbly and windy, loose thread. 'You shouldn't make things up, Baldur,' said Baldur when he was sitting on the edge, 'and you mustn't shout. In fact, you gotta be very quiet!' he cheekily cried immediately afterwards, on purpose, and this he repeated once more: 'In fact, you gotta be very quiet!'

He was sitting by the lump of paint again and looked at the way his thread was fixed to the hair from the paint brush. Disapproving, he shook his head and then walked over to the fence post. He looked down and then back again, at his thread, then upwards, suspiciously, and then he prepared himself to walk down along the post. But before doing so, he muttered something which made him look rigidly ahead of himself for the full length of the descent along the post.

'I'm a calculator, dammit!' he muttered.

Once he had landed on the ground, he continued to sit there for a while, quite motionless. What nonsense, to set to, on a fence like that. You ought to set to work in the shade and make an entire net at a stroke. What a job that would be. Such a tremendous job. Nobody else could do that. Such a grand thing one does in silence and awaits the results just as silently. He who touches shall wither, thought Baldur. Space is the lust to play, the net is will!

3 q r = 2 π g, it suddenly occurred to Baldur D. Quorg – how? – the mind, too, rewards with fruit. Nervously, he began to rub his front legs together, during which he screwed his eyes half shut and his mouth contorted grimly.

'Right,' he softly said, inwardly, 'right.' And then he looked around him to see if anybody was listening and said, half out loud: 'And thus the cadavers abided in ropes', and because of this a meagre thing turned into something solemn after all.

Without minding his thread any further, he ran away, along the top edge of the fence and then down, back to the ground again and a good way across the ground too. Cantering along like this, he cried out a few more times: 'Right' or 'Quite so' and then he came to a halt in front of a wall which he ran up instantly until he reached a beam. That beam formed part of the roof. He went the length of that beam, too, to where the gloom cast by the roof became very deep, and then he reached a little door in the coping of a farm barn of which the wall made up the bottom most part.

He now climbed up to the upper rim of that little door until he had reached the middle and there he halted and began to concentrate.

Having sat there a while, an older spider appeared at some distance away from him. It was quite a big one, and he was called Simon P. Quellyn. He had been at work on a web for a while already and rather felt the need for a chat. Creakingly, he rubbed himself with his legs down his hindquarters and then he said, all of a sudden: 'I'm just lumbered with it!' Baldur nodded, and it pleased him that his youth was apparently now behind him for Simon P. Quellyn spoke to him as though to an adult. Baldur adjusted to this, therefore, and said something old too: 'Just so.'

'There's me having to yank that lot from my arse,' Simon said, troubled. 'And nobody's grateful to you for it,' Baldur replied instantly, with a bitterness that turned out particularly well.

'Spot on!' cried Simon P. He regarded Baldur for some time, appreciating him.

'Are you going to start here too?' he then asked.

'As long as it's getting time for it,' cried Baldur.

'Spot on!' Simon said one more time, but he said nothing further and, unexpectedly, he dropped away again on a fresh thread.

Baldur watched him go and saw that the other spider had made considerable progress already with a large and extremely sturdy web. That spider's skill was evident. His threads were nicely taut and the joins looked unassailable. Simon P. Quellyn saw perfectly well that Baldur was watching him, and though he didn't make an issue out of it and continued to work just as calmly as before, it still gave him pleasure. He had learned that one must always keep calm and that excitement leads to mistakes, but on the other hand he knew that the danger of excitement is ever present when one is busy with a construction in the certainty that it is unsurpassably good. 'It's always wait-and-see what makes a beeline for it,' he used to say to himself occasionally in the past. He never did that now any more, for the slightest allusion to fate's favour can itself be of unfavourable influence. The emotion of satisfaction, too, can be so. One ought not to undergo such an emotion therefore, if one truly wishes to draw the favour of fate towards oneself! Thus, Simon P. Quellyn ignored from then on any possible appreciation from Baldur D. Quorg.

The latter, having watched for a while, let himself drop too. With a pounding heart! This was undeniable for, even though he had been talking bitterly and like some one of experience, as had been demanded of him, *this was to be his first web*!

When he had let himself drop some way, he halted with a jolt.

Now the thing was to begin to rock back and forth until he was able to grab the side of the door with his front legs. For, if he didn't do that, he would have to drop down altogether and then climb up that side with a good length of thread behind him, there to make his first join, having first drawn in a long and useless length of the thread, to be his first construction thread running from half way down the upper edge to half way the side.

And what use's that palaver to me? thought Baldur, so he began to rock back and forth. Swinging about like that, he did think it a pity after all that Simon P. Quellyn was busy in the same door opening, for the fun of this adventure was being marred a bit by the necessity of having to act experienced. The conversation with Simon marked the end of his youth, and now he had to calculate and keep his mind on things; but had all of this not been the case, the swinging would have rather amused him.

Swinging, Baldur looked at Simon but, sitting on a cross-thread, he was just at that moment busy on a join and he needed all his attention and didn't look round. Then, despite himself and therefore with an angrily contorted mouth and very much under his breath, in case Simon should start to look after all, Baldur sang:

'3 q r = 2π g
Baldur swings here full of glee,
2π g = 3 q r
B. D. Quorg swings, oh, so far.
Pincers in the force field pounced,
Onward, spiders: flies announced!'

What a rotten ditty, thought Baldur, for he hadn't kept an eye on the door and had swung into it with his back without having been able to grab hold of it. The following swings he executed in silence, doggedly, and then he was able to grasp the side. He fixed his thread well indeed and then he had the foundation for a web.

'Not bad for a beginning,' observers might have muttered and would have certainly had they had known that this was indeed the very first time; in the main, spiders use trees or bushes with a good number of side branches offering a generous hold. But Baldur didn't miss the fact that there were no observers cheering him on. Now he'd fixed the first thread, he no longer had a need for Simon's proximity either, what with his chatter. Now Baldur was looking at that lovely foundation thread, he felt that he wasn't one for company at all, really. He climbed, making thread, up into the corner of the door. Having landed there, he suddenly spotted he had made a mistake. During this last part of the climb he shouldn't have made any thread but should only have started in the corner from where he ought then to have walked over to the beginning of his thread, half way along the top edge, then to have stepped on to his construction thread in order to make a join half way along that thread with the first cross thread running from the corner. But now he was in that corner already, with a huge strand of thread flying from his body, and Baldur became dark with rage. There's me having to yank it from my arse, he now thought too, quite like Simon just now, and he let the piece of thread go, which now hung, pointless and disfiguring, down the side of the door. He quickly began a new one which, with exaggerated care, he fastened in the corner and then, spinning like one possessed, he walked along the top edge of the door to the start of his diagonal construction thread, quickly nipped along it to half way and then, quietly and thoroughly, he made his first thread join.

There now! But who could take pleasure in a first result like this while, rumpled and pointless, that unused length of thread hung down along the side of the door, like a mistake and a stomach churning waste? Baldur didn't rest, therefore, and worked on at once. He didn't want to make any more mistakes. Not ever again. He spun threads, first three from the corner to other points on the first construction thread and then, in corners other than that one, threads from these to the top and side of the door. Once he was done with this, he climbed back up again and oversaw the whole thing. It was hard to speak of a 'whole thing', for that matter, but when Baldur pondered this further, he had a terrible shock for he noticed that he had made a far bigger mistake than that first, wasted thread: were he to expand his web on the other side of his construction thread, then he would inevitably touch Simon P. Quellyn's web. But that wasn't all. He also saw that, in the time Baldur had needed to climb up to the top edge of the door, Simon had made a join with a thread from his web, quick as a flash, on to Baldur's construction thread.

It made Baldur go rigid. What was it again he had cried in his first thread, in the fence, about 'silent flyers and augurs'? 'What a stench the world is,' he now cried out. He didn't really cry as much as shriek: 'What a stench the world is, what a whining stench of unwillingness.' He decided upon the following: in due course,

Simon P. Quellyn would have to come up along thread c6 of his web for a new connection to join r3 to the wood. Baldur would go and sit there, but tucked away slightly, so that the climbing Simon would not be able to see him before sticking out his head above the edge. Then Baldur would strike.

He only thought of the word 'strike', not of killing, murdering, destroying or of pinching off the head. To strike is sufficient and all other concepts are needless.

Thus he waited.

Simon P. Quellyn would have to come soon. He still had to go past v6 and then half way along to c7, parallel to c6, make the join there and then back and up on the wood along c6. Simon had been going about for a while, thinking what to say to Baldur this time, once he had reached the top, and he had decided on an amiable remark. He would say: 'Loads of catches here,' for he had used one of Baldur's threads and perhaps he would then be at peace with the fact that Simon had taken advantage of his work, for a plentiful catch could be expected *anyway*.

Baldur's calculation was exactly right. The moment he thought: watch out, he might well now appear, Simon's front legs came up over the edge. Baldur struck, but only at those front legs, not at the head. Simon drew back fiercely, but Baldur was still able to pinch one off. Hurriedly, Simon slid down a fresh thread from join r3 to the bottom of the door, and disappeared there, one leg short. A fight was pointless now for Baldur's strength was young and hard.

Baldur watched him go and he now surveyed the new situation. The way Simon had made use of one of his threads, he now could deploy what Simon had wrought. Quellyn was certain not to return, for no one fought with half a front leg.

But the formula for his web was no good any more. Both q as well as r had changed and the tension which would now fall on the foundation thread was too great.

The thread needed to be doubled and this was what Baldur was going to do, quickly. He worked until dark and then he went to sleep in the corner and next morning he began afresh, the moment it became light. The threads were barely moist; the spot in the roof frame was as favourable as possible and in the course of the morning the highly complex web reached completion. Baldur withdrew into the centre of it and there he began a battle against the thoughts occurring to him. He looked along the threads of the web. Bar that wasted one along the door, there were no flaws in it, though the form wasn't pleasing because of the annexation of Simon's part. Baldur ground his jaws together, for he had to do something to quell the satisfaction gaining hold of him even so. He ground them so hard that the desire to have something in between to be ground down overtook him, trembling. Oh, blow me, what a web, he thought. What an achievement, what an overwhelming good, what irreplaceable worth. And in spite of his firm intention never to recite a rhyme again, one arrived nevertheless:

> 'On my threads sit I, the Marshal:
> Calcium hidden well, not partial.
> No one shall rip free from here,
> Pot-roast ready, mine the cheer.'

A nice little ditty but dangerous to give in to that gift. It was for the second time, though, that Baldur had raised the subject of calcium and he went and thought a bit about this now. He must have hit on it because of the hard grinding of his jaws and that urge to grind something down, but he felt that there had to be something else behind it as well. Something that, amongst other things, was connected with the quickly forsworn youth and the doom he had felt when that one front leg of Simon P. Quellyn's was snapped off and dropped down so unexpectedly and pointlessly. A strange rhyme, Baldur thought, that of the marshal on his threads. He raised himself up and considered the reach of his net and the marshal's eye in charge of it. But just when this made him tingle for a moment, something happened again that confirmed his abhorrence of life.

A fat wasp who had been getting up to heaven-knows-what in the loft of the barn, came flying out with a great racket. It touched thread g5, stood on its head there because it got caught for a moment, but then it began to beat its wings and twist its hindquarters so impetuously that the thread first gave and then shot loose from join p2. Gone, the fat wasp, and the entire g-section of the new web had been distorted, and dangled there feebly. Baldur was instantly on the edge of the tattered part. He ground with temper and trembling watched the wasp, who had a good length of thread trailing behind him, go. 'Gunk!', he cried, as loud as he could. 'Gunk, blundering stop-squirt, blubber gunk.' But the wasp had gone and it was very quiet now, after all that noise.

Baldur shut his jaws. He was almost vomiting and rather wished that it would be calcium then.

'Never, no one,' he then shouted, hoarsely. And with this, Baldur D. Quorg indicated that from now on he would never engage with anyone ever again, didn't want to see anyone again, wished to speak to no one and to look no one in the face again.

Then he began the repairs.

But what is it to repair something that has been perfect and had tension, and had been woven and joined exactly according to the formulae?

What is it to repair a work that has come forth from nothing through calculations and through industry and strength and through bodily material, by one's own thread? What is it to repair threads that existed in space like crystallised silence and are now destroyed and disjointed, and which from now on can only tarnish a creation, a true creation?

The web was repaired. Indeed it was. But it was no longer a net that could be compared with what once had been. It was a solution Baldur had thought up for the repairs. The only good one, even, for when the repair was done there was cohesion in the web again and it transmitted the vibration of every movement made, in or against it. But that vibration was no longer clear and gleaming and faultless: it was dull and laboured. It had become a practical aid.

While Baldur was still busy, he felt the net tremble a few times. There was prey therefore; he must set out after it. But he didn't; he went on working first. He used the auxiliary formula for restoring tensions, but he calculated them sadly, for the web was no longer a thing that was there for ever, a thing that allows no thoughts of decay, a thing *there*, the way you yourself are there.

The wasp was no longer a gunk but a scourge and a continuous betrayal. Only when it became dark did the repair reach completion and only then did Baldur go along the threads to the point where they had got caught: the flies Guwel, Roesk and Drod and the gnats Zuuwkin, Resie, Zamiel, Luuk and Frizoen. They were almost dead already when Baldur struck so they were barely startled any more. Baldur then withdrew, not into the nucleus of the web but into the corner of the door. He bit off the pointless thread still hanging there so that it floated down. But this made no headway. The web was too tattered for that. Baldur closed his eyes; he slept.

It is dark and dead quiet. Countless is the number of living creatures. On this side of the earth they are almost all asleep, most of them very well hidden and impossible to find. Baldur D. Quorg is impossible to find too, for not only he has crept into the dark corner of the loft door below the roof of the farm barn, but also beneath the dust and a piece of dead leaf that has been trapped there for ages already and is decaying. His first web hangs motionless across the door and since he has devoured Zuuwkin and the other gnats, and Guwel and Roesk and Drod, there are three more gnats, flying in the night and wanting to go into the dark of the barn, who have got caught, that's to say: Zarina, Loes and Rufkin. These are now dying there and, nervous and frightened, they look around them. If they should set to work thoughtfully – as thoughtfully as Baldur works – they would be able to free themselves, but they set to work wildly and jittery. Rufkin has said so once or twice: 'If you think everything through in advance then you actually do things very stupidly, in retrospect. But I'm just always so pleased I'm alive.' When it gets light they will all be dead from fatigue because they wanted to get out of that web so wildly all that time. They will not be given a monumental tomb though Rufkin was one whom life blessed frequently.

When Baldur finds the three gnats – for that matter, there are sure to be more by that time – the web will still be new and fresh. He will devour his prey but probably without being triumphant, for when he emerges from beneath his leaf and sees the web glinting in the light, his satisfaction over the construction has passed and it will be clear to him how vulnerable his work is. And so it is. If they are going to fetch sacks from the loft today then the farmer will swipe that web out of his way with a single stroke of his arm; it could also start to rain hard or a chicken, in its boundless folly, could go and try to get into the loft. There's a great chance, when it gets dark again, that the entire web will be dangling about in mucky tatters, rubbish and dirt; and who will comfort Baldur then?

He is still asleep, but when he wakes later on a new experience will await him: the fact that he can move provokes unease within him. The hinges of his legs and grabbers and of his neck and his hindquarters displease him, that's to say, the circumstance that everything there is able to move. It is as though the night has taught him something of the meaning of 'calcium hidden well' in his marshal-on-the-threads ditty. Life should be more insignificant. And it should lie like a small control centre in the calcium box of his head with for its sole instrument his eyes with which to leer and to determine how rightly he has foregone more of life than necessary in order to reject all.

But everything did still move and Baldur ran out on to his threads. Two gnats had joined the three of that night: Diek and Snuis. These were still alive and Baldur stayed and watched them for a while before he struck, and he devoured them as like-minded ones, for it was clear that they pleaded for the end when they made out Baldur on the thread.

The web in the door remained in use for ten days or so, but then sacks indeed had to be fetched from the loft, and the first tore the net in the corner as if it had never been there. Baldur managed to escape and disappeared into the same skirting board Simon P. Quellyn had fled through. From there he set off on the journey down: he walked a long, long way across the ground and then reached a pear tree in the yard. Here he made his second web, from the lowest branch to the trunk. Much smaller than the first but magnificently constructed, too, and refined in structure. When it had been there for a day, a cock who crowed every morning in that branch of the pear tree, sagged backwards rather oddly, so that he plunged from that branch and, fluttering, tumbled right through the web.

Then Baldur made a web in the window of the farm's living room. This was fantastic, for a light burned there in the evening and the gnats arrived in throngs. But the farmer's wife was very tidy so, after two days, she appeared with a mop, and that was therefore that.

After his sojourn in front of the window, Baldur wove a web against the hen-roost. A dangerous place, one would say, but he stuck it out here a very long time, for the chickens never flew into that roost, walking studiously through the little archway instead; many gnats appeared in the swayingly warm air of the chicken coop and nobody was mad enough to go and wield a mop there. Baldur was only forced to give up this web when it had become too old and too dirty and too bedraggled to be used still. Not that he was still relying on the warning system of the vibrations in the web when something flew up against it. He leered, for although he could move he yet played the game of the calcium box where the little control centre had been stored which wanted to spy exclusively. Sometimes, because of this, he was already at his victims' side before these were actually well and truly stuck to the thread. This gave them an easy death, still quite ecstatic because of that trembling air from the hen-roost.

When Baldur left this net, he made one in a little window of the pigsty, then one near the hay stack, then one near the big barn once again, and then another one again in the pear tree. He grew older and bigger and his body became harder and more calcified, and the hinges became more of a struggle. On rare occasions he would kill another spider and occupy its net. He never thought any more, except when making a web; but construction, too, was in fact an almost automatic thing to him and he made no mistakes. He no longer swung and he made no rhymes. And it was as though his bitterness had become a new organ inside him, producing calcium.

One day, he left the yard and went out on to the road. knowing quite well that booty would be thinner there, knowing quite well that there would be no protection from wind and rain. Walking along the road he tested his jaws. These were rock hard and a touch grainy; for the first time in ages there was something like satisfaction in Baldur, who closed his eyes for a short while and did not leer. Then he climbed a tree and, having arrived on the first branch, he deliberated a little. It would have to be not too high up and not too low down. And it would have to be open. It became a masterpiece of constructional daring. There was no unevenness to it, the joins were accurately placed down to the last millimetre and they sat so tightly around the threads that it was barely possible to discern the ties. It was as though a mathematically creative hand was laying down a form for all time, for eternity, unsurpassable.

When the web was done, Baldur D. Quorg went and sat at its edge and he leered. Nothing came into it. It was as if nothing was flying any longer in the world. On the road, too, there was nothing to be seen. Baldur sat motionless and after a while he no longer leered. He looked at his joints. The sockets were smooth and white. He stretched his legs and looked again: it was possible to efface each movement. Beneath the calcium roof of his skull, his brain lay in a calcium box. It had become smaller and no longer allowed much thought. More space had risen up around it, in which there was perfect silence. His heart was still beating and propelled something through his body and through the channels in the calcium. This was cruel, and again Baldur repressed the satisfaction and made the bitterness work, so the propulsion that continued might deposit calcium too. Something flew into the web that shivered like a *carillon*, but Baldur did not look. Even his leering he had to surrender, he understood.

It became dark and started to blow. But the web held out

splendidly and the force of the storm pressing on it was distributed so magnificently across all the threads that there was not the slightest threat of it breaking. Late that evening, a horse and cart came down the road. The farmer himself, driving it, had to smile from time to time. He had wanted to go by car but he hadn't been able to get it going and then he had left in the little carriage that had stood for years already in the stable, without being used. 'Take the carriage then,' his wife had said. Now he was on the dark road and they were heading for home. The lanterns did not give much light and the horse's hooves on the road were so calming that anyone would have had to smile. The whip was in its holder, to the right on the box, sticking up in the air, but the farmer did not think of using it. He had taken it into his hand for a moment at first, when he had driven away from the yard and they had all roared with laughter at that coachman in his carriage and they had cried *prrrt, prrrt* to make the horse run. But on the road the farmer at once had put the whip back in its holder and there it was now, in just the same state, and now he was going, very calmly and inevitably and, who knows, righteously, right through the web in a tree, close to the farm, of Baldur D. Quorg.

There wasn't a sound.

The web was left hanging from the whip like a pennant and Baldur calmly clambered down the whip to the floor of the box. There he settled, the hind legs leaning on the wood and the front ones resting against the two planks making up the corner. He was sitting beneath the whip holder. When the farmer got back home, he put the carriage in the stable. Not in the big one but in the little one that had been built up against it, and which was much chillier and more draughty and which only contained things that were old and no longer used. The farmer did put the leather cover, lying on the box to protect the coachman against wind and rain, right over the box. In deepest darkness, beneath that leather cover and in the even deeper darkness underneath the whip holder, sat Baldur.

He has been sitting there a fortnight now and he is still alive. He hasn't moved during that time, it is true, and his eyes are closed. It is darker there than blackest black can depict but should he wish to, Baldur would still be able to open his eyes. That's no movement worth mentioning and he would be able to close them again too. He would not see anything and we would not be able to perceive him either. But, were we able to see in the dark, then we would still notice that the bitterness in those eyes no longer glows, almost no longer exists, and is about to be expressionless calcium.

No one observes this death. Nobody visits the farm, by the last train and the last bus, by cars standing at night on the verge, on bikes put askew against the barn. There are no people standing in this draughty barn in the dark so that you see the fiery tips of their cigarettes flare up or describe arcs when they take their cigarettes from their mouths. And so there isn't any hushed conversation either. As dark as it is, that's how silent it is too, and so deserted, and there isn't a single sign of life except for that of the wind blowing across the earth precisely the way it already did millions of years ago.

The spider's heart is still beating.

That's annoying! When Baldur no longer leered, his much shrunk brain switched to observing this beating. It became hollower all the time and it made an echo beneath the calcium, reverberating dome of his skull.

Now that dome had to be freed of everything still there within: Baldur's brain. So it shrank and withered away.

Thus the heart tolled away perception. Both grew dim in time with one another, for the beating of the heart diminished and the echo died away. The dome became larger and empty. And silent.

Millions of years ago the wind blew the way it does now. It could not set anything in motion except the waves and the dust. At that time, in a swamp or deep down in the sea, in vaporous light or in a violet darkness, movement came about. Movement which was sealed into a form; movement that became beating, the beating of a heart, the beating of Baldur's heart, the tolling in this dome of calcium that is empty and silent once more.

Calcium.

It beats one more time.

Calcium.

And now . . .? No, no more now. It is over.

A dead spider! It is as though the shapes have become vaguer already: the legs, the maulers, the head, the body. Granules are what remain. Barely, really.

'No one, never,' Baldur said, and this was right.

O wondrous life that began to move in a swamp or a sea.

O sweet promise of a heart that beats; this was Baldur D. Quorg, spider.

The Full Diagnosis

Frans Kusters

I awoke from a deep, dreamless sleep. At the foot of my bed stood
four figures: two men and two women, all of them well past fifty.
They wore starched white coats; in front of one of the women's
throats hung a paper theatre mask. They looked pale with fatigue
and didn't move a muscle. Why, I could not say, but I was quite
sure that the foursome had been observing me for some time already.

'Am I ill then?' I uttered, seeking to support myself on my
elbows. Barely had I posed the question when, that instant, they
lost all interest in me and, to my amazement at first, but soon to
my indignation and annoyance, began to gambol about like little
children and to grab one another by the hair, the nose and the
ears. These can't be real doctors, I thought, they're nursing staff; if
they get caught here, they'll be given the boot, you bet.

'Would you please cut out those pea-brained goings-on!' I cried.
'Let somebody tell me what's wrong with me, instead.'

My words did not have the desired effect: on the contrary.
Things got ever wilder and more vicious; they rolled about on the
floor more than that were on their feet, and where only recently
there had been boisterous and teasing laughter now the first cries
of anger, fear and pain resounded already. As far as I could see,
each fought for himself; where there were any alliances, these
never lasted longer than a few seconds. The most remarkable of all,
however, was how the women kept their end up.

I would have to get out of bed and try all that was possible to
put a stop to this bizarre and horrifying pantomime. I had already
thrown off the covers but suddenly all my attention was taken up
by the shirt I was wearing. It was so beautiful, that shirt; it was
made of dark-grey damask and the patterns woven into it changed
at the slightest movement I made. I just continued to stare at that
dark, mysterious fabric that was so soft I could barely feel it, and
the banging and shrieking seemed to be coming from very far
away, now.

Then a very bright light shone in the room and a small, slight little man was standing on the threshold. I quickly wrapped the blankets round both my shoulders and the moment I went and lay down again I saw that the men and the women had let go of one another and, contrite, were brushing the dust from their coats and smoothing down their hair. Flanking the little man on both sides, they took up positions at the foot of the bed once again.

'The *chef de clinique*,' the woman without the mask whispered, bending forwards. Nothing in her appearance or behaviour indicated that, just now, she had had to perform a tremendous feat of strength, and this applied to her three colleagues likewise.

'Am I ill then?' I asked once more, raising myself upright.

It was like flour, the head of the *chef de clinique*, cocked incessantly from left to right, and the exaggeratedly wide-open eyes within it were large and moist.

'Young man,' he spoke severely, 'now just you take it easy. With us you're in very good hands. We know exactly what's wrong with you. We know what it is, how it comes about and how it progresses. We've even got a name for it. It's just that we're not quite far enough advanced to combat it effectively. As is the case with cancer, I mean to say, and important discoveries are made in both areas, daily, so best not despair.'

He was silent and grasped his black, almost square moustache between thumb and index finger.

'The hairline recedes,' he went on, having cleared his throat, 'the body sags and wears out: that's our diagnosis.' During those last words he took a stethoscope from his doctor's coat, tossed the gleaming instrument into the air, caught it, and nonchalantly put it away again. Then he bowed his head a moment, glanced fleetingly and irritatedly over both his shoulders and indicated by demonstratively drumming with his right-hand fingers on the back of his left hand that he considered his visit to have come to an end.

'The patient has a right to the full diagnosis,' one of the men protested. He added a curse to his remark and it was because of this that, as if by magic, I recognised him and the other three. They were Hans and Monica, Margreet and Rudy, my best friends. Disbelieving, I looked from one to the other. No wonder I hadn't recognised them at first sight: they'd become thirty years older, at least. But it was them: no doubt about that in the slightest. Hans and Margreet were standing on the doctor's left hand side, Monica and Rudy on his right. Yet Monica belonged with Hans and Rudy with Margreet. The *chef de clinique*, too, I had seen before at some time or other, I realised, but I no longer knew on what occasion.

'Out of the question,' he said decisively. He took a step backwards. 'Ladies and gentlemen,' he continued, 'you doubtless know that there are other patients awaiting us. Would you mind following me, please?'

Monica laughed encouragingly at me. Hans stared fixedly ahead of him. He had taken out glasses with half lenses like you see politicians and successful businessmen wear at times. Margreet whispered something into Rudy's ear; he nodded gravely.

'Oh, help me then, please,' I wailed, 'haven't we always been friends? Why won't you tell me the full diagnosis?' But they turned away and followed the strange little man who, with coattails flapping, had almost reached the door already. 'Patients come and patients go, the full diagnosis endures even so,' he cried over his shoulder, giggling. It was not clear whether that remark was intended for me or for his assistants instead.

They looked at me one more time and then they were gone. Only Hans halted on the threshold, looked around restlessly and then retraced his steps. The light had become less bright again now. He sat on his heels next to my bed and without losing sight of the doorway he began to speak, softly, hurriedly. There was also a touch of solemnity in his voice as if he was reciting an old and affecting poem.

'Listen,' he said, 'the full diagnosis runs as follows. The hairline recedes, the body sags, the parts wear out. The arrival of nocturnal guests. They knock on the back door; two shadowy figures against rain-stained, ink-black glass point at stomach and mouth and chew through all the food that now still stands on the kitchen shelves. Husband and wife they are, clad in rags; you don't know their names and why precisely you must be the one to regale them. And why specifically at night, not by day or in the evening hours. You give them ham: they want honey; you give them honey: they want ham. Behind their backs, you walk to and fro, an apprentice waiter who will never learn the craft. No, they do not eat, they just pretend, so their arrival has nothing to do with hunger. Only you have heard their knock on the door, only you have opened up to them. You don't know how long they will stay. They do not eat, nor do they speak. And you're afraid: you walk up and down the kitchen, busily.'

He was silent and regarded me fleetingly. 'I have to go now,' he said, 'farewell.' With the flat of his hand he stroked the metal bars of the bed, and before I was able to say anything he had already left the room. And the door swung to behind him and clicked shut.

Decorated Man

Harry Mulisch

The base was in the rock. From the horizon the ocean came and lay there deep inside the rock where the submarines, gleaming, rose and fell with the tides. From the workshops, further into the rock, the noise of machines, shouting and loud music resounded.

Brightly lit by electric light, a group of sailors in overalls stood on a floating platform and watched the periscope, just above the water's surface, making its way from the tropical sun into the dusk. She rose a moment later, the dripping tower (Y253), the gun on the bow, and then suddenly, with a lot of splashing and gushing, the entire hull, the longest they had ever seen. A second submarine was fixed to the foredeck, a pup, a sweet little thing with triangular little wings, no more than four metres long.

The quarters for officers and men, the warehousing, the offices and radio rooms lay deeper down. The electronic brain that provided the base with all its meteorological and strategic data lay in the furthest bowel of the rock that protruded, bare, from the empty ocean.

Inside, Bernard Brose looked fixedly at the grey hair, brushed diagonally across the skull, of the admiral behind the desk. He was leafing through some typewritten papers, stapled together. He looked up.

'This is an order,' he said. 'We can't take any risks. It must succeed. Do realise what's at stake: the Beast's on board. With his entire State Department.'

Brose stood to attention and slowly swung forwards so that he had to crush his toes down to the floor in order to stay where he was. For a moment, he marvelled at how, all his life, a human being managed to balance on two legs like a tightrope walker.

The admiral raised an eyebrow so that his monocle dropped into his hand, resting on the table top. He altered his tone.

'You'll bring the war to an end, Brose. On our side alone, the war has already cost forty million dead to date. Far away beyond the horizon, three quarters of our cities lie in ruins. Your town has been wiped from the face of the earth for ever. Both your parents perished in the bombing. Your brother died in action at the Northern front; his corpse is floating around the pole in an iceberg somewhere. Of your two sisters, one was murdered, the other died of typhoid. Your wife was in a train that was shot at, one which ran from one pile of rubble to the next.' The admiral – he had looked among the papers from time to time – began to twiddle the monocle between his fingers and once again he changed his tone of voice. 'You will exchange your life for forty million more lives at least, just on our side alone. You will live on in memory as one of the greatest heroes in the history of mankind – no, not a hero,' he said, gesturing with wide-spread fingers, 'something else ... more dangerous ... I'm still searching for it.' With his eyes, the admiral scanned the space next to Brose; then he got up and came out from behind the desk. 'I envy you, Brose,' he said and he laid his hand on Brose's shoulder for a moment in passing as he walked to the door.

Brose, his little finger unchanged along the seam of his trousers, turned on his heels to continue facing the admiral. The admiral's hand rested on the doorknob.

'I could not take any risks,' he said. 'Had I asked for volunteers, would you have come forward?'

'Yes, Admiral.'

'But I didn't.'

'No, Sir.'

'It's an order.'

'Yes, Sir.'

The admiral opened the door and offered his hand.

'We'll meet again before long, Brose. You've been appointed a Sub-Lieutenant.'

Brose took the hand and clicked his heels. It was cool and dry and pleasant. All of a sudden he hesitated.

'Is it an order, Admiral?'

'It's an order.'

Brose felt the hand continue to grasp his.

'When must it take place, Sir?'

'The day after tomorrow. Tomorrow you can operate the craft and try it out. It's dead easy. She's just arrived. She's just being unloaded right now.' The admiral did not let go of Brose's hand, looked at his watch and said: 'At precisely this moment the Beast is boarding ship.'

The Y253 from the fatherland was lying alongside the landing stage, a great creature covered in crawling parasites. In the distance lay the motionless ocean, turning a little pink. A piercing tone began to whistle through the vaulted space, a signal that dusk was falling outside and that the lights would be doused in ten minutes' time except for a series of feeble lamps screened off on their seaward side. Leaning motionless against the rock face, Brose watched the bustle of unloading. The craft was already ashore and being driven off to the workshop on a lorry. It resembled an aircraft more than a submarine. Nobody knows she's intended for me, Brose thought. All this fuss is because of me. This time, the day after tomorrow, I'll be dead.

This was hardly a thought, however: it was a line in a foreign tongue, learned off by heart. In the past, every New Year's Eve, awaiting midnight, his father would recite great chunks from the Odyssey in Greek; he and his brother and sisters listened, breathless and laughing by turns, to the incomprehensible white and yellow sounds spiralling up from his mouth like smoke. It had been exceptionally impressive, but it had also had something to do with a boundless desolation and sorrow — and with great effort he had learned the first two lines his father had written down for him phonetically, off by heart.

Ändra moi éneppe, Móesa, polútropon hós mala pólla
Plánchte epéi Troïës hiërón ptoliëtron epérsen.

The day after tomorrow he would be dead — but he wasn't ready to think this yet, not by a long chalk. He had never been able to do his homework except at the very last moment. It would turn into a thought the moment he broke into the Beast's ship with his craft. In the instant of the explosion, language would surrender the secrets of its grammar.

He could have eaten at the officers' table, but he went and sat in his old place; he was a bit quiet, listened to the radio and later that evening he lost a game of chess because he had never learned the opening moves. The others smoked and played cards, or they read. The morse from the radio rooms hovered in the walls, and down below, in the workshops, hammering and the whine of the torpedo lorry from the storage halls resounded. The entire rock was just a den of energy and destruction.

A few men began to sing near the canteen. I'll never go to bed with a woman again, Brose thought — but it wasn't a thought. He drew on his cigarette and thought of his wife, riddled with bullets at a carriage window in a motionless train in the middle of the countryside. It was all of it nonsense. She had never existed. What existed was the sea, a dozen submarines and the Beast's convoys.

He got up and began to walk through the ice-cold striplighting of the corridors. He wasn't a volunteer, but he would have been had the admiral asked for one. Like him, volunteers had to keep it a secret to the very last moment: who had been selected. Beneath the black vaulting, he saw a vessel disappear under water in the middle of the pond and slowly draw the trail of her periscope towards the sea. He had a feeling she wouldn't return. In his bunk, he thought: Why didn't he ask for volunteers? He must take no risks, he'd said, but was he actually taking any? There had always been at least ten, usually twenty volunteers for assignments without hope. He had always been among them and had never been selected. This had happened twelve times but, though the ones selected had never returned, the number of volunteers hadn't declined, not ever.

The sleeping quarters were still empty. He looked at the bunk above and wondered what was bothering him. Suddenly he thought: There's been a mistake. He should have asked for volunteers. He's not allowed to give an order for something which is one hundred percent certain to result in death. And all of a sudden he had the feeling of preferring to top himself rather than follow the order. That was loopy. What did it matter whether he did it voluntarily or was following orders? But it seemed to. He sat up, leaned on his knees he had drawn up and tried to discover what this was.

It was dead quiet. He was surrounded by stone on all sides and not a single sound from the workshops penetrated here. For an instant he saw himself sitting there, viewed from without, somewhere far away on the ocean: right inside a rock rising up from the sea.

He couldn't discover what was bothering him and he went and lay down again. One thing was certain: the Beast must be killed and here was the opportunity to kill it, the Beast with his concentration camps. Perhaps these were no worse than those in his own country, but it would in any case mean the end to the war. The Beast never travelled by air — he didn't like it — but an air or missile attack on his ship was impossible because he knew how to defend himself more broadly and comprehensively than ever a ship had done before. Nothing (the craft excepted) could approach closely enough for his ship to even be on the horizon.

Brose felt his eyelids drooping. If I could flee, I would do so, he thought, even if the Beast does remain the Beast and even if there is no weight in an order to do something one would have done voluntarily in any case. An order like that isn't an order, and the one who gave it is none other than my own will having turned admiral . . . With a sense of satisfaction, he fell asleep.

And yet, that night, Brose saw himself fleeing down endless, cool, striplighted corridors, walking on the sea in an admiral's uniform, and he saw his mother's house, half of it torn down but half still standing, his mother in the severed rooms, and a friend from his schooldays who had come to fetch him to go by car to the heath, but nothing had come of it.

In the chart room he bent over a huge table and followed both the index fingers of the commodore, the one indicating the Beast's route, the other his own. At a spot, hundreds of kilometres out into the ocean, there was a red cross, marking where they would meet and the war would end. The admiral was standing next to him and had his eyes fixed abstractedly on quite a different spot on the map.

When Brose looked up at the general officers on the opposite side of the table, he suddenly knew all the nonsense he'd been thinking last night. He wasn't the point, the Beast was. Whether he set sail voluntarily to destroy him or was obeying an order, and what subtle differences flowed forth from this perhaps, that was in no proportion whatsoever to the issue at stake: the end of the war which had already lasted nobody-knew-how-many years.

Among the gold and the stars, he walked over to the wall where a sketch was hanging of the ship the Beast would be travelling on. She wasn't a cruiser or a battle ship, but something that could only be termed a steamer: an unarmed tub which no freight company would keep in service any more. This was one of the whims the Beast had to set against his inhumanity. It meant nothing. All depended on penetrating the tremendous cordon around him. In the afternoon he practised with the craft. She was back on the Y253; with a helmet down to his collar, in a leather suit full of belts and chronometers, he crawled inside, was fitted with an oxygen mask and everything was bolted down around him. He had just enough room to sit upright; his head protruded above the hull in a little dome of moulded quartz, and near his eyes there was a little periscope he could raise and retract. The men helping him looked at him questioningly now and then but didn't ask a thing.

With all the officers on the landing stage, the Y253 let herself sink and he sank with her – soon he saw the surface of the water rise above him and disappear. Not for a second did he think of what it was all about, that tomorrow he would see the sky disappear above his head like that for the last time. He felt only the tension of the experiment.

After a minute the water suddenly turned pale green. They were out into open sea. Continuously, he checked the instruments in front of his eyes and spoke into the microphone that was in front of his mouth. Ten minutes later he was given his position and he fired the engine; he felt severe juddering, and with a broad smile round his mouth he noticed he was starting to move. He dived to a depth of a hundred and fifty feet where the light turns so incomprehensibly blue, like that of a dying flame, and then, navigating by his illuminated instruments, he hurtled through the sea along a precisely charted trajectory for a quarter of an hour. His heart was pounding and he laughed loudly into his oxygen mask. A little later he began to sing. Something that would have to be a fat fish slapped against the dome and was gone. Brose laughed and bounced up and down, singing. On all sides he felt the boundless mass of water slipping by as though it were stone, but he was outsmarting it! Never before had he felt so free.

He switched off the engine, made the craft rise and raised his periscope. He was exactly at the calculated spot in front of the cave, and slowly he sailed inside. The Y253 was lying alongside the landing stage again. He came to the surface by her side. Laughing, he stepped ashore a moment later and shook the gravely extended hands of the general officers. Wide-eyed, the admiral looked out to sea.

The departure was at six o'clock that evening. For the third time, the craft was atop the Y253 and the crew were already on board. Brose sat on his bunk in the sleeping quarters and put the photographs of his wife and family in his pocket. Moments later he brought them out again and tore them up. His eyebrows raised, he looked at the shreds of paper between his feet. He looked at them and thought nothing. There was a gleaming sky, blown quite clear of everything, in his head. When he looked up, somebody was standing in front of him and said that he was to take him to the admiral.

Brose followed him along the plastered corridors; it was as though they had become just as long as in his dream. He was astonished that they made it to the admiral's room. The admiral was sitting at his desk.

'Take a seat, Brose.'

Brose sat down and he marvelled, one way or another, at his own presence in the air, on earth. The admiral was silent for more than a minute and looked at Brose's throat incessantly.

'In a few days' time,' he then began, 'the war'll be finished. Others have discovered that the Beast was going to travel, what route he would take and which ship. Staking their lives, scores of agents have been at it for months for this. Their work's unthinkable without the totality of our intelligence apparatus, which in its turn is unthinkable without state government. When it comes down to it, the death of the Beast will be the doing of our entire wretched nation. But the central role, Brose, is the one you play.'

No, thought Brose, the order I was given does that. He managed to think: but that's my own will – and went on listening.

'One of those agents,' the admiral said, 'met his death, but this death was not an important one. He could also have got away with his life. He played a game. We all play a game – except for you. You are the only one who knows in advance that he will die, *irrevocably.*'

I do? thought Brose.

'And this is why you die a different kind of death; not a hero's death, for you're not doing it voluntarily, but a death with the force of a law of nature.' The admiral dug his monocle under a nail, and continued: 'In a few weeks' time we'll all be back home again. Except for you. Most of us still have a relative somewhere, or a friend. All of my own family are still alive; I'm a rich man: they didn't have to die like dogs in the cities, like yours did. But the one who has nobody any more, he too will find a wife, soon enough, and have children. Don't get me wrong, Brose. In a few years' time, probably even sooner, all of us will really have forgotten the war. This rock will change into a fairy-tale holiday resort for millionaires. I drew up the plans for this myself and they have been approved. Further things have been approved. All over the world, plans are being laid for the next war, and when it breaks out, about twenty years hence, this one will have become *completely* pointless: our victory too, the death of the Beast as well. And in the meantime, we'll all be lying in bed with women again, have parties, be drunk, earn money, buy cars and go on holiday.'

The admiral looked him in the face and narrowed his eyes a little.

'But when we think of you, Brose – and very seldom this will be – it'll be to us as though we're looking into a different world, and shivers will run down our spines. We will see you, all of iron, standing in immeasurable space, for ever. In you, I will have immortalised war, for your soul is unable to go anywhere. And then we'll put our beautiful cars by the side of the road and for minutes on end we'll be incapable of driving on. We'll see the tarmac shimmering and smell the woods – but somewhere you will exist, made of iron, part of all possible scents, of the wind, beyond all forests . . .'

Filled with people, explosives, soundings and messages, the Y253 made its way at a depth of fifteen feet through the ocean to the area the Beast would travel through. Though no one knew of his promotion, Brose had eaten with the officers. No last repast: the usual fare. With the exception of one single officer from the base, all the faces were unfamiliar to him – incomprehensible, reticent faces from the fatherland. Little was said. Sailors everywhere stood with their faces to the walls and checked the instruments among the pipes and wiring, the nerves and bloodvessels of the vibrating ship.

At nine o'clock he was given a cup of coffee; he slumped forwards on to the table and fell asleep. The doctor checked his pulse and had him taken to his bunk.

From one direction, the convoy of the Beast approached, from another, at rectangles to it, Brose, in unfathomably deep sleep, five metres below water, surrounded in iron.

He woke at four in the morning. The officer from the base was standing in front of his bunk.

Surprised, Brose sat up. He existed. His leather suit hung over a chair. While he dressed, the officer sat on the bunk, his head in his hands.

Brose stepped into the trousers and didn't believe a jot of it that he existed. It had to be his imagination. A few times in his life he had thought about it and had doubted. Now he was sure. The *others* were the ones who existed; he did not. Even in the days when his father was still reciting from the Odyssey, when the firecrackers and Japanese thunderclaps were lying ready, he had felt that he didn't exist: that somewhere there must be a world where he belonged and where he could exist, but that he had lost it, that losing his way, he had roamed beyond it, and that now he only existed as an intermediate form, a transition, a thing of the imagination in between two worlds ... He went along with the officer to the commander, a stranger from the fatherland. On a map, he was shown the spot where they were in the ocean, the supposed position of the Beast and, one more time, the route he was to follow when the time had come. Until nine o'clock in the morning, the Y253 would still be transporting him in the craft, but then she would be in range of the outermost cordons and would no longer be able to surface. Not a word was spoken that was not relevant. While the sailors were helping him get into his straps and instruments, the vessel began to rise. Brose looked at the commander. He was standing there smoking a cigarette, watching a dial. He was a component of the submarine. When the iron ladder slid into view, he saluted, touching his cap, and turned his back.

Silently, the Y253 slipped through the night, on top of the water, in the warm wind. The darkness lapped softly against the hull. Five, six sailors ran forwards across the dripping deck and opened the craft. Hurriedly, they helped him in and fitted the oxygen hose, but before they were able to close the dome, the officer from the base, who had come up along with them, began to shake Brose's hands and to pant incomprehensible words and sentences, almost invisible in the night, allowing his head to droop, then tossing it back, mumbling, panting, weeping. And Brose nodded back, weeping, open-mouthed, all tears ...

When the fog in his head dispersed, everything was empty; the dome was over his head and behind him the steel creature was twisting down its manhole cover. All of a sudden, he felt the boundless night around him, the world in which he didn't exist. And as everything began to rise, left and right, and the water lapped his dome a moment and then rose above him – in that silence Brose suddenly knew that man is an animal in space, dividing gods and joined in battle with them, his mind turning into machines. With his head in the dome, deep under water already, his teeth began to chatter in the face of the immensity of the miracle he suddenly saw.

He saw man drop in across the silent earth, full of restlessness, thoughts and words. In a flash, he saw him live among the animals, erecting mysterious signs and fires to heaven, and then gradually he saw the words step forth from his head, phantoms slowly becoming visible in all the plains and vales as machines, vast factories, power stations – cryptic, unfathomable extensions to his body: his legs that thought themselves into being wheels, his arms into ships, aircraft and cannons, his skin into helmets and bunkers, his heart into electricity, and his ears and eyes into radar and telescopes. A smoking, swirling, sparking human body of steel, stretched out over the earth, in it, under water and tumbling through the air, his own words like bombs and raining down fire upon him . . .

Open-mouthed, gliding deep through the black water, Brose looked at the decorated man: standing, legs wide apart, his face turned to the East, on top of a decomposing monster with wolf's eyes and Christ-hands, a space for his eyes and a map beneath the roof of his skull, grown invisible beneath the weapons and tools of his deep faith, a roaring tree of light, a fire-god of the stake.

'Time is eight hours, forty-nine minutes, twelve seconds. We are situated at the edge of the convoy's first zone of defence. Its centre is estimated to be at a distance of nine miles. It's moving in a North-North-Easterly direction at a speed of fifteen knots. There are many aircraft in the sky. Your position is . . .'

Rigid, Brose listens to the voice in his ear. It was hard and dry: the commander's. His legs were made of blue, transparent ice.

'We'll be going about in a hundred and twenty seconds' time. Detach yourself in sixty seconds. Do you read me?'

Hoarsely, Brose said:

'Yes.'

'Time is eight hours, fifty minutes, four seconds.'

Brose began to shake and, listening intently to his headphones, directed his eyes towards the instruments. The soft noise of metal on metal already sounded down below. In a moment, the wire would break: he had no radio on board – it would be too dangerous. He heard someone walking. Metal continued to tap against metal.

'Detach yourself in ten seconds.'

All of a sudden he heard shouting and running, to and fro, disjointed sounds like those of a brawl. He put his foot on the starter, peered at the chronometer and listened with his whole head.

'Ah! . . . come . . . not the . . . – *Brose!*'

Thumping, groaning: the officer from the base. He wanted to protest, undo it all, to make the world a better place – '*Ha ha ye ya lala!*' Brose shouted, slamming down the starter. Trembling embraced him and a moment later it was so quiet in his ears as though an entire solar system had disappeared and got lost.

He dived to a hundred and fifty feet and thought: I could turn around and blow up the Y253. But the commander would have borne this in mind. Like an eel, he wriggled and zig-zagged his way away from him now, into the fathomless space of water – not to protect himself but his ship – himself. Never would he find him.

But it didn't enter Brose's head to go and find him. His eyes on his instruments, he shot through the water. It had become lighter, a soft-blue dusk with many little fish in it. His knuckles were white clenching the steering wheel. Minutes on end, he roared on. He didn't exist. He was a figment in the admiral's mind, and another in the commander's and again another in that of the officer from the base. In a quarter of an hour's time, for an indivisible moment, he would be a figment in the cranium of the Beast: a figment of tearing iron, fire and death. That was the most extreme purpose to which a human being might grow. Nobody existed any other way than as thousands of different figments tearing each other to pieces in the heads of other figments – *fata morganas* in a desert dream. Brose breathed agitatedly into the hose and looked wide-eyed at the gauges. Man builds himself in, in his words, grasps the joystick and flies through the air or the water like a god, he thought. His eyes grew large. The craft was *his body*. He had turned into iron. With his body he would break open the flowing body of the Beast. The imagination of the human soul was too large for a bundle of flesh and blood. It had found itself more spacious accommodation. In the beginning was the word and the word has become machine. Somewhere in a clean room, an electronic brain would suddenly punch out a saving message of redemption for mankind, the message of the new body and everything would bend its knee to it: – *Deus ex machina*.

Brose's head glowed like phosphorus. More and more frequently, he slid underneath hazy, dark patches hanging like thunder clouds above him. He kept away from being beneath them as much as possible to evade their radar. But he would be a quick, unknown sea creature to them at most: he, an iron body with sufficient explosive power to obliterate a metropolis. Suddenly it began to rain silver before his eyes and for seconds on end fish drummed against his little dome. When he had passed through the shoal, the dark patches had greatly increased in number and the sea was full of hollow pounding.

I'm deep below the convoy, Brose thought. It suspects nothing. It's a colossal, floating creature, held together internally by wireless nerves. A signalling aircraft, a train thundering across points, a ship with people inside: these are creatures of a higher biological order than a human being. Offices, the cuckoos of singing churches, smoking factories, cinemas shaking with laughter, are bodies with forms of consciousness above the comprehension of man, the way the cells of a body know nothing of the individual they collectively have formed. Brose thought and thought; he thought so as not to think. Cities, states, continents . . . Before his eyes he saw consciousnesses piled up like an inverted pyramid disappearing ever wider and hazier in a darkness forever darkness. He thought: the entire earth's becoming a body with a consciousness, and soon the solar system and then the Milky Way and, after billions of years, all solar systems in the universe: an omnipresent character grown from the human soul chased away from house and home — and then, who knows, other universes too . . . worlds where one belongs . . .

Was this still thinking? His brain worked like his razor when connected to a voltage too high for it. He looked up. The firmament was choc-a-bloc with threatening, billowing shadows. The water had changed into ear-splitting thudding. It was nine hours and four minutes. He had travelled eight miles. Half a minute later everything above him was suddenly green, empty and quiet again. Startled, Brose looked at his instruments. Had he gone off course or had the fleet changed direction? A corpse-white fish flashed past — the ghost of a fish. Five hundred metres further on, a small diffuse cloud hovered again. At top speed he shot underneath it from the side and then ran into the convoy again. He hurled his steering wheel round, veered back in a sharp bend and reduced speed.

He was in the eye of the cyclone. The little cloud was carrying the Beast, a silence surrounded by space, the Beast with his State

Department. At that same moment, an electrical charge hovered in his belly and legs like when he thought of the woman he would go to bed with later on. Then, thirty metres above him but twenty metres below the surface, he slowly saw a colossal iron shadow looming up. His body reacted sooner than his mind – when he was able to think, he was already in a perpendicular spin at full power, down into the deep. Twenty centimetres above his head was the water. He felt the pressure rise rapidly: he felt it by the dancing indicator which began to light up as the darkness increased. There was no difference between the little dome and the roof of his skull; it could withstand a pressure of thirteen atmospheres – death lay at the red line on the dial. At a depth of three hundred and sixty feet, he levelled the craft, hurtled with buzzing ears a few hundred metres in the direction the convoy was steaming in, and there he waited, leering about, with his instruments as so many senses. Light fell through a church window in deep dusk, almost absent but penetrating ultraviolet. No submarine appeared. No depth charge exploded. He hadn't been seen. Were he to continue to circle this spot, the centre of the convoy would be above him again in exactly two minutes. What was he to do?

But he thought: the murderer is a figment in the victim's imagination as the victim is a figment in the murderer's. But every bullet that strikes, too, is a part of the murderer's body, piercing that of his victim. Each murder is an obscenity, an intimate embrace, a sex killing. He saw his wife riddled with bullets and thought: murderer and victim are two figments, mating.

Then Brose wanted to see the Beast. For a single instant, he wanted to see his steel body above water stretched out over the ocean. Then he would hurl himself upon him. The Beast was lost already any way. Even if he was discovered and shot at from a mile's distance, his explosion would toss the entire fleet melting into the air and slurp all the aircraft like liquid aluminium, down to the deep. If he couldn't reach the Beast's steamer, he would pitch himself on to the submarine or a ship at random. It made no difference. Cautiously, suspicious like a deep-sea fish that at last wants to see the sun for once, he began to rise. The indicator ran back slowly and sun hovered in the water once again. The engine's trembling was no longer there; what he heard was the quiet flow against the dome of the water, an impassive element the moon is tugging at. A small shadow began to take shape above him: just one, no more. It was the ship of the Beast. Brose rose and let the shadow pass over. With a little snap, the rushing in his ears disappeared. The submarine was nowhere to be seen any more, nowhere the churnings of its wake. Brose began to shiver and suddenly he spiralled up to fifteen feet below the surface. All of a sudden there was a bright green transparency, a sphere of glass. On his chronometer, he checked when he would be exactly midway between the steamer and the convoy. It was possible that a ship or an aircraft would open fire at once and put an end to the Beast and his fleet. Slowly, he rose to six feet, to three feet – and then, all of a sudden, he rushed his dome out of the water.

He shouted. In an ocean of light, the convoy lay there, from horizon on horizon. The sea was quite built up with hundreds of silver-grey battle cruisers and dreadnoughts, heavy in the water, with supernaturally turning radar aerials; in amongst them countless light cruisers, flotilla leaders, destroyers, mine-sweepers, corvettes, gunships, frigates, all smoking and baying cheerfully: an immense city on the glinting water – and above it the blue, booming sky, full to overflowing with aircraft, tumbling, playing, descending and rising up from their matrons of mother aircraft carriers. A chalk-white seaplane touched down, foaming, between the ships and a jet fighter whistled over him, low down; high, high up, heavy bombers drew crosses and pentagrams against the sky. Brose looked and looked, no longer capable of stirring himself, one second after another. The unutterable body of the Beast! And the heart, the black steamer with her fat plume of smoke at the centre of the empty circle: it was dressed and full of music. Oompah-music, moving off thinly across the sea, she sang as she sailed along. Sobbing, Brose clenched his steering wheel and began to dive. For an instant he saw the irrepressible feast split in two; it foamed around his head and the water closed over him. He had seen the sun for the last time. That too is no more unbearable than never to see a certain pebble in a foreign country again.

Under water, Brose realised he was still alive. What had happened? He must have been seen, the little quartz dome must have shone in the water like a gem. Perhaps the defence was over-organised: they had taken him to be one of their own craft. Maybe it didn't cross their minds that the enemy had been able to penetrate so deeply. Perhaps everyone here at the centre was far too jolly to keep an eye out.

He moved along with them, at the same speed as the convoy, as

215

if he belonged to it – like the deadly germ in a body tough as iron. He had nothing to fear. He put up his periscope and trained on the Beast's steamer. She was sailing three hundred metres on ahead of him, covered in bunting. Brose looked at his instruments. He still had fuel for a good three hours but oxygen for two, at most. He had panted, wept and shouted too much.

Thus he sailed along – in his head, once again, the fleet, an architectonic swarm of secrets, the sky full of finger tips and glances, and in front of his eyes a gleaming little film of the heart, with its plume of smoke, but the music inaudible.

And suddenly he got the hiccups the way a pope once got it from two thousand years of Christianity. Malevolent hiccups, from deep within his entrails, every three seconds; at each hiccup into his hose, the machine shot forwards with a jolt, a defect in the engine, so that the little steamer jumped from the mirror and returned there, trembling. He held his breath, swallowed, shifted in his seat, tensed his stomach muscles, but the hiccups continued, like a clock. Nervously, he fingered the steering wheel and with dismay he felt how the hiccups began to tear him down, stone by stone, propeller by propeller – his dismay was disintegration itself already. Along with it came the fear; that same instant, a white pillar of smoke rose up perpendicular within him. With trembling hand, he retracted the periscope and gave full throttle. The ocean began to seethe around him. It was coming, it was coming! His life lay stretched out in metres before him. Softly the throbbing of the ship awoke in the water – in the distance, her shadow was born; the throbbing soon grew louder and created the ship. There she hovered, keel down, her propeller grabbling helplessly through the water. Black, thunderous, she stormed towards him. Brose hiccupped to the point of shaking – death to the Beast! – saw a broken shoelace, a corner of the balcony of his burnt house, his father's hair parting, and full of revulsion, he drew the steering wheel towards him. With the roar of welded armour plate, rust and shells, the ship rolled by overhead, gliding into the silence beyond him.

Hiccupping and weeping and making noises, Brose came to himself, still in the silent space. Automatically, he turned and desperately tried to find the way within himself. At the last moment he had dived underneath. Why, why? The fleet ought now to have been hanging in the sky, aflame, and the war to have been over. Why had he dived underneath? Not because he could

not die — he *could* die — everything suddenly had become impossible. No hero's death — an impossible death. *He could not die.* He
hiccupped — it was almost turning into vomiting — he put out his
periscope and sought the Beast. The moment he saw him he
chased over towards him.

Emerging the other side he had turned into a wreck. Death to
the Beast! His mouth was full of vomit, dripping into the hose.
Everything was nonsense! His will was an admiral with a monocle
and he had no one in the world any more! He looked for the ship,
retracted his periscope and, roaring along through the water, he
murmured desperately:

> *Ándra moi éneppe, Móesa, polútropon hós mala pólla*
> *Plánchte epéi Troïés hiërón ptoliëtron epérsen . . .*

Thus Brose hurtled, hour after hour, now from one end then from
the other, from the front, then from the rear, below water, towards
the steamer of the Beast continuing, impregnably defended and
full of oompah music, on her way to the mother country.

Finally — he had lost track of the convoy for ages now and was
wildly roaring back and forth, pointlessly, at great depth — everything went black in front of his eyes, he slumped forwards, let go
of the steering wheel and, without oxygen to hiccup still, he slid
slowly down to the deep, hour upon hour, with his craft, gently
turning and somersaulting like a meditating fish; the little dome
was tenderly being pushed in, and at the end of the journey he
came to a halt, almost unnoticeably, in an oozy world of ink and
illuminated monsters, extinct millions of years ago. There his craft,
languid and sleepy, dug itself into the sand, along with him.

Once every few centuries, however, soft floating and humming
would suddenly set in during that night, a mirage — this was he
himself, a realisation of existence, a boundless amazement: *Bernard
Brose — Bernard Brose.*

Souls Errant

Carel van Nievelt

Her last breath had been peace, as had her last glance been love. Peace and love likewise reposed in the marble smile which the finger of death had etched around her pale mouth. Still and painless, as if in a soft swoon, she had slipped away in the mist that no gaze will penetrate.

But such battle had preceded that reconciliation between living and dying! – Battle by the body, the young body that wrestled and contorted itself to shake off the annihilator who, unsuspected, in one of his grimmest guises, had ambushed it. Battle by the heart which had to part from him whom it loved and whose life was but one within hers. Battle by the clouded brain that in its feverish delirium felt itself to be accosted by visions of terror, terror of that which, hideous, depicted itself in the human imagination gripped by its most bitter fear.

Yes, had she not, only the night before, risen up from restless sleep and tortuously gripped the hand of him who did not move away from her couch, and had she not spoken to him in a hoarse voice, eyes wide and staring, of the tortures of hell?

Reinout, my beloved, save yourself! she had said unto him.

Save yourself! It is all true what the Christians teach, the things we have rejected so foolhardily. I have seen it: my soul in its oppression has revealed it to me. Reinout, there is a God, a zealous God, a fervid grey-beard on a bank of clouds. And at his right hand is his son, Jesus of Nazareth; and around them both are legions of believers singing hosannahs to the strumming of golden harps; and deep beneath their feet burns the eternal pool of sulphur, full, full of doomed ones, wringing their hands and gnashing their teeth. Reinout, I have seen it all. I died: I sank away in that which is unfathomed, but like a bubble of air in water, thus my soul shot up to the Eternal Throne. They dragged me before the radiant judge: brazen, like the tone of a trumpet, the judgement sounded from his mouth: 'Down with the adulteress who has not sought grace through the sacrificial blood of my Son! She has despised my word and rejected my covenant. Forgetting herself in unlawful passion, she has desired the flesh over sanctification. She has been dissolute and hardened in all this. Into the pit with her!' I cried out to the Saviour for pity but angrily he turned away from me: 'Too late! Was I crucified for naught? I know not them who have not known me.' And then I was seized and cast down; flames writhed around me, a fiery fume became my breath, waves of sulphur slammed together above my head – I burned! ... Here, internally, it is still here – the fire, the fire! ... Reinout, save yourself! Flee into the desert wilderness and do penance for our sins! Do penance, Reinout, and pray for me! For, I burn! I burn! All is true what they preach in their churches. Our lust was our fault and our unbelief is our doom!

Olga! he then cried, steeling himself against the abundance of his suffering, stop! Here: drink, my darling! It is thirst that scorches your throat, it is the fever that makes you dream of this devilry and which stirs up the memory in your sick mind of this misbelief of your youth. Drink, sweetest one, drink!

No, no! No water will quell this fire, this fire will not be extinguished. My Reinout, save yourself! Do penance! Pray for me!

Olga, come to your senses! What do you fear? Have our lips ever lied? Was our unbelief not honest, was our love not true? – And even were it all true what you believe to have heard and seen – Pray tell, have we not both sinned *together*? If the glow of hell is marked down as the penalty for that which did us both such good, made us so blissful in each other's possession – oh, my all, my love, shall I then not be with you in the fire? ... Olga, look at me! Am I not your only one, your faithful one?

A sheen of comfort had passed over her face.

Yes, my Reinout! she had sobbed, you shall be with me: you shall be with me for ever. No God nor devil can separate us, for we have become *one*, *one* flesh and *one* desire, *one* mind, *one* quest and *one* meaning, in everything, in everything! ... Oh, a wild joy, my beloved, arises in my soul, joy over the pains of hell. It was terrible! I feel the flames even now, still their glow scorches me. But better, oh, a thousand times better this than annihilation! ... We shall burn, Reinout! But I rejoice, I rejoice in that torture! For, even then *we shall not cease to be* for one another: we shall be together, together for eternity!

Exhausted, she had sunk down; tremors jerked the course of her slender body, beautiful even in the throes of death: the end seemed to have come. In time, though, these spasms had abated; the fever relaxed its grip and a merciful slumber settled on the feeble eyelids. Already he believed her to be spared; already the hope of rescue coursed like drunkenness to his temples. Woe is him! This calm was but the sign that life had given up the struggle with death. The wrecker had completed his work on this young body; now, he left it there and set off to strike down fresh victims.

When Olga now opened her eyes one more time, the peace of resignation rested upon her being. Yet, to him who regarded her with the glitter of the happiest of expectations, she, barely noticeably, shook her chill bespangled head. Then he knew everything. Like a bird, pierced in high flight by the hunter's arrow, he thudded down into the dust, convulsed.

All pain has passed away, she murmured, and the fire is put out ... Reinout! you were right: that was a false vision, yes, the one of those flames and that sulphurous pool. That was not the truth ... I now see green around me, green everywhere. I hear the rustling of the leaves. I hear the rushing of a brook. The air is cool and smells of fresh herbs ... Farewell, my sweet, farewell!

Olga, Olga, do not leave me!

I await you, Reinout, my own! Seek me, seek, and you shall find me.

Then that smile had come, with that look of leave-taking from which one more time everything shone out to him, everything he had loved in her and had idolised, what had enchanted and moved him in her, that which had rendered him blissful: her mildness and her care, her beauty and her glowing sensuousness, her undivided sympathy, for his failings too, her boundless devotion, even to his faults — in short, her warm, mild femininity giving itself away to him and which was his, entire and without reservation; to him, and to him alone. Thus she had rounded the edges of his angular character and sated his timid passion; thus, as a friend and a lover, as a walking companion and as a mistress, making his lonely soul clamp tightly to her love for all eternity.

And now ...

He bent over her and drank from her lips her final breath. Then he sat staring rigidly at her, how she did not speak any longer, did not look up, did no longer move. And suddenly, in a weeping groan, he had fallen face down and had slammed his teeth into his fist, and he had beaten his head against the floor boards until his sensibilities failed him.

*

Seek me, seek me and you shall find me!

These words were the first that his consciousness summoned up once he had returned to life out of his stupor of days' duration – solely to die, he had thought – but now, after all, precisely because of these words, to life proper. For they gained ascendancy over him, these last words of the one loved above all. At first, they had been but lisped murmurs, murmurs he sensed when falling into slumber and on awaking; at night while he gave free rein to his despair and by day, too, when, in order to not to lose his reason, he sought to escape himself for a moment, into the sound and fury of the world. They whispered in differing tones: pleading, jubilant, wailing and threatening in turn. Now they would be close by, then they would be distant; now inside him, then out: in the wind that touched him in passing, or in the throbbing of his temples; at times as if coming from heaven on high, then again as from the depths of an abyss. Often, when he, lonely, was taking a walk, they appeared to assume an intangible and indescribable presence which hovered out ahead of him and signalled him to follow – yet when he pursued them, there was nothing. At first, this made him fearful; later, it filled him with a vague, half-fearful, half-hopeful expectation – until, finally, it had gripped him like a storm, a hurricane of desire, driving him on.

Seek me, seek me, and you shall find me!

And there was another dying word of hers that would not leave him, that time and again rang out at him from his innermost depths like the solemn booming of bells from the darkness of a forest:

We have become *one, one* flesh and *one* desire, *one* mind, *one* quest and *one* meaning: no God nor Devil can separate us!

If he made a connection between those two utterances, then hazy light would loom in the night of his distraction – a hazy light of reunion. Like the dawning of a revelation, it loomed up in front of him, him, the unbeliever. He no longer weighed up and rejected, he no longer fathomed and denied; he solely felt that it *was*. The stumbling words of his beloved had assured him of it. Yes, yes, this is how it must be! There is a law of reunion, a law like that of decomposition. Of the deceased human being an *essentia* remains: a distillation, purely spiritual, of that which he has felt and loved most intensely. According to the nature of that essence, the extent to which it is either strong or feeble, ethereal or earth-bound, all who have lived do find a place again in the life of nature; and as between the chemical elements on earth, likewise between the hearts of mankind, thus there can be a choice relationship between these *essentiae*, powerful enough to attract them to one another, at times so powerful that it operates through the curtain which still separates life from death. Therefore, those who here on earth have belonged to each other entirely and uniquely, and have been one in everything and faithful to the end, these the grave cannot keep apart and their love, stronger than death, carves out a path to one another. For, between their beings there is an affinity which continues to act in nature even after the decomposition of their earthly life.

Seek me, seek me! the voice repeated once again. Then he readied himself and went. His body threatened to fail, incapacitated through fasting and fretting: but that sacred desire clamped wings to him – and he went, as if carried by spirit-feet.

Whither? – Would he, with his own fingers, tear down the thread which still bound him to the clay: with his own hand rend asunder the veil hanging there in folds between him and *her*? – This would have been a short path to take, yet not the right one. No! No act of violence would lead him to her, for she would have had no part in that act and only *unity*, unity in everything, in what were the things of life and of death, would be able to reunite them in a higher harmony. Thus, no suicide, no effort of irascible impatience that would alienate her mild spirit from him. He wished to seek her, patiently, fervently, trustingly, without rest – seek her, and seek her – until she let herself be found by him.

Onward, then! A last pilgrimage to her grave.

Over the bed of green sod with which he cloaked her, he bent his head down to earth. A long time did he remain like this. The scarlet of sundown melted into night; the dew, pearling on the flowers, soaked his clothes and the chill wetness from the leaves of grass sprayed into his face. He, however, remained, his forehead on the earth as if his hearing wished to penetrate the silence of that which was below, yet to catch a panting of her breath or beating of her breast.

Olga! he whispered, do you still repose *here*, close to your poor body which my heart and senses have loved so dearly? Tell me, Olga! Here I am. Come to me! Come!

There was no answer in the garden of the dead.

And more densely did darkness make its quarters on earth: a pale mist extinguished the twinkling of the constellations which set out after each other, circling heaven's pivot. Then came the night wind, suddenly, with a sad, wild sigh; and the trees, in their sleep, shivered at its touch; and it stirred about in the mist and shredded it into whirling figures that chased one another across the heath. And in the moaning of the gusts across the tombstones, Reinout's ear thought to perceive the sobs of souls who sought and sought one another, yet could not find; for, though they had loved each other in life, they had not loved enough, not entirely and uniquely, not in *everything* . . . Thus, the night passed. The wind inclined, to sleep among the shrubs; the mist melted away and with it the swarm of shades, fleeing the morning which, ahead of Hesperus, had already arisen with joyous glitter. He, however, was still sitting there and awaited a sign.

Olga! he cried, if you are not *here*, where then must I seek you? Tell me, show me, oh, my darling!

Then he heard, from far in the distance, he did not detect from where, the sweet note of a bird, so soft and yet so clear, so alluring and yet so chaste. A shudder coursed through his limbs. No nightingale fluted thus, no blackbird ever sang like this. There was no mistaking it: that note was hers. Jubilant, he jumped up:

She lives, she knows me, she has heard me and calls me to her! Olga! Olga!

Seek! the voice resounded. Not on the graves. Higher, further away. Seek her, seek her, and you shall find her!

Wings sprout from his shoulderblades so that he rises up like the lark toward the dawn. For that sweet call came from above, he now believed. There, up above, he would greet her, glad and sweet as though she was already on earth, a singing spirit in the eternal light-blue.

He rises — higher than the highest mountain colossus, higher than ever a thing of clay has penetrated the unknown, boundless expanse. Earth, beneath him, becomes like a garden in which sea straits are the glinting paths and islands the flower plots while the ocean lies stretched out like a green meadow across which the white clouds move slowly, like grazing sheep.

But above and around him is the realm of emptiness. In vain, he looks out for the dwellings of the blessed spirits; in vain he is abroad to hear at close quarters the sweet tone that called him.

Soon the night will enshroud him again. Moon and stars bulge from the dark vault of the spheres, lighting with swollen size and a shine not seen before; meteors hurtle past him, barely at hair's-breadth, searing hot – a wild chase of heavenly vagabonds, as though slung into space to annihilate the bold one who dared to hazard as far as this on to the racecourse of the planets. That which he seeks, however, is not here. Here no wind blows, no shade's wing rustles here. This is where the beingless void begins.

And when morning dawns, ashen, rises higher still. Even higher does he wish to search for them, those glorious dwellings of the beings-volatile. He rises up, but he does not find them. The more he now wishes to approach the source of light, the further it draws away from his yearning striving. Alarmed, he shrinks back. He has reached the limit where the light is present no longer, solely the darkness. The sun is but a dull-glowing disc, the stars but golden foliage: atoms, glimmering specks, as though lost in immeasurable space; and that space itself – that space into which the children of earth look up in faith when they dream of their blue and warm and blessed Heavenly paradise – that space itself, night: black, eternal, beingless night.

Will he penetrate even further? – How, were this hollow darkness but a Styx which he must cleave through in order to end up in the fields of Elysium? . . . But no boatman offers him passage; Nothingness stares him in the face and a terrible fear strikes him with paralysis. Imagine he cannot find the way back? Imagine he must remain here, hovering like one doomed and lonely, in punishment for his self-seeking and his seclusion on earth? . . . His wing-beat becomes impotent; the cold makes him rigid; a grievous oppression threatens to stifle the spark of life in him; already, he believes himself to be dragged along by one of those cosmic currents which will make him roam the tides here in everlasting peregrination. Suddenly, life seethes upward inside him at full strength, for in the icy dead-silence he has perceived a note, a note arisen, barely audible, from the bottomless deep: the bird-note of the beloved one, now lamentatious and afraid, as a quail's that, mid-sea above the water, cannot find a resting place for his exhausted wings. And the voice, too, he heard calling out, inside himself:

Reinout, Reinout! Whither do you roam? Why do you seek outside the earth that which was born out of the earth and must belong to her for ever? – Leave heaven to the stars! Descend,

Reinout! Seek me still, loyal and awake, with all that is in you — and you shall find me!

So shrill and frightened had that note sounded now, and so fathomless, it seemed, from the deep: — the note of a soul in pain: wailings for salvation *de profundis*. Oh, God! could it be that she yet must suffer punishment for her sweet sins? Could hell be a truth while Heaven was nothing but lies? . . . Zounds! He wished to go to her. Dizzyingly quickly he shoots down and coursing for a pillar of smoke that twists up towards him from earth, he plummets down into the blazing crater of Mount Etna.

Glow and flames, smoke and ash. Rivers of molten ores; seething lakes of lava that sink and rise up again in waves upon the breath of a subterranean high tide; rocks that splash down in a bubbling pool, pulverised on its foundations by the black-searing fire; walls that burst apart with a thunderous bang; blue-flamed sulphur pits; hissing spurts of boiling moisture; shafts which open themselves out into even deeper, even hotter a glow. Verily, as Heaven is to be found in the expanse of the skies, the location of hell is no delusion and is to be found, not too far away.

But Reinout's plaint here, too, only evokes echoes in the void. Though salamander's brood may populate this Tartarus, creatures of flame, raised in fire — but to the souls of man the hot abyss is as inaccessible as the chill vault of heaven. He reposes, the errant one, he reposes and he seeks, until the flesh threatens to char on his bones. He calls out, till the lower-most eddies resound to it. No reply. Even the bird-note has not the power to penetrate and reach him in this horrible dungeon. The voice alone admonishes him once more:

Not here, either, Reinout! Only that can exist in fire which was born in fire. Do not seek her in death, nor in destruction; seek her in life if you do still want to find her.

In life, then! In life he will seek his deceased one — in life which he himself is to leave as, he feels it, the last powers of the body are sinking away from him.

Resurrected from the pit, he finds the sun beautiful, the stars charming again, and the cloak of the fields more glorious than ever. He kisses the good earth who is his mother, his progenitress, his origin and his destination, and his home and hearth for ever.

Earth, life, earthly life, *where* do you keep his deceased one in your womb? – Silence! Is that not the sweet, the salvation-promising note, trilling from the distant place, greeting him? – O place of reunion, how long still the search?

Onward, he wishes to go again, around the world; and the West wind who takes pity on this tired errant one, lifts him on his wings and carries him across the ocean. And everywhere in air and water he scrutinises for signs of reborn human souls. He sees them emerge from the splashing waves, turning to spume on the crests, rolling along some way with the surging deep, then spitting apart to merge again with the brine; – these are the souls of brave seafarers who chose the sea to be their tillage. He hears them cleave the sky in swarms, like albatrosses with their broad, swishing flight; – these are the souls of heroes and warriors who ride coast to coast on the hurricane. He believes to be able to see spirits of rulers, lording mighty on storm-defying cliffs; to see spirits of poets striding across the flat mirror of musing lakes that glance up to heaven. But she whom he seeks, he does not detect among them all.

It is done: he can go no further: on the sandy beach he collapses, fatigued to the point of death. With a hoarse roar, the surf slams down at his feet; grub-grey the Northern hemisphere oppresses the sombre yonder; two sad spruces, banished from the green forest, stretch out shivering above the wanderer's head their rip-stripped naked limbs. Melancholy, the desire to die is all. And in the clouds a hunt comes into being; white crests speed from the West across the suddenly impetuous spate; it drives through the dead needle-foliage like a moan. These are souls, errant souls who cannot find what they seek. And he listens – he knows them – he cries out after them:

Wait for me! Wait for me! Presently I will join you, travel as one of you. For, searching, I am not worthy of finding and my Olga knows me no longer!

But hark! – now, finally, at last – the bird note! . . . And this time no longer vague, from an undefined beyond, but clear and certain, from yonder way, landward, in from the South . . . Bird-voice, will you now be his guide, now he is about to undertake the final journey?

Yes, steadily the calling sounds ahead of him, soft and clear, in inexpressibly cheerful tones in the grey evening quiet. It shows him the way – and that road he does know; and through the tearful joy of reunion his failing heart relearns to beat. For once upon a time he trod this road with *her*, this road which now will lead him back to her.

This is the German land, the land of hills and forests, of grapes, of songs, of forest poetry – but to him, particularly, the land where they found each other and possessed each other, where they had sung and swooned and, engrossing themselves in the soul of nature together, had revealed their souls to one another. The land of their love, the land of their happiness, where, in quiet togetherness, had it been permitted, they had wished to end their days.

And yonder is the forest of grey beech trees that climbs grandly up the sweet slope of the ridge of hills. A parvise of scrub encircles it, quite impenetrable; but for the errant one the tightly twined branches rustlingly part, for his footstep a green arch opens, only to close itself behind him – and he sets foot beneath the silent vault of the druid's temple, timid, shy, like the sinner wishing to pray crosses the threshold of a sanctuary. The night wind sighs. There, the roof of twigs trembles and rustles. Moon rays, broken through the weft of foliage, marble the smooth trunks: shade figures float to and fro in the dark perspective between the rows of pillars, and myriad spatters of light, sprinkled across the moss, are like staring eyes that direct the question toward the stranger:

Man or spirit, what seek'st thou here?

He, however, no longer seeks. For from the darkest of treetops, perfectly close by, the bird-voice trills toward him: a melting mordent, a swelling, jubilant crash. Staggering, he approaches. He drops to his knees.

Olga! his lips stammer, I am here! . . . Then a green glow of light dawns before his breaking eye, a Gloria of nightingale notes rushingly envelops him, intoxicating, a wave of forest-flower scents rushes towards him, a balmy wind like one that caresses the fields in June nights appears, whirling, to take him up on high – and, enshrouding, a rain of leaves descends from the verdure on to that husk now abandoned, left behind in the blueberry bushes, wet with dew.

Looking Back: the Weapon

Hélène Nolthenius

'... but you have been acquainted with this a long time already, M'Lud, as the members of the jury have been also. It cannot have escaped your notice that the conclusion the Public Prosecutor has reached holds no water. Only the adder that bit my wife might be accused of culpable homicide, at best. At the place where I found her, she was dead; had been for years even, perhaps, I don't know: there's no time down there. Black-haired I descended, white I returned: *that's* what I know. Culpable homicide! My life it was that I risked to give her life again. What the Public Prosecutor means is not that I drove my wife to her death but that I failed to drive her *from* it. I don't seek to deny this. I should only wish to deny that I looked back out of negligence, or because I doubted the promise of the gods. I *knew* my looking back would be fatal. You, Mrs Prosecutor, would have to accuse me of murder ... had Eurydice been alive at that moment. I looked because I did not want her back.

'... May I continue? Your interruptions, members of the jury, would gain in quality were you to shout a little more tunefully. M'Lud, what I should like to explain in these last words you have permitted me is this: that solely the living learn from death. The spirit of one who dies stultifies. Growth is no longer possible. Death encapsulates the spirit the way the Egyptians did the body. It is right like this. How else would the dead endure the horrors of the underworld? The living who descend are spared nothing, however. I, ladies of the jury – I have passed straight through hell. That I survived this I owe to my music, to my *kithara* here. The point at issue is that my music, too, has returned to earth white-haired, and that Eurydice has not wished to understand this.

'Alright: you do not do so either. Your expertise in this matter reaches no further than the tinkling of the tambourine and the shriek of the Phrygian reed pipe; but any professional can tell you that the work of my youth relates to what I play now as does the plain surface to the cube. Death gave it a new dimension.

'Begging M'Lud's pardon: that's no digression. Had my wife paid attention to this, she would now be alive. There was no place for that kind of attention in the mummy of her child's brain. She was dead, after all.

'I have heard my journey down described as the adventure of a lovelorn strolling player. Perhaps it may have started that way: as an adventure and a challenge. I had celebrated triumphs in the upper world so why not in the nether one too? Such hubris did not last long, however. The deeper I penetrated the darkness, the more deeply the darkness penetrated me. The song that mollified the hound of hell darkened with each subsequent variation. All the pitiableness of those who heard it sucked tightly on to the sounds. The yearning of Tantalus, the toiling of Sisyphus, the exhaustion of the Danaids. But so did their crime; their remorse too, likewise the irreparable nature of their deeds; and surrounding this the relentless hissing and shrieking of the Furies who stole after me like beggars do after a stranger. My journey must have taken months, months during which dismay made me into another person and my *kithara* into a new instrument. How otherwise would I have been able to penetrate the grimness of Hades and melt the frozen tears of Persephone? That which I sang for them was the very last song before my voice gave way. Beyond suffering made sound, there is nothing more. That's why the gods *had* to hear my prayer. They advocated against it; they warned me of the dangers; they pointed out to me that my wife, blameless as she was, did not feel unhappy in their realm. But they had to hear me: such is the power of music.

'Eurydice was fetched from the pasture of asphodels where she had woven wreaths in the half light. She left her girl friends in no different a manner from that which she was wont to do in the sunlight among the narcissi. To me, too, she at once picked up the thread of conversation where she'd left off, as though nothing had happened. As you know, I was not permitted to see her. The gaze of one living destroys the last germs of life in one dead, like a deadly ray. I was not allowed to look back but there was no question of doubting the divine word: I could hear her, couldn't I! Her little mouth never stopped. It never did on earth either unless she was sleeping. I had relished her euphonious chatter though I seldom heeded it. It gave me a feeling of peace and domesticity. It still did so when we began our trek upwards. It might be that the reunion – in sound, I should say – had something of an anticlimax after all the horrors. But that she was with me again, this made me deeply happy. I loved Eurydice so very dearly indeed. The promise the gods had asked, that I should remain faithful to her for life: I gave this with a laugh, one I thought back to many a time later.

'Perhaps if the way back had not taken so long. Perhaps if I had been less tired and not so shattered by what I had experienced. Perhaps if Eurydice hadn't disturbed my thought with questions that required an answer — on fashion? About a kitchen recipe? I don't know any more. If only she had realised something, a hint even of the unparalleled thing taking place there, or had even had the remotest attention for the cries of woe of the shades which wafted like vapour around us ... well, yes; and if only those shades themselves had left us in peace. But those shades were jealous. They became malevolent. They pressed ever closer around us so I could no longer see the path. There was nothing to be done about it: I had to forge my way back like I had done the way down there: with music. The moment I began to play, they recoiled and became silent, enthralled by their own, sung suffering. Just one kept holding forth, undaunted: my wife.

'She had done so in the past too. When she wasn't dancing to my music she'd be talking right through it. In the past that didn't matter so much. It was background music I created in the past. The Muse who had made me the darling of thousands was a popular one. Curious: I only realised this at that moment, the moment I could no longer bear Eurydice's chatter. It must have taken weeks, my attempts to explain to her what had changed. As often as my tired arm let the *kithara* droop I would repeat that there is music ... *that I had been the first to create music which cannot suffer disturbance*. Music which must be listened to, must be experienced, which is born from all the joy of the world and all the agony of hell. Music that has priority. Music before which all other things must give way. Did I say that Eurydice didn't understand? She did not *wish* to understand. I had tamed Cerberus, had comforted Sisyphus, even moved the Furies. My wife chattered. And slowly, slowly her tittle-tattle turned into reproach and accusation. She loathed what I played. She was not sufficiently dead not to feel the threat of this new music. She became jealous of it: my art had become her rival ... and I began to realise that she was right. The woman I had fetched from the deepest of night would upon her return never again be number one to me. It was this the gods had warned me for. This was the reason why they had me swear fealty to the sulking child trudging on behind me. They knew that the radiant being who had entered their place would have to leave hell a fiend of that ilk. Because only the living learn from death and the dead cannot follow such growth. And I saw what would have to happen, irrevocably: two lily-white little hands in a strangulating grip around the throat of my art. That's when I looked round.

'Members of the jury, you are about to retire to consider your verdict. A formality. I know your conclusion. In my youth I, like anyone else, have consulted the oracle. When I learnt from the jailor that all of you: prosecutor, judge and members of the jury, belonged to the extremist women's group I kept Eurydice from, I knew that I had met the Maenads who according to the prediction will kill me. This is why I have made no attempt to make you well disposed. Likewise, I shall not plead for mercy later on. Those who serve Justice cannot condemn me: to kill one dead is no crime. But you do not serve Justice: you serve Fate. I am at peace with that Fate. After all, Eurydice's place has not remained unfilled: now they are the Furies of self-reproach who pursue me. It cannot be long now or their hissing and shrieking will drown out my music. There is but one place where they will leave me in peace. That place has been given me by Hades, the All Providing One, to look forward to. Far away in the nether sea lies the blessed isle of the Syrens, the Muses of Death. There, those who have served the Muses of Life repose for eternity. M'Lud, members of the jury: your verdict and sentence is my letter of safe-conduct to Elysium.'

Werther Nieland

Gerard Reve

On a Wednesday afternoon in December, when the weather was dark, I tried to wrench loose a downpipe at the rear of the house; this didn't work, however. With a hammer, I then smashed a number of thin branches of the red flowering currant on a post of the garden fence. The weather remained dark.

I couldn't think of anything else to do and went on my way to Dirk Heuvelberg. (As far as my memory went back, he had always lived next door to us. At four years of age, he was still unable to speak; until his third year he had gone on all fours. I also still recall how, when we were little, he would come running up to our kitchen door on outstretched arms and legs: his arrival he would announce by screaming. If invited to do so, he would eat horse turds off the street. Later on, he was still able to move quickly on all fours and even then he didn't speak with ease. He was eager to tell, with a certain pride, that his tongue was too long and was on too loose a string: to corroborate this assertion he would make loud clapping noises with it. On that autumn afternoon, too, in the back room of his house, he still spoke with difficulty and indistinctly, in stumbling bursts of words. His stature had remained small. I was eleven years old at the time.)

A yellowy-pale boy was visiting him whom I did not know. He was standing in front of the window and he greeted me hesitantly and timidly. 'He's Werther Nieland,' said Dirk. They were building a hoisting machine from a meccano set, one they wanted to have powered by a windmill, but this they hadn't started on at all yet.

'Better make the windmill first,' I said. 'That's much more important. Once you know how much power there is, only then can you work out how you must build the crane. And whether you should take a large or a small wheel. For that matter,' I continued, 'you have to choose someone who's boss during the building. Best would be someone who lives in the house next to the mill for instance, or close by.' I uttered this last sentence softly so they couldn't hear it. A silence arose for a moment which filled the small dark room. (It had dark brown wallpaper, all the wood-work had been painted dark green and there were terra cotta crocheted curtains hanging there.)

While the silence continued, I scrutinized the new boy. He was skinny and gangly in appearance and a little taller than me. His face wore an indifferent and bored expression; he made his thick, moist lips protrude too far. He had deep-set, dark eyes and black curly hair. His forehead was low. The skin of his face was uneven and displayed flaky bits. I had the desire to torment him, one way or another, or to injure him on the sly. 'Don't you think so too, Werther, that we must make the windmill first?' I asked. 'Yes, that's fine,' he replied indifferently, without looking me in the face. 'He's an animal that likes to have a nibble,' I said inwardly, 'I know this.' Both of us, while Dirk was busy screwing something down, looked outside into the newly dug garden; an old washtub and a few weathered planks were lying on the bare earth. A mist of moisture and settling smoke hung between the roofs. I went and stood close to Werther and, without either of them being able to see, I made half-suppressed punching movements in his direction.

Though Dirk, too, did agree with my proposal concerning the windmill, we didn't go and build it but continued to sit together without doing a thing. 'You don't have to start making a windmill if you don't want to,' I said. 'But that's very stupid, 'cause you can learn a lot from it.' Dusk was falling. 'Werther, listen,' I said. 'D'you live in a house where a lot of wind comes past?' He did not answer. 'Then I could come and help you,' I continued, 'then we'll make a windmill you can run appliances off in the kitchen. I can do that, easy, 'cause I've got time. And to promise a thing and then not do it, that's something I don't do.' I was feverishly intent on ways to visit him at home.

Werther took no notice of my words, perhaps because I didn't speak loudly enough and because we were listening to vague music from the wireless coming through to us from the front of the house.

It was already late in the afternoon when we went outside and ambled along, the three of us. The street lamps were already lit. Werther declared he had to go home; we continued to accompany him. He lived in a self-contained first-floor flat on a corner where the development came to an end and which had a view on to the wide parklands that stretched out as far as the dike.

'Sure enough,' I said, 'when it blows here, there's a lot of wind: I can tell even now. Do you have a veranda?' Werther did not allow either of us to come along upstairs, however. When he was already standing in the doorway, I went up close to him and hurriedly asked, without Dirk being able to hear, when I could come to make the windmill.

'I'm allowed to have boys visit me on Saturday afternoons,' he said, and he closed the door.

When I got home, in order to ponder, I made my way into the box room near the garden, where I kept secret documents. Here I wrote in pencil on an old piece of wrapping paper: 'There is to be a club. Important messages have already been despatched. If there's anyone who wants to muck it up, he'll be punished. Sunday, Werther becomes a member'. I hid this sheet under a chest, where it joined other inscribed papers.

That same evening, in the kitchen, I discovered a broad flower vase of clear glass without ridges or curves, one which really was a round aquarium in fact; I was allowed to use it as such from then on. Next day, I put the sticklebacks I had gone to catch immediately after school inside it instead of throwing them into hedges or down sewers or on to the street, as I was wont to do. I looked at them through the glass which seemed to enlarge them slightly. Soon they were boring me already. I scooped them out, one by one, and with a paring knife I cut their heads off. 'These are the executions,' I said softly, 'for you are the dangerous water kings.' For this activity I had selected a sheltered part of the garden, obscured from the eyes of possible spectators. I dug a little hole in which I carefully buried the dead creatures in a row, their heads joined up to them once more: before filling it in, I sprinkled it with petals of old faded tulips from the living room.

Thereupon I went to the canal once more to fetch a second catch. On the way back it seemed to threaten to rain; this failed to materialise, however. When I had returned to the garden, I suddenly thought the cutting off of heads a cumbersome and time consuming job, so I began to construct a chopping implement from meccano parts into which I wanted to screw down a razor blade; in doing so, however, I had an accident.

While fixing it, my left hand slipped and the index finger was driven with force along the blade: it was sliced open from the tip to well past the middle; the wound was deep and bled profusely. I became dizzy and nauseous and went inside.

My mother bandaged the wound. 'It was a razor blade,' I said in a plaintive tone of voice. 'I wasn't even playing about with it: I wanted to make something from it.' I understood that the small animals that told each other everything, after all, had caused me the accident.

'You'd better be careful with that,' my mother said. 'Best not to go walking outside with that if it's very cold. You know what happened to Spaander.'

(He was an acquaintance who once had suffered a similar injury. He lived in the Vrolikstraat and made a living sharpening people's knives and scissors, going around town in a cart. This man, while sharpening something, had happened to cut his thumb out on the street. Bitter cold prevailed; the soaked bandage became hard and, without him noticing, the thumb froze so that half of it had to be amputated. Though it had nothing to do with it, my mother, when relating this event at length, would tell me as an encore that his son, in the one single room their dwelling boasted – this fact would be held up to me, time and time again – was studying to be a teacher without allowing himself to be distracted by chit-chat. 'You see: now that's what I call pluck,' she would then say. I knew that, even if our house were made up of ten rooms, I would never be able to learn anything. Each time the man came to us, I was allowed to see the stump of thumb and feel it. He would always come alone. 'He has a fool of a wife,' my mother would say regularly. Over and over, she would tell how, through some prolapse or other, this woman had got a very large paunch for which a medical corset had been prescribed. Because she went out to work daily and the corset impeded her, she had not worn the corset for more than a day. 'When she's washing the floor, her stomach hangs down to the ground,' my mother related. 'And she's thirty-four years old. Isn't that dreadful?')

She impressed the accident with the thumb upon me once more at length. 'You mustn't go about in the cold, not in any circumstance,' she repeated emphatically. When a mild frost set in, she even wished me to stay inside all weekend, but a solution was found in the end: from pale-blue flannel she made a little protective cover for the bandage, with two ribbons tied round the wrist. I would now go out into the garden again for hours.

I did not complete the chopping implement: the parts, wrapped in newspaper, I put away in the box room. The water in the glass vase had frozen: the fish were stuck, rigid, in the middle, close to the surface inside the clump of ice: the vase itself had cracked. I studied the fish closely. 'They're magicians,' I said out loud, "course I know that.' I buried the vase, with all that was inside it, as deeply as possible. 'They can't come up any more,' I thought. It had turned Saturday already.

In the afternoon I made my way to Werther's house. It was freezing a little but there wasn't a breath of wind. Standing in the porch, I didn't ring the bell immediately but studied the green painted door. Above the little nameplate which read 'J. Nieland', there was a circular enamel sign with a five-armed, green star surrounded by the inscription *Esperanto Parolata*. I listened at the letter box but heard nothing other than the rustle of silence. The draught brushing my face conveyed a vague, indeterminate scent I believed never to have smelled before; it reminded me of new curtains, matting or upholstery, but with something unknown mixed in. 'This scent is made by magic power and is kept in a bottle,' I said inwardly. I rang the bell.

A large woman with a broad, pale face answered the door. She remained standing at the top of the stairs without saying or asking a thing. 'This afternoon's Saturday afternoon,' I called out, 'and I could come. I've come for Werther.' The woman did not move but merely nodded a moment. I ascended the stairs. When I arrived at the top she still didn't say anything but only looked at me, searchingly.

She looked odd. Her wrinkled, oldish-looking face had a mouth which apparently was unable to close completely: coarse, yellow teeth remained visible. She had little eyes, like a chicken's or a pigeon's; these stared deep from their sockets and moved almost imperceptibly. The upper half of her head was surrounded by drab, fluffy hair.

'I'm Werther's mother,' she said suddenly, smiled, and all of a sudden she made a few tripping dance steps on the floor; I thought for a moment she'd tripped up, but this couldn't be the case. The landing was dusky, doors with yellow frosted glass opening out on to it. For an instant I thought the scent was being generated to stupefy me and lock me up in a chest.

'You've got a sore finger, I see,' she said. 'I'd better take off your coat carefully.' While she was helping me, she again made those strange steps. 'And who are you?' she asked. 'A friend of Werther's?' She caught hold of me by the neck. 'I'm Elmer; I could come this afternoon, Werther said so,' I said hoarsely. I couldn't go down any longer as Werther's mother was standing in front of the stairwell.

236

'Werther said that, did he now?' she said. 'I no longer have a say. You're naughty rascals. Are you naughty sometimes, too?' 'I don't know,' I said softly. 'You don't know, do you?' she asked, taking me by the shoulders, squeezing them and giving me a few mild slaps on my bum. Then she pushed me on ahead of her, into the kitchen.

Here, Werther was standing in front of the windows of the veranda door, looking out. With a little fork, he was eating bottled mussels from a dish. 'I'm Elmer; you know me, I was coming,' I said quickly. 'We had to build the windmill.'

The kitchen was very bare. There was only a small wooden table standing in it.

Without replying, Werther continued to spear mussels and eat them. 'Their little trunk-thingies are the nicest,' he said, holding up a mussel with a pale, trailing appendage. 'I eat them last.'

'Is his trunk-thingy the nicest?' his mother asked, who had remained standing at the kitchen door. 'And you eat it all? How mean. How would you like it if I ate the nicest bit of you?' She smiled and snorted. Werther stared at her for a moment and then he began to giggle.

Werther's mother gave me a fork. 'Have as many as you like,' she said. 'You can take off the trunk-thingy if you don't like it.' At this, Werther laughed loudly. I speared a mussel, but in bringing it up I twisted it round into a position that prevented a trail from hanging down and brought it quickly to my mouth. It didn't taste nice to me and I now focussed on fishing out bits of onion. His mother followed my movements.

'Werther, we've got to start on the windmill,' I said, for I wanted to get out on to the veranda. He did not reply. 'If there happens to be someone who's good at building windmills, you've got to make use of it,' I went on. 'It's stupid not to make a start in that case. Someone who knows a lot about windmills should become the leader at once.' I spoke softly because his mother was listening. Werther asked whether we could get down to some work on the veranda.

'You can't,' she said curtly. 'I don't want woodwork and mess there, what with all the muck you walk into the house.'

'When you've left the kitchen we'll do it anyway perhaps,' said Werther. 'Indeed?' she asked. 'Then you need to be punished bare-botty again, and your nice little friend too.' Werther produced the beginnings of a smile but then he looked down at the floor. His mother came towards me a little and said, loudly: 'Elmer,' – it surprised me that she had remembered my name so soon – 'they're *such* rascals: real scallywags, that's what they are.'

She took a piece of grubby white cardboard – presumably the bare left-overs of a calendar – from the fireplace, turned it over and in front of the window she began to decipher a text written down on it in ink. 'At the time, it has to be five years ago at least, I used to write down what they did, now and then,' she said. She then began to read out loud:

'While I'm in the kitchen I hear Werther in the garden. Quite so. He's there with Martha. He's on the swing. Then she wants to get on again, and when she's on it, he wants to get on again. Such teasing!'

'We were living in Tuindorp Oostzaan at the time,' she remarked by-the-by. 'Have you ever been there?' 'No, I've never been there but I do know where it is,' I said, carefully. She read on:

'There's snow everywhere so no shortage of pranks. They're terrible squabblers. Werther is the strongest, for Martha gets it rubbed in the most. She's made to taste defeat. I stand in the kitchen and I hear and see it all, though they don't think I do. I see it all, believe you me. Though they don't think I do, the little devils.'

Her eyesight had to be poor for she held the cardboard right up close to her eyes. She scoured ahead rapidly and continued:

'Now it's summer. Everything's in full flower. Werther's off to the swimming baths with Martha. Yesterday they did their swimming dry, in the bedroom. He was given a pair of swimming trunks, blue ones. Proud of them as anything, he was!'

Here the text appeared to have ended. Silence fell. Werther looked out. His mother put the cardboard back, halted for a moment, and all of a sudden she said as she looked at the table: 'I liked writing that down. It's handy 'cause you can read it again some time later.'

'When was this exactly?' I asked. 'Five years or so ago,' she replied.

'Yes,' I said, 'but doesn't it mention a day or date?' 'No,' she said, 'it's all completely for fun, of course. Only recently there was someone who said it had been very good to write that down. Who was it again, Werther?' He thought. All three of us were standing still.

'We're going inside,' she then said. She pushed us out ahead of her towards the adjoining room; there was nothing else in it except for a table with a ping-pong net and four little benches. I stood there for a moment, undecided, for I didn't know whether I was allowed to go on ahead into the room facing the street, the sliding doors of which were open; but a small man sitting there with his back towards us in a red, plush easy chair, gestured to us. He was Werther's father.

Only when he moved did I notice him. 'It's quite alright for the two of you to come and sit here, Werther,' he said, 'as long as you watch what you're doing a bit.' He had a gaunt, yellow face, lined and with drawn down eyebrows. His grey eyes looked tired or sad. He spoke as if reluctant, as if speaking wore him out. He had narrow shoulders. I calculated that he must be smaller than Werther's mother.

He was apparently doing nothing but think, for there was no book or newspaper lying on the little round table in front of him, nor was he smoking. I didn't know whether to shake his hand or not; I clumsily moved my feet a few times and then I sat down in one of the easy chairs. Werther went and stood by the window.

Whereas the room we had passed through was almost empty – only a thin scrap of matting lying on the floor there – this one was filled to overflowing: there were six side tables with lace doylies, at least, benches and foot stools; wherever this was possible, crocheted cushions had been put down. The wallpaper was dark and had a design of large, brown autumn leaves. There were eight wall lamps: two metal ones, two fretwork ones in the shape of a pointed hat and four cylindrical ones made of parchment painted with sailing ships. On the mantelpiece over the fire which made the doyly flutter because of the heat, among three gnomes, a shepherdess and a porcelain toadstool, stood a brass statue depicting a naked worker with a hammer across his shoulder. 'As long as you don't sit there scratching the armrests with your nails,' Werther's mother said. She went back to the kitchen.

'Are you at school with Werther?' his father asked. 'No,' I replied, 'I'm a friend I think.' At this moment the sun came out and sharply lit up his head and the thin neck that also turned out to be covered in lines. On his skull, in the hair cover, a sparse patch became visible of which the skin appeared to be scabby and inflamed. As I observed this, I got a feeling of hate and pity both at once.

Werther stepped back from the window. 'When I leave school

239

I'll be going to the literary-economic High School,' he said. 'What things do you learn there?'

'Many languages,' his father replied. 'Languages, mainly.' 'What sort of languages?' Werther went on asking. 'French, German, English,' was the man's short reply. His hands were moving on either side of his chair as if he wanted to begin plucking at the material. I saw that on the inside of the feet the leather uppers of his shoes were parting from the soles.

'And no Esperanto at all?' Werther asked. His father merely shook his head.

'And what kind of language is that,' I asked partly addressing Werther and partly his father. The latter straightened himself and looked at me severely. 'Do you really want to know or are you just curious?' he asked. 'If you're really interested, I don't mind telling you.' 'Yes, I'd really love to know about it,' said I.

He looked at me again, hesitating a moment. 'In the previous century,' he then said, 'in 1887, if you want to know exactly, a very great man − I don't mean in the sense of being tall, but plucky, very learned − he made a language out of a whole lot of other languages. Werther, you know who that was alright.'

'Zadelhof,' said Werther. 'Doctor Zamenhof,' corrected his father. 'Louis Lazarus Zamenhof. If you're interested, I can tell you lots more about him. He was a man who lived in Byalystok, in Russian Poland. No less than four, five languages were spoken there. And he decided to put an end to that confusion of tongues and so he compiled Esperanto, the world language. He took something from all languages. 'And' is 'Kai' − there's an example for you. 'Kai' was taken from the Greek. That's how he did it.'

'That sign with the star, on the door, that's about this,' Werther said.

'When someone from some foreign country or other comes here and he's learned Esperanto, then we can talk to one another and we understand each other,' his father went on. 'That's the great work of Doctor Zamenhof.' He fell silent a moment.

'But there are still too few people who are prepared to put their shoulder to the wheel,' he now said, half to himself, pondering. 'For, all too often I run into acquaintances who ask me something about it from time to time. But when I say: you must go and learn that language then they don't. They think it's too difficult to learn those words, they say.'

He let his hands rest between his knees and peered at the carpet.

'Would you like to learn?' he suddenly asked me. 'I don't know,' I replied. 'I don't know if I could.' 'You don't have to start immediately,' he said, 'but if I give you a brochure – that's a kind of little book – to take away with you, you'd be able to understand that, wouldn't you?' 'I don't know,' I said. 'That isn't Esperanto,' he pressed on, 'but it tells of how that Doctor Zamenhof thought it up. That's very interesting. I'll give you one to take away with you later on; but will I get it back? It has to be paid for normally, when someone buys it – fifteen cents.' For a moment it seemed as if he was going to get up to look for it but he continued to sit there.

'We're going to play ping-pong,' Werther said. He took me along to the room we had passed through, pulled out the leaves of the table and took the bats and the ball from a cupboard. 'I don't know how it goes,' I said. He explained the rules to me but I only listened superficially and peered out to one side: on a veranda on the opposite side of the gardens a big alsatian was walking to and fro, barking occasionally and persistently poking his head between the balusters; doing so, he would get stuck and, whining, would wrench himself loose again. I realised that he couldn't go anywhere and couldn't even jump over the balustrade because his run-up would be too short.

We began to play. Werther's father had continued to sit there the way we had found him.

When we had been at it a while, Werther's mother came in from the kitchen. She went and stood next to the table and followed the ball with her eyes. When she had done this a little while she began to make grabbing gestures but she didn't snatch it, just. 'Mother, you're ruining the game completely,' Werther said. Instantly, his mother stayed her hand and regarded him with a staring gaze. 'You look nice when you play so fervently,' she said; 'you're quite a pretty little boy really. Or a pretty boy, we'd better say.' At these words, Werther stopped playing and quickly looked at his father in the front room. He was still sitting motionless, his back towards us. The ball dropped behind Werther on the ground. His mother picked it up quickly and pretended to walk away with it. Pressed by Werther, she put it back down on the table again, however.

'Something like that's fun,' she said to me. 'I like pranks just as much as you two do. When we used to play outside, we'd make such fools of ourselves! You didn't think so, did you? I could have fun like nobody's business, I could. I'm mentally young, you know.'

She took away my bat and assumed my place. 'Now me against you, Werther' she said. She did quick shakes with her upper torso, as though she was listening to music.

They began to play. Having missed the ball four times, she tossed the bat on to the table though the match had not ended yet. 'Werther's the champion,' she said. 'Congratulations.' She stepped up to him with outstretched hand but when he wanted to grasp it she made a feint, passing his hand, and she grabbed him in his crotch for a moment. He giggled and jumped away. 'You're the lovely Werther,' she said. He had jumped towards the sliding doors and was looking at his father. The latter turned his head. 'Did you hear that?' he asked. 'What was that, father,' Werther asked in a frightened voice, 'I didn't hear a thing.'

There was a moment of silence. Werther's mother took up the bat and swung it airily to and fro, as if she was conducting the music. I looked down at the floor. 'The chest is opening up,' I thought.

Outside, a kind of bellowing yowl resounded. From time to time its pitch would rise. For a moment I thought it was a low siren but then I realised it had to be a voice. 'It's here in front, in the street,' Werther's father said. He got up. We all walked over to the window.

On the pavement along the municipal garden stood a thin man with a dark-green, hairy coat. He had a bony, weathered face displaying an embittered expression. In his right hand he held a large, tin loud-hailer: a megaphone, I knew. We had only just arrived at the window when he put it to his mouth and let out a long drawn out, deep noise that sounded like 'Hoo!'. He twisted his head slowly from side to side. Thereupon he cried out: 'War draws near. Be on your guard!' He left instantly at a fast walking pace and disappeared round the corner.

I didn't know whether I should laugh or keep a sorry silence. I did realise that it must be impossible to understand all that happened and that there were things that remained mysterious, causing a fog of fear to arise.

'It's that potty Verfhuis chap,' Werther said. 'The one who lives on the Onderlangs.' His mother shook her head with a pitying expression. 'It's a morbid inclination,' she said, 'a morbid inclination.' Werther's father said nothing and went and sat in his place again.

A potent fear came over me, that he would go and find that booklet now. (I believed he would then read something from it to me and, if I didn't understand, seal me into a barrel or a sack.)

'We should go to the kitchen,' I said softly to Werther. 'I have to speak with you urgently, alone.' We made our way there. Silence reigned; only the gas beneath a kettle hissed quietly. Almost no sound from outside penetrated either.

'I have made several discoveries,' I said. 'It's alright to tell you. If you come along to my house now I can show you things that are very important. I also have a burial vault that's real.' I desired to get out of his house as quickly as possible. He assented but first he wanted to go and say that he was leaving.

'You mustn't do that,' I said emphatically, ''cause it's a secret. That's how enemies could come to hear of it and they'll start to follow us then.'

Without a sound, we descended the stairs and hurried away. Back at my place we first sauntered round the garden. The slight wind made the shrubs rustle almost inaudibly. We went and hung from a branch of the laburnum until it broke off and we planted it upright in the soil. Then Werther asked where the burial vault was. I took him to the box room where we went and sat on an old mat and draped jute sacking in front of the entrance so nobody would be able to look in. 'This is the burial vault of Deep Death,' said I. Werther said nothing and looked listlessly into the half light. 'We have to found the club,' I said. 'Then we can make burial vaults. For they're much needed.'

All of a sudden I remembered that I had found a dead starling the previous day which I had hidden under leaves in a corner of the garden. 'We have to go outside,' I said, 'the ceremony's about to begin.' We sought out the dead creature after which I made a wood fire. On this I burned the body from which foaming brown juices bubbled up. A charred lump was what was left, smelling strangely; I put it in a boat-shaped date box. In a little earth mound I raised quickly, I dug a blind tunnel, the walls of which I reinforced with bits of wood: I slid the box inside; having sealed the opening I sprinkled the top of the mound with fine coal ash. 'The secret bird has gone into the earth,' I sang inwardly. I repeated this sentence many times but dared not utter it out loud.

'We must found the club,' I said once more. 'If we wait too long with it there'll be enemy clubs already; you know that too.' Again I had him come along to the box room where I now lit a candle.

Then I wrote our names down in an old pocket diary I had brought out from underneath the chest. 'Now the club exists,' I said, having read out our names slowly. 'It's called the Burial Vault Club, the B.V.C. Everyone who's a member, in his garden we can make a burial vault. That's very important.'

'You understand, of course,' I continued, 'that someone has to be the boss who, for instance, says when there's a meeting. Best to be someone at whose place the club has been founded.' Werther nodded but I didn't believe that he was listening attentively. I got up and went and leant against the wall.

'I'm the chairman,' I said, 'that's already been written down. You're the secretary but that has to remain a secret. You'll become secretary of course, but the chairman does everything that needs to be done: it's always like that.' Werther now asked whether the club would only concern itself with the making of burial vaults.

'Club members also make windmills,' I said, 'this has a lot to do with burial vaults, as of course you understand.'Cause the one who can make a burial vault, who thought of it first, he's also the boss of the mills. If there's someone who wants to mess up the club, his prick'll be cut off. Let me tell you exactly what kind of club it'll be.'

I, however, no longer knowing what else to say, looked for old shoe laces, divided them between us and lit them. Having blown them out we sniffed the smell they continued to spread, smouldering. I blew out the candle so that by swinging our arms about we were able to make fiery lines and circles that produced a faintly purple light in the dark: for a good while we continued to sit there lost in thought. I felt sad. 'We should go to the sand,' Werther said. He was going to meet Dirk.

We went on our way, the three of us.

When we reached the plain behind the dike, the wind had risen slightly, blowing little clouds of dust along from time to time. As we made our way, we jumped in and out of potholes during which we searched for objects the diggers might have left behind but there was never anything more than an insignificant plank or a half buried newspaper.

When we reached a generous pit, quite deep, I requested them to join me and sit down inside it. It was cold; the wind pushed a puff of sand into our hair. 'This is the first meeting of the club,' I said. 'The chairman is going to make a speech.' I waited a moment. 'Dirk, you have to say something and then yield the floor to me,' I said, "cause you're to be the assistant secretary.' He, however, said nothing and plucked at the roots of some grass. Again some sand was blown on to our heads. 'You can become assistant secretary,' I went on, 'I can see to that. It stays a secret of course because the chairman does everything that needs to be done. You must now yield the floor to the chairman.' He remained silent. I now addressed my request to Werther. 'Elmer, go and make your speech,' he said.

I got up and began: 'Honourable members. The club has been founded. It's called the B.V.C . . . So there's a club but that's not all there is to it, not by a long chalk. It must not become a club of which we're merely members; it must be a club with clout. A dormant membership is no earthly good to us. And members who, when the chairman asks them to say something, don't: they're a complete waste of time. They'd better resign.'

'We should pull a tree down over there,' Dirk said, pointing at the municipal gardens behind him. He took a long strong piece of rope from his pocket.

'You're an enemy of the club,' I said. 'You must be bound.' We grabbed hold of him, cast the noose, already present in the rope, round his ankles and dragged him around in circles. He held forth in a tearful voice that we should let him go free, instead of which we clambered from the pit and pulled him by the rope over the edge. Because the rope was cutting into his skin, he now began to cry terribly so that we let go of him and ran away. When it turned out he wasn't coming after us, we began to amble along normally and continued our way across the bare plain.

'It's his own fault,' I said. 'He wants to mess up the club 'cause he's the spy; this happens frequently, that someone first behaves as if he wants to join the club and then goes and tells everything to the enemy.'

We now arrived at a boggy bit of land which we called the wilderness. Here, in a shallow brown little stream that seemed to well up from the earth and which ran through a pool with reeds into a ditch, we made a dam from stones causing a dirty little waterfall. Then we tore it down again and, hidden behind elder bushes, we threw the stones at little flocks of sparrows until we hit one. It was impossible to tell whose throw it was. Though the bird seemed to have been crushed, it turned out, once Werther had pushed the stone away from it, still to be trembling slightly. We kept looking at it glumly. 'This is the secret bird of the spies' club,' I said, "cause they've founded one. They're very wicked; they don't dare to do anything themselves and they send birds to collect letters.'

We stayed and waited in order to take the creature with us to be burned once it was dead, but the movements wouldn't stop. In the end I quickly built a little pyre from bits of old reeds and asked Werther to lay the creature upon it. 'This is the punishment for spying when our club's building waterfalls,' I said, once Werther had acceded to my request. I lit the little pyre but the flames went out each time. In the end all my matches were finished and we left it behind, smouldering. The light was already fading to dusk. We walked along in silence in dejected mood.

In the vicinity of Werther's house we entered a little grocer's shop where Werther bought some licorice. I wanted to wait outside at first but he urged me to come with him. It was dark inside and it smelled of damp earth.

While we waited for someone to come to the front, I became convinced that a trapdoor must be hidden behind the counter, giving access to an extensive subterranean space. Here the earth creatures lived who crept along between the tree roots that served as pillars. Without Werther seeing it I held on with both hands to a rod that ran along the counter, so I wouldn't suddenly be dragged below ground without being able to resist.

At last a pale little woman with grey hair came forward who went to count out the licorice. 'Excuse me please, excuse me,' Werther suddenly asked in a slow, stupid voice. 'How do they actually make licorice?' The woman said she didn't know.

'They make licorice from special flour,' I said. 'And from herbs that grow under trees: those are actually the most important, 'cause there's only a little bit of flour in it.' In fact, I hadn't a clue as to its manufacture. 'I think it's odd, you not even knowing that,' I went on. 'You're quite a dunce really.'

When we got outside I said: 'You can stay in the club if you know a lot. You'll have to get out otherwise. Members who are stupid are no good to us at all.' We sucked the licorice and trundled on with no clear plan. 'We must see to it that it becomes a good club,' I added, dully.

We reached the shelter at the terminus of the bus route. Here we went and sat shivering on the muddy floor and remained silent a good while. Finally, in order to say something, I asked how old his sister was. 'She'll be nine,' he said. The wind had increased slightly and slipped rustling past the wooden walls.

'I've got a brother and he's run away from home,' I said: 'he's on a ship.' Once I had assured myself of the fact that Werther was listening, I went on: 'He's just as old as I am.' Werther now asked why he had run away.

'It's quite a story,' I replied, 'and a very sorry one.' I waited a moment.

'I've never told anyone before,' I continued, 'but I don't mind telling you, but you mustn't tell anybody.' This he promised. 'Fine,' I said, 'but if I tell you and you give it away then you'll be cut to death – you understand that don't you?' He nodded. 'It's really too late to tell it all now,' I said, 'for the afternoon rushes to an end: darkness is falling already.' (These last eleven words I remembered as having read them somewhere.)

'That brother was a real rotter,' I began, ''cause he always acted mean. He's cut off fishes' heads. And then my mother locked him up in the cellar. He climbed out through the window when it was dark. He took almost noth'n with him, just the blankets from his bed.' I waited for a moment and added:

'D'you think I enjoy telling you something like this? Then you're mistaken. It's something really bad. That's why I'm so sad this afternoon. D'you know his name?'

Once again I waited a moment. I couldn't think of a name off-hand. 'He's called André,' I then said. 'And the ship's the Prosper: that means they sail forwards.' (I had read the name on a dredger.) 'He's sailing far, far away but when he comes home he'll bring back an animal and that's for me.'

A bus driver chased us from the shelter. We ambled to my house. 'André once brought me back a parrot,' I said, 'which he'd bought. It would say anything you did. But it died. All animals die anyway.'

Having reached my house I invited him to the box room again. 'There's going to be a big festive gathering of the club at my place,' I said: 'we need to discuss that.' When we were sitting on the mat behind the jute sacking once more and I had lit the candle again, I said: 'It's really, really bad what happened to my brother then, but one mustn't always be sad. This is why the club is having a festive gathering tomorrow afternoon at my place. I'll prepare a wow of a programme. You must see to it you're on time, otherwise you run the chance of arriving and it's already started. I'll be making a big speech.'

'Can Martha come along?' he asked. 'That would be possible,' I said slowly, in a grave tone of voice. 'We might make her a prospective member; she can become a proper member later on then.'

247

Mute silence flowed in; the cold was making us stiff. 'I'll show you the photograph of that brother,' I said and I requested him to wait while I went inside.

In the living room where dusk was already settling, my mother was sitting near the window, snoozing. Carefully, I took the frame in which a mass of little photographs had been arranged behind glass from the wall. In doing so I lightly knocked both the blown eggs hanging on either side from thin wires. (These were a large white ostrich egg and a smaller, black egg of an emu. Each time there was some horseplay or something was being thrown, my mother would cry: 'Mind the ostrich egg! Mind the egg of the emu!')

On my way to the box room I chose a small image of a boy on bare feet beside a large dog, in a kind of park. (I didn't know who it was.) 'This is André,' I said, 'this is that brother I've had so much sorrow over and still have now.' Werther inspected the photo thoroughly but then he also began to study the others. 'They've got nothing to do with it,' I said and snatched the frame roughly from his hands. Doing so, I banged it against the doorpost so that a crack appeared in the glass, in the corner. I said nothing and returned the photos to their place in the same unnoticed way I had taken them in.

On leaving, Werther declared he would be coming next day. I did not accompany him further on his way than the exit to the garden and took my leave, mumbling.

Until meal time, out of the mat from the box room, I built a tent at the edge of the garden, up against the neighbours' bicycle shed; in the middle I planted a heavy concrete block in the soil.

'This is the centre of the temple,' I said softly. I set down an old, cracked casserole on the block and made a little wood fire inside it, slipping into reverie as I did so. A lot of smoke developed. I took the old blue cover of an exercise book, smoothed it out and, having gone and sat down in the tent, I wrote on it in chalk: 'To André, who's a brother. On the ship, On Board that is. They must give him this letter'. I rolled up the sheet and cast it into the flames.

Now something strange happened: in the adjacent garden, footsteps approached and halted right next to the tent. I put the lid on the casserole. There was some mumbling and immediately following that a bucket of water was tipped out on to the tent. I sat there quite motionless and didn't make a sound. The water did not come in but ran down in noisy streams. Then the footsteps removed themselves, a handle rattled and a door closed. I thought it possible that the casting into the fire of the letter and the crashing down of the water enjoyed a magical connection but I could not understand it. Until I was called to have my meal I continued to sit there, shivering. 'He stinks,' my brother said when I was sitting at the table: 'He's just like a ruddy bloater. He only does filthy things. It has to be filthy or else he won't do it.'

I spent the next day decorating our bedroom. I fixed branches of Christmas trees I had brought in off the street to the wall with drawing pins and braided them with strips of white paper. Then I was going to install the wire for the lights.

A good while back already I had been allowed to buy a sixty cents doorbell transformer but until now I had not been allowed to use it because my mother didn't trust the device. I was now allowed to on condition that I showed it beforehand to an acquaintance in the neighbourhood, a small, hunchbacked tailor called Rabbijn: he had the reputation of being knowledgeable on the subject of electricity. 'Yes, that's an ordinary transformer,' he said at once, but he held me up a long time, telling me how the poles had to be connected even though this was clearly marked on the bakelite casing. His wife, who was racked with rheumatism and could barely move her swollen fingers any more, looked at the device with her poor eyesight and said: 'You shouldn't play pranks with such things.'

Her husband now asked me whether I knew that there were people who took the covers from electric sockets and held their fingers to the poles for fun.

At the same time he told of what had happened to him a few days previous. In his work room, which looked out on to the garden, he had fixed up all kinds of loose wiring which hung like washing lines around the room. One late afternoon, while he was cutting, holding up the cloth to get some good light on it, he had cut through the wire connecting the lamp. A bang and a flame had occurred; he had received a violent shock and a short-circuit had been caused instantly. Neighbours in the adjacent garden had come rushing in and had described the light phenomenon as being a 'blue spurt of fire'. He himself was convinced that a layer of worn lacquer on the eyes of the scissors had saved his life for him.

On returning home I fixed up the transformer and connected three bicycle lamps to it which I allowed to be half hidden by the fir branches. On a piece of cardboard I drew in coloured crayon: 'Join the B.V.C.' and hung it among the greenery. Finally I switched on the current. Then I asked my father to come and have a look.

A hand in his pocket, he looked round with a mocking expression curled round his mouth. 'What's the B.V.C.?' he asked. 'That's a secret which only the members know,' I said in apparent triumph but in fact depression had taken me in its grip. It had begun to thaw and it was raining lightly.

At the table on the landing I went and wrote a programme that ran as follows: '1. Meeting opened by the chairman. 2. The chairman welcomes those present and explains the purpose of the meeting.'

I couldn't think of anything else after this. For a long time I continued to sit staring in the half light. In the end I added: '3. Speech in which the points to be touched upon are: a. a club with clout; b. no dormant membership; c. nobody may act funny to members or to the chairman; d. a department will be instituted for building and technology, primarily for mills that run on wind; the head of this is called the mill-wright: he has to be someone who has built many mills before.' I made a neat copy of everything and rolled up the paper. Then I surveyed the decorations and the burning lights. Silence was all around; occasionally the voices of children in the street or the barking of a dog would penetrate, as if only from a distance: it was as though the grey sky, like dull felt, dampened all the racket.

It was past three o'clock when Werther and his sister arrived. She was a pale, podgy little girl with a flattened face. She wore a knitted dress of orange wool that emphasised the cumbrousness of her figure even more clearly. She spoke in a whisper almost, after which she would burst out giggling time and again. We went and sat on the beds in the bedroom.

I had switched off the lighting in advance but now I lit it all of a sudden. Martha said: 'O-oh'; Werther looked round, silent and indifferent.

I got up, went and stood behind a table and unfolded my piece of paper. 'I hereby declare the great festive gathering of the B.V.C. *open*,' I said. With a ruler I banged a few times on the table. 'Come in,' Martha said and began to giggle. 'Isn't Dirk coming?' Werther asked. 'I think not,' I replied, curtly.

'As chairman I welcome the esteemed members and the prospective member,' I said. 'Hi-de-hi,' said Werther. 'Let me set out the purpose of this meeting,' I went on. 'It's not the intention that our club should only have afternoon parties: we shall have to have other meetings, about serious things. We must end up with a good, strong club, a club with clout. Dormant members we can do without. Members who are just members but otherwise only make mugs out of everyone, are a waste of time. The next issue I wish to speak on is the fact that there are members who act funny to club members or to the chairman. That's not on. Esteemed members! A department is to be instituted for building and technology, primarily for mills that run on wind. The head of this is called the mill-wright: he has to be someone who has built many mills before. Or someone very good at installing electric wires for lights 'cause that's got something to do with it. That's what I had to say,' I concluded, scrunched up the paper and went and sat next to Werther. 'The afternoon meeting has begun,' I said vaguely.

Half a minute past during which no one said anything. 'When does it begin?' Werther asked. 'Only a few members have turned up,' I replied. 'It's a shame to perform the entire programme for just the few attending.' Werther now proposed picking up Dirk. The three of us went to his house.

He answered the door himself and halted, standing silent in the doorway. 'I shall address you,' I said. 'A while ago we were on the dike and some less pleasant things took place,' I started off. 'It would not be profitable at this point to work out who's the guilty party,' I went on. 'But this afternoon we're having a tremendous club party at my place. Of course you understand that the assistant secretary cannot stay away: the entire committee must be there. It's going to be a splendid afternoon which will live in our memories for a long time to come. I shall also be making a stunning speech.'

After some persuasion he came with us. When we'd arrived back upstairs my mother brought tea and sugar frosted biscuits. After we had drunk tea a silence fell that seemed never to end. I stepped up to the window and looked at the sky. Unheeded I went downstairs to look for my brother. 'We're sitting upstairs and we haven't got a programme,' I said. 'Won't you play something on your mandolin?' 'No,' he said. 'But we haven't got a programme!' I said emphatically. 'No,' he repeated, 'I won't do it.' I continued to press him for a good while but he stuck to his refusal.

When I arrived back in the bedroom it turned out someone had opened the deep cupboard. I had locked it but had left the key in the door. I used the cupboard for two purposes: because it was so dark and quiet, I wielded my member there, or I kneaded little pots, jugs and ashtrays from modelling clay which were left there to dry. A bright light without a shade lit the small space so I could close the door behind me completely. (Most times I would lock it from the inside.)

They had all forced their way in and had brought out pots in order to look at them in daylight. 'We won't break them,' Werther said. He studied the base of an ashtray on which he had discovered the inscription T.A.P.F. 'What does that mean, *Tapf*?' he asked. It was an abbreviation of The Antiquity Pottery Factory, but I didn't dare to say this.

'They're just letters,' I replied. 'But I see the same ones each time,' he insisted, for he was having a look at the base of the other objects too.'Quite possible,' I said. 'But we'd better put everything away again.'

They were showing signs of putting the items back again when Werther dropped a little pot that fell to bits, unrecognisable, with lots of powder forming in the process. 'That's a pity,' he said and stood there looking at it. I began to pace to and fro, fretfully. When everything had been put back in its place again I locked the cupboard, put the key in my pocket and went and sat on the bed. Again a silence forced its way into the room.

'We're going out again now,' I said and switched off the lights. We stomped down the stairs and sidled in silence to the front door. 'I've still got some homework to do,' I said dully. They halted just beyond the doorway. 'You'd better go away now,' I said, 'I'm staying here. You've got horrid habits.'

Dirk went off to his house but Werther and his sister continued to stand there. Without a word, I thumped him hard, which made him cry out; I then quickly jumped inside again and shut the door with a bang.

In the empty bedroom I stood at the window a long time. Needles rained down sparsely from the fir branches. 'The silence sails like a ship,' I thought.

It was raining next day. In the afternoon, after school, I found a note in the letter box that proved to be from Werther. The text ran: 'Elmer. Don't bother coming to my place any more. You thump because you're mean. The club's finished because I don't want to any more. Werther'. It had been written in pencil on half a sheet from an exercise book.

At once, I called Dirk to come outside and showed him the paper but moved it about and kept it exactly at a distance he would just not be able to read from. 'This's something secret that's just arrived,' I said. 'It's a letter. We must have a meeting at once.'

We made our way to the box room. Here I let him read the text. 'As a good member of the club you've understood, of course, what the matter is here,' I said. 'He's a frightful spy. He has stolen into the club to tell all to the enemy: that's how he wants to smash the club. He's been at it a while already. He has gone and opened a cupboard at the chairman's to chuck nice things to bits. That was to muck up the club. We have to bury the list of members in a secret place.'

Dirk continued to peer at the note but said nothing. While reading he picked with nonchalant motions at a scab on his knee.

'Did you know a club with two members is a very good thing?' I asked. 'It's really even better than three members.' Dirk dropped the note and felt along the ground until he had found an empty treacle tin; he tried to lift its lid with his nails. All of a sudden I began to hate him.

'You have to be got rid of too,' I said. 'You've been put up to things as well; I can see that clear as anything. You, too, want the club to end. From now on you're suspended.' Dirk said nothing and went on messing with the tin. I got up.

'You've got to get out of the meeting,' I said. 'If you want to get into the club again — but that's very difficult — then you must send the chairman a letter and beg forgiveness. Would you do that?'

I left him no opportunity to reply but began to kick him, holding back. 'You just ruin everything,' I said. When he didn't get up, I drew him upright by his arms and pushed him outside. I watched him go as he trundled off in silence.

It wasn't raining any more but the atmosphere was damp; there was no wind though banks of mist slid past slowly above the houses. I went back into the box room. On a piece of cardboard I wrote: 'There are enemies of the club everywhere'. I buried it, folded up tiny, in a shallow spot which I marked with an elder branch I had picked.

I no longer spoke with Dirk and Werther for some time. Because the cold weather wouldn't go away, I no longer visited the box room but made my way frequently to the loft. Here I would sit on my own for long periods at a stretch. I called the space 'The Enchanted Castle' and nailed a cardboard sign to the door bearing those words drawn on it in crayon.

On a Wednesday afternoon I once let in a little grey cat that had been sitting in the rain on the roof, coughing. I locked the creature up in the drawer of a large cabin trunk and left it there for hours. When I opened the drawer again, the bottom, pasted with floral wallpaper, was soiled with sticky slime. I threw the animal back on to the roof across which, coughing in spasms, it disappeared from view. 'It has coughed and must therefore be tormented,' I said out loud, watching the cat go through one of the little windows I would often stand looking out at to think the while.

If I had nothing to do I would keep myself occupied in the loft shattering the soft plaster on the wall, hacking at it with an axe. I would become sad each time and, if I had my glass cutter on me, I would try to scratch my name into a little window pane but this failed most of the time; I would go outside again then.

In the street behind ours, in a house the back garden of which bordered ours, a boy called Maarten Scheepmaker had come to live. When he had been living there only a little while, I was busy making a fire one afternoon. He approached and asked whether I was allowed to. That was how we got to know one another. I could visit him at his home.

He was the same age as I, but smaller and stouter. He went about dressed very slovenly, and he didn't have his lank, greasy hair cut short enough. He already had a thin moustache as well. He bore a strong body odour which I ascribed to the fact that he went about as heavily dressed indoors as he did in the street and kept his scarf knotted round his neck too. I liked visiting him for he had strange, noteworthy habits.

In his little room facing the street crossbones hung from thin wires at shoulder height, and beneath a glass bell-jar, on a tuft of white cotton wool, lay the breasts struck off from a pink porcelain woman's statue: its ruined remains were lying in a box beside it. Around and above his bed, in the middle of the room, he had made a canopy from cloths and carpets and the walls were pasted with panoramas that had been cut out of magazines and picture postcards of sunsets above mountain landscapes.

Except for the bed and a single chair there was no furniture in the room because all the remaining space was taken up by junk one had to pick one's way through: he liked to tinker and build.

I regarded him as an inventor. At a time when I'd only recently known him, he told me one afternoon that it was possible to catch a lot of fish in the ring canal by causing an explosion under water. In my presence, he prepared a complicated machine consisting of an old cocoa tin in which two nails he had magnetised had been mounted; spanning the two tips was a chain of iron filings. An electric wire had been connected to each of the nails which, well insulated, left the tin in such a manner that there was no surrounding space remaining which water or air could penetrate. He had first poured a thick layer of a potassium chloride and sugar mixture on the bottom of the tin.

'That's one of the biggest exploders,' he said.

His intention, once he had submerged it in the water, was to transmit electricity from a battery which had to set the iron filings aglow after which the charge would ignite. We were ready with our preparations when his mother came in.

She was a small, ugly woman with a tired face and drab, shapeless hair. At first I had thought her dangerous but she was amiable. She had heard us talk of our plan and she expressed her concern over it. 'What am I to say at Elmer's when you have been hauled off?' she asked. 'D'you know a number of people have been shot for things like that?' She forbad the execution of the plan and left the room again.

I could not understand her pronouncement but, repeating the words to myself, I felt an oppressive gloom rising. I no longer desired the plan to go ahead. 'We'd better do something else,' I said. 'A club needs founding, for that matter, perhaps you know that too. That's very important. Then we'll stay here and found it at once.'

I spoke these sentences softly but hurriedly while looking Maarten cautiously in the face. 'The chairman has to be someone who's already made clubs before,' I said: 'he'll appoint a maker at once. That's someone who's good at building things. He makes all kinds of things for the committee and the chairman, things they can keep. He must also make a lamp that can't go out.' (I believed it possible that such a thing existed.)

Maarten didn't appear to be listening. 'Perhaps you don't like a club,' I said knowingly, 'but that was just the same with me, too.' Without saying a word, Maarten inspected the tin. He declared he wanted the explosion to go ahead.

At dusk we went to the water's edge with all the necessaries.

When he connected the power, nothing happened however. Hauling it up, only the electric wires surfaced: the tin with all the components had disappeared. I showed myself to be disappointed and put forth my conclusion that the assembly had been poor so that everything had worked loose before the power had been connected. Maarten, however, asserted enthusiastically that the explosion had most definitely occurred but had taken place at great depth so that the gasses had condensed and dissolved before they were able to reach the surface. He spattered as he spoke and wiped saliva from his chin for he was dribbling with excitement.

For a moment I began to doubt whether the machine had ignited or not; again, however, I reached the conclusion that this hadn't happened but I did not want to say it anew. I concerned myself with the question whether Maarten believed his own explanation. Whether or not this was the case I could not ascertain but I understood that in either case there would have to be misery.

We retraced our steps; Maarten asked me to come inside with him but I said goodbye. In the loft I began to draw up a document. At the top of the paper I wrote: 'The new club Maarten must join. He has to become a member'. I continued to sit there thinking but couldn't think of anything else to write down. I folded the paper up and put it in a flat cardboard box; I hid this under a roofing tile next to one of the roof lights.

On another occasion, a Saturday afternoon, Maarten presented me with the possibility of manufacturing a rocket. He still had a little aircraft bomb made of wood lying about somewhere; it had been painted silver and had four fins at the rear; it was a toy from way back.

He drilled a hollow in the rear part into which he hammered a tube. This he filled with the same mixture as had been used in the previous experiment; to prevent it running out, he sealed it by sticking a paper disc to it through which he threaded cotton yarn soaked in methylated spirit.

'Does it go at once with a bang or does it first begin to hiss?' I asked. 'Both,' he replied. 'It's bound to go some twenty-eight metres or so into the sky, or even more.'

In the garden we built a pedestal from a few bricks; it ended up on the paving behind the kitchen. He set the rocket down on its tail fins, nose in the air, and put a little ball of paper underneath which, with a serious face, he lit; then we stepped back circumspectly.

The flame reached the fuse and the charge, and fire began to shoot from the tube, hissing. The rocket tipped over, continued to hiss a moment and then fell silent. Some smoke spiralled up, dispersing rapidly. 'It's empty,' I said. Maarten picked it up. A grey-blue, white-edged scorch mark had appeared on the paving stones.

'There was just enough force to make it fall over,' I said, but Maarten didn't agree with this. 'It was caught on something,' he declared with certainty. He maintained, and stuck to it, that both when standing upright as well as when it had ended up lying down, the bomb had been held back by something which had prevented it from taking off. I did not believe this but I didn't wish to say so.

'Let's fill it up once more and then set it off again,' I said, but he rejected this proposal. 'I have to check everything properly first,' he said self-importantly.'Besides, it has to cool down too. Or did you think it didn't get hot inside?'

He had taken no precautions whatsoever to keep the experiment a secret so that his father who had come to the backroom window had seen everything. He didn't come outside however and didn't even make a single gesture. He was a fat, heavy man with puffy cheeks and bags under his eyes; he had short, bristly hair. I thought he resembled an old mouse from a story book I still possessed. He stared, dreamy and abstracted, into the gardens.

It was late in the afternoon and it was already getting dark. In vain I tried to stave off the sadness that was approaching.

Maarten inspected the rear of the bomb and picked at it. I longed to trip him up or to destroy something of his clothing: he would then, so I thought, begin to cry in an almost soundless manner.

With the announcement that I had to eat, I left and made my way to the loft where I continued to hack at the wall with as little noise as possible. I scraped the grit into a little mound; I began to hack away with a purpose and made a hole which I excavated with a piece of iron. Then I inscribed an old suitcase label with my name and date and I stuck it, rolled up, into the opening. Finally, I wanted to stuff the hole with an old newspaper. As I was tearing it to pieces I ran into a death notice, some lines of which I read mechanically. The final sentence, before the signatories, ran: 'He has accomplished his long pilgrimage'. I had to think about this a long time. Inwardly, I repeated the words slowly and began to sing the lines softly. I tore out the notice, chewed it up fine, and pushed the wad into the gap in the wall. Then I looked for the glass cutter but couldn't find it. While leaning my forehead against one of the little windows and stirring my member, I listened keenly to the sounds in the house. 'The day is full of signs,' I repeated continually, inwardly. I considered inviting Maarten up to the loft.

On another Saturday afternoon, we were sitting in his room. We hit on the plan to go and catch ducks in the park on the watercourse running alongside the cemetery. Few people went there in autumn and winter. Maarten turned out to have an air gun with which we could shoot darts or lead pellets but though they penetrated with ease a cardboard box we were firing at in practice, the weapon had no great reach. Maarten, however, was convinced that we could strike birds, other animals and even people with it, mortally so. 'You thought you couldn't shoot someone dead with this, did you?' he asked. 'It's not even that difficult. It just depends where you hit them.'

There were, he asserted, eight spots on the human body where a shot had a fatal outcome. I asked him which these were but he gave no answer to this. 'You can certainly aim a hundred metres off,' he said, 'and then it still has force.' We went to shoot an apple; the darts and pellets didn't pass right through the fruit but disappeared, barely damaging the peel, into the core where they were hard to find. I doubted the power of the weapon.

To gain some idea of the gun's possibilities we then began to shoot at each other according to rules we had agreed. Each standing on opposite sides of the room, we would aim at one another beneath the canopy: thus it was impossible to hit each other in the face. We used darts. By drawing lots, it fell to Maarten to fire the first shot.

He hit me in the middle of my chest. The dart, having pierced my clothes undamaged, struck a small, perfectly round speck in my flesh. It hardly bled and barely hurt at all. It brought me to anger, but I hid this.

I myself took a long time to aim but I knew that the shot would fail. I struck Maarten on the right half of his chest but even his skin had not been touched. When I walked up to him to investigate the result, the little projectile turned out to have been arrested by a pack of papers in his inside pocket. It *had* pierced almost all the pages. I gained the desire to take these papers from him and make him plead for their return, for I believed they contained secrets. I didn't touch them however.

In the evening, after dinner time, when darkness had fallen, we went on our way. I was allowed to bear the gun and wore it next to my bare skin.

The park, which wasn't surrounded by fences, lay before us, deserted. Because it had only been laid out a few years previous nothing had grown tall yet: we had an overview of the clumps of shrubs and low trees. It was drizzling.

We left the cinder path and walked across the edge of grass so our footsteps became almost inaudible.

Soon we reached a spot where scores of ducks were sitting hunched together on the shore. I cocked the gun and shot into the gathering. A few ducks were startled by the sound and made a few steps in the direction of the water but nothing else happened. I loaded a second dart and gave the gun to Maarten. At his shot all the birds fled quacking into the air. We searched on but there wasn't another duck anywhere. In the end we roamed around a bit to see whether something of interest might be found anywhere in the park but we didn't run into a thing.

'You can't shoot through a layer of feathers,' I said. I declared the undertaking, though pleasurable, to be useless. Maarten fought my arguments emphatically. He maintained that my shot had missed but that his had struck a duck in the chest at which little feathers had flown about. 'You saw it, didn't you?' he asked. 'That those feathers burst loose and flew up?' 'I didn't see it all that well,' I replied feebly; I knew it couldn't be true.

He now added to this that the stricken animal couldn't continue flying but would have to come down slowly, to bleed to death. Doubtless we would be able to find it next day, so his expectation ran. We walked back in silence.

I went along with him to his place. His parents were out. In his little room he didn't connect up the electric lamp but lit a candle. Then he took the fitting from the ceiling and connected an instrument to a lead that crackled and made blue sparks. He had brought it out from a chest. The moment it worked he blew out the candle after which we continued to watch in silence.

There were two meccano arms with carbon rods from an old battery at their ends; the rods had been brought close together; in between hovered a blue, rustling little flame. The whole thing had been mounted on a plank which Maarten set on the ground. He invited me to come and sit next to him on the edge of the bed to watch. We pushed the cloths of the canopy aside.

'It isn't even a strong current,' he said. 'I've put resistors in it. It's perfectly alright to touch the rods; it won't give you a shock.' He invited me pressingly to touch them but this I did not dare. To divert his attention, I asked whether the device would ever go out of its own accord; he gave no answer to this. I sniffed the scent of the sparks and stared into the dark. Maarten's face could only barely be made out in the blue dusk.

A moment later his parents came home. He rapidly put the device away but didn't light the candle. He listened and asked me to stay put, not moving a muscle. We breathed cautiously. His mother took a step inside, tried the light switch and muttered something; she halted a moment. I had my hands in my crotch and listened to the silence that began to rustle. My heart was pounding for I believed that, once we were discovered, something terrible would follow.

When she had left again, Maarten still did not restore some light. We continued to sit in the dark. 'We have to talk carefully,' he said. I opened my mouth but was silent. Staring with wide open eyes into the darkness, I squeezed my genitals to find out how much force I need apply before it hurt. I believed I had to flee. 'I have to go home,' I said hastily: 'or else I'll get what-for.'

Maarten showed me out through the window. I ran home quickly and crept up to the loft. Though the electric light was fine, I lit a candle I kept in the cabin trunk. Then I opened a window, brought out the cardboard box from beneath the roof tile and took the sheet of paper from it. I left the window open to listen to the wind making a gate rattle somewhere, for it had begun to blow.

'I am in the Enchanted Castle', I wrote in pencil on the reverse of the sheet, 'but it is the houseboat of Death. I know that: it is going to sink into the deep'.

Draught blew in which set the candle flame a-swaying so that the shadow of my head was swung to and fro across the white surface of the wall. It looked like a big black bird that had no wings, yet because of a mysterious power it could fly and it awaited me to do me harm.

Folding the paper I fell prey to doubt as to the question where I might best put it away. Adding it to the rolled-up label in the wall I thought risky because perchance my brother might discover it. Neither did I think the spot underneath the roof tile could be trusted because the boys in the neighbourhood could see me hide the box from their gardens and betray where it could be found to my brother. I decided to keep it, folded up tiny, in my trouser pocket. The thirteen cents I left in the box which I put back in its place. Until I had to go to bed, I remained sitting by the candle.

Late next morning, Maarten came to fetch me to go and find the duck said to have been struck. We set out at once. In case we saw fish in the water, I brought along a little net and a jam jar. The weather was just as dreary as the day before; it seemed as though dusk was already falling in the morning.

We carefully searched the area we had been the evening before but found nothing. I wasn't expecting to and only looked around mechanically. The grey sky gave the water of the watercourse a matt, cloudy colour; I believed it possible that weed-encrusted watermonsters lived on the bottom – something I had thought earlier – that could come up to drag us down into the deep by our manly parts. I looked regularly at the surface of the water therefore.

When we were forced to abandon the search, Maarten declared that we were too late and that the bird had already been taken by others. I did not contradict this. We walked on and passed a narrow, shallow side-ditch where we went fishing with the net. There wasn't much to see. I did bring up an oblong, beetle-like creature with little pincers. It was about half an index finger long. I dared not touch it, but lifted it with two sticks; then I threw it away as far as possible from the water into the grass. I wasn't easy about this, however, so I found the animal again and ground it into the soil with my heel. 'It's a rotten mean creature, I read so,' I said to Maarten. 'It has to be killed.' In fact I wanted to make the beetle's return to the water impossible, for he would doubtless inform the watermonsters about me otherwise.

Soon we reached a shallow spot where clearly attempts had been made to make a dam; everywhere there were bundles of brushwood and stones in the water that had become shallow. Here I discovered a big gramophone horn in the shape of a calix, most of it under water. We fished it out. At its broadest point it had a diameter of three quarters of a metre, no less. It had been painted green on the outside, pale pink within. The paint had flaked off here and there. 'It's mine,' I said, ''cause I discovered it. If you find something, for example, and you're the first to point it out then it's yours.' I rinsed the horn clean, knocked the water off, and hollered into it. Then I went and acted daft with it. 'Listen folks,' I cried, 'to perform for you now the great elephant Jumbo. Ta-ta, you sods!' We ambled on meanwhile. I put the horn across my shoulder with its opening facing backwards so I could continue to holler into it regularly. 'The one who has this horn is most powerful,' I thought. 'Maarten,' I said, 'listen. We've talked in passing about the club but it's got to be for real now. We mustn't wait at all any more for you know only too well that they're making hostile clubs everywhere.' When he let my words pass, I went on: 'If we found the club this afternoon we've got a horn for starters. And a club with a horn is very good indeed, in fact — you know that too. We can blow it when the meeting starts. It is of course best if the chairman does that. By this you can see it's a good club.'

Maarten barely seemed to be listening. With my net he fished a few minnows from the ditch and put them in the jam jar. 'When we have a club we can also catch fish and make a pond together,' I said, half despondent already.

At that moment an unknown boy in blue overalls was coming towards us. He was a head taller than me, at least, and had a pale, bony face and very pale blond hair. He came up to me with a leering expression, halted in front of me, studied the horn and tapped against it with his index finger. I began to tremble.

He had small, sunken eyes. On his upper lip I saw scabby swellings like those of a skin complaint. He grinned malevolently, tapped, a little harder this time, against the horn and asked, taking no notice of Maarten, how I had got hold of it. I gripped the instrument convulsively and couldn't think of anything to say at first.

'We fished it out of the ditch here,' I said. 'It'd been lying there for ages 'cause it'd been thrown away: it belonged to nobody.' I wanted to continue speaking but ran out of things to say. I looked at Maarten but he said nothing 'Well, as long as you know it's mine,' the boy said. 'It's not up to you, taking things away I've left here for the time being. D'you hear, laddie? Just you hand it back here: chop-chop.'

'We need it badly,' I did still say, softly, but I knew the horn was lost. The boy grabbed it, took it from me and sauntered off. We halted and watched him go. Then we walked back home. The rain, which had been almost unnoticeably fine until now, became a little denser.

'Ah, never mind,' I said, 'it was a bummer anyway. No use to anyone. You could see. Anyway, I have an uncle: he has loads of those horns: I can have as many from him as I want.' Maarten didn't reply; he held up the jam jar and peered at the fish.

'We must found the club instantly, this afternoon,' I said. 'Then we'll make an army – all good clubs have one. The chairman of the club becomes the chief: it's always done like that.' Maarten shook the jam jar and continued to be absorbed by the fish.

Reaching my house, I requested him to come along to the loft. There, I opened the little window and showed him the box beneath the roof tile. 'That's the club's secret place,' I said. 'All the things that are written down we keep there: that's the cave 'cause nobody can get at it.'

I looked for paper, put it on the cabin trunk and invited Maarten to draw up the first document together. 'First we must have an army,' I said, ''cause a club without an army is noth'n.' I requested him to wait and quickly wrote down a few things. Then I read out: '1. There's a club army that can track down too. Should there be someone, for instance, who keeps on nicking horns then we go after him. Then he gets taken prisoner'. I saw that Maarten was looking at the stuffed-up gap in the wall. It had stopped raining; patches of light slid past in the sky.

'So now the club's been founded,' I continued loudly. 'It's called the New Army Club, the N.A.C.' This last sentence I wrote down behind the figure 2 . . . Maarten was listening now, so I thought, but I didn't believe he was enthusiastic.

'You have understood, haven't you, that it's very important that we make an army?' I asked. 'If the club wants to we can take that sod who's nicked our horn prisoner.'Cause I know his name and where he lives.'

'Who is he then?' Maarten asked. This question put me on the spot. 'That has to remain a secret for now,' I replied, ''cause the army isn't quite ready yet.' Just what I did mean, precisely, wasn't clear to me either. I quickly folded the sheet, laid it in the cardboard box and put it back beneath the roof tile. 'It's completely hidden,' I said. 'You really don't need to be afraid that someone'll find it. Should it rain, for instance, it'll stay dry 'cause the roof tile's over it.' That instant, I took the jam jar Maarten had put down on the floor and emptied it out on to the roof tile. Maarten uttered a fleeting cry but then watched quietly with me how the fish were washed away and disappeared down the guttering. 'They go in the ground because they're very dirty creatures,' I said inwardly. The jam jar I tossed into the garden where it flopped down to earth without breaking. I closed the window and went and stood behind the cabin trunk as though it were a shop counter. From here I looked at Maarten who continued to look out of the window. 'He's the cat and has got to go into the trunk,' I thought.

'You don't have to become a member at once, today,' I said persuadingly. 'If you're not quite sure, you'd better wait until tomorrow.'Cause coming into the club right away is easy enough but then you'll become a dormant member, perhaps.'

Maarten began to feel along the gap in the wall and pull out the paper stuffing in tatters. I made him stop this. 'That's something else that'll be included in the club's regulations,' I said: 'you're not allowed break anything in each other's houses. The one who does that has to leave.' I wrote down at once: '3. When there's a meeting in someone's house nobody may break anything. Anyone who does has to leave.' I read this to Maarten, took up the axe and began to knock plaster from the wall a good way beyond the hole. All of a sudden Maarten said that he had to go home, and he left. While he was going down the stairs I watched him furtively and then slipped quietly up to the loft again. I took out the paper I kept in my pocket, struck out what was on it on both sides and wrote: 'PLANT TORTURES. While it's still fixed to the plant, you can nail down a thin branch to the fence. Then it will slowly die. You can also cut into it and put ink on so it gets inside; then it goes a different colour completely and dies, but it takes very long.' I left a blank space and wrote a little lower down, in a new paragraph: 'If there's a toadstool you can light a fire of matchboxes underneath it. Then it gets roasted underneath while it's still in the ground 'cause it's still standing there.' In the final paragraph I put: 'If there are spiders on the plant you must make a fire underneath it too. Then they can't get away any more.' Having folded it, because I no longer thought my trouser pocket sufficiently safe, I put it under my vest on my chest.

I called our cat, one with grey and white markings, upstairs and cherished her for a while. Then I fetched a few bits of biscuit from downstairs and put a tall, square little chest, which once had contained tea, in unstable equilibrium on the edge of the stairs with the opening towards me. I fed the cat some bits of biscuit and tossed the last few into the box. The cat walked into it, disturbed the balance with her weight and plummeted down inside it. I followed the fall assiduously. I returned to the loft to read the document concerning plants afresh. When I was on the verge of folding it up again I heard my brother coming upstairs, so I ate it.

It was rainy on Monday morning as well; in the afternoon it stayed overcast. Having come from school, I wanted to go to the loft but my mother turned out to be busy up there, hanging the washing. Despite the chill, I now went and sat in the box room. When I was getting too cold for comfort, I lit a tin can with methylated spirit and looked into the rarefied, motionless light. 'This is the devotional flame,' I said solemnly. I caught a daddy-long-legs and tossed it into the glow. 'Sacrifices are being made from all sides,' I said, half singing the words. From time to time I cast a glance into Maarten's garden.

When I saw him, I put out the methylated spirit and sauntered up to him with indifferent tread. He was standing there in his rain coat looking up at the sky. 'Is it going to rain?' he asked. 'I think so,' said I, 'but not much.' Hurriedly I went on: 'It doesn't matter whether it happens to be bad weather, for I've already got a club room where we can have meetings: we're allowed to use that always.' Maarten continued to look at the sky. 'It's there,' I said, pointing at the box room. 'There are members, perhaps, who don't think it's that good, because it's cold, but we're allowed to have a fire. That's a flame in a jar. It stands in front of the chairman and it doesn't go out yet so you don't have to throw anything on to it.' I asked him to come with me to see it but he announced that he had to run an errand, to a clockmaker's, to collect a repair. I went with him.

As we walked along we said nothing for a long while. Finally I broke the silence. 'You can still join the club,' I said. 'Or don't you think the New Army Club's a good name?' I pointed out to him that a fresh meeting could be held in that case. When he replied that he thought a club of two members who, moreover, lived close to one another, was preposterous, I proposed a drive for new members. 'I don't want to be in a club at all,' Maarten said in the end. We were silent for a long while again. Once more I was the first to speak. 'Are you someone who's very quickly frightened?' I asked. 'Not at all,' he replied. 'Even so, I thought you weren't very brave,' I persevered. 'You don't look very brave really. I don't believe for a moment that you're really tough.' He said nothing back. Up until the shop we didn't exchange a word.

A narrow little street was where we needed to go. We halted in front of the shop for there was something in the shop window we had to stay and look at. It was a composite piece of machinery which I first took to be a pair of scales. On closer inspection it proved, however, to be a machine without any useful purpose and only intended to amaze the public or to amuse.

At the top, metal balls of varying sizes plunged at intervals into a brass bowl at which point a large hand indicated their weight. Then the balls fell into the compartments of a paddle wheel propelled by their weight. The traction of this wheel was passed, slowed down, to a very long arm going up and down a distance of a few centimetres, protruding from the machine. This supported two parallel carriageways, separated by fences, for a little racing car which ran incessantly up and down them, first the one, then the other: at the extremities niftily constructed connecting bends saw to it that the little car could turn without colliding or tipping over and run back. This little vehicle moved me. It was a little red car bearing the registration 'W13'. On a black pennant the driver was holding, it read in pale blue letters: 'Death Ride'. His head was wrapped in a crash helmet and a leather mask that hid his face. In front of the whole thing stood a sign in capital lettering with the text: 'This Perpetuum, Racing Car Track, was assembled from 871 parts in 14 months (all Parts home made too). By a handicapped miner who seeks to provide for his livelihood in this way. Cards are available at 20 cents each or from J. Schoonderman, Beukenplein 8 hs. SC14,4,1,75 for ten.'

Faded picture postcards bearing a depiction of the apparatus were lying roundabout. Quite a bit of dust had fallen. 'It's a fine thing,' I said. In reality I felt a great sadness approaching. 'I must go and see someone,' I said hurriedly when Maarten was preparing to go in, 'I'd forgotten about that: I've run out of time.' Before he had been able to reply I had already set off at a trot and left the little street. When I was sure he wouldn't catch up with me any more I went and stood by the ditch along the road and looked out keenly for pieces of wood, but I saw nothing of the kind floating about. In a porch I stayed and waited for Maarten. When he had passed me, I followed him at a distance all the way home. 'I'm walking behind him but he doesn't know that I'm following him,' I said to myself.

Getting close to home I peered around carefully and discovered Maarten in his garden. I couldn't get to the loft yet, so I decided to stroll around for a while. It wasn't very cold; the drizzle felt lukewarm. I walked past Werther's house and made my way to the parks by the dike. Here, having looked round a bit to make sure, I entered the little spinneys.

Here and there, the ground, which was juicy and sucked tight to my shoes, was covered in moss. I chose a spot where, without being visible to passers-by, I could watch Werther's house. Here I sat on a small trunk that had snapped, one that hurt me sitting down, and I embarked on some reflection. It turned out that I did have a stub of pencil but no paper on me. However, I discovered a damp cigar box on the ground. On this I wrote: 'I'm sitting in the spying tower, looking out at Werther's house. At the moment I can't see anything yet. When I spot trouble I shall send a messenger.' I trampled the box and drove it, stamping my heels, into the soil.

Just as I had finished doing this I heard laughter and hollering coming nearer. I saw a woman run past along the broad cinder path who slowed up occasionally to turn a full circle. At first I thought she did this to look behind her, but it more closely resembled some combination of dance steps. Before I'd been able to make an accurate observation she had already gone past. I stepped out from the bushes into the open, in order to watch her go; just as I was standing on the path a collection of at least thirty hollering children reached me, apparently following her. I mingled with them and dashed along in their midst. We began to catch up with the woman. Reaching the street, she stepped on to the pavement and halted. All her pursuers came to a halt at some distance from her. I was one of the last.

The woman turned round, bowed and took up the edge of her skirt on either side. When she straightened out again I saw that she was Werther's mother. A great fear crept over me. Afraid she would recognise me in the multitude, I bent down a little and crouched slightly. 'She isn't wearing a coat,' I thought.

She began to execute rapid steps on the spot during which she repeatedly struck the soles of her shoes loudly against the paving stones. All of a sudden she raised her skirts about her head, almost losing her balance in doing so. When she had let them drop again she halted a moment and then began to make shorter, more restrained little steps, humming as she went.

Two women now arrived from a porch near by, one of whom wore a white cap, like a nurse. The other had put on a coat. They took Werther's mother carefully by her upper arms. 'Mrs Nieland, you really must go home quickly,' the woman with the cap said.

'It's far too cold here. It's late already. You really must go home quickly.'

They continued to hold on to her. She did show signs of putting up a struggle but did not resist with force. We came closer.

'I'm dancing in time to the music,' Werther's mother said. 'I'm the dancer Agatha.' She said this in an ordinary, businesslike tone of voice, but immediately afterwards she went on resentfully with: 'Everyone shouldn't think they know what dancing is. Dancing is quite a different thing to what people think.' The two women pulled her along with mild coercion. Her dark floral dress billowed occasionally in the wind which lifted her fluffy hair repeatedly. I wanted to walk away but could not bring myself to.

Suddenly she began to shout. 'Education!' she cried. 'That's no education at all! Not in a month of Sundays!' Her face looked tired and flushed, but she smiled continually. The two women drew her along more rapidly now and brought her inside the doorway to her house.

Adults had joined us now, too, among them the corner shop tobacconist. He looked on but said nothing.

Though it was no longer necessary, I had mechanically continued crouching at the back. A girl gave me a push so that I fell over. 'Just taking a crap were you?' she said. The door to Werther's house had closed. I walked away slowly, a few steps, and then I ran home. I understood I would have to think a great deal.

After dinner I lit a wood fire in an old iron barrel in the garden and stayed with it, standing there. The sides became red hot. I called Maarten to come and see. We peed against the iron, creating clouds of steam. When the fire was becoming spent he proposed to sail a large cardboard box that stood in his garden, on the water, its contents burning. We took along the necessary and went to the watercourse. The box, filled with wood shavings, pieces of cardboard and dry branches, and weighted down at the bottom with a paving stone, we balanced on the water, set it alight, and pushed it out from the edge. Because the wind was unfavourable it sailed back slowly. We gave it another push but this time, too, it slowly returned. Maarten said that, had he had the air gun on him, he could have sunk the box with one or two shots. The latter slowly burnt down to the water line, became saturated and went out with a hiss, whereupon it sank. We went and sat down on the bank.

Though it was dark we could see smoke rising above the

cemetery which blew in our direction. It smelled of smouldering, imperfect combustion. 'That's where they burn the bones,' Maarten said. 'When the dead have been underground for seven years, the flesh's off the bones.' He added detail to this. The bones hanging in his room he had, he maintained, fetched from the big piles of bones in the cemetery when the ditches were frozen over. He had done this in collaboration with others. They had taken skulls along as well but had lost these then because they had begun to play football with them on the ice on their way back, without knowing that cemetery staff were closing in on them, from behind. They had managed to escape at the last minute but had been forced to abandon the skulls. It had been thawing, and when they returned the ice had cracked already.

I didn't know whether it was true what he told. Lastly, he maintained there had still been hair on some of the heads. This detail, I thought, could not possibly be invented so that I now believed his entire story. 'The day has three signs,' I said inwardly: I believed that Werther's mother's dancing, the sailing back of the cardboard box and Maarten's tale of the bones were connected with one another in a mysterious way.

When we got back home I took Maarten along to the loft and switched on the electric light. As we were going upstairs, however, I already longed to be alone. Maarten looked round searchingly and studied the cabin trunk. 'That's the secret chest,' I said. 'You're not allowed to touch it.' I went and stood behind it and took paper and pencil. 'I happen to have to write something concerning the club,' I said, regarding the paper as if it bore a message. 'The messenger has brought an urgent message. I have to deal with it but a non-member may not be present.' I looked at him pensively. 'You've got to go,' I decided, 'it can't be helped.' Maarten left without a word. As he descended the stairs, I said: 'You mustn't come here any more 'cause I can't possibly have anything to do with enemies of the club.'

I lit a candle, doused the electric light and wrote: 'The Army Club. What the Club can do. We can sail boxes that burn. That's good to pester the water monsters. 2. Go to the cemetery when it's freezing and fetch heads and bones. If it's not freezing we'll build a dam. This must be done by members who know a lot about graves and building. At the head stands the chief, that's the chairman of the club. 3. Go and take a look in the spinney when, for instance, someone comes by who runs fast and begins to dance.

You can see this 'cause she hasn't got a coat on.' The final item made me ponder deeply. I put the date underneath what had been written, put it away beneath the roof tile and took a fresh sheet. I decided to send Werther a letter and wrote: 'Werther, I have to speak to you urgently because it's very important. Danger threatens. I'll wait for you tomorrow at four. At your house, on the corner. Elmer.'

I was given permission to go out on to the street for a little while. When I was standing in Werther's porch, the same smell blew out at me as the one I had noticed inside his home. I pressed open the letter box but instead of dropping the letter in, I listened at it, keeping an eye on the street. Only a draught rustled past my ear and I didn't hear a thing. I continued to listen even so. After some time I heard the rub-a-dub of footsteps crossing one of the rooms, and hushed voices. I considered opening the door with a pass key I possessed and to go and sit at the foot of the stairs, but this I did not dare.

Suddenly a door opened somewhere on the upper landing and I recognised the voice of Werther's mother. 'I've got a good deal more power than you think,' she said loudly. 'I've got the green gem stones which . . .' (A number of words got lost here.) Then the door was slammed shut again rather forcefully; I could still hear voices but too faintly to distinguish between them. In the end, I flicked the note into the letter box and went home.

The following day, in the afternoon, I was standing sentry at the spot indicated. I had come walking quickly from school and I knew I would have to run into Werther for he attended a private school twenty minutes' walk from his home. When I saw him coming I ran towards him and walked along with him during which I held forth at length. 'There's a very bad misunderstanding,' I said. 'That has to be cleared up. We aren't enemies at all but there was someone who wanted to break up the club: he was sowing discord.' (This last expression I had read somewhere shortly before.)

Werther wasn't angry any more and heard me out affably. 'We must meet tomorrow afternoon,' I said. We had ended up on the pavement in front of his house. Here he halted hesitantly. 'We have to talk,' I said, 'that's necessary.' All of a sudden, his mother poked her head out through a little window that could not belong to a room nor to the stairwell. From here she began a conversation.

'Hello boys,' she said, laughing. I wasn't sure whether her behaviour was commonplace or most extraordinary. 'Mother, you're just like an acrobat,' Werther said. He sniggered for a moment but then looked straight up again.

His mother made a few dotty, shaking movements with her head, then stuck out her chin and asked: 'Isn't that your little mate Elmer? Have you hatched a plan again? You're a right pair of likely lads. Why not come upstairs.'

Werther seemed to hesitate but when his mother repeated her request we climbed the stairs. His mother was already waiting for us on the landing. By looking round carefully, I worked out where the window might have been and concluded it had to open out from the lavatory.

'I had been looking down for quite a while already,' she said, 'but I said nothing. I had actually wanted to throw water on to your heads. Would you've liked that, Elmer?' she asked.

'It would've been a giggle,' I said, looking at the floor; 'it's still a bit too cold for that.' I felt uncomfortable.

We had made our way to the kitchen. 'Cold water is good for horrid dreams,' she said. 'Werther, why don't you tell your friend what you keep on dreaming all the time.'

Leaning with one hand on the window sill, she did a few tripping steps. 'Come on, tell,' she urged him. 'He's a strange laddie, isn't he?' she said and grabbed Werther by his hair. 'Are you strange like that too?' she said. At once she seized me by the hair also and gently shook my head. I dared not make the slightest movement.

'Well, ehm,' Werther said, 'there's a man after me all the time. He's got a big bread knife and he wants to cut my lips in two with it.' He indicated this with his index finger using the same gesture as the one with which you ask for silence.

'But we've been to the doctor, Werther,' his mother said. 'Yes, Elmer,' she said, turning to me, 'we've been to the doctor with Werther-kin. He's over sensitive. Every afternoon or evening, he has to be washed with cold water. I'll run the bathtub ready. He's got to be undressed completely, of course.'

At this moment Werther's sister arrived home. 'You can have a bath together,' his mother said, 'then I won't make the water as cold.' She began to fill a large bathtub she fetched from the veranda, running the water through a red rubber hose, and she told Werther and Martha to get undressed.

'It's quite alright for you to join in,' she said to me. 'No, that's not necessary,' I said. 'I had a bath only this morning.' (This wasn't true, however.) 'You're welcome to have another one here, you know,' she said. 'Then you lot can have a bit of a rough and tumble afterwards to really dry off. You don't have to get dressed at once.'

She spoke with apparent indifference but in reality there was something compelling in her voice that made me afraid. Werther and Martha had begun to undress. They put their clothes on the kitchen chair. It struck me that Werther undressed himself very tardily and would look round all the time, embarrassed. His mother urged him to hurry.

'You never have to be ashamed of anything about your body,' she said. 'It's a very ordinary thing. Elmer's having a bath with you – or isn't he?' 'No, not now,' I said quickly, 'it's not necessary.'

'If you don't want to, you don't have to,' she went on, 'but it's very good for you. You surely dream horrid things too sometimes, don't you?'

'I've dreamed of a whale,' I said. I regretted this announcement instantly and understood I quite simply should have replied in the negative. 'But it wasn't horrid at all, quite the opposite,' I added speedily. I considered how I might suddenly run from the house, but didn't do this for I might trip up on the stairs. Martha, who was already naked, declared she was cold and ran to the living room.

Werther's mother decided that they didn't have to go into the water at once: they were allowed to walk about undressed for a while.

'Why don't you go and wrestle inside,' she said. 'Then I'll come and watch to see who wins.' Werther hesitated to rid himself of his underwear, however.

'You really don't have to hide your thingummy,' she said. 'Your little friend has one too. Or doesn't he – what?' I nodded feebly and searched for any word to say but failed to utter anything. I tried to shuffle imperceptibly to the corner of the kitchen. Suddenly, however, she approached me from behind, swung an arm round my neck and felt with the other, over my shoulder, downwards; I could feel her breath against my neck. I stood quite motionless: at the slightest resistance, I knew, she would stick a thin knife or a long needle into my neck until the marrow had been reached. It took a few seconds before she reached the goal of her fumbling. Then she let me go and jumped towards the window. Her face was red.

Werther looked into the water in the bath. There was a moment's silence. 'That thingummy of yours has a purpose,' she said. 'It's there to do something with that isn't anything weird at all. Birds do it too.'

The front door was being opened and somebody came up the stairs. Werther's father. He looked into the kitchen but said nothing. Then we saw him go into the living room but he left it rapidly too, to go up the stairs. He turned back from this instantly again, entered the kitchen and halted, standing there in silence. I considered greeting him but dared not do this.

The man continued to stand there in silence as though he had complex considerations he must shed light on. 'Mother,' he then said without looking anyone in the face, 'Aunt Truus'll be coming tomorrow to collect Martha and Werther for the little circus.' He had uttered this sentence uncertainly, staring out through the windows on to the veranda as he did so. Werther's mother said nothing and didn't appear to be listening. 'Agatha,' he said. Now she looked up all of a sudden. 'Who'll be collecting Werther and Martha?' she asked. 'What's all this? What's it all in aid of?'

Werther, quite naked now, was standing by the veranda door. I considered what it would be like were he to go outside and jump off. 'He'll become a dead bird,' I thought as I regarded him. I thought he was feeling cold.

'Agatha,' Werther's father said, 'I'm telling you this to make you remember. When Truus comes they must be ready. So they can go along at once.'

'So she's going with them to the circus?' she asked. 'I'm coming too in any case, no problem.' 'Agatha,' Werther's father now said at once, 'we were going to be home tomorrow afternoon, weren't we? We were going to have a chat about things; we'd agreed on that, remember? Course you do.' 'Oh,' she said, 'yes. We're home tomorrow afternoon. That'll be nice. But if the circus is really fun, I might go along after all: just for a little while.' She smiled and spoke ever more quietly until she stopped, unnoticed.

'Werther,' the man said, 'listen. I'm telling you this in case your mother forgets. Both of you must stay home after lunch and not go out getting yourselves dirty.' 'Yes,' said Werther, staring at his father. The latter went on: 'Then Aunt Truus'll come to collect you and she'll go with you to a kind of little circus. You'll remember now, won't you?'

'Werther was coming over to my place tomorrow afternoon,' I

now said, suddenly. 'First, I was coming to him and then he was going to come with me.' For a moment I wasn't sure whether in fact I had uttered the sentences.

'Well, you come along too then,' Werther's father said quickly. 'Werther, he can come too.' Werther's mother was standing there wiggling and looking with a rigid smile at the mat.

'What is it we're going to, father?' Werther now asked.

'Look, Werther,' he replied, 'it's a kind of variety, a little circus in miniature. With small animals. There's a man with a dog that jumps through a hoop. You can stay to have supper at Aunt Truus's. Agatha, they can have their evening meal at Truus's.'

Werther's mother, not listening apparently, began to giggle. Suddenly, without addressing anyone in particular, she said: 'But d'you think that's education? That's no education at all. It has nothing to do with anything.' She continued to stand there.

'Werther, go and get yourself dressed, there's a good lad,' his father said. 'Why not go inside. Take your clothes along with you to the stove.' Werther disappeared. I would have liked to have followed him but didn't dare. The three of us remained. Werther's mother began to hum.

'Don't you have to go home yet, lad?' his father asked me. 'Yes, I really ought to,' I said, sniggering to save face. With a hand to the back of my head he pushed me out of the kitchen and closed the door behind us. Without real force yet inescapably he drove me along. We reached the landing. 'Best be off quickly now,' he said, 'or you'll be late.' He didn't look at me. I stepped on to the first stair. 'Sir,' I asked, 'what time must I be here tomorrow afternoon. Didn't you say I could come too?' I thought it possible that, with a kick, perhaps even against my head, he would make me plummet down. He hesitated a moment and then said that I had to come at two o'clock. 'What's your name?' he asked. I gave my name, said goodbye and rushed downstairs, for I was afraid that he would go and look for that brochure.

At home, I told about the invitation. 'We're going with an aunt of Werther's to the little circus,' I said. 'What kind of circus?' my mother asked. 'It's a circus in miniature,' I said, 'a kind of variety with lots of small animals. With monkeys and rabbits. There're dogs as well that go through a hoop.' 'You haven't asked that aunt whether you could come too, have you?' she asked, worried. 'Course not at all,' I said. 'That aunt wasn't even there at his place. They themselves said I should come along.'

274

The following afternoon she gave me 35 cents in a wrapper. 'You must give that to that aunt,' she said. 'You don't need to go along at those people's expense.' I felt through the paper that they were a 25 and a 10 cents piece.

When I rang the bell of Werther's house at ten to two, his father answered the door. 'I'm Elmer,' I said, 'I'm coming along this afternoon.' 'Would you mind waiting downstairs for now?' he asked.

It took a very long time. From time to time I thought they had left already. 'How's it possible his father's home in the daytime?' I thought. At last Werther and his sister came out. They were accompanied by a woman who resembled Werther's mother slightly but she was younger. She did have the same little eyes but she had an ordinary mouth and wore her hair in a bun. I wanted to shake hands with her but wasn't given the chance.

'We're late, kids,' she said, 'let's be off.' There was a strong wind and it was raining. On the way to the bus stop we were heading into the wind so there was no talking. When we were sitting in the bus, the aunt said to me: 'So you're friend Elmer? How nice you're coming with us.' I was already holding my hand out a little to pass the money to her when the bus started off. We said nothing during the ride. Werther's aunt offered peppermints round regularly.

We got out at the terminus and walked to a tram stop. The weather had turned dry. Beneath the glass shelter of the stop it was quiet. Werther and his sister had taken a seat on either side of their aunt on the narrow bench. I ambled up and down in their vicinity. They were talking softly. 'Yes,' Werther's aunt said, 'I'm coming to live with you for a while. D'you like that?' I listened.

'Mum's nervous,' she went on, 'perhaps you've noticed that too. People get like that when they're very tired. I'm coming to you to help out a bit.'

'You really don't need to think it horrid or to have a shock should mum happen to say something you don't understand at all,' she continued. 'You see, she's tired and then thoughts get mixed up. You know what I mean: you ask something and she answers something quite different than you mean.'

'Yes,' Werther said, half whispering. He let his gaze flit to and fro, restlessly. I prepared handing over the money but the tram was approaching so I didn't get down to it.

Our journey's destination turned out to be a low, café-like

building bearing the name 'Arena' in neon lights. I couldn't imagine a circus being there for there was no need to pay even at the entrance. I thought of drawing Werther's aunt's attention to this but she escorted us into the revolving door with such certainty that I just had to assume she knew the way.

We reached a low, elongated hall with its chairs not arranged in rows like in a theatre or cinema, however, but clustered around tables. There were some thirty or forty people inside, drinking or eating something and watching the stage which had been half built out into the auditorium. On it stood a man with a fearsome face. His head seemed big, his hair stood straight up on end and he was looking at the tip of his nose. He had turned the toes of his shoes towards one another. Bright, coloured beams of light shone down on him. He was silent and appeared to be waiting. People giggled. Just as we were sitting ourselves down at a table the music of an orchestra struck up and the man sang in an awkward, drawling voice: 'I'm the goofy, I'm the simple, I'm the nitwit Jopie!' He held his mouth as if he was vomiting.

It turned out to have been the final line to a number, for the curtain fell and people clapped. Of the four of us, only Martha laughed.

I studied the price list on the table. The cheapest item was lemonade which cost fifty-five cents. It gave me a shock and I wanted to put the paper away but Werther's aunt had already seen me reading it and asked whether I would like something. 'No, not at all,' I said quickly. Meanwhile the curtain rose for a new act. It seemed to be a kind of play; I didn't understand it. It began as follows: in a room with a screen and a desk, two men in white coats were waiting. Thin rubber tubes dangled from their pockets. 'A doctor's life's a hard one,' one said. 'Never ever a nice bit of totty at surgery time,' the other said.

Werther's aunt signalled the waiter and asked him for a programme but there wasn't one. 'It goes on all the time and each time there'll be something different,' he replied. Werther's aunt ordered a coffee for herself and lemonade for the three of us.

The play continued. A fat lady entered with a girl, presumably her daughter. She wished to be examined and undressed herself behind the screen. She came out from behind it a few times to look out to the left and the right. She had taken off more clothes each time, clothes she had hung out over the screen from the inside. Every time she appeared, people laughed loudly. The girl stood

276

looking at the floor with her fingers in her mouth. 'Can you play mummies and daddies?' one of the doctors asked. 'How does that go?' the girl asked in a stupid, petulant tone of voice. The people at the tables laughed.

I became afraid and decided not to look any longer. With great difficulty I drank from the lemonade which was fizzing up my nose. Werther's aunt seemed to notice. 'You don't have to drink it against your will,' she said. I got out the money now and planned to cast the sum wrapped in paper into her handbag.

Meanwhile I spied on Martha and Werther. Martha appeared to think everything that happened on stage to be colourful and funny. She laughed repeatedly. Werther, however, stared out ahead of himself with a gloomy look.

Using the tubes I recognised as those of a stethoscope, one of the doctors examined the lady now only left wearing her corset and shoes. Meanwhile he muttered comments which drew laughs, here and there, but we were sitting too far off to hear them.

I wanted to cast the wrapped-up money with as fluent as possible a movement into Werther's aunt's open handbag but the throw missed and it dropped on the ground. She heard it and picked it up. 'Did that drop from the table?' she asked me. 'I don't know,' I replied. 'Someone's sure to have left it,' she decided, having opened up the paper. Great shock gripped me for it turned out to have been written on. She read it out: 'Milkman, a jug and a half please, will settle up with you tomorrow.' It contained nothing further so I felt somewhat more at ease again. She decided that it was pointless to make an effort to track down the owner. 'You three may buy some sweets with it,' she said.

The doctor had finished the examination and declared she was healthy. Then, without her having undressed herself, he examined the daughter. 'She needs an injection very badly,' he said. 'Gosh, how can you tell so soon?' the mother cried, 'she hasn't even taken anything off yet. 'No,' the other said, 'we can tell from just seeing her.' Then mother and daughter made to leave.

'Your daughter had better come to the surgery tomorrow afternoon, alone,' the first doctor said. 'Is it expensive?' the mother asked. 'No, not at all,' the doctor assured her, 'she'll have that injection for nothing.' 'Can it do any harm?' the lady now asked. 'No, not at all,' the doctor assured her. 'They do occasionally get fat for a while,' the other one said, 'but that passes of its own accord.'

The audience roared. Werther's aunt called the waiter. 'Will the animals still be coming?' she asked, 'the dog with that hoop?' 'No, madam,' the man replied, 'that was last week.' 'So what's on now then?' she persisted. She learned that the programme consisted of sketches, tapdancing and acrobatics. Werther looked on intently during the conversation. I suddenly got the feeling that perhaps he had the same thoughts as I did: that possibly, without anyone knowing it – for it was being kept a secret – we were brothers.

'This's not very suitable,' his aunt said. 'We'll leave.'

With extreme willpower, I began to drink down my lemonade. A finale developed on stage: having left to applause, the woman returned with her daughter and the orchestra made thumping drum rolls. Suddenly all four of them put on wigs, seemingly made of dusters or cotton wool, and stepped to the edge of the stage. The music struck up a slow, dragging melody. All four, in time to the music, began jerkily to thrust their hips forwards and backwards, singing in harmony: 'Roger here 'n Roger there 'n Roger please, all day; if Roger's still available, it's Roger now till May.' They bowed at the end, the music drumming once again. We went outside.

'It was really nice last week,' Aunt Truus said, 'but this's not quite suitable.' I wondered where we were trundling off to. 'Why don't the two of you go off and buy something,' she said all of a sudden, giving Werther the money and she sent him and me together into a grocer's shop. There were rather a lot of people standing there. 'Werther,' I said as we waited, 'you must come with me on Sunday to my uncle and aunt. I've been with you this time so you may come with me on Sunday. You've really deserved that.' We bought dates and sticks of rock and spent the entire amount. I wanted to request him again to accompany me on Sunday, but we'd already left the shop and returned to his aunt. She approved our purchases. It began to drizzle. Werther divided up the dates but I didn't like them. 'I'd better go home again,' I said. His aunt tried to talk me into staying with them but I didn't give in. 'I have to be back early,' I said. In the end she gave way and asked whether I had money for the tram. 'Oh yes,' I said but I had none on me. When she wanted to take me there, I said I still wanted to look at a few window displays and would then take the tram myself. I left with a fleeting wave of the hand. When they were some way off already, I walked back and asked Werther if I could count on him on Sunday. Before he had answered, I had run off already but in this short time his aunt handed me a stick of rock which I accepted. I began to travel the very long road home on foot and ate the stick of rock, without relish.

'Did you give that aunt the money,' my mother asked. 'Yes, she's got it,' I said. 'Was it nice?' she asked. 'Yes, it was a giggle,' I said flatly and went up to the loft. Here I wrote a note to Werther, which read as follows: 'Werther. You must come along on Sunday afternoon because it's great fun. Come to my place as early as you can. When you get home the letter will be on the mat already.' When I went to deliver it, the same rain prevailed as when we had set out. In front of Werther's house there was a white car; some people stood talking beside it. I passed them, entered the porch and popped the note into the letter box. The moment I had done this I heard the clump of footsteps on the stairs and noisy voices that developed into cries. 'Now hold on, easy,' a high-pitched man's voice said, 'and don't let go.' I listened at the letter box. Thudding, half stumbling noises sounded, as if there was a struggle. At this moment a man from the group standing by the car approached me and chased me off. I ran some way into the park and sought out the spot where I had been on the lookout before, and I settled down on the trunk. The same way as previously, I continued to spy on Werther's house. Nothing extraordinary happened, however. The shrubs gave inadequate shelter so I started to get wet and went home.

Early that same evening Werther came to bring a reply in a letter which he handed to my mother. She called me but when I reached the door, Werther had already disappeared. The note ran: 'Dear Elmer. I'd love to come with you. I'll come to you; you mustn't come to me. I'll come over to you before it's Sunday. You must not come to my house. Werther.' This letter made me think.

He didn't turn up for the rest of the week. I thought he had forgotten the entire appointment and began to write a new letter, but I destroyed it.

On Sunday, when I had installed myself on the lookout in the loft, I saw Werther approaching at almost half past two. We set off. 'You're sure to like it,' I said: 'that's why I have brought you along.' The truth was that I didn't want to go to my uncle and aunt on my own. They had asked my mother why not send me over this Sunday. They lived in an upper-storey flat on the Tweede Oosterparkstraat.

My uncle sold goldfish in the market. His stock stood in large tin baths on the veranda at the back. When, sitting on my heels, I looked at the fish swimming among the floating water plants, my mood would always turn sombre and I would feel desolation encroaching. The house was situated close to a corner and the veranda only provided a view of a blank wall plastered white. (Thin, blue smoke would settle in the gardens frequently.)

We spoke little on the way. The weather was dark but dry and windless. I foresaw that the afternoon would run a bad course.

My aunt greeted us warmly and gave each of us a piece of Christmas cake. My uncle wasn't home. She went and sat at the window and brought out her cithern. Underneath the strings she laid out a trapezium shaped sheet of music which didn't contain notes but little balls connected by a jagged line. When the sheet had been placed accurately, the little balls, each lying beneath their relevant strings, indicated the plucking point for the melody.

As always, she began with the song about a frog that was eaten by a stork: she sang slowly and loudly.

Werther sniggered for a moment and stood there listening with a stupid expression on his face. I leant against the alcove door.

At the end of some verse or other, of which the final words ran: 'Mr Stork, Sir', I could no longer contain myself and I just had to look at the brass vase with peacock feathers on a small, three-legged table at the entrance to the alcove. I knew that great sadness had appeared and made my way on to the veranda. There, everything was as I had foreseen. This time, too, there was a hazy veil of smoke between the rows of houses. I looked into the tin baths, dipped my finger in and studied the wall. I knew I had to go back in again but that this, too, would provide no relief.

'That's the wall,' I said out loud, 'and these are the tin baths. The cithern is inside with the song on it. And in the vase the peacock feathers are.' I wanted to start and sing it softly but it wouldn't work. I went back in through the kitchen; my aunt went on singing the song. Without switching the light on, I went and sat in the lavatory and waited. In the end I came off and stayed and stood listening in the hall. The song had finished but now the cithern was playing something else, without any singing. Without a sound, I descended the stairs and went on to the nearby footbridge above the railway. Here I stood for an hour, watching how the smoke of the locomotives mingled with the strands of mist. In the end I clambered down from the bridge again and took up my post on the corner from where I could keep an eye on the house. I stayed and waited here for I did not want to go up there again. After a very long time Werther came out.

Unseen, I followed him for several streets. Then, jumping out at him from behind, I gave him a fright. He was cross for a moment but didn't remain so. 'I thought you'd gone to fetch something somewhere,' he said. 'Where had you gone?' 'I can't tell you that yet, not right now,' I said, 'though I would like to: it simply has to stay a secret.' When Werther failed to reply I said, to fill the silence: 'It's horrid, the way they live there, I think. Did you like it upstairs?' He replied feebly that he didn't. We walked on. 'We're going to move,' he said suddenly. 'To the Slingerbeekstraat. That's in Plan Zuid.' I didn't reply. Without my asking anything, he told how the removal would be taking place within a week. He mentioned the number of the house as well.

I was silent a long time. Then I said: 'You've got to be very careful with removals 'cause there're people who move and then they end up in a lesser house than the one they first lived in.' Neither of us said anything after this.

'D'you know why I stayed outside?' I asked after a while. "Cause I think you're boring this afternoon. That's what you are all the time, really.' Before he could reply, I ran out ahead and hid myself away on a corner. Again I gave him a fright but in doing so I collided with him, which made him fall. It turned out he had grazed the palms of his hands a bit. I apologised and declared it had happened by accident but in truth his injury gratified me.

From now on we kept silent as we walked along. He looked at the ground with a stern expression. I tried to make him laugh several times but didn't succeed.

Approaching my house we took our leave with a bit of a mumble.

I no longer saw him after that. I did, every day after school, walk past his house without ringing the bell.

The sixth day there were no longer any curtains to be seen. I made my way home and took a piece of paper but merely dashed a few scrawls across it. Then I took my brother's bike and rode to the Slingerbeekstraat.

It was slightly foggy, and the street lamps had been lit early. I had remembered the number.

It was a ground floor flat near the corner. The sign with the green star had already been attached to the door.

Without getting off, I slowly rode past the windows and then turned back. 'They live darkly,' I said, softly.

At home I roamed the back garden and pulled the tops off the withered remains of the Michaelmas daisies. Afterwards I fetched the axe from the loft to hack thin branches to bits on top of the fence.

The White Woman

Arthur van Schendel

In a small town with little canals and tall elm trees lived a man who for his entire life had only observed people without having anything to do with them. It was said that he was timid, not a philanthropist although he always subscribed to good causes. Never had he had any other pastime than books and reading; from morning till night, year in, year out, he had long reposed in worlds far from this one. Otherwise he was ordinary – no criticism implied – and the two old servants who had known him from his birth lived contentedly in his house. By day and by night he was in his room with the books, occasionally looking out at one of the windows at the back on to the garden, occasionally at one of the windows at the front on to the canal.

One evening at the window he saw black clouds scurrying in the dark; bare branches were being tugged at and the lantern light on the bridge moved up and down. It was chill; he smelled hail. He drew the curtains; he heard the swishing of the branches outside. Seated near the lamp he opened a book on stars, a page full of figures, numbers without end. And he read:

A white woman, on the eve of Spring, sat in the half light of birch trees on a hill by the sea. The trees were motionless. A light flickered in the sky, the sea lay down below in the mist: not a murmur. Beside each tree a strand of vapour rose up, a shape with its arms crossed in front of the head. The strands entwined, the shapes moved from one tree to the next. The leaves rustled, the vapours trembled, a glistening descended. Down below by the sea a voice cried out, a form stood there, a wave flopped on to the beach. The white woman held her hands in front of her face and descended. Then it was night and black and nothing could be heard except for a wave breaking.

His hands were stiff, his feet cold. He had the feeling that there was ice in the room, strange at this time of year. And casting up his gaze from the page beneath the lamp light he discerned the white in front of the curtain of one of the rear windows; he only saw the white of a garment and of a foot stretched out in front.

And when another foot had appeared he straightened up and saw the figure had approached to where the lamp light fell. He knew this was no human being, no woman. He rose up and saw the face but, because of the moisture before his eyes, he was only able to discern something deep and dark swathed in white as white as snow. She drew closer and she raised a hand; he heard a voice and at this sound he felt the warmth of tears.

The time has not yet come, she said, perhaps later, then shall the time be. She sat down on the floor in the light of the lamp, hands folded in her lap.

He was a modest man, he dared not ask who she was and whence she had come. But the darkness of her eyes opened to him so he could understand all that she said, and though tears still slid down his cheeks he sat quietly at the sound of her voice.

You hear that I can speak, hence I must be an 'I' like every other creature but it has been a long time since I have known this. I also have memories of a time long before this, when I existed I don't know where. Perhaps it was the place of sorrows for when I think of this from a distance I hear sighing, moaning, weeping, everywhere around, as if multitudes throng and plead in the darkness and one voice sounds that might be mine. In the silences I have heard so much weeping that the thing I long for most is that sound. And at times I have thought why – thoughts without end and worse than all the weeping. Without those thoughts I could never have believed that I might be a human being, not here, no, not here or there, a human being who must be or who has been. Then I see an image before my eyes and it is as if the sun begins; I no longer ask whether it's true or not. I cannot speak of this, that once I may have been a human being, cast out young from mankind and always yearning, always hearing the crying, crying here, crying there, crying within my innermost being.

Her voice became high and plaintive: Why is it that it is so cold here? Tomorrow I must be here, then shall the time be, why so cold?

She rose and had rapidly disappeared in the darkness of the curtain.

Then he heard feet on the steps of the stairs: the maid servants were going to bed. He opened the curtain at the front, saw a hail stone strike the window, the black branches swishing in front of the lantern, but his vision was blurred by the tears in his eyes.

And again in the evening he sat beneath the lamp with his head bent over the book, reading about stars, their courses and distances. And again he suddenly felt the cold to be present there, and casting up his gaze he again saw the whiteness in front of the dark wall. The figure approached more rapidly and when she was sitting he made out the whiteness of the hands and the feet; they seemed hard yet without weight, white as hail without a sheen. She spoke: Dusk is where I have been waiting and no sheen can be there. We acquire sheen when we touch something, something standing on a foundation, here or yonder. The thought has asked whether this is why all the weeping must be. I know I long to touch the world and people but from the depths I must weep that this should happen. Why the fear? We both know that we cry and hear crying everywhere and that we all wish to come. We know the one cannot be without the other and that there must be pain when two meet together. Not two dust specks together without sorrow. That is where warm and cold, light and dark begin; there fear commences. Read in the book whether it says anything about life; mankind thinks of nothing else, after all. Is it this for which we hear sighing, weeping and wailing? Why we call out, want, fear? Is this why the tears fall from your eyes? That will be it, for from afar I recall something about tears. It was dusk, there were trees, tears falling hence upon me. There were eyes all around and voices that sobbed. I think I was young then. But perhaps I remember because I long so, and no longer know yea or nay.

And again the tone of her voice rose to a high plaint: Cold, cold, it is becoming colder than before. I knew it when I longed for this house.

And when he had wiped the tears she was no longer there. He heard stumbling and whispering on the stairs; he quickly opened the door and he saw the two maids going up slowly, pinafores held up to their faces. Reaching the window he drew the curtain aside. There was nothing to be seen outside but the lantern through the branches, a cloud, a star. And that it was cold, this he felt too, colder than at other times on such spring evenings. He sat down again and pondered, but all that he thought was sorrow without end.

Next evening, at the window, he saw the thinnest crescent of the new moon floating in a vapour, its light already yellow however. When the young moon gleams clearly, he thought, fine weather is in the offing. He looked at the houses beyond the branches, all their doors closed and a lamp lit here and there. He noticed he was lonely, he sighed and drew the curtains. A servant knocked; she asked whether he had called, was there anything he wanted. Sir's so quiet, she said, it's upsetting us. No matter how softly you speak to yourself it can be heard downstairs. No, he said, your ears deceive you, I'm not talking with the books.

Silent, she lit the lamp and he went and sat down with the book and waited. The page turned over slowly.

And when the white woman was sitting there on the floor with her head raised up to him he looked straight into her eyes; there was something there deep down, something with a blue glow. About her face and hands there was something that moved.

Why cry and wait? she asked. After all, I have heard it ages ago, I have been driven here a long time. I know it because I wake up and notice how far the darkness is from the light, how much night differs from day. Of yesterday's event I know about sitting here and how much time has passed between then and now. Something has gone away, something has slipped down and I clearly remember that yesterday there were cries and I myself cried too. Today I have understood that there has been a moment, now past. And today it was full of rumours, many voices, many sobs, and weeping, more than I could hear. I don't know whether the waiting is here or there; I don't know whether it is I who waits or someone else. That is new and strange, the thought of another; it makes me soft, small, cold. It has hurt in my eyes and within me there is something: that tomorrow I shall know the great fear, darkness gaping open.

She laid down her head on the floor and wailed with a feeble sound, monotonously. Bending over her, he listened as his tears fell; he heard her softly asking each time: Why is it so dark? Why here? Why here? Why so dark?

He rose upright for he could not bear it; he covered his ears. But she had gone: there was only the crepuscular light and the floor was empty.

There was a knock on the door; he went and saw the two servants, each with a tip of her pinafore in her hand. Did Sir call? asked the one and she trembled. Did Sir know how late the hour is? asked the other pleadingly; we're so afraid. He did not know what to say. But when they continued to stand there he said: Now just you go to bed.

The following evening rain was falling silently, the cobbles shone near the bridge, the sky was drab. Behind a window, beyond the lantern a reddish light gleamed. Past that house it was dark with trees and a dog began to howl there, high and long. Occasionally, when the howling grew fainter, it had the deep sound of a big dog, then it began afresh, helpless, intolerable. A figure, slowly mounting the bridge, halted and then descended into the dark of the trees. There was a sigh. He wondered why he stood here so often, watching, always in the direction of the bridge, watching the dark passage beneath the arch and its twin reflection on the canal water. The dog suddenly ceased howling; not a soul to be seen.

He drew the curtains, lit the lamp and took up the book. While reading he looked round repeatedly but there was no one. And he read, page after page, until he noticed he had been sitting there a long time. He thought: Has it been a delusion of the senses? He thought even more, about this and other lives, about near and far, about now and tomorrow. And when he looked up she was sitting on the floor. She kept her white hands clenched tight together. Her voice sounded feeble and indistinct, tired, without hope: I do not know why I come here; I do not know where I must go and what I must think. I want to but I dare not. I have had peace here; it has been a moment and now another must come. Forget me; I shall forget you too.

Her head fell forwards; she sobbed noiselessly. And he did too, hands in front of his mouth.

Then he heard different sobs; he looked and saw the open book on the table, the floor without the whiteness that had been there. There was loud urgent knocking on the door; he answered hastily. The two maid servants were standing there holding on to one another. Sir, Sir, oh merciful heavens, Sir! cried the one, and the other hid her face. But they touched him and became quiet. The one said: we heard Sir talking with something worse than we are capable of thinking. Quiet yourselves, he replied, go to bed and good night. They went up the stairs, slowly, dabbing their eyes.

He drew back the curtains and looked out into the night again. It was quiet. But beyond the bridge there was the small sound of a child just beginning to bawl. The branches moved in the wind. He mused as to what it was: something worse than one was capable of thinking; he mused whether truly he had seen anything at all.

The Unbalanced King

Willem Schürmann

It was a cheerful summer's day but the king felt in sombre mood.

Slowly he passed along wide fields, far from the city, without accounting to himself for the fact that he had been roaming for hours already. He saw toiling labourers in the fields, and something like self-reproach for never having worked rose up in him. How wonderful it must be to rest after a day of intense toil, he thought, but he realised that he would never be capable of such heavy physical work for his head reeled even when he only bent down for a moment.

Used to haughtily making his way upright, he could not imagine a hunched posture without a feeling of humiliation and effort.

He had never humiliated himself nor ever made an effort.

His parents had never demanded anything from him that even smacked of subservience and the wise teachers who had provided his upbringing had themselves solved all the difficult problems they had set him.

Only for the results of their investigations had the wise ones requested his attention; he knew the solutions to all the sums, but how these were done he did not know.

He was said to be a wise king and he did not trouble himself about the question as to why he had earned that name, but one day, when he was sitting at a window in his palace, bored, he had suddenly become restless in the silence that none of his courtiers dared disturb.

He looked at the turrets of distant castles and attempted to laugh off his restlessness. Why am I restless? he thought.

Yonder live my subjects who do everything I order them to. They would gladly sacrifice their lives for me . . . for . . . I am their king.

But *why* am I their king and *why* are they loyal to me?

It's perfectly possible that they hate me . . .

The sun went to its slumbers, the gold slipped from the sky and still he sat there peering out ahead of him, lost in thought.

Then, without having himself announced, he made his way to the queen's apartments who, surprised at his unexpected arrival, received him with suspicion.

'Ma'am,' he asked, 'can'st thou tell me why I am king?'

The queen, mindful of a trick question, replied hesitantly: 'Thou art king to command.'

The king went and sat down in an armchair and let his head rest in his hands.

Finally, he had a minister called in.

'Your excellency, why am I king?' he asked.

'Thou art king by the grace of God, by birth and by the love of thy people, Your Majesty,' was the immediate reply.

'And why do the people love me?'

'Because thou art wise, Your Majesty.'

'How do they know I'm wise?'

'Your Majesty, when thou show'st thyself to the people even the smallest child, at once, sees . . .'

'My people always see me from a great distance.'

Without pausing for thought the minister then said: 'Regal is thy presence, Your Majesty, for thou art regal both in bearing and deportment. The impression thou makest upon thy people is of an almost divine eminence. By thy movements all feel how far above them thou art through refinement of thought.'

'So I am different from others?'

'Your Majesty, thou art a king.'

This answer, too, could not satisfy the king.

He spent sleepless nights and dozed his days away in musing.

And now, too, while slowly making his progress along the wide fields, he was engrossed in questions without finding a solution to a single one of these.

As nightfall approached, he set himself down, exhausted, on a rock by the side of the road.

The labourers passing by saluted him politely but not with uncommon reverence. Nobody cheered. One or two said: 'G'day to you, Sir.'

They do not see I am king because I'm wearing neither crown nor robes of state . . . so the minister has deceived me, the king thought, and he fell asleep from fatigue.

Suddenly, he woke with a start because of the rattling approach of a cart.

It was morning.

Shaken, the king got up, attempted to walk, but the cold of night had so stiffened his legs that he decided to ask the driver of the cart to run him back to the city.

'Whoa there, my good man!' he cried.

'Well?' the coachman asked, as he brought two bony horses unwillingly pulling a green, covered wagon, to a halt.

'Drive me to the city!' said the king.

'I've just come from there and I have no time to lose,' was the reply.

The king was about to make himself known when, painted in bright letters on the torn hood of the wagon, he saw: *Karel de Man's Theatrical Company*.

The coachman was already applying the whip to the horses when he restrained him, saying: 'My friend . . . I would dearly like to make your company's acquaintance . . . might I ride along with you? . . . I will reward you handsomely for it.'

'We can do with rich people, we can,' the coachman laughed. 'Get up on to the box but don't wake the *artistes*, for we have to perform tonight. And because you're rich, you can start by giving me something up front.'

The king, amused by this unusual familiarity, handed him a gold coin at once, stepped on to a wheel, heaved himself up next to the wagoner and a moment later the cart rattled on.

As they went along, the coachman told of how the company had performed in the court capital, where receipts had been paltry. And that's the king's fault, he said, for he knows nothing of art.

'What plays does your company perform?'

'Royal Tragedies of course! Don't you know Karel de Man is the finest king in the country? Every child knows him!'

'I see,' said the king.

He had thought of going to the mayor in the next town in order to return to the capital in the mayor's coach, but during the ride he changed his plans.

This adventure was one of rare enchantment to him, the wagoner telling him tales never heard before, and strange smells, of paint, old cloths and sharp scent, arising from the wagon. The fields seemed wider to him than ever he had seen them before. The sun shone more cheerfully and the king would certainly have sung out loud had he known an ordinary song.

Impatiently, he awaited making Karel de Man's acquaintance. In him he would see that he was not the only regal human being!

With gold coins, he urged the coachman into noisy song, hoping the actor would wake up, but the latter continued to sleep peacefully in the jolting cart.

At last some movement commenced under the hood and suddenly the leather covers fell down with a thud.

It was a peculiar spectacle the king then beheld. In the wagon, beneath faded rugs, heads resting on torn pillows, men and women were sleeping closely packed together.

A young chap, having jumped down on to the road, ordered the coachman to halt, uttering many strange-sounding words in so doing, words that – to the king – seemed pithy insults for which, in angry mood, he had often impotently sought in vain.

'Who's that sitting up there?' asked the young man.

The wagoner jumped down from the box, whispered something into the questioner's ear, and then spoke loudly: 'A proper tleman! Might I present to you . . . our young lead . . . Sir? . . .'

Just in time, the king read a name on a billboard in front of which the wagon had halted.

'And where are you going?' the actor asked.

'I'd like to join the company.'

'Ever acted before?'

'Royal parts,' replied the king.

'Which company?'

'Freelance.'

'Don't let the old'un hear that you do his livelihood,' the young man said, 'in that case he's sure not to take you on. You don't know what actors are like.'

The royal *artiste* who, at the collapse of the hood, had raised himself up a moment, stretching, was lying there snoring peacefully again, but the eldest of the ladies had smoothed down her rumpled clothing and she approached, smiling amiably. The young lead introduced her as the *mère noble*.

Following her, a slight young girl arrived, laughing – the *ingénue*, so the young lead said, and it struck the king that the old woman who had to play the mother-parts behaved like an innocent slip of a thing while the girl busied herself with appearing to be a woman worldly wise.

He, however, had no time reflect on this curious matter for the player of father-parts approached him genially, a tremendously fat man in peculiar clothes.

He had a red face with heavy double-chins that trembled at

every word he spoke; his lips were thick and dark, the corners of his mouth black, and his teeth had the colour of old ivory. He was wearing a green velvet smock and his crooked fat legs, in yellow stockings that reached up to his thighs, seemed to bear his heavy torso with difficulty. His podgy left hand in which he held a small cap with long feathers, he moved elegantly to his heart.

'I am well-known,' he said, 'but who art thou, noble stranger in silks who honours our terribly poor company with thy respectable presence? Dost thou come out of love for the lovable young girl standing next to me?'

Demurely, the mother-part lowered her eyes.

'Dost thou bring us subsidy out of love for art, or art thou a rich merchant who, in his spare time, has written an ugly play?'

'I seek to join your company,' the king replied.

'Hast thou money?'

The king nodded.

'Then there are no objections! Art is a beauteous young damosel. To every man seeking her company she is a credit . . . but . . . possessing her bears a heavy price . . . From the poet she demands his lifeblood . . . from the merchant his rolls of gold! We are her representatives and hope ye be a prosperous merchant, for we cannot live on lifeblood.'

Thereupon, the king proposed to celebrate their acquaintance with splendid wines and precious fare in the nearest town.

They invited him in to the wagon and the coachman applied the whip to the horses.

It was a cosy, jolly ride.

The mother-part, who had powdered herself with dexterity, pressed her plump body warmly against that of the king; the youth told risky jokes which the slight young girl listened to with gleaming eyes; and the father-part recited the names of the many dishes he was mad about.

The star of the company continued to sleep.

Toddlers by the side of the road who recognised the wagon cheered the players, and as they drew nearer to the gates of the town, more and more children came pouring out towards them followed by callow youths, girls, old men and old women who surged around the company in groups.

The young lead banged the drum with glee, the fat father sang a cheerful song and the mother-part flirted seductively.

The king feared that people would recognise him but there was nobody who took any notice.

The people demanded the appearance of the star and he, woken from his stupor by the cries of 'huzzah', roused himself, searched hastily for the torn, red satin sandals he had put away beneath his pillow, put his hand with a flourish through his stubborn, auburn locks and beamed at the people.

His laugh was cheerful and sad, all at once; his lips laughed but he kept his eyes cast soulfully up to heaven. With a broad gesture he swept a dark-red cloak round his shoulders and his auburn beard fluttered in the wind.

The king thought him a preposterous king, but he made a great impression upon the people. He opened his mouth and a suffocating waft of brandy struck the king in the face. With pathos he spoke of 'beloved citizens', 'noble patrons of the arts' and 'loyal paladins' while his lips laughed and his eyes looked soulfully up at the heavenly expanse as if he was seeking his significant words in the clouds.

The bass drum emphasised each of his sentences with a heavy stroke.

The people were elated and more admirers arrived from all sides.

Only when they were sitting at table in a little hotel did the *artiste* seem to notice his new travelling companion.

A few times, it had seemed to the king that the actor had seen him much earlier on, but the latter, once he had been told that the stranger would be treating them to precious fare, professed his regret not to have been able to welcome him sooner. When I feel inspired I do not see the people, he said by way of an apology.

The acquaintance made, he showed himself to be a charming man. He ate a great deal of the precious fare, drank numerous cups of wine and deprived the generous stranger of not a single detail of his illustrious life.

With tears in his eyes, he related many touching events, with the assurance that there was no more serious artist than he. I do not say this out of vanity, said he, but a man who is aware of his value must not pretend to be less than he feels himself to be.

The king thought him to be an interesting man but felt himself to be the more regal personality.

When the star was talking about the masterly interpretations of his royal parts, the truth was burning on the king's lips, but the *artiste* made it easy for him to keep silent about his dignity for he spoke with such fervour and with such short pauses for rest, that no one other than he was able to utter a word.

The other players apparently couldn't care less; they adopted attentive expressions but their actions proved that they only gave heed to the popping of the bottles a dexterous landlord was ridding of their corks.

The feast lasted for hours.

The mother-part acted more sweetly as time went by, the father one became sleepy and the young parts began to make love, visibly.

Then, slurring his words, Karel de Man gave the order that, because of the absence of one of the *artistes*, the first performance would not be taking place till next evening.

Having become maudlin with drink, he called his host an exceptional man who proved by his attentive listening to be able to appreciate genius, a man he would gladly call his friend.

And while he was uttering these charming words, the king thought: This man, celebrated as the most regal actor in the entire country, seems to me to be a most petty *bourgeois* creature. He reeks of cheap drink, wears highly unkempt clothes, his hands are clumsy and his nails have been gnawed down disgracefully. His gait is unrefined and his entire appearance indicates low birth.

This parody of a monarch renders the quality of kings ridiculous. The people led astray by him must through truth learn to see the absurdity of his delusion. I myself wish to play a royal part. My prime minister said: It is enough for thee to show thyself to thy people so that all shall see at once that thou art king. If this be the truth, the audience in the theatre must notice instantly that a true king is walking the stage.

'I want the truth! I wish to act!'

Then, in reply to the actor's flattering words, the king said: 'I, too, am uncommonly pleased to have made the acquaintance of a gifted man. Your name is known in many countries and often was the time when I longed to be allowed to address you as a friend. I am very rich ... and the rich man often has curious whims. My ideal would be to play a royal part in your stead for just one night.'

The actor began to laugh uncontrollably, put his arm round his host's neck and said in his ear: 'Such a fool you would make of yourself, my dear chap.'

But the king, who wanted the truth at any price, cast a purse full of gold on to the table. 'I wish it!' It sounded like a command.

At the sight of so much wealth, all the artistes sidled up close to the speakers.

'Let him act!' they cried.

'But it'd be ridiculous! We'd make immortal fools of ourselves,' warned Karel de Man.

The father-part, stroking the heavy purse, spoke: 'What harm can it do to be ridiculous when you possess those sweet, yellow discs.'

'But art . . .' the star resisted.

'Is so much gold not to art's benefit?' asked the king. 'I wish to give double that! Think of all the fine things you will be able to buy!'

For a moment, Karel de Man thoughtfully let his long tresses slip through his fingers; then, smiling, he asked: 'And how many times would you wish to act?'

'Once will be sufficient.'

'Let him act,' cried the others.

'A bodice of white lace,' the mother-part whispered, lovingly stroking the king's knees the while.

The innocent young thing whispered something at the ear of the young lover and the father-part spoke softly to himself: 'Down coverlets . . . caviar . . . mocha, and Havana cigars.

Having hesitated a long time, Karel de Man then decided: 'So be it! Once! No need for me to worry, for the difference between us is too great.'

'Indeed it is,' said the king.

Then he was given his part and he left at once to go and learn it in a small chamber.

Late that night the mother-part came knocking softly on his door. 'D'you know your part already, lovey?' she asked, 'and might a simple little woman be of service to you?'

'Not yet,' whispered the king through a crack.

A sigh was the reply to this.

On a small stage, among tattered cloths representing the walls of a palace, the king would celebrate his triumph.

Never before had he been so cheerful; he knew his part and did not doubt the success of his enterprise.

Truth would vanquish make-believe!

He felt he was about to do a great deed.

Laughing, he allowed his face to be smeared with grease. A heavy beard was stuck to his chin. His eyes, lined in black, enlarged unnaturally, had exceptional sparkle and his perfect teeth glinted brightly in the fiery red frame of the painted lips.

Long lengths of cloth pinned to his shoulders were his robes of state. A gilded crown rested on his hair.

No one would recognise his face!

The majesty of his person would have to prove his right of kingship.

Through a little hole in the curtain, he saw many faces he knew: the mayor's, the governor of the province's and those of many dignitaries with whom he had often been bored to tears at table.

These men will instantly recognise the monarch by the grace of god, he thought, but the star, standing in front of another spyhole, spoke, *mezza voce*, while peeping at the same people: 'What on earth will all those fine gentlemen make of it.'

Nervous, he continually talked to himself, for the calmness of the stranger had made him fearful.

He had drunk much that afternoon to divert his thoughts, but he had remained surprisingly sober.

The purse with gold weighed heavily in his trouser pocket.

When the curtain was raised, he withdrew, trembling, into a dark corner whence he could see everything that was happening on stage.

The contents of the play were romantic.

A nobleman who loves a simple shepherd's daughter, vows to marry her, but the king, not wishing their union, has the lovers condemned to death, later – touched by their glorious faithfulness – to grant the ardent couple his forgiveness and their lives.

Instantly upon their appearance, the lovers enthralled the audience. The simple father of the girl arrived and there was unstoppable mirth until the caring mother came tripping in who, by her heartfelt tenderness, moved many people to tears.

Then the king strode, well-controlled, up close to the footlights.

'Odious creatures,' he said loudly, but his first words were lost in a storm of bravos.

'Odious creatures,' he said once more with greater conviction, for the expression of enthusiasm with which they received him he put down to the gloriousness of his appearance.

Never had he been more conscious of his power; the great clauses of his role he spoke with splendid certitude and he moved the train of his robes in an uncommonly elegant fashion.

It was quiet at first and then, slowly, a hubbub began in the auditorium and suddenly it rang out from the densely packed crowd: 'It isn't De Man! It's someone else! He's got nothing of a king about him!'

The king did not let himself be put off by that cry. Witheringly, he looked into the auditorium and with the certainty of a man who knows he will gain victory, he continued with the euphonious lines of his part.

Mocking laughter began to erupt.

The king paled. He saw the dignitaries shake their heads at one another, winking, but he continued to speak.

The laughter became even louder then, and with the despair of one who is being deprived of his rights, he shrieked his words into the hall after this. But the laughter became uncontrollable and the more fervently he trod the boards, the more shudderingly the people moved about, gripped by hilarity.

Hysterical screams were reaching him.

Yet he went on.

It's the uncommonness of it that strikes them, he thought. They'll appreciate me better later on. But long after he had left the stage, people were still sniggering.

'I'm not a king,' he said softly to himself, passing by Karel de Man sitting in his dark little corner rubbing his hands.

'I told you so, yesterday,' the actor said with something of commiseration in his voice.

Proud, the king straightened himself out, for suddenly he felt the humiliating nature of his position.

'The second act will prove to you who I am,' he said, haughtily.

'Ridiculous fool!' he heard the actor mutter.

The second act brought him even greater disillusionment and the third the king could not bring to an end.

Protesting loudly, the audience left the auditorium.

Affably wiping the greasepaint from his defeated opponent's face, Karel de Man said, in order to comfort him: 'A man is never too old to learn ... You might still turn into something quite acceptable, perhaps ... Come and see, tomorrow, and then learn from me how a man of refinement does it.'

The king said: 'Dear friend, I'm quite knocked for six. I cannot understand how you can be more regal than I.'

'And that's your mistake,' the actor laughed.

'Then I shall come and look, and if you are truly a worthy king, I want to learn from you,' replied the king simply.

'His arrogant pride borders on insanity,' thought Karel de Man.

The night the king now spent was one full of strange feelings.

In his little hotel room, he went nervously from the wall to the window and from the window to the wall, his head sunk deep down on to his chest, his warm hands clenched stiffly together. Accustomed to the wide marble halls of his palace, he felt as if imprisoned in the small, pokey space. He dared not pace about loudly for fear of waking the actors sleeping in the rooms around him, and all the time he was seeing the grim faces of the crowd, mocking him. He heard their laughter and the sound of his own voice reciting the dramatic verse. It seemed to him that he could speak this far better now, that his voice could sound deeper and richer, that his posture had not been sufficiently regal, and yet he was certain never to have taken so much trouble to appear a man of importance than he had that evening.

He had never declaimed his speeches from the throne in as carefully prepared a manner as this, had never understood their words as well. Those speeches had been received with acclaim, and writers, in rich and lengthy paragraphs, had praised the warmth of his voice. Time and again, courtiers had come to do him homage, many of them even with tears of emotion in their eyes. He had never doubted their sincerity; now, he no longer believed in anything.

He felt himself closer to the people than ever before, but now he understood the people, he feared them. Humiliation, shame, fear: he had learned to understand all ordinary human feelings. It seemed to him as if he had suddenly been transplanted into another world.

'So I shall get to know real life through ordinary people,' he thought. 'Through Karel de Man's success, I shall have to see how my people wish a king to be. An artist shall make me an artist-king. So from De Man it is that I must learn; therefore my future behaviour shall be according to his example.'

He had forgotten the actor's strange manners and he no longer thought of his oppressive smell of drink.

But when that tardy night had slipped away and the cheerful star patted him in greeting on the shoulder with the affability of one having the advantage, the king could no longer consider him so full of hope to be his master.

'Ah yes,' said De Man, 'acting comedy seems easy but it's a great art. In order to be a good actor one must be able intensely to imagine oneself placed in all possible circumstances. If you want to depict a king, it is necessary to imagine oneself to *be* king, Fantasy must become reality! *But . . .*' and he blinked mysteriously . . . 'the regal must be *within* you above all. That is what you lack, my good fellow, and I saw this at once.'

Then the king felt the desire to shout out loud who he was, and it was only with difficulty that he was able to control himself.

For the rest of that day, he stayed with the actor who continually rattled the ducats buried in his trouser pockets and who bought all kinds of things in a multitude of shops, things he called articles of luxury by which one recognised the man of refinement. He bought a multi-coloured collar, spats, pale-green shirts, handkerchiefs of floral-print silk and a long, carved meerschaum cigar-holder. He also purchased strong scent because a rich scent is indispensable to a civilised man.

Of everything offered him for sale, he took the most expensive, and while making his choice the ducats tinkled the song of riches in his trouser pocket.

The father-part spent his share on his favourite dishes, of which there were many he had never tasted before, and the mother provided herself with colourful dresses.

The king had pleasure from his money.

De Man said to him: 'It's a pity that there are so few patrons of the arts, for artists such as I are a rarity. It's a disgrace that I cannot always sit on velvet.'

The mother whispered: 'I also bought a *saut-de-lit* of Brussels lace . . .' and in her eyes the king read all-promising gratitude.

The lover-parts did not speak but ate chocolates from one another's lips.

The *artistes* spent their day relishing their suddenly acquired luxury and made their way to the theatre, singing joyfully.

In the dressing room where he, too, had been decked out, the king saw how Karel de Man made himself unrecognisable. The artist stuck the same beard that he had worn to his face; with the same crown he adorned his hair, and he pinned the same red cloths to his shoulders in which the king had moved about the previous night.

Once again the hall was full, for it had been made known in the town that the star himself would now play his role.

'Of course,' spoke he when they came to tell him of the large influx, 'how could it possibly be otherwise?'

The father-part sang a jolly ditty and the mother, enchanting in her new lace underwear, came to ask the king whether a freshly bought posy of roses in her hair honestly didn't look peculiar.

At the stroke of eight the curtain went up.

The king was sitting in one of the last rows of the stalls, which were full to bursting, and he had to crane his neck in order to see the stage.

Once again, the lovers spoke intensely of marriage and faithfulness, the father arrived to make his clod-hopper comments and the tender mother wept so touchingly that the audience was much moved.

Tension mounted as the moment of the king's appearance approached.

'Oh, behold: the king,' cried suddenly the mother-part and at that moment the star stepped out from the gloom.

It was an impressive moment.

Calmly, he proceeded forwards, lips clenched.

'Odious creatures is what you've got to say,' thought the king. 'He's not saying anything; drink has put him off his stroke! He has forgotten his part.'

But a moment later he understood why the artist had kept silent.

He allowed the audience to complete their jubilations, did not bow, made no move, but waited, his face a tense mask.

Then, in the silence that followed the impudent clamour, the tightly clenched lips suddenly tore apart. The words 'Odious creatures!' he cried out with mighty roar and his eyes glinted wildly.

Then it went quiet again.

The king bent far forwards. His gaze burned on to the king of the stage, he kept his eyes wide open and he cupped his hands to his ears.

He saw Karel de Man's wrath mount, heard the slow swelling of his voice to a roar, followed with eager eyes the broad gestures, saw the gathering of the faded, red cloths that looked in the distance like velvet wings, shook his head in time with the king's thudding paces and trembled at the sight of his glittering pupils.

The actor had turned into an entirely different being.

His voice sounded rich and dark, his words were of a different construction than in ordinary life.

He did not say single r's but rolled them instead, and of the n's he did not forget a single one. The r-become-r's gave a special expansiveness to the words, it rendered them more difficult to say and by this an effect was achieved as if each syllable had been carefully considered.

The s's hissed into the auditorium, the 'i' had a sharp, penetrating sound. The 'a' sped forth from a wide-open mouth and for the letter 'o' he pursed his lips to a little tube.

The king repeated the words after him and attempted to imitate the facial gymnastics, but a young lady sitting next to him forbade it in an angry voice.

The audience sat listening with bated breath.

The king saw how the monarch became steadily more angry on stage. At first, it was only his voice providing the anger, but in due course everything about his body began to betray his unbridled temper. The eyebrows joined and parted brusquely; the nostrils billowed out as though they were elastic; the lips shrank, rounded, tensed; the chin hopped forward and cowered, while the twinkling fingers interpreted the fierce rushes of emotion. The cloak shrivelled, widened out, billowed and hung down straight as the sound of the words demanded. The legs of the actor arched and stretched. The feet moved rhythmically.

Now on tip-toe, then stomping his heels, the indignant king made his way across the boards. His beard waved wildly about his face and the hair danced above his eyes.

It was a terribly tiring job to follow all the gestures but the king did not miss a single one. He saw rivulets of moisture running down the actor's face and heard how the audience murmured approvingly as the colours melted and merged on the mobile countenance.

Women pressed their handkerchiefs to their mouths, men moved their heads, nodding, and on all faces he read admiration.

When the king had spoken his proudest words, the curtain came down but it had to rise at once again.

Loud cheering resounded throughout the auditorium.

'Oh, *what* a king!' they cried and a sobbing young lady shouted: 'Ecstasy!'

The king was left staring gloomily ahead of himself. He had seen how the governor of the province had risen to applaud the *artiste*, that the mayor was beside himself with admiration and that many dignitaries were still nodding satisfaction, long after the curtain had come down.

'So this is majesty?' he thought. 'Is this the way my people want their king to be? . . . And will I ever be able to learn this, what is

301

thought to be fine and regal? I tire quickly, I have never bothered with gymnastics and my mouth is much smaller than this man's.'

Then he heard a nice young girl say: 'This one's quite different from that creep yesterday! He is the spitting image of the king himself . . . He really *could* pass for his brother.'

'Indeed,' agreed a neighbour.

This surprised the king highly, and with longing he awaited the second act to see this curious likeness for himself.

The second act, too, enraptured the audience to great admiration but only in the third did enthusiasm rise properly to its peak.

In the final scenes, the actor gave himself completely. His glorious delivery sounded as tireless as at the beginning, his hair whirled wildly around his head, he made the robe wave about like the gown of a belly-dancer and he twisted his body into many con-tortions.

'Delicious! Masterly!' were the cries.

The rolling r's, the penetrating i's and the clear a's were of wondrous effect.

'God save the king!' cried many in the galleries, and when the play had ended, people were loath to leave the auditorium.

'Well?' asked De Man, when the king entered the dressing room. 'Have you now seen what a king is?'

'It was an overwhelming success,' said the king, 'but forgive me for daring to make an observation. Weren't your movements a touch frantic for a dignified prince?'

The actor laughed: 'Are *you* now trying to teach *me* how a king behaves?!'

And to the fat father, ridding himself huffing and puffing of his stockings, he said: 'The man hasn't the slightest notion of physical expression! What did you think of it?'

'I always think it's tremendous!' was the reply, but the father could say no more for a servant was just bringing in the platter with one of his favourite dishes.

Now many people in fine gala attire came to pay the artist their respects. In the foul-smelling room, past bowls of dirty water in which floated thick tufts of hair, they moved about with relish.

Modestly, the king retired behind a curtain and heard one of the gentlemen, in whom, by his voice, he recognised the governor of the province at once, say with conviction: 'Mr De Man, Sir, you are a splendid being! You could even teach our king a lesson or two.'

*

Then the king removed himself.

Once outside, he hastened his step.

The cold of night did not bother him. A lovely warm feeling had taken possession of him. He could have sung with joy.

Far outside of town, he turned round. He raised his hands high, and proudly his voice resounded: 'Starrrs, shine down on thy king forrr whom the mysterrry has been solved.'

The stars twinkled in the sky. The cows lowed in the fields.

Proud, he made his regal progress to his palace.

The guards at the gilded gate did not recognise him at once, so strange was his bearing, and in the marble corridors the lavishly gold-adorned footmen stared at him in great surprise.

It seemed as if the king had grown larger. The indifference had vanished from his features. His chest puffed out, head thrown back, one hand by his side, the other stretched out commandingly in front of him, fingers spread wide, his heels stamping on the mosaic floors, he made the impression of one ostentatiously proclaiming his dignity.

His eyebrows were gathered in a frown, his eyes glinted and strong-willed furrows outlined his mouth.

The old duty-chamberlain who had fallen asleep in the hall in front of the royal bedchamber, tired from days of waiting, was gravely startled by his thunderous voice. The crystals in the chandeliers glittering in the morning sun tinkled.

The pikemen at the doors rushed forward and the king's favourite dogs gave tongue.

A smile passed around the king's lips and with impressive stateliness he proceeded solemnly past the startled individuals into his bedchamber.

There, he laid himself down to rest in an impeccable, physically expressive attitude and, while he slept, the tiding went from mouth to mouth in a whisper: 'The king's returned but he seems almost intoxicated.'

When finally, after a long wait, the stroke of a gong announced the king's order to approach to the softly conversing ministers, they, curious, went to pay their respects.

They did not find him in his housecoat sitting listlessly at the golden table, like on other days, but strong-willed, upright, fists clenched on the armrests of his Florentine chair. He sat there, legs wide, broad in his coronation robes draped in elegant folds, a crown of golden laurel leaves on his curiously coiffed hair, his head thrown back haughtily.

So much did his altered appearance surprise them that they remained bunched together at the entrance to the room, staring at him.

This pleased the king greatly.

'Apprrroach, my Lorrrds, apprrroach,' he commanded, and on the features of these highly surprised ones, his eyes sought out the effect of the distinguished sound of his words.

Slowly, the ministers approached but remained carefully bunched together.

'You arrre surrrprrrised,' said the king, 'fearrrful, prrrobably, because we seem alterrred to you.'

'Oh, no, Your Majesty,' the ministers stammered.

Then, with broad gestures, the king stepped up to them; his brow wrinkled, his eyes rolled wildly beneath his fearsomely bunched up eyebrows and in a tremendous voice he roared:

'Do not lie, odious crrreaturrres! We have become a differrrent perrrson. Werrre we in times past merrrely king by birrrth, today we arrre this deliberrrately, thrrrough knowledge of life and the superrriorrrity of ourrr perrrsonal genius. The days spent by us in grrrave and weighty study have perrrforrrmed a wondrrrous meta-morrrphosis upon us. Frrrom now on, we arrre king with rrroyal allurrre! Yourrr unrrrefined gesturrres displease us grrreatly! What seems strrrange to you in ourrr charrracterrr is the neverrr demon-strrrated essence of trrruly rrregal rrroyalty. Teach yourrrselves to move exprrressively! Learrrn thrrrough us the corrrrrrrect prrronun-ciation of the worrrd. Study yourrr a's, yourrr e's, and arrrticulate the rrr's with distinction. Frrrom now on, ourrr courrrt will exude trrrue rrroyal rrrefinement!'

Then the king made a splendid gesture. He drew himself up tall, pointed wrathfully at the richly decorated doors and waited until their surprised excellencies had disappeared, their backs hunched.

Following this, without altering the expression on his face, he went to the huge full-length mirror and studied the distinguished impression he must have made on the wisest men in his realm.

The ministers, once outside, rushed, their backs hunched, to their own council chamber, closed the doors there circumspectly, stretched themselves to the length befitting ordinary human dig-nity, patted their ears in which the many fierce sounds uttered by the king still rang and regarded each other, smiling.

'Priceless,' the prime minister spoke first, and instantly the others dared to hoot with laughter.

They deliberated in hushed voices for a long time. One brought up the suspicion that someone had intoxicated the king's mind with a mysterious poison, another irreverently suspected His Majesty of overindulgence in drink, a third let it be known that in his opinion they were dealing with a case of One being of unsound mind, but all were in agreement that the actions of the monarch were exceptionally amusing and each time they reminded one another of the details of his poses, the laughter became uncontrollable.

'Oh dear . . .' the prime minister said at last, trying to force his face, once again, into the grave creases befitting his office: 'Wisdom or folly, it is our conviction that we must co-operate with the king and therefore I don't believe that this attitude will be a permanent one. His Majesty, doubtless, was jesting, *but*,' and he placed special emphasis on the word 'but', 'we must not take this jest with too much mirth. We must watch over decorum. I myself shall acquaint Her Majesty the Queen with what has taken place.'

Then the sound of many trumpets sounded through the corridors of the palace.

The king was going to display himself to his people. Already the guardsmen's horses were stamping and pawing in the forecourt. Outriders in red uniforms jigged up and down, soldiers in glinting cuirasses controlled the gawp-happy populace that had poured in, in droves, and a general stood motionless, sabre drawn, ready to salute the king.

They expected the king dressed in simple clothes as usual, but he appeared on the high dais cloaked in an ermine robe.

He bore a golden staff in his hand and he bore a crown of laurel leaves on his neatly crimped hair.

The ovation the people gave him was, for this reason, of exceptionally long duration. But the king did not make his way immediately to his coach as usual. He remained on the steps to his palace, waiting, the way he had seen the actor do the night before, until the people had grown tired of cheering, then to make royal gestures on the marble elevation.

He extended his robe widely, stretching out his hand with the sceptre toward the sky, and his face showed the expression of the most regal possible pride.

The people, surprised at his movements, watched with bated

breath, and by this silence the king understood that he was being highly admired. He repeated the gestures therefore; he shrouded himself in the ermine, raised himself on tip-toe, suddenly let the robe drop, brought his hand to his chin, stared into the void, remained motionless a moment only then to move again most elegantly. He twirled round a few times, stared at the sky, peered over the heads of the people at the fields, greeted the entire surroundings with wide-spread arms and stepped, now on tip-toe, then stomping his heels, towards his gilded coach.

The people were more and more surprised. Never had a king been seen like this before and when, slowly driving by, he looked at his subjects with adoringly staring eyes, they thought the expression on his face so extraordinary that they pressed round his state-coach as though he were a jolly fair-ground quack instead of the inaccessible bearer of authority.

The pikemen had difficulty in keeping the people at bay. Wildly, the people thronged closer.

The king, egged on by their enthusiasm, displayed his most splendid poses of all. He rose from his seat, made countless elegant waves of the arms, shook his tresses, twinkled with his fingers, grimly contorted his mouth only to smile amiably again instantly, whipping up the people to ever greater boisterousness.

The roar of the crowd could be heard streets away, and the city's population ran in huge throngs to meet the curious procession.

A fierce crush arose: horses reared up on to their hind legs, people ended up underfoot and the king went on with his physically expressive poses ... until the people could no longer be contained. They broke the ranks of soldiers, opened the carriage and forced him to go into the crowd.

This gave him a shock.

People embraced him, wanted to induce him to dance and they cheered in a disgracefully irreverent manner.

Pale and unnerved, he suddenly understood how much his dignity had been damaged. He wished to free himself of the embraces but he got stuck in the crush.

Cuirassiers had to relieve him.

Sabres unsheathed, they hacked their way into the multitude now running amok.

In a distraught condition, the king reached his palace. Faithful retainers led him to his apartments and in his bedchamber, burying his pale face in his trembling hands, he sank down on to his bed.

With reverent gentleness they relieved him of his torn robes, asked in hushed voices for his orders but he did not stir. For the second time the shameful feeling of humiliation oppressed him. It was as if his throat was being pinched shut and the blood throbbed at his temples.

His head pressed deep into the spotless pillows, he could still smell the vile smells of the people and, trembling, he could still feel their rough touch. Through his closed eyelids he saw cheeky grinning faces and his ears were filled with noise, buzzing.

They let him be, and knowing himself to be safe in the silence at last, he dared to move.

Then he roused himself, went over to his chair by the window where he had felt doubt for the first time and, staring, he looked out into the darkening beyond.

The queen entered by the door, pushed open softly, and approached with small, careful steps.

'My poor Lord,' she said, and her voice sounded so intensely compassionate that tears welled up in the king's eyes.

'My poor Lord . . .' she repeated and at once she pressed his hand tenderly. 'Why art thou so imprudent to display thyself to the people when thou hast taken too much wine?'

The king did not defend himself for he did not wish to speak to her of his doubt, but when the queen had departed he called for the old Councillor of State who had been his first teacher. To him he confessed his adventures. And the old Councillor said:

'I, too, after the full, carefree years of my youth, have attempted in the first period of reflection to assay my self-worth. By appearances I sought to give myself more esteem, but life taught me that we are what we are; never more, never less, and it taught me that, by wishing to achieve more than one is able to, one can only succeed in humiliating oneself.

'Thou art called king, but thou canst not elevate thyself to royal kingship through acts of outward display.

'Time shall pronounce judgement.

'Be thyself, and if thou art of royal quality this shall be evident by thy true deeds. When thou sought'st to bring reality to the realm of appearances, thou wast ridiculous. Ridiculous, too, wast thou when thou sought'st to hand victory to appearances in real life.

'Should the actor, acclaimed and lauded as make-believe king in the realm of make-believe reality, wish to play the same part in the real world, he would be as preposterous as thou wast on his stage.

'This is the first pre-condition for he who wishes to be a balanced human being and seeks to make a success of his life: ask not the why of things, accept the things the way they are, and act simply, with honest conviction, according to circumstances.'

When, after a year had past, the king had grown calm again, he ordered Karel de Man's theatrical company to attend court.

The celebrated *artiste* came at once and was received in special audience. The star, who now acted very modestly, barely dared look up at the monarch, but when he did so his eyes acquired a deeply thoughtful expression.

'Tell us what you are thinking,' said the king. 'We demand that you should tell.'

'Your Majesty,' was the hesitant reply, 'I thought of a ... forgive me, pray, Your Majesty; I once knew a rich man who believed himself capable of personifying a king. He resembled Your Majesty so much that at first sight . . .'

'And was he regal?'

'Begging Your Majesty's pardon, he was an upstart Mr Average. Only his face resembled yours but in his manner, bearing and expressions he was annoying, uncouth . . . but conceited he was to a high degree.'

'Are you quite sure we were not that man?'

The actor grew fearful of having said too much.

He stammered: 'No, Your Majesty ... for I should recognise you amongst thousands by the majesty of your person.'

And the king gleaned from his eyes that he was speaking the truth.

That evening, Karel de Man acted in his most powerful play but, though giving the best he was capable of, he could not manage to make more of it than a modest success.

That same governor who once had applauded him warmly, that same mayor who had ridiculed the king, those same dignitaries who had praised him once loudly, thought him, now they knew themselves to be in the king's presence, a ridiculous prince.

The king has thought at length about these contradictions, but he has never reached any clarity in the matter.

Affection

Jan Siebelink

In his mind, he imagined that the little room filled itself with the racket of his revolver blazing away, that cracks ran like dark rivers through the glass of the mirror and that both of them, he and the woman, fell apart in shards ... With a smile on his serious, contorted face, he listened to the reverberation of the tumult above their destroyed bodies which had remained intact nevertheless. The smile vanished, his hand slid along the bedspread hanging down to the ground, sweat forced its way out from his forehead.

A few years ago, Van Baak had entered an ironmonger's shop and had stood a long time looking at a showcase sealed with a padlock, at the rear of the shop, in which firearms of many kinds were displayed. He had just made his so-manieth visit to the sexologist ... 'Allow your imagination to wander a bit, let it do the real work, and do take plenty of time ...' He knew in advance that it wouldn't work out, but the doctor acted very busy, made telephone calls, rinsed bottles, walked to and fro, washed his hands at length: all actions undertaken with the intention of distracting him so he would not get the feeling that the doctor was waiting for him, was expecting something from him. His mind had to be trained 'lightly' on the sex act, so 'lightly' in fact that the success of that act would not seem of the slightest importance ... 'Close your eyes! It stimulates the imagination and gives you peace ...' But he did not close his eyes; from behind the plastic curtain he followed with revulsion the grotesque shadow of the doctor; that particular time he got an erection; its cause did not lie in the evocation of the sharply defined image of a lascivious woman. The busy doctor irritated him boundlessly. Chill anger crept up inside him; if I had a revolver now, he suddenly thought, I'd wrench open the curtain and then, him, I'd ... Calmly, he slid open the curtain; the doctor turned round, smiled, rubbed his hands and said: 'You see: perseverance's the thing!' With his index finger he tested the hardness; Van Baak looked at the nail which was smooth and pink with fine spots of calcium.

'Splendid!' the doctor added. But under the caressing finger and the approving gaze, his sex withered.

And he had gone for a walk in town, right hand in the pocket of his unbuttoned raincoat, finger on the trigger – in reality he was clenching the key to his front door – and he shot . . . an uninterrupted hail of grey bullets . . . he felt himself grow strong, a strange power seemed to take possession of him, the sombreness in his life was solved at a stroke . . . he even had to restrain himself from dancing a few steps . . . the disdainful expression on her face would disappear. The trick, discovered just now, did not turn out a success; he could riddle her with bullets, shoot like a daemon: in vain.

He never could have imagined that something like this would happen to him. Even as a boy he had been convinced that terrible afflictions lay in wait to assail his body; he was forty-two: anything was to be expected at that age and gratitude was a fitting thing for each day without pain. Thus, he had been prepared for many things – not for this. He well remembered that evening when it had gone wrong for the first time; he blamed it on the combination of tiredness and booze, and her discovery, too – he could not deny this – of an entire year's worth of 'Knock-knock, knockers', the big-boobs mag, underneath a folder of bills in his desk drawer; and shortly afterwards she had come into his room (a blush of shame rose to his cheeks again) and he had not been able to stuff the booklet out of sight quickly enough; it had fallen from his trousers, down in front of her feet . . . 'I'm the one watching every penny – Sir buys expensive, filthy little books . . .' They lived in a small place near Utrecht. She worked for social services in Amsterdam, visited broken homes, rang up ever more frequently to say that the consultation was running over time, that she wasn't coming home, and in the end she moved in with a man she had helped with his divorce. In letters she wrote from time to time another reproach came to the fore. That they had remained childless was his fault. The sexologist had once confided to her that his semen was too meagre.

It would happen that he would lean in town against a lamppost, right hand in his coat pocket, and that for a moment he was really of a mind to buy himself a firearm, but people had looked at him so penetratingly and he'd hurried off into the suburbs. He would never buy a firearm, and that moment of repentance had given him childlike pleasure because he was mild-mannered by nature, but particularly because he could now give his imagination free rein if need be; without danger, he could observe all the effects of a shot fired, down to the last detail, as his whim dictated.

He became a regular visitor to the house boats on the Zandpad. Most of the prostitutes knew him alright: always carefully dressed, but never without an unbuttoned beige raincoat.

The noise had sunk away into the drab bedspread. Except for the woman who, sighing, moved her leg, it was quiet inside. Outside, birds uttering sharp cries flew in across the water; in dense swarms they would dive, over the road situated higher up, over the fence in the verge, rotting away, over a crumbling wall — the last remains of a little farm — down into the depths where the fields began and faded away, further on, to a dead plain with a block of flats under construction.

The mirror with blister marks was the sole luxury in this bare, repulsive room; he turned his head and his eye fell on a poster depicting a naked woman in a curious vaulting position. At one time, the walls had been papered; the remnants were still stuck to the faded, badly fitted slats. On the table by the door stood a table lamp without a shade and a portable radio; he heard the birds again and he pressed himself up against the woman; with his head held to one side he could continue to see the shine that gave a depressing intimacy to the room — the fo'c'sle in fact. Under the lamp lay two twenty-five-guilder notes.

It was always asked for immediately upon coming in. Van Baak had adopted the habit of taking the money from his wallet in advance and to come in with the money clearly visible, mumbling, half-stooping, as if he had just found it on the path that led steeply down from the road to the boat. The money he was holding in his hand wasn't even his! And now those notes were lying there just so, brightly lit under the lamp, he could barely remember having put them there. Of course, his behaviour was very childish, but this playing with illusion had become a necessity to him.

There was a further advantage connected with this course of action. What he was holding in his hand was the sum he wished to spend. He had no more for that evening. In order to answer the call, financially, of this increasingly compelling 'extravagance', he had to draw cash more and more frequently. Van Baak was an averagely paid white-collar worker.

It was quiet outside now, too; the boat rocked and in that

moving silence he expected, any moment now, that the woman would let fly at him. He would get in there first: he turned his face towards her, almost closed his eyes and said: 'It won't work.' He raised himself and leant on his arms.

'Don't give up so soon.' The eyes beneath slate-blue eyebrows in the thin face had a friendly expression. He heard the birds outside again; in the dusk they would be gleaming black and round; birds or people, in great numbers they were always terrifying. He had never been inside this woman's place. He always took a great deal of time to take his pick, but today the chattering creatures flying over so low had frightened him. Without looking, he had fled in here. He shifted his weight from one arm to the other, lowered himself beside her, spotted a shallow fold, like an eager child's mouth, in her neck, and he was moved; his nose caught the scent of her perfumed hair; he was afraid that he would have to cough, and he looked in the mirror again, his head in the hollow of her arm. When the woman was lying down she had very hunched shoulders too; she breathed heavily; he thought she had asthmatic bronchitis.

'Come,' the woman said hoarsely.

'It's no good today,' he said. 'I don't need to try: it's because of the birds.' He lay perfectly motionless, actually expecting that she would begin to laugh, derisively.

After a good while, she said: 'And you haven't been drinking?' Her voice was calm; it seemed resilient because of the asthma.

'No.'

'Been working too hard, have you?'

'Yes,' he admitted. 'I'm sorry.'

'When you're tired it's always difficult.'

'I do believe I'm tired,' he said softly and weepily. He raised his head, stared at the bare wall above the pillow. Her hand stroked his back; he stretched his legs, laid his head back down on her shoulder.

'Are you nervous?' she asked.

'Yes, I should have stayed home today.'

'You must relax and not think — look at me.' He looked at the ageless face; she pulled his head towards her, pressed it against herself; he felt her thin neck and her bony hand slid across his body. 'It's no good,' he said. 'My eyelids are trembling — I'm tired, I'm terribly sorry.' She looked him in the face, made a slight movement, and he thought she shrugged her shoulders.

'I'm restless . . . if the birds hadn't been there . . . it was just as if they were coming out of the water: vicious, black creatures. He acted a bit hard-done-by, made a helpless gesture with his hands. 'You're afraid but don't you go thinking that there's anyone who'll take any notice of your fear. You, yourself, will have to . . .'

'I can't help it.' He would have liked to stroke the woman's hair but its hard sheen of lacquer prevented him.

'Better luck next time,' she said and remained lying down.

'I'm making a fool of myself.'

'You'd never been to me before?'

'No, I walked in, just like that.'

'Walked!' She had a thoughtful way of smiling. 'It looked as if they were after you; like a bat out of hell, you . . .'

'The birds . . .'

'They settled this afternoon, opposite; they seem very vicious.' She thought and then she said: 'It's as if they want to fly themselves to death; perhaps it's only at dusk that they shriek like this.' She looked at him for a moment and said: 'There's something very sad about you.'

He got up from the bed.

'Why are you in a hurry all of a sudden?'

'I'm ashamed of myself.'

A cat came out from underneath the bed; it rubbed against his legs, it purred; it was airless in the low room and the table lamp was burning; he stroked the creature. In the mirror he saw that she, too, now left the bed. To save face, he asked: 'D'you loathe it?'

'Why?' She was standing in front of the wash stand.

'With all those men?'

'I know who I take in.'

'How many a day?'

'Curiosity killed the cat – but fine, if you want to know: things are very quiet now but on a day with lots of regulars I quickly hit thirty or so, but I do make things easy for myself at times.' He stroked the cat. He had gone and sat on his heels next to the bed; he began to put his shirt on.

'So how d'you do that?' She began to laugh, a hoarse laugh that ended in a fit of coughing; she let water run into the mitten flannel; he saw in the mirror that she closed the tap, allowed the flannel to slide into the basin and came towards him; the cat's body was warm.

'She's a timid puss, actually; she'll only allow me to stroke her. She loves you; I think you must have a lot of friends.'

'I've got no friends.' He waited. 'I've got too powerful an imagination.' He did not understand quite what that last sentence amounted to right now; he was surprised for he felt at ease in a strange kind of way.

'You're an odd-un.' The cat shivered; the birds were silent.

'How old are you really?' Across the back of the animal, his eyes trained on her, he said: 'Forty-two.' He got tired of hunkering down and, with the cat, he went and sat on the bed; the woman had walked back to the wash stand. He looked at her sunken back.

'Forty-two,' she repeated. He squeezed the cat hard below its backbone. It jumped away, moaning; making itself small, it crawled away beneath the bed.

'What on earth're you doing now?' She looked him up and down from head to toe, but he couldn't discover anything disapproving in her; only her voice was upset. 'I made an unexpected movement,' he replied despondently and he bowed his head.

'You don't half look glum, you do – I've never had a man like you before.' She acted a little annoyed. The woman came and sat down beside him; footsteps sounded outside, it had begun to rain; he knew what the sky would be like this autumn which had set in early: from behind the flats, dark clouds would come sailing in, winging their way up like tremendous beasts, lit from below by the last rays of the evening sun; it was as if all those clouds were gathering for an attack upon the endless row of dripping, rocking boats, in order to smother the shrill cries of love. He looked in the mirror and was startled: he was still holding his revolver in his hand; it was not heavy, what with its slender, cobalt-blue barrel and the flame-grained grip. He got up and walked over to his raincoat hanging on a nail against the door, and he put the gun away, deep in the coat pocket. The woman followed him and shook her head. The rain was falling, hard and monotonous; again he heard footsteps, someone was listening at the window; the image of the feverish sky returned; he was sweaty and he saw that his hands were trembling.

'Actually, what's the time?' She took his right hand, rotated his wrist forty-five degrees, and looked. 'Ten past seven. Quietest time of the day.' She put his hand on her bare, knobbly knee. 'Try just one more time.' He looked at his shirt which he was busy buttoning up.

'Never mind, keep it on.'

'Yes,' he said, without conviction. He lay there looking at

himself again and at the woman who was doing all she possibly could.

'Just think of nothing at all and don't do anything either; you're all wet with perspiration.'

'It's hot.'

'The room has low ceilings; it soon gets too hot with the electric fire on.'

'It's hard to regulate the temperature in such a little room,' he said, 'an electric fire has just two settings.'

'Don't move,' she ordered; she acted very strict, almost the same tone as his mother's, way back.

'My wife . . .' he said, and was silent.

'Well . . . ?'

He was silent. 'You don't have to tell me anything, but *if* you want to get something off your chest, I can listen, I've learned to − , I'm here, I sometimes think, more to listen than . . .' He went on being silent.

'Fine . . . all the same to me . . .'

'No,' he said, suddenly.

'What, no?'

'It won't work, honest . . . I'm s . . .'

'Is that you apologising again?' She acted cross again; looked at him in the mirror. 'No need to be ashamed of yourself: you're just tired, we're all tired at times.' The rain clattered on the roof and against the little window pane. 'Please don't pull such a helpless face: you're just like a child.'

'I shouldn't have done it today − I might have known.'

'You're in a bit of a state: you ought to go home.' He got up at once, walked over to the chair his clothes were lying on and, with a rapid gesture, pulled his trousers from it. The woman continued lying down and said: 'See: now you're acting all panicky again.' He stared at the money under the lamp, on the table by the door − he only need stretch out his hand.

'Perhaps I'll already be back again tomorrow,' and a little laugh spread across his face.

'I won't let you in.'

'You'll let me in alright.'

'Yes, I will let you in,' she admitted and she smiled, thought-fully.

'Just imagine, me being so tired today of all days, when I'm here for the first time.'

315

'Now you listen here,' she said, 'it's time you stopped that whingeing.'

'Could I have some water, please: my mouth's dry.'

'That's what it's there for.' He walked past the bed the woman was still lying on, held his head sideways underneath the tap and drank; he saw the money; why hadn't she put it away at once? He drank greedily, wiped his mouth and said: 'I'm sorry.'

'Put a sock in it, *please.*' She put a long cigarette between her lips. It had become stronger of late, this mania of apologising for every word, for every deed.

'D'you know what it is with you?' He shook his head. 'Lack of self-confidence.'

'Perhaps.' Half hunched over, he stood by the wash stand, in socks and a buttoned-up shirt: preposterous and unworthy, full of revulsion at himself. She said: 'You're still afraid and the birds can't be heard, haven't been for ages.'

'I'm always afraid,' and he put his trousers on. 'I have to do battle a great deal,' he said with an ironical laugh. It seemed as if the woman was thinking about something.

'It's very odd,' she said, 'I'm never frightened. I get customers like that more often and then I think to myself: why haven't I got it? That fear — and then I sit trying to work it out and I almost seem to get frightened and then I say to my self: 'Bugger it, my girl, get a grip on yourself: you're letting yourself be wound up by all those men . . .' She waited. And then she added: 'I'm only frightened of my chest going tight.'

'Fear is frightful,' he said. He wanted to say some more, but nothing would come to him.

'If I get ill, I'll take things as they come: you die willy-nilly, only you shouldn't give in to it.'

'D'you always talk so much with your clients?'

'Sometimes.' And the money was just lying there under the lamp. If I had it back, he thought, if . . . and he went on dressing himself, slowly, but his hands were trembling so much he had to stop for a moment. It wasn't raining any more; he thought he heard footsteps again. The woman had got up; there was a tap at the window. He put his raincoat on. 'You do look neat,' she said. 'I know who I take in.' He laughed a little sheepishly and said: 'My money doesn't grow on trees . . . I'd best be off,' and he walked to the door. She was too quick for him. 'Wait,' she said, pushing him aside. 'I'm not done yet.' He stood by the door, hunched, slave-like

316

almost, and the revolver felt heavy in his coat pocket; he waited. She moved in his direction and at that moment Van Baak still wanted to make a remark, about the cosiness of the room or about her, that they weren't all like her, that she had so much patience, that with others he was back out on the street in five minutes, usually, but he said nothing and looked at the door. He heard her taking the money from the table, heard her fold it up slowly – he didn't dare to look; she was standing behind him, she touched his arm, breathed with difficulty, her hand slipped into his coat pocket, she clutched his fingers, he let go of the key and felt the money. 'Go on, off with you,' she said, 'and see you again some time?'

She unlocked the door.

The door closed behind him, the curtain was drawn open and she followed him with her gaze; he clasped the money in his hands – it was still and empty around him; he didn't have the courage to look. A cool scent hung above the road; the moon forced its way between the clouds, casting scraps of light on the dead plain and revealing a foaming drainage-canal. Perfectly alone, he stood in the road the was wind passing over. With the greatest possible difficulty, he kept himself upright; mysterious light had gathered behind the wall as if there was a fire there, that's how bright the glow was, and then he saw that he was not alone. Figures, almost invisible because of the moving shadows the boats cast on the road, looked at him with curiosity; some were on their haunches: ominous, motionless phantoms; a frog floated in the muddy stream of water between the road and the verge. Why were they watching him? How many men were waiting there? Had he stayed inside too long? Did they have it in for him? What did they have to do with him? A man with a briefcase and a walking stick loosed himself from a hollow of darkness, walked in the direction of the woman Van Baak had just left. He halted in the middle of the road, walked back as if having second thoughts, came to a halt again. Within the safe shelter of his hands, he lit a cigarette; his face lit up above his hands, in his eyes the surprised look of someone wondering how he has ended up there. He prodded the gleaming stomach of the frog, then walked resolutely to the window and went inside.

Van Baak remembered that the cat had not showed itself again; he proceeded slowly in the direction of his car; he no longer had any interest in the eyes fixed on him, nor in the plentiful light the moon was casting behind the wall. The house boats looked bloated because of the moisture; he averted his gaze from all of this, took a few more steps. In his hand he clutched the money she had returned to him; she had let it slide into his hand and he had had the feeling as if it was sliding up inside his body . . .

Once again, he began to walk down the road; by his watch he saw that it was seven-thirty; he still had an entire evening ahead of him; a flock of birds passed along, high and far away against the grey sky.

He turned round.

A woman made up of large, brown spheres tapped against the window, slowly and seductively; the rain began to come down again; plumes of vapour rose from the water as if big animals were breathing in the winter air; a swan, created from small white blossoms, attempted, hissing, to rid itself of a condom that had wrapped itself round its beak. He nodded.

Tears came to his eyes and, with a rapid movement, before the dark woman opened the door, he loaded his revolver.

Leviathan

P.F. Thomése

1

Only after some time did the hunters notice that they were no longer walking along a path. Drink whispered and giggled in their ears so that they did not know it had become as quiet as death itself around them. They wanted to shoot, for they had not yet shot a thing all day. From time to time, one of them would train his gun in order to feel the butt against his cheek. With the barrel he would describe the flight of a grouse or the course of a rabbit. But all who rustled and fluttered concealed themselves in the trees and the scrub, so the gun was shouldered once more, with nothing to show for it. The hunters tottered on, and they did not know that they tottered – their drunken thoughts sped on ahead like fawns' hooves on moss, enticing. The dogs, curious, looked round continually, following the hunters' trail, thinking that it led somewhere. Behind them, the landscape fell apart into dunes of dusty sand.

Taking turns, the hunters bore along a dirty, linen sack. Inside it, they were transporting the stone head of Saint Hieronymus of Noordwijk which they had won on the way, gambling. The sack was heavy and stank of fish. Occasionally, they would have to rest because their fingers were becoming cramped with all that lugging. Yet, they would get up each time again and not forget the sack. Though they did not want to take the sack along, they actually did so.

The loose slopes slipped away beneath their feet. In vain they sought to gain a hold on the weeds that shot loose, on the prickly thorn bushes and dead tree branches.

Only when the sky darkened and the storm arose, in wild gusts which made the dune sand fly up, did they notice that, by God, they did not know where they were.

They halted near a weathered enclosure because they had seen its woodwork before, but when that had been and which way they

319

had then gone at the time, this failed to spring to mind. So they stood there, indecisive, near that little fence in the wilderness while the storm battered the dunes and lightning flashed in the distance. It surprised them that there was no shelter anywhere: just now it was beginning to hail and sandstorms made further progress impossible. In his mind, each of them cursed the others, but himself as well, because he had gone along with them, off to nowhere. As well as they could, they hid behind the fence, the hacked-off head of the saint between them. Because of the wet, the sack had begun to stink even more and now their dress coats, too, smelled of fish. The dogs were in a panic and howled in desperation. The hunters were hardly worried at all, as nothing serious had ever happened to them. In their heads still hummed the boasting of a while ago: of hunts on the manor of so-and-so, and of women with doe's eyes who were soft and plump like rabbits. Rolled up tight, their faces in the hollows of their arms, they let the tempest pass over them and they did not notice that the plumes on their hats had snapped.

The storm raged terribly. A little further on, lightning struck and a hamlet disappeared in its entirety in the roaring, spitting flames. At sea, fishing smacks were engulfed by tidal waves and the boats on the beach, too, had disappeared, for there was no longer any beach there. Already the sea was swirling over the top of the first dunes. The hunters were oblivious. They lay there, huddled behind the fence, and were too far away to hear the bells of Noordwijk-op-Zee raising the alarm.

Around them, gusts of wind sliced away at the dunes and thus freed a path for the flood.

It lasted too long to the hunters' taste. It was already late and they wished to be home before dark. They were also worried about the dogs which they had not seen for a while now. And when the storm abated for a moment, they crawled out and stood upright. No mean thing: their joints were stiff and their heads ached with stabbing pains. They were cold and their sodden clothing itched on their bodies. After bickering a bit about the sack – whether they would not leave it behind after all – they were on their way, sack and all.

First, they had to climb the dunes to see where in fact they actually were. The sand was loose and heavy, giving their unsteady legs support. But before they had reached the top, a brusque, heavy gust of wind forced them to lie down.

Flat on their bellies they crawled along and thus they reached the highest point.

Perhaps they might better have stayed behind their fence, for what they saw did not improve their prospects. It was not just the sea which was all around them and foamed at the mouth like the prophecies of Isaiah, rising and lighting up beneath the darkened heavens, but it was that beast in particular, fearfully large and near, so large and awe-inspiring that it seemed almost biblical – it regarded them and gave a leering grin at so much insignificance. It was not clear what they could do, for behind them, too, was the sea. The fact of the matter was, you might say, that the sea was had only failed to reach where they were. It was curious, too – and this only dawned on them slowly – that their case was a hopeless one. There was indeed a fishing smack floating in their direction, but before they had had a chance to see it properly, it was smashed to pieces by the waves.

The dune held up for quite a while still, and because it lasted so long the hunters got up hope. The biblical creature came no closer, though it did not go away either. Now and then, it submerged as if to hoodwink the hunters, and then it rose up again revealing its immense back. It seemed to the hunters that the beast was the instigator of the violence of the sea. It appeared to smash down on the waves with its tail and that way propel their surge. Occasionally it would open its jaws and they could see a disgusting tongue of flesh. Possibly, were they able to kill it, the fateful tempest would cease – and the water would return to the sea and they would be able to continue on their way through the dunes. But the hunters had never shot anything larger than a deer and they feared that the beast, once struck, would only burst forth in fury. Still, they grabbed for their field bags and wanted to load their guns. The gunpowder was wet, however, and they did not even make the attempt.

They thought they would soon be eaten now – and this set them off crying. The hunters wept, their bellies shaking, and they barely noticed that the flood swept over them.

The sack with the saint's head, too, disappeared into the depths of darkness.

2

When morning was approaching, the storm had died down and a haze of light began to dawn beneath the low, heavy sky, the

Admiral set out with a number of other fishermen to take in the damage on the beach. Their clothes were soaked and they were freezing with cold. They had little hope that there would be anything left of their little vessels, but they were relieved to be able to flee from the devastated hamlet. Its eight hovels had all been wrecked and had then collapsed. The women were now busy bandaging wounds with wet, stinking rags. Others took pity on the horse that during the lightning had got into a panic and had broken its legs. They had heard the creature all night but it merely trembled now. Someone sliced its neck open and allowed the blood to drain into the sand. While the horse was still convulsing, people began to cut off the meat in strips.

In the distance they heard the bells of Maria-ter-Zee, tolling for All Souls.

The Admiral thought of the candles that would be burning there and how those lights would make the gold, silver and brass gleam, with sparkles shooting up so that it seemed as if you had tears in your eyes, and the saints, too, had tears in their eyes — tears of sadness, but also because things had ended well, after all. The Admiral no longer attended chapel: he was one of the new faith. He walked with God. The new faith did not gleam: it was dull and black and resigned, like a funeral cortège. Thus, head bent, he walked with God through the gruesomeness of life. Yet it alarmed him that the chapel which had likewise been built of wood had not been sent to perdition during the tempest. He walked out ahead of the men and was silent. They, too, were silent: they preferred not to have their forebodings confirmed.

The coast was beyond all recognition. The flood had forced the water to surge deep inland. Dunes had caved in and been swept away, and on the flattened remains they found the blue pulp of dead jelly fish. The fishing smacks were nowhere to be seen. For that matter, there was not a sail in sight on the entire sea. It lay grey and empty in the morning light. They could have gone back now but they walked on, in the direction of Noordwijk-op-Zee.

Ahead of them cantered the Admiral's little son. The hump-backed lad, commonly called the Humpkin, rose and dipped from dune to dune as if he was trying to escape from the little dune on his back. The Admiral was revolted by that little hump which had sent his wife to her death. He was revolted by that simple little lad that had been born from death — with its little-old-man's-head it had waited between blood-soaked thighs to see whether it would be allowed to live. The Admiral had not known what to do. He had taken his fishknife and fetched the mite in a gush of blood. There was nothing else he could have done: it had been that hump that had stuck in the mother's womb. Nobody had taken against him for this but he had turned dour precisely because nobody had made him take the blame – and he hated fate, a fate that was indifferent and took his beautiful young wife from him and provided an ugly hump in her place.

Humpkin, meanwhile, tripped on ahead and seemed to have no notion of the burden weighing down on his shoulders. It was the father who was weighed down.

For years now, the Admiral was being undermined by doubt which had rendered him taciturn and evasive. The fishermen took this to be gruffness and believed that their boss thought himself to be too high and mighty for them; they did not know that inner confusion and despair were what impeded his sociability. He had thoughts he could not utter so they continued to wheel about in his head without encountering contradiction. They dragged him along and left him stranded, not knowing the way.

Where he was lost, there it was writ that God had taken the truth away from the world and had set hope in its place.

The doubt had been sown in the days that preachers of the new faith had come to smash up the idolatrous statuary. Their word seemed true and the misdeeds of the false church appeared terrible to him. But when they had entered the convent garden of Saint Barbara, he had hesitated – and from then on he would continue to hesitate. It had been a languid summer's afternoon and nightingales were singing in the shrubbery. He was touched by the industrious plenty and peace that reigned in this garden. The herbs in their trimmed borders, the flower beds, the hum around the bee hives, the tuneful chatter of birds in the orchard – these were all there and it was good that this was so, for it was beautiful and devoid of people. The convent walls were cloaked in clouds of vine and honeysuckle, and in front of the convent stood shady lime trees. He knew he ought not to be there; he smelled how the scent of flowers, herbs and ripe fruit were being driven out by the smell of fish steaming from him in the afternoon warmth. Behind his back he felt the men's presence spread out. A cloud slid in front of the sun – but it was as though it were their shadow passing, chill and sombre, over the convent garden. Lizards slipped by past their feet; startled birds fanned out into the sky. Rustling everywhere, and snapping twigs.

It befell him that his feet were booming through the convent corridors and that his eyes saw the idols break. There was baying and screaming and the shattering of glass. The fishermen chased after the sisters, down corridors and up staircases, sanctity crunching beneath their feet. He stood in the chapel among the wrecked prayer stools, torn altar cloths, among the shards and powdered rubble. There he stood and he recognised the head of the saint of Noordwijk who looked at him and did not seem to understand all this either.

He felt a draught rush by, past his ankles, slipping away through a crack.

He had thought to rescue the saint by taking him with him. Often he had prayed to him when God was wrathful and made the waves foam. He knew Hieronymus was an idol and at the same time he knew that it was sacrilegious to touch a saint with one's own hands. He knew he was doing wrong, no matter what. But was this going to make him leave it lying there, defenceless, and wait for the others to trample it to dust?

He didn't have much time to think, for a moment later fire roared up from the thatched roof and smoke billowed through the corridors.

He wrapped the head in a strip of altar cloth and slipped away through a smashed window in the sacristy.

From then on, he had kept the head in a cupboard, together with his wife's worthless paraphernalia.

He wondered whether it had been wrong to take only the head. Possibly the torso was roaming about somewhere, haunting, soulless. But he had not seen the torso lying anywhere. Now, that head was lying on its side on a shelf as if it was a hunk of cheese or some kind of hat. It was the preposterousness which worried him, and he became convinced, by and by, that he had done something irreparable, something only to be atoned for by punishment. Though, indeed, he had converted to the new faith, he feared that God would take but little notice of that. The wayside preacher had said that He 'shall expunge from the land the names of idols, that they be thought no more'. And yet the head of Saint Hieronymus lay in his cupboard and each day he would think of him. And each night, when fear rattled at the shutters and groaned quietly in the wood of his alcove bedstead, he feared both retribution and vengeance.

Then ˙ ˴se three gents, those simpletons had knocked at his

door and they had got themselves drunk on the brandy he had sold them too dearly. The Admiral loathed such gents because they gave him the feeling that everything about him was wrong. They made him envious and caused him to feel sad for all he was not and would not become. The way they sat there on the wooden bench, with their boots of burnished leather and those hands gesturing you-know-what – it gave the Admiral satisfaction to ply them with brandy until their tongues writhed helplessly like fish on dry land. To frighten them, he had taken the head of Saint Hieronymus from the cupboard, but he himself had become afraid; the gents were not startled, on the contrary: they, with their rotund little tums, had had to laugh uncontrollably and wished most insistently to cast dice for 'that patron saint of brandy drinkers'. The Admiral wondered whether perhaps they were of the new faith that they dared mock a saint in so carefree a manner. And his loathing grew the greater because they seemed so at home with higher things and were not afraid at all, as if they had been able to strike a deal, somehow, with up-above.

Shortly after the gents had left, with the head of the saint in an old sack, the storm had risen. For a moment, the Admiral rubbed his hands with glee at those waddling bunglers who would only find a hold on each other's flapping coattails – then he forgot them, because his house had begun to creak ominously.

The peril his house was in notwithstanding, his neighbours came to seek shelter with him. His house had two floors and seemed almost impressive in the midst of the fishermen's hovels which most closely resembled tents, what with their posts and their canopies of sailcloth. But his house could not hold out against that battering North-Westerly either, and he was forced to seek refuge in the cellar. Here, there was only space for a few: the others had to go outside again to find what shelter they could under the oily sailcloth the storm tore at and the tempest hailed down upon.

It was dark in the cellar and airless, and everyone sat bent down because of the flotsam timber shifting and subsiding ominously overhead. Buried in this grave, they had listened to the voices borne along by the storm. No praying, just occasional cursing, for everyone wished to hear those voices which were the voices of the lost, roaming dead. They had heard them more often at sea when the storm came from the North-West, from over yonder where the world disappeared in mist and where heaven and earth seemed to touch. Now, too, they listened to the voices again though they knew that these could not be understood.

In the end it had quietened down and shortly afterwards they had heard the familiar shrieks of common terns.

Now the storm had abated it seemed as if everything that once had been, had been taken away. The saint of storms had taken away their dwellings and their ships, and he had taken away the paths and made them roam in the wilderness. The fishermen wailed and cursed, but the Admiral was only tired. He knew that this was as it was meant to be: one builds that which will be lost anyway – and that it is useless to know this. He would erect his two-storey house again, ridiculously puny with its thatched roof beneath the gruesome expanse of heaven. He again would lead the fishermen and they would believe themselves to be going somewhere because they followed him – the way they all followed the Lord and did not know that he was wrathful and had taken away the truth from the world, only leaving hope behind.

They had been trudging along all the while, heads bent, bog-brained with tiredness, looking on without noticing how their feet left imprints behind in the wet dune sand, feet meandering across the smooth sand, fanning out, crossing and trampling each other without discernible cause. The men walked heavily, as if they were carrying something. There was something solemn about it, something rather ceremonial, the way they progressed in this stricken dune landscape, something terrifying, too: the misshapen child out in front like a messenger of doom. The bells of Maria-ter-Zee still tolled in honour of the mystery of death and, seen from a distance, the little troupe resembled a funeral cortège, impressed by something of which the meaning eluded them.

Down below, the sea allowed its waves to unroll listlessly on to the bare coast.

Thus they went on, oppressed and introverted – and because of this, they only saw the stranger when he was nigh upon them. He resembled a monk, but if so, one from an unknown order. Around his shoulders hung a drab blanket which was bound tight round his middle with a frayed length of mooring rope. His head was bald, the bald pate hard and smooth as brass. He did not speak nor did he look them in the face. He pointed towards the sea. And then, only then did they see what they might have seen a long time ago, for it had been there all the while.

On the beach lay, fearfully large and alive, the Leviathan.

3

Jan van der Does, the young Lord of Noordwijk, unwillingly took his leave of his Leiden host and in the company of a number of literary friends he left for his seigneurial demesne. He would rather have stayed to let himself be admired a little more as the scholar and particularly as the poet Janus Dousa, renowned in the Republic of Letters for his elegant *Epigrammata*, but duty called – duty he had inherited and which he bore like Aeneas his father. He hoped to amuse himself with his companions on the way; the previous evening they had sat up late and had argufied over the question of whether the classics might ever be surpassed. But now he was trotting along muddy roads, he had no longer any desire to shine. Because of last night's storm he had not had a wink of sleep, and he was tired and ill-tempered.

Actually, he would have stayed in Leiden a few days more – some learned visitors from Leuven were expected – but his host had filled his head with worries. At first, he had wished to know nothing about them, but as time went by he had become worried nevertheless – now he was even in a hurry to get back home.

The road was barely passable, thick mud and deep puddles forcing him into the verge. At walking pace, occasionally at a trot, the riders went along, one behind the other, each sunk into his own thoughts.

Dousa was reminded of his return from Paris, when it had been autumn, too, and he had felt himself to be like Ovid on his way to Tomi, his place of banishment on the Black Sea. *Longa via est: propera! Nobis habitabitur orbis ultimus, a terra terra remota mea*[1]. In his head these wondrously beautiful verses, yet around him, on the carts and the barges, Dousa heard the shameless jabber of merchants, soldiers and fat monks – and he felt nostalgia for his student days in Paris where such stupid folk quite simply did not exist and where everybody spoke about books as though they were their personal friends. It was in a Zeeland barge, squashed in between farmers with baskets full of vegetables and decapitated geese, that he had seized upon the plan that he, too, must write a *Tristia*, emulating the great Ovid.

[1] 'Make haste, the road is long. From now on we shall live a' the edge of the world, in a distant land remote from mine.' Tristia 1.3 *Tr*

327

But now, riding through the autumnal Rhineland, he recalled anew why nothing had ever come of those Noordwijk lamentations: this bleak region, this *orbis ultimus* where the wind always blew, this was not just any place on the edge of the world, this was *his* land and he belonged here. Here he knew everything like the back of his hand: the church spires of Noordwijk, Katwijk and Rijnsburg, the flat countryside with its canals and ditches, the dunes, the trees of *'t Hout*, the sea. What remained was the melancholy that fate had put him here and not in Paris – that the fine, glittering life was there, but not for him. In books, however, he found solace; words to him were more real than that which he saw, and this was why he had memorised as many poems as possible in the libraries of Paris, Leuven and Antwerpen, so that he, no matter where he was, would only need to close his eyes to float away on words to wherever he wanted. He knew Ovid and Horace, Juvenal, Martial, Propertius and Tibullus – he only regretted that they did not know him and did not know that here he was, trudging through the mud on horseback in that no-man's-land, well past the frontiers of the Roman Empire, lost in the mists of time, but that he was doing this with their poetry in his head nevertheless. Definitely.

Behind him trudged his travel companions, comparative dunces who could not distinguish the Vulgate from classical Latin and who spoke with hollow reverence of 'the language of God' while, in their heart of hearts, they would like best of all to be covened together inside their chambers of grand rhetoric, huddling around those crooked little Dutch rhymes of theirs. They had come along this time because they didn't mind staying at the country seat of a real humanist for once. Dousa tolerated such folk because Noordwijk was remote and his great friends Giselinus and Silvius did not come down that often. He had a need, from time to time, to promenade in educated company amidst the surrounding countryside, conversing on the *bonae literae*. He was continually uncertain about his own work, too, and hankered after judgements, opinions, even if only those of a few dotty rhetoricians. Without them, he would grow lonely, standing in vain on the look-out in the hope that the postilion with his brass horn would bring a letter from afar. Even Ovid, who had kept company with the best in happier days, would write in the language of the Geti at times, because he, in the midst of barbarians, would rather be the greatest poet of Tomi than nothing at all.

Occasionally, however, Dousa would fear that his life was founded upon a misunderstanding and that he had gone the wrong way, irrevocably — like a midge at sea that flew on because it had wings and noticed too late that this world was too large for it.

When they entered Noordwijk, riding across the wooden little drawbridge, he ceased his cogitations. Here he was lord, and he had to endure that his head would be taken up by others' lives forcing themselves upon him with their obnoxious insignificance. The villagers cheated him as regards their rents, tolls and excises; they poached on his hunting grounds and stole from his winter supplies — and still they were not ashamed to bother him about one thing or another. He permitted it because things were easier that way — he had a distaste for business and certainly for business of base quality. His contempt for material life, among which he also reckoned this illiterate clodhopperdom to be, was so great that he preferred to hide it, which meant he passed for an amiable man.

He wished to reach his manor farm as soon as possible. To prevent his being addressed, he spurred his horse on with the consequence that dogs jumped up, barking, and ran along bothersomely amidst the horses. The villagers came out of their houses to see who was going with such haste along the *Gooweg*. On seeing it was their lord, they waved and cried out after him. He replied with mud splattering up from beneath the horses' hooves.

Before he had reached the little lane leading to his estate, he was brought to a halt by the bailiff who tended his affairs during his repeated absences and who appeared to have need to speak with him urgently now. Pieter Woutersz was an insignificant man who was in awe of the house of Van der Does, sworn vassals of the Counts of Holland, with a coat of arms quartered: in the first and fourth, nine diamonds gold on red; in the second and third, the Noordwijk lion on silver. Dousa was irked by this servile creep whose meticulousness made things boil down to the fact that Dousa only needed to confirm whatever-it-was of concern at the time, which meant that things happened the way Woutersz wanted them to. The man had the irritating habit of speaking of 'we', which gave Dousa the feeling of being involved in an unsavoury *tête-à-tête*. He would likewise always refer to agreements which Dousa could not recollect at all. In such cases, Dousa had the tendency to put himself in the other's position thus forgetting his own interests, in the end agreeing to something that was only to his disadvantage. Afterwards he would then ponder for a long time still why he had said this and not that, and why he had not put Woutersz in his place in particular.

As is more often the case with thinking people, a curious phenomenon would occur with Dousa in that he made a rather slow, even dunce-like impression while in reality his thoughts had rushed a long way ahead of the conversation, which meant that what he said already had nothing to do with that which he was thinking at the time; the words, uttered casually and carelessly, were to him but a small step in a dizzying train of thought, but to a blunt soul such as Woutersz these were the only things that mattered. It was like Zeno's paradox about the contest between Achilles and the tortoise: once Achilles has caught up with the tortoise the latter has already left again. Likewise, Woutersz kept ahead of him all the time. The thinker's thoughts were faster than reality yet they never caught up with it.

This time, however, that jobsworth did not know what to do with himself, and it gave Dousa pleasure to continue at walking pace, just ahead of the bailiff, so that the latter had to speak up beyond his powers and could not be sure whether he was being understood. The lane was narrow and no matter how Woutersz manoeuvred on his big *Gelder* stallion, he remained uncomfortably situated, half hidden behind Dousa, while the bare little twigs of the trees lashed his face.

Quite soon, Dousa lost himself in thought and he forgot his retinue. He remembered his plan to acquire land on the North side so that his estate would reach to the *Lijdweg* and he would be able to withdraw altogether within the seclusion of his domain. He relished the trees, some of which were showing their bare skeletal shapes and others were adorning their last days with a glow of gold-leaf – and it annoyed him that he did not know the names of the trees. He resolved to enquire into this and to make a study of nature. One did, after all, first have to study things individually before being able to fathom the whole. There was so much one passed over unheeding, there was so much there without one being aware of about it. Those trees just stood there and quite simply begged to be understood by him. Suddenly, Dousa was gripped by the impatient desire to know how they came into being, how they grew and why there were trunks and branches and all that leaf-cover that died and was reborn. And above him the sky stretched out in incomprehensible blueness. He was in a hurry; he wished to lock himself away in his library as soon as possible to delve into some books. Plodding along here, snail's pace, in the company of useless souls, was wasted time: all time not devoted to study was wasted time.

He had not noticed that the bailiff had overtaken him and he was startled when his way turned out to be barred: Woutersz had taken up position at right angles to the lane and he burst in brutishly upon Dousa's thoughts. He spoke confusedly, probably because he had been made to wait so long for his opportunity and now he was standing in all his glory in front of his lord, he no longer quite knew what it was he had been waiting for. His sentences reached out for something that always remained unmentioned; they twisted and turned and became encrusted with words they were unable to shake off. It pleased Dousa to let the uneducated bailiff wrestle to such an extent with the language as though it were a thing too large for him to grasp. But in due course the confusion of his otherwise so punctual bailiff began to worry him nevertheless, and when he was asked to accompany the bailiff, he did not demur.

There were horses trampling and snorting in that little lane, reins were tugged and flanks were prodded with heels; for a moment all stood at right angles to one another and no one knew who wanted to go where – but the next moment all were off at a canter in pursuit of the hurrying Woutersz, and the bailiff led along the literary scholars in ignorance.

Again they went along the *Gooweg* and turned off right, down the *Heiligenweg*. At St Hieronymus-In-Deserto they reduced speed, for in the churchyard the pit was open and the priest was busy sprinkling the dead with holy water as if something was still meant to grow forth from that corpse-cradle. A dog was bothersomely running about in front of his feet but the priest dared not give the creature a kick, bearing in mind the sacred actions undertaken. The dog sniffed between his legs and tried to get near the pit, something the priest countered with half-hearted movements. From a distance, a few stood watching. In front of the wall of the charnel house a choir had been arranged. With booming men's voices it sang a *Dies Irae* that fell quite dead under the bare sky.

Through the open church doors they heard the true believers hurling abuse. They had been locked up in the lofts above the galleries where previously the skulls had been stored. Dousa had been surprised that the church had decided on this course of

331

action, but the priest had explained to him that he himself had urged the inquisitors to be allowed to lock up the heretics in the former charnel lofts so they would serve as frightening examples to those still erring. The prisoners had disturbed the liturgy with their hollering – and they would even chuck their excreta down during the eucharist. Churchgoers had complained but the priest had been adamant. He saw the Christian faith as a kind of wager-of-battle with evil, and he took pride in drowning the noise of the heretics with communal singing and thus have the corpus christi gain victory under a bombardment of heretic filth. When the faithful stayed away in great numbers, the priest reviewed his teachings and from then on, at the sacred hours, the prisoners would be bound and gagged or even knocked unconscious.

Beyond the church the gallows began. These stood among the trees so one would only see them when watching out for them. From the odd one a forgotten skeleton would be dangling, but most of them were empty because the followers of the new faith had been warned in time and had been able to go to ground. The empty gallows stood along the *Heiligenweg* and along the *Oude Zeeweg* in the dunes; like herons at the water's edge, quiet and assured, they stood, all the way down to Noordwijk-op-Zee.

Along this road they continued on their way.

The friends from Leiden, who had been looking forward to cosy chats in a summer house, were getting fed up now and they asked where all this was taking them. Dousa did not know. I don't know, he said, and cantered off after Woutersz. You go from here to there, he thought, from there to yonder, but you get nowhere, for it is the world that is sliding from underneath you – and if you look back you can see it disappear. Dousa wanted to hold on to this thought – he might be able to use it for a poem, perhaps – but when suddenly he was made to sidestep a dead tree-trunk, it had already evaporated. He did still try to track it down, but it was not to be found. How curious, the way thoughts came and went as you progressed, as though the head was making its own journey through the landscapes of the mind.

Somewhere between two gallows the bailiff halted. This was where they had last been seen. He was talking about the three cousins of his lord's wife who had gone out hunting and had not returned from the storm. At first, Dousa did not know what this was all about. The cousins, the Van Zuylen cousins, said the bailiff; they had gone out hunting and had not returned. Dousa thought:

is *this* what I had to come along for all this way, for my wife's cousins? The Leiden friends, on the contrary, seemed to take the greatest possible interest in the case. They bounced back out of their decline. All kinds of details they wanted to know, such as the shoes the hunters had been wearing and whether or not they had gone on horseback; they wanted to know times and distances – and they whispered among themselves no end. Dousa did not understand how they could get so bothered about a load of cousins, and another's at that. The thought of those missing evoked in him an atmosphere of fleshiness: fat little hands gesticulating in full rooms and wasting time with a great ado about nothing, and he concluded that their disappearance amounted to no great loss.

Already, Dousa wanted to turn back on the spot but Woutersz gave him a sign. There was more: they must go on.

The ones from Leiden who had expected to be turning off down the dune track, retraced their steps, non-plussed. They would gladly have set off on a man-hunt for the disappeared gentry, with lots of trampling of hooves on the dull moss and cries of 'this way!', and an exciting catharsis with three run-through corpses in a thorny thicket. They did not understand how the two others could allow this spectacle to elude them, but they followed on, without protest. They were beginning to suffer saddle pains, for that matter: they were used to sitting down, but not on horseback. They were tired and Dousa, too, was tired, and this made them amenable.

All rode on, following the bailiff down the deep cart tracks among the gallows. The bells of Maria-ter-Zee sounded in the distance. The sky darkened, the wind got up, and soon it began to rain. It suddenly seemed much later, now drab-grey clouds blacked out the sun. As if the low sky lay heavily upon them, thus the horsemen bowed their heads. The birds, which at the announcement of the bad weather had been skimming criss-cross above their heads, had disappeared. Where do birds actually shelter, Dousa wondered. Behind the dunes roared the sea. It was here that the land met its end.

From a taller dune they saw what they had come for: the floods of the past night had swept away the dune-side facing the sea and the water had streamed freely into the fishing village. The chapel was awash; against its walls two little boats bobbed up and down. They saw people sitting on the roofs of the houses; other houses had collapsed. A few men waded through the knee-high water, pushing along possessions a-top pieces of driftwood. But when they took a better look they saw that these were not possessions but corpses which had been tied to planks and doors, corpses which were being taken to dry land where they were laid down alongside other corpses. Then they would be untied and the wood would serve once more as a floating bier. There was no hurrying here which was why things looked as if this was the way they were meant to be. From a little distance away a few old dears were watching the way things are always watched when something changes place. So they were not watching the corpses lying there, a little gawkily, with feet that could walk no longer and hands that could no longer grasp and a head that never again would understand why it had ended up just there. The spectators had no interest in the corpses, abandoned by the soul, unprotected and defenceless, now seeking shelter in the void of the sky, no, they were watching the men pushing bier after bier through the black water, but it could also be that they were watching the raindrops, splashing and drawing rings, and the wake of the bier, drawing lines instead, and how the wind wiped all of this out.

The bailiff pointed downwards and asked Dousa what was to be done about this. How was he to know? How am I to know that, I who do not even know where birds take shelter in autumn when it rains and the trees are bare. I don't know, he said, and the bailiff did not know either.

Because they were getting cold up there on top of that dune in full force of the wind, they went on. There was more, the bailiff said, further on, down on the beach. And they saw the beach through a breach in the dunes and behind it lay the sea the way it always does. They descended; the horses slithered and were startled when they stepped into the cold water. Everybody watched the horsemen going along, one behind the other, through the water. The men with the biers stood still and looked up at the horsemen, and the old dears on dry land, too, watched how the gentlemen high up on their horses passed by them. Only once the gentlemen had passed from view did they continue with recovering the dead and watching the black water the dead were being fished out from, and only then did they hear the bells tolling because the birds did not sing and the women did not sing at their stoves and because the souls were lost and could not be found again.

The beached whale lay motionless, waiting, and the bystanders looked on and waited too. They stood at a safe distance and they had brought along knives and axes — just in case — even though they did not know whether they would be able to kill it, given the tremendous dimensions of the creature. Neither did they know what to do should they unexpectedly succeed. Most of all, they wished it would go away so that they, too, could go away. But it did not go away, and neither did they. The rain tapped on their caps and fell noiselessly on both land and sea. The drops splashed on the whaleskin, slick as oil, and pearled down; it seemed as if the whale shivered but it was the rain, splashing. The ones who had been standing there longest maintained that they had seen it laugh. The corners of its mouth twitched, they said. Why it had laughed, they did not know. Bloated and cumbrous, it lay on dry land and birds skimmed over the top of it and pecked at its skin. Had it not laughed, one might have thought that it was dead, the more so as it stank like the grave. No one would then have to be afraid of the whale, but for the fact that it was so large, it deprived all that surrounded it of its meaning.

Because the whale was so unconscionably large and the bystanders therefore insignificant, the feeling crept over them that this had something to do with God and that He had sent the whale as a sign.

At the same time, a stranger had arrived on a dogcart. Nobody had spoken to him for he had not ventured in their midst. He kept himself apart and did not seem to wonder at the calamity that gripped the community's spirits and kept them low. From a distance one might believe him to be a monk, but on looking closely one saw that he was not wearing a habit but a horse blanket, bound by a rope round his waist. Because of this miserable blanket some saw in him a mendicant monk from an unknown order, others thought he was an anabaptist, but no one excluded the possibility that here might be a case of the appearance of a saint. This was because of his head which was bald and as smooth as the polished wood of statues, but it was especially because of his eyes. These were of an impenetrable grey which reminded one of the indifference of November skies: these were eyes that had seen too much and from which all wonder had been erased, eyes that looked from a yonder as from within a different world. Since the whale had appeared he had stood on top of the dunes and looked down on all. The curious ones on the beach were afraid of him and at the same time they hated him because he stood on top there and looked down on them. It might be that he was looking with his autumnal eyes at the beached whale, it might be that he was looking down on the bystanders who hid themselves behind each other's backs and waited for that which eluded them for the time being. It might also be that his eyes were tired and found rest in the far beyond. That was why they hated him: because he left them in uncertainty.

The appearances numbered three: the storm, the whale and the saint on the dogcart. According to some, however, they numbered four: the storm, the whale, the saint and the floods. Again others came to five or six or seven — and thus the truth fell apart into multiplicity.

When the Lord of Noordwijk rode on to the beach, all faith and hope was placed in him. He was a well-travelled and well-read man and though they themselves were neither one nor the other, they suspected that these matters were connected with the truth. To them, truth was something in which they would never have a part, something which revealed itself in matters incomprehensible, the way one can see lightning but not where it comes from, and they suspected, without realising this, that truth kept itself hidden in a distant yonder, in an unknown realm which might only be found by following the, to them, unfathomable and obscurely twisting paths of script. They themselves were not capable of thinking things any other way than they were; they lived in a world which was self-evident, no matter what — even doom had acquired something familiar so that it had become unimaginable that there had been a time when the whale had not been lying on the beach and that there had not been any corpses floating down the streets.

Dousa was startled when he discovered the whale, but because he saw that bailiff Woutersz, who had been here earlier, was observing him from the side to sound out his reaction, he let as little as possible be seen. So this was why the man had kept silent so mysteriously on the way here. And for a moment he held Woutersz responsible for the total disarray in his demesne. This was a pointless and unsatisfactory impulse, as he could not stand disarray even if this might be charged to Woutersz's account. Therefore he recovered himself and sought a description or an all-encompassing idea which would give meaning to what he saw. He brought Pliny to mind — with the classics he always had the experience of entering an ordered space, each word in its own place within the indissoluble context of grammar. However, his large memory notwithstanding, he was unable to remember whether there was any report in the *Naturalis Historia* of a *balaena* or a *phallaina*, as the whale was called in Greek. Nor could he remember himself as ever having devoted any extended thought to the phenomenon of the whale. It was, in as far as he had any image of it at all, a mythological monster, a creature of fable like the griffon, the centaur and the flying horse — and he was surprised that, without ever having seen such an apparition before, he had recognised the creature at once. How curious, he concluded, the way everything became curious if only one thought about it for long enough. So now a whale had ended up within his thought. But the whale swimming about in his mind was a different one from that one there, stinking on the beach, and he could not understand how this was possible. How could that whale have ended up in his head — and why was it different from the one on the beach? He felt he was approaching the essence of something, though he knew not of what, but soon the perception had already lost its coherence.

The waiting populace was disappointed that their lord was so indecisive. It had been hoped that, following his arrival, something would happen, but everything stayed the way it was. Perhaps it was because he had dismounted and now was standing just as low down as the rest, because now for him, too, the cold drew up from the ground through the soft leather of his boots, a cold which was like paralysis.

Dousa was aware that he was failing, and in his insecurity and impotence he was irritated by the bailiff who, in the light of the gravity of the circumstances, was sitting there, incomprehensibly calmly, on top of his overly tall horse. Woutersz — Dousa realised with a mixture of envy and contempt — was a man who divided up the world by responsibilities, and who only bothered himself with his own affairs. Because of this, he seemed devoid of fear or uncertainty concerning higher things, for the way he saw it, this was the responsibility of the church which attended to such matters in God's name — as if the life of a bailiff was not spent in a state of darkness, too, and as if in the case of a bailiff each glimmer of light, too, would not also show up that shadow cast ahead by death.

This was probably a correct characterisation of the bailiff; in the matter of the whale, however, the bailiff was not at all so sure of himself. He had checked on the privileges but his researches had brought no clarity. The coast belonged to the manor of Noordwijk, but was this at high or at low tide? And the sea the whale had come forth from and of which he was a part, as it were, that sea was no one's – something the bailiff found highly unsatisfactory. Moreover, there was the possibility that the whale was the property of the King of Spain, though it was not likely that he would be coming here demanding his rights. The fact that, all this notwithstanding, the bailiff still sat relatively calmly on his horse was because of the restful realisation that the Lord of Noordwijk bore more responsibility than he, no matter what, and that it did not even appear impossible to pass all responsibility on to his shoulders altogether.

This last thing he did not dare do; perhaps it was because of his meticulousness, perhaps because of his servility, but when his lord asked him what needed to be done, he did not reject his own responsibilities but gave as faithful as possible a report of his official findings.

Dousa did not understand what the bailiff was going on about and he frowned when the King of Spain was being dragged in with all his majesty, a thing that – Woutersz realised this – made rather a foolish impression here, at the edge of the world with that stinking cadaver – or was it still alive?

Still, it did not strike Dousa as unpleasant to have to listen to the useless minutiae coming from the bailiff. It was as though something slipped from his shoulders, a heavy burden or, to put it in the bailiff's terms, a responsibility. Now the ever-accurate Woutersz did not know what it was they must do either, one was permitted, as it were, to stand deedless on the beach beneath the unfathomable dome of heaven in an almost grand realisation of one's own insignificance, a realisation that offered him a way out for the conscientiousness that rested upon him.

And thus nothing happened for some while.

Surprisingly, the Leiden friends were the ones to break that arrested state, stepping forward out of the background. Some clamour arose among the bystanders though this was borne off at once by the wind so that nobody knew what had been said. This was not of importance, either, for it had been understood what might have been intended by those not-understood words: that people were tense and unsure about what those unknown gentlemen were going to do. The gentlemen from Leiden, as rhetoricians having an understanding of display, bore the wishes of the public in mind. Hands on their backs, as befitted scientists, they made for the whale and what is more, to stretch the period of uncertainty, they also gave it a wide berth walking round it, creating an atmosphere of weighing-up-possibilities by making lovely tutting sounds with finely pursed lips. Perhaps they would have been frightened otherwise, for close-up like this the whale reached from the corner of one eye all the way to the corner of the other and beyond, but losing themselves in their roles they forgot that they themselves were the ones who were standing there and, like the public, they now believed that they were three scientists from distant parts who wished to take a more detailed look at the anatomy of this wondrous fish. The scientists regretted that they had no access to a measuring rule, for it was writ in the Bible: 'Here is wisdom. Let him that hath understanding count the number of the beast.' The understanding was there: this they had themselves, and the beast was there, too, but without a measuring rule no wisdom would be theirs. So as not to forget themselves, they decided to measure the whale, in as far as this was possible, by their own bodily measurements: the yard, the foot and the span. Because of the solemnity with which they went about their business, their performance gained something preposterous about it, it became an unintentional mockery of the incomprehensible. All three arranged themselves beside the whale and at the same time placed their lower arms against the flaccid, wet skin of the tail. The one in front stayed in place and the two hindmost overtook him to join those in front. Then the one in front kept his place and the two others went and stood in front of him in their turn. Thus they went on, in this unequal mating dance with the whale that stank of putrefaction. Because they were continually muttering numbers all the while, the display acquired the darkness and malevolent character of a satanic rite.

The spectators, who were not sure whether this was allowed, this curious and probably even blasphemous mating dance of three gentlemen and a whale, looked in anxious expectation to the lawful authorities who, however, seemed to think everything was in order. Still, the bystanders did not have much truck with it and when the scientists noted down their measurements – something which, for want of a slate, they did on the beach, drawing numbers in the wet sand with their heels – the spectators feared something terrible, that is, they feared the number that is the number of the beast and though none of them could read, there were those who believed they saw the number. Six hundred, threescore and six. Six hundred, threescore and six, lisped the wind. Six hundred, threescore and six: everybody was whispering it, but no one understood what it meant.

Unperturbed, the scientists continued with their measurements. They had the dimensions of the sides and the tail and they were now intent on a method of measuring its height. No mean thing, that, and their hands clasped their chins in a sign of profound thought. The whale was taller than they themselves so they would have to climb one on top of the other in order to reach the highest point. But what were they to measure with? Finally, they had it. Two of them, one having climbed upon the other, allowed themselves – to the horror of the spectators – to fall against the whale, at which the blubber trembled a moment, and then the upper one reached with his hand to the highest point. Then they let themselves slide down the whale, went to lie down on the beach, head to toe, that hand stretched out, so that the third, hopping alongside on his haunches, was able to measure the combined length using his lower arm. The result was noted down in the sand.

A number of separate body parts were still to be measured, like the snout and the trunk-like sex, but they had the bulk and at this they were highly satisfied. They had the feeling that, thanks to their calculations, the whale had been explained satisfactorily, and they considered its presence as being obvious.

Among the spectators, however, resentment arose over the self-satisfied demeanour of the Leiden gentlemen which they had experienced as mockery and blasphemy. The most sombre among them, who knew the eyes of the saint to be directed at them, feared that now something terrible had been provoked and they averted their gaze; others, more practical folk, thought that intervention was necessary and they directed their hopes towards the lord and the bailiff, with impatient expectancy. These, however, had fallen prey to paralysing doubt. Dousa in particular, though this was in his nature, for his spirit was like a blind man who feels his way with soft fingers; but the bailiff, this otherwise so punctual and in his punctuality, in a way, so simple a man: he too was at his wit's end, beset by the confusing feeling that the King of Spain had let him down.

With dull helplessness, Dousa and Woutersz were obliged to watch as resentment in the people flared up into anger which, through lack of direction, caused confusion. There were those who demanded that the whale be towed back to sea with the help of nets and horses; others believed it would be better if the whale were to be killed because, in their eyes, death was the only effective solution. In all the zest of their anger they were apparently forgetting their fear of a judgement from God, for one of them even went so far as to declare the saint with the dogcart to be the guilty one. In so doing, he did bring down the indignation of others upon himself, it is true, but it had been said, nevertheless.

And so, each had his own opinion; there were those who had a number of opinions and some even had contradictory ones.

There was one person who remained quietly on the sidelines. He was the Admiral. He had been standing here from morning, free from the frightened curiosity that had held the others in its grip. And now, too, now they were brandishing their axes and crying for nets and horses, he stood apart for he knew that this was all irrelevant. At most he was surprised that it had come about like *this*. And in a curious way he had been proud as well: proud that God had sent the feared Leviathan for him, a humble fisherman. The Admiral waited for a sign and there had been a moment when he had thought that it was there. This had been when the beast of vengeance had laughed. Nobody who had seen this had understood it, except he. It had laughed at the saint on the dunetop and it would not have surprised the Admiral if, in a secret understanding between them, they had also winked at one another. The Admiral had not been afraid then either, for in his opinion he deserved to be punished, not only for the theft of statuary and heresy, or for what he had inflicted on his wife, but especially because he could no longer believe in the truth.

He was tired and he wanted to sit down, but he thought: they will be coming to fetch me soon, so he continued to stand. He was very tired and did not understand why the others made such a fuss. He could not care less: he regarded everything from a great distance. Perhaps he was already dead. He had thought this that morning, too, when he had crept out into the open from his cellar: that he had died and that his soul no longer had a body to carry him. He would indeed not be surprised if he had died already, and in that case he thought he was entitled to go and sit down. He sat there and it occurred to him that it might be more pleasant to lie down. This was why he let himself slip over backwards in the wet sand. It was cold, but not unpleasant. He felt himself grow stiff and without sensation, the sounds became dull and far away, and above him was the sky, dull and far away, too – he thought of the candles in the sea chapel, how beautifully they glowed, and then he slipped away.

It no longer concerned him that the others had decided to fetch nets and cart horses. Humpkin, who had been sent on ahead, wanted to greet his father, but because he was lying there asleep, he let him be instead.

Not long after Humpkin had left, the North-Westerly began to roar. This did not necessarily signify much, but the people had become jittery. Dousa and Woutersz, too, thought it advisable to break up the gathering. Only the ones from Leiden hesitated: they had written their calculations in the sand and they did not know how they were to take them along. There they stood, at the high water mark, bent over their figures, rehearsing: Six hundred, threescore and six; six hundred, threescore and six – that is what it sounded like. Dousa would have liked best of all to have left that little lot behind, but he felt obliged to call them. They mounted and went at walking pace past the throng going laboriously up the dune path.

Nobody thought of the Admiral lying asleep on the beach, left alone with the whale, while the saint stood on top of the dunes, looking on.

5

As Humpkin chased along with the wind in his back, and he thought he was going somewhere and did not realise that in fact he was leaving something, and when the procession, too, had moved on a good way, that is to say on the way back, the fishermen noticed that their leader was not among them. They would have preferred to keep this to themselves for, being in the protection of the others and especially of the grand gentlemen who seemed actually to protect them with the mighty flanks of their great horses, no one felt like sacrificing himself by going the other way through the cold and the wind. People continued on their way and it seemed the Admiral would be left to his fate. It was being said that he had already gone on ahead, though nobody had seen him go on ahead – nor did anyone believe it, but things were easier that way. In the end, more from impatience over the indecisiveness of them all than out of concern for their boss, two reported for duty, a one-eyed one and one who still had both. They turned round and went in search. The wind, which turned out to be a storm when you had it against you, and the rain beat their faces. The one clenched both his eyes shut, the other his single one. Thus they diminished their view; it was as if they were inside, inside themselves, peering out through a crack. They did not see much and this was a good thing, for that which surrounded them was too spacious for them anyway. Behind their backs, the procession withdrew and were they to realise it, they could feel they were being deserted. But they merely continued because they continued, and they were going to do something because they had to; they were cold because it was cold. They did not feel deserted because they did not think about such things.

Thus, these two went one way and the rest went the other – and all had the conviction that it was the right way, the way they were going.

The weather turned even grimmer. It seemed as if the storm was trying to sweep the countryside empty and that the rain gushed across the land to erase the last traces. Seen in this light, those going along the road – both the few going the one way as the many going the other – gave the impression in their doggedness of resisting with full commitment their disappearance.

One might also say, however, that, going along the road, they were already disappearing.

When the great exodus reached beyond the village by the sea, the survivors left their houses and their dead and joined the trek, pot luck. They did not think of it as disappearing: they thought they were on their way somewhere.

Those on foot got sorely in the way of the horsemen; time and again, the gentlemen had to rein in their horses – something they did with reluctance for, best of all, they would have preferred to have left those superfluous and useless dolts to their fate, but one thought that the other thought it was their duty as gentlemen to stay here and to watch over the rearguard of mankind. Dousa was surprised that these people – who could not read nor write and therefore had to be thought of as equal to the horse he was sitting on, less than that even, perhaps, taken that at least you could still ride a horse – could force their way into his life, just like that, as if his spirit was a hostelry where one might barge in, muddy feet and all, no questions asked. Like an ugly word in a poem, this was the way one ought to be able to scratch out all those ugly and superfluous people. What was he to do with that little lot? Woutersz, more businesslike (in the case where his lord's thinking might best be compared to a bird, probably a crow, his thinking might best be said, if it had to be a bird, to resemble a chicken scuttling about round the house, trained on the low-down-to-earth and not realising that it had been able to fly at one time), this good bailiff thought that the obtrusive refugees might be housed in the convent of Saint Barbara. This was, it was true, a wreck without a roof, since the heretics had set fire to it, but for those fishermen, who according to him were all heretics, it was good enough. He thought that was just the thing for fishermen to do, to fall into heresy: on the boundless sea, which was no one's and therefore no rule of law applied there, the divine did not reveal itself in sacred forms and appearances so that it was almost understandable that those seamen began to get all kinds of ideas into their heads. Perhaps there were a few among the populace getting under their feet here, who had defiled the convent at the time and had decapitated the Saint of Noordwijk. In that case it would even be an act of justice to have them spend the night in the ruin of their own creation.

Dousa just let the bailiff talk. And when the latter fell silent, he assented with a slight, absentminded nod of the head. He had already forgotten his irritation as regards the homeless again. The sight of the whale had made his thoughts heavy so that these sank away repeatedly into the depths of his thinking where it was dark and oppressive like in a cellar or a deep pit, and where he could no longer hear the bailiff.

The gentlemen, each ensnared in their own way in the unrest of incomprehensible thoughts, did not notice that they passed the place where the three hunters had last been seen. They had no eye for it, not even the ones from Leiden. In their defence, it might be put forward that there were so many empty spots that it could hardly be called negligence either that they did not see this particular one where the hunters had been and were now no longer present – though it was a trifle hard on the hunters to have to disappear without being missed by anyone.

Meanwhile, the procession made such slow progress that it began to look more as if people were standing still. That hunchbacked fisherman's brat walking out in front, he was a long way ahead already. The footsloggers shuffled through the leafmould and the puddles of rainwater. It might have been a sorry sight, but the gentlemen were not in the mood for compassion; their desire was more one of beating the hordes with sticks. As though their horses were having to drag a cart without wheels through the mud, this was what they felt like – a heavy and in fact superfluous task which only occurred because that damned cart just happened to be there.

Precisely because they could not make progress, the gentlemen thought with regret of all those things they would have been able to do if they had not been obliged to be toiling their way through the mud here, and had it not rained; and it seemed as if it was because of the mud and the rain and the others that, irritatingly, they had ended up in an incomprehensible confusion. The Leiden friends believed themselves to have been thwarted in their scientific work; they missed their numbers which they had been forced to leave behind near the whale and which now would certainly be wiped out. And the falling rain fell like a curtain, depriving them of their vision. But Dousa, too, sinking away into his thoughts as if into a deep sleep, felt uprooted and harried. He wanted to be with his books, in the shelter of their spines standing like watchmen around him and giving him cover against the unthinkable and incomprehensible that was life outside. Even the bailiff, a down-to-earth man after all, was in a kind of hurry to escape. He was no man for whales and now there was nothing here he might call upon, he longed for the return of the familiar and he believed to be able to find this again were he to return to the place whence he had left, that is to say, home, where the world was but a thought, an ordered thought that was complete and with which, therefore, he no longer had to bother himself.

Thus, the gentlemen all had a place – elsewhere, yonder, over there – where truth would be. And instead of making them despondent, the notion of over there, yonder and elsewhere gave them hope and an urge to go on as if they did not know that, rather than a case of going on, this was a one of escaping, of trying to escape the hopelessness.

And the homeless followed, full of trust, and they did not know that there was no roof either in the place where they would be housed.

Further on, or further back (for this was becoming ever more difficult to distinguish) the two fishermen reached the end, or the beginning, maybe, of the road. They descended the path to the sea and arrived on the beach. The storm made them bend over like porters and this was how it came about that amidst all the empty spaces they did not notice the empty space the whale had left behind. Nor did they see the empty space on the dunes where the saint with the dogcart had been standing. The place where the Admiral was lying was, in a sense, empty too, but this the fishermen only noticed when they felt how cold death had made their leader. It gave them a shock, but not too bad a one, for one of them had already seen many go before and the other, by way of a down-payment, had already surrendered his own eye. And yet, encountering so much motionlessness, they did not know what to do. The Admiral was not stiff yet and it appeared as if he could live if he did his best to do so. Only his eyes betrayed that nothing would come of this — a gaze that did not reflect, or it would have to be that which someone dead could see. This was why his eyes were closed with careful hand, not because the deceased might thus be comforted, but so as not to have to see the empty space into which he must stare forever.

Were one to look at one deceased for a long time, one might think him lonely and helpless, the way he lay there and did not understand what had happened to him. Just take his shoes: made from sturdy leather and fit for brisk walks, but no one could tell any longer where they had been and where they had wanted to go. All had been for nothing and it seemed that this was why he lay there, so mute and lame, as if an indissoluble despondence had come over him. Each morning he had put on his shoes to go somewhere, doing this on the assumption that it served some purpose, and he had not known that his life was like that of a traveller who stays the night in a hostelry along the way: when he breaks up camp, there is nothing that remains, except perhaps for a broken shoelace, a torn-off button or a stale crust of bread. That shoelace or that button might mean something: a present from a former mistress whose passion, like the shoe and the smock, had worn out; or an heirloom, dutifully worn until threadbare, even the crust of bread might have a meaning, but there was no one who might know — and a girl would turn up to sweep them up, a blonde girl who thought of a cheerful future; she perhaps would polish the button to a shine and keep it, but the shoelace and the crust of bread would be thrown away. Thus the deceased would have to allow that what once had been his life would fall apart into mere objects such as laces, buttons and crusts of bread which, of no use to others, were thrown away as rubbish, and that only a shiny button would remain, for instance. One might say that the deceased, through that which is taken from him, becomes another, in a way, but one might just as easily say that he can no longer be designated by words such as 'another' and that he might best be compared to a torn-off button – the button of a traveller who spent the night along the way, the button which was picked up by a blonde girl, not to sew it back onto the smock it had burst from, but because it gleamed so beautifully and – for the time being – because it was such a pity to do away with it. And yet the deceased would have to allow that even that button, dulled through neglect, would be thrown away, one day.

Something the deceased had to allow, too, was that the fishermen hauled him upright, and tried rather awkwardly to lift him, treatment under which, had he still been alive, he would definitely have felt uncomfortable. Because they were not convinced that the deceased was not aware of anything, the fishermen apologised in between their groaning and sighing. That he could no longer walk was an established fact and because of this he came off the ground, upsadaisy, by his ankles and armpits. Lugging him was no great burden to them, going across the firm, wet sand, but when they got to the dunes they were obliged to lower the corpse and they dragged it, each to an arm, through the sand. His head lolled crookedly to one side and sand got into his hair and on to his mouth and eyelids. At the top of the dunes they had to catch their breath for a moment, for the corpse was rather heavy after all. Had they not been so busy catching their breaths there, it might have amazed them that someone deceased is just as heavy as someone living. A soul, which is life, weighs nothing. This could have been one of Dousa's thoughts, but he was further ahead and did not know that death was dogging his footsteps; he might have thought that, as a dead body weighs just as much as a living one, one has carried the burden of death along with one all that time, without knowing, and that in dying one only loses something, something weighing nothing, a trinket, perhaps even less than that, a mere trifle, something that perhaps may never have been. An incomprehensible thought, the way everything became incomprehensible were one to think about it for long enough. But the fishermen did not think. They got up again, lifted up the corpse, and continued on their way.

After some time they noticed that the corpse began to stink of excreta. Because it was stinking so badly they could have thrown the corpse into the bushes; however, they did not dare do this for they knew that the dead must be buried near a church because the soul can only wrest itself free properly in hallowed soil. Also, they were gaining sight of the procession with the horsemen so that it did not seem that far any more, even though the procession still had a goodly way to go.

The horsemen only noticed that they were being impeded in their progress; they did not know that behind them the two fishermen, stinking death between them, were coming ever closer.

Only the Leiden friends had a tendency to look back, not because they had begun to smell death, but because they knew their numbers were in the sand, defenceless. They repeated the six hundred, threescore and six, giving voice to it in three-part harmony, so that their knowledge seemed to be stored more in the tongue than in memory, the tongue hopping agilely back and forth from teeth to roof of mouth, ringing out Leiden science in an almost oracular, and in any case artful fashion. Because of the continual repetition, the numbers threatened to lose their meaning, however, which was why the Leiden gents preferred to turn back most of all: to see whether the numbers in the sand really did exist. The bailiff, too, was one who had to see a thing in order to believe it. A limiting characteristic which preserved him from inflammatory thoughts and from thoughts in general, for that matter. Now that he had not seen the whale for a while, its terrifying aspect already began to fade in his memory and it would not be long before the wondrous fish would have been reduced in his head to the neatly arranged measurements of a greasy old herring. This, too, explained his dullness: even though he had actually seen a whale, he would still speak of herrings, not out of modesty, definitely not, his character was in fact as bloated as *rolmops* that have been in pickle for too long, but because his thinking was incapable of containing anything larger.

Dousa had gone to ride some distance away from the others, perhaps in order not to have to hear the hollow sounds of the gents from Leiden, or not to have to smell the bailiff's sour pong – he could not smell the stench of death yet, in any case, even though the wind was in his direction. Like this, at a distance from the others and distancing himself from the unimaginable whale, his thinking regained its familiar lightness. His thoughts burbled up like bubbles of air from the dark depths and burst open at the surface, merging with total airiness. The arrival of the whale was, for the time being, an incomprehensible event, it was true, but Dousa was convinced that there would be a time when he could confidently surrender himself to complete knowing.

And so each had his own thoughts on the whale and nobody knew that the whale had disappeared long since, and that behind them two men were lugging a corpse, stumbling under the weight of their burden and walking ever faster because of this, and nobody knew that there was nothing there to be understood – except for the deceased, perhaps; maybe he had realised it, just for an instant, before the incomprehensible enclosed him forever.

Out in front went Humpkin, to fetch the nets – and behind him, his dead father was being dragged through the dunes, and Humpkin knew nothing at all of this and thought that something big was going to be caught with those nets.

The Stone Face

Simon Vestdijk

The third house, standing out from the night and at the same time, as though with a reticent gesture, allowing the light from my torch to skim untouched along its gable, was larger than both the other ones. A hat-like roof rose up in the pallid darkness; some low outbuildings stood to one side. It was located quite close to the road, and when my eyes had grown slightly accustomed to the sparse light, I discovered that the entrance was situated in a side road, or it was possible that the road my path would have to lead to was the main one, for it was hard to judge the width of either of them. For a while, the problem of those two roads took the place of what ought to be so much closer to my heart, but then, interrupting this idle ponder with a jolt, I began to think intensely about my situation.

I must have lost my way. My host had warned me, for that matter, about this part of the road – oh, how I now longed for his dune villa with the two table lamps below which our wine had gleamed! – but he had warned me about the fierce dogs, not for what I was about to experience now. Experience: already with a certain foretaste of mysteries which appeared to lay themselves down from the night wind on my tongue, past which my own wine-breath engulfed me.

Assume I knew the region. Not as a part of this area of dunes to be indicated at random, in which case I would have to have been there before, but as something one has read about long, long ago, or has dreamed about, and of which one has always borne along the vaguely drawn model. Every landscape knows such road complexes which, like Gordian knots in an innocent looking net-work, wait for years, indeed for centuries even, for a traveller who will become ensnared in them. Mostly there is a windmill in the vicinity, one lacking sails like a guide who has given up and draws in his arm. Cats skulk around there. They ought to mark these places on maps in a special colour, but no. Because they must not resemble each other – that would be too easy by half! – each of them displays different inessentials, in this case those large, detached houses, almost feudal, which marked entire tracts of their surroundings in their survey as being dark and inaccessible, or that lonely garden – it's known even though it isn't seen – with the two broken plaster statues in it and many gusts of wind where the summer house once stood ... And I wondered why, in darkness and in such ambiguous places, the world has to be so different, so much deeper, more despairing, and with the particular kind of feigning that determines the honesty of night ... Let me dream some more, I thought, until I'm past this house, for its intentions towards me can't be that good ... Two plaster statues, broken – but of identical manufacture? ...

Let's assume, let's believe the wind indeed returned to that garden and created a life from nothing, one which was lost again and yet is still there, even though it is not seen by day ... Again, I tore myself from ponder that could serve no purpose: the long-winded and free translation of four glasses of wine and wild conversations ...

Right in front of me, the road seemed to break off all of a sudden; an edge shimmered there; cobbles, far apart, made way for a little wilderness of thistles and rubbish; there the cats would have to stalk through, there the windmill had stood or the burned down farm or what-you-will. And there too, probably, was the centre, the junction, the most lonely of all, where all the strands conspired; I had expected to get there and yet I could not reach it even though I was there now ... Again my thoughts grew confused.

The torch, my sword of Alexander, would have to find everything from now on, and free me of this confusion. For a few moments this distracted me: a round patch of light that becomes elliptical, stretches out an arm, embraces the night expansively and, hesitating, hovering, beating almost in time to the pulse, returns, half way, and then fragments itself in a pale rain of light on leaves and gravel, or feels along boards down which splinters, gnarls and heads of nails run towards it as though deranged. But then the house drew my attention again, the way it stood there so tall and remote. Long, straight walls, walls to walk along after a nocturnal conversation that asks no sorrow of us, only petrification ... In what way the gable had been decorated or overgrown, I could not make out at first. Soon, however, my torch discovered the capricious, lissome creepers which, struggling, bent upwards as though they were seeking a window or a hand – each branch, each leaf quickly provided with a Chinese shadow behind, which moved away a little, crept back again and instantly became more distinct. Stone frames, I made out, around the windows, in front of which the shutters had been closed. Still I let my cone of light rise and fall a few cycles, meanwhile already forming the intention to walk on and seek the road in accordance with my friend's instructions, when the shine attached itself to something above me, and me along with it, as though I was being directed by a power in, or attached to the house which had seized the torch. I looked more closely, *there*: a grave head of stone.

I was surprised. There was even a kind of hilarity that gripped me, a sequence of bouts of laughter somewhere in my body which, for that matter, were unable to penetrate my still half-inebriated consciousness. Be that as it may, I felt at once to be thrown together with the stone head as though with a chum in trouble: he, too, was lost, one might assume; he, too, – I now suddenly saw the creepers as vines – must be inebriated, lost, and cast out by life, though it would not be easy to ascertain whether he was all these things by day as well, when walls, plants and stone ornaments lead so different an existence than at night. No, little could be said about that. For example, did he like living in the light or was he a loner, a shaded one? He remained almost invisible by day, behind those tangled branches sprouting in all directions, like over-abundant antlers, from his skull. Thus he lived as though in a cool grotto. But now, at this nocturnal hour, my light seized him in the right place, unlocked his eyelids, flared his nostrils, and finally, when my hand had begun to tremble a little less, it showed his forehead lofted high above the broad shadows of the eyebrows climbing it like tired thoughts. Vague was the direction the eyes were looking in, though what they expressed spoke clearly of the satisfaction of knowing someone to be below who wished to shine on the forgotten one of this house! A quiet smile, a few lines in the corners of the eyes: and already I no longer felt any regret about my nocturnal jaunt. Firmly, I directed the torch to engender new life this way in one who, through the chill association with leaf and stem, could only still be accustomed to the colour of green mould, who for years now had no longer found any profile and who now tasted the light as though from behind vines. I had been drinking: he too must drink; I gave him plenty. The branches swiped back and forth in the wind but I didn't allow myself to be chased off, no matter how much they flailed and waved. I had found a confidant.

Who was he? Did this house have more of such heads? But no, this I didn't want to believe; and how could it be possible, for that matter, now that I had found him and wanted to stay with him till morning, not wanting to leave before all loneliness and deprivation had been shone from his face! . . .

But my cone of light had slipped away, suddenly, because of an uncontrolled movement of my hand. Search now! High and low, left and right: of course he still had to be there . . . *There*. I struck his face as though with a snow ball – he laughed. So young that face now looked, younger than a moment before, and the creeper's branches now suited him better. And even though my hand trembled mercilessly, I wanted to carry on for as long as possible, for it seemed as though he changed in the beam of light, becoming ever more youthful under my hand, fresh and revived like a god of antiquity. Was I myself creating him from nothing? Was it possible to make statues of marble or stone assume any age by any kind of lighting? Whatever the case, I was the creator, no matter what; he owed everything to me, right down to the vines which, shimmering red, grew up contrastingly from within the green under the magic power of my circle of light. And, though the night wind was cooling down so that I shivered and had to button up my clothes more tightly, again and again I engrossed myself in the stone face that gleamed with inviolable youth.

Inviolable? Having reached a peak which did not seem easy to surpass any further, it was now as though he resisted something, as though he attempted to surmount something which my torch would have to assist him with. Carefully, I aimed the beam of light in such a way that branches cast as few shadows as possible, but there was always one which would not allow itself to be passed, a fat, hairy one: I could make it out clearly from below. Then, when I dropped the torch a little, he suddenly resembled someone drowned among seaweed and polyps, pallid and swollen, but how rapidly could that image not be dispelled! He lived and revived, time and again, feverish and inextinguishable; he drank my light, radiating it in all directions, though I was never able to chase away that high shadow running from his eyebrows across his forehead because I was standing too low down. Then I stepped back to try it from a greater distance: in an instant he had disappeared. No wonder, I thought, that he can only seldom be seen by day; what would he not give always to have such a life, the way it was now! From time to time it seemed again as though a smile was playing on his lips, but now it continued to be a smile of youth, self-evident and effortless: youth doesn't have enough wrinkles yet to smile truly; this was the natural smile of sleep and innocence I had conjured up there in the twinkling of an eye.

But the night strode on and with this a creeping change came over his face, one which had announced itself already a few moments earlier when shadows were playing across his features. Wrinkles returned, crystallised, first hiding themselves in the corners of his mouth and eyes, then shooting across cheeks and forehead; pitiable grooves waged war on one another, still cancelling each other out for a while, but then everything moved unstoppably towards old age. How to preserve him from this? I kept my hand as steady as possible; there was no film of moisture on the lens of the torch; no chill mist floated by. For a moment he stared at me as though reproaching me, then he sank even more deeply into his own destruction, assailed by fatal decay I had so gladly wished to hold at bay, for I felt that everything was at stake now, that in a few minutes' time he would be beyond saving . . . Perfectly lonely it was, all around me: no dog barked, no light anywhere, the house seemed uninhabited. I had every chance ahead of me, if only my will would remain sufficient! Even now I hoped for him, indeed I believed, I demanded, that the cycle of mounting youthfulness would begin again; but it was not only ageing from which he now suffered: pain too, sorrow, despair, mortal terror . . . Every expression of human woe I saw pass over stone that night, vague but unmistakable and not suited to any explanation other than of the woeful afflictions they evoked within myself . . . Then again, it was as though he was on the verge of coming down to whisper his secret to me which would rob me of all peace; he pleaded, he prayed, his cheeks hollowed, beard stubble grew rampant, grizzling in the light; had he had a body, he would have knelt down or writhed about in agony, but his body was no longer there any more, surely: the house was his body, the ground upon which the house was built, the fields around it, the night . . . And how old and far away and irretrievable the night is! . . . And then, all of a sudden, I understood that he must be the one, doomed to restlessness, who controlled this landscape and who had lured me here in order to have me share in his misery. I was seized by impotence. I wished to get away but could not. Trails, fragments of my initial thoughts coursed through my mind, and behind them a fresh thought arose, not to be caught in words yet, a thought I was not yet ready for, as all my attention was being taken up ... My arm stiffened; with muscles growing more powerless all the time I trained the light on to the same spot. And his eyes just stared, stared – and slowly they sucked me towards him ...

At that moment I heard the crunching of gravel: footsteps! Instinctively I cast down my torch. I expected a cry as though I had wounded him or had torn a bandage from his face. However, the first change evoked by those sounds now took place within myself. It was the thought of a minute ago which, in its full stature and accompanied by all the signs of sobering-up after my mild intoxication, stepped forward as though around a corner of my consciousness. In three seconds I knew everything again, in three seconds I had fallen back thirteen years, right through the night, right through time. Hurriedly, the thought let itself be viewed from all angles like a beggar showing his wounds, who fuses with the giver, who forces himself up against him and most of all would like to pass on all the diseases ploughing his skin, just to be sure of the compassion he's asking for ... Disease, death, a death bed? ...

Indeed, an entire night I had watched over him, fighting sleep and boredom. A long night of emptiness, and one in which no thoughts of any importance could have touched my spirit. When morning approached, he called me to him, with his feeble voice, and then I saw that he had become young like the stone statue earlier on, smooth and untroubled before he would die, as though he wished to overtake a distant past chunk of his youth, and in doing so was not content with thinking and dreaming alone but had also adjusted his appearance. He was barely able to speak any more by then, and half an hour later it was all over. But who knows with what child's game he had been occupied with a few minutes prior to his death, in what childish difficulties he had still entangled himself? Who knows what toil it cost him to go so far back in his life that was already barely a life any more! How strange and not to be unriddled, this return into himself, this completion in which life, winding youth like an ultimate loop around deepest old age, ties itself in a knot which can never be unpicked ... And I? That I saw it and did not understand! That he was my father and yet someone else – an ordinary, untragic death bed without gestures, and which I had thought little of during those thirteen years – and that I only understood now it was too late, even – after this warning, this announcement – too late for the one who had provoked that memory ...

Noises . . . Outside of myself again!

A door was opened, conversation: a woman's voice. At the same time, blinding white light flared up, drawing forth an unreal, hard garden, one I could not have expected to be there. Gruesomely rectilinear yew hedges, shaved bare, cut through the night, their leaves snappy and tightly packed together like little scalpels; each bit of gravel seemed to glint individually, without cohering with neighbouring ones. In front of me lay the beginning of the drive, a drive for machines: white, smooth and soulless. When I moved a little further to the left, I noticed the electric light above the door which was half open; an iron boot scraper lay on the step. A male figure moved along the drive in my direction, youthful and slim, but his gait was almost stumbling; behind him, slower, a much older woman, with grey hair the light gleamed through, silvery, who now called out a second time: a name I didn't understand . . . But the young man had already reached me and grabbed my arm:

'He's dead and you could have saved him! Why didn't you come sooner! He's dead, he's dead . . .'

His voice sounded hoarse and tremulous; I looked him straight in the face, which was still catching some reflected light, a crooked, confused face, deathly pale, with eyes like chasms; and all surrounded by long, black hair. With his unmoulded features from which the nose, lonely and helpless, appeared to detach itself, he seemed a boy of not yet twenty. Now the old woman joined us, my presence not getting through to her, apparently:

'Come, come back home now; you shouldn't . . . That's the last thing, you're not at that stage yet, you can't go back yet . . .'

Half sternly, half soothingly, she put her hand on his shoulder. But again he turned to me:

'You could have saved him, you're too late, why didn't you persevere for longer, why . . .?'

Full of hunger, all reproach, his eyes regarded me; his hands were folded as though he would pray to me, or only to give me strength even though it did seem too late for everything . . .

What was I to reply? I sensed nothing uncommon in what he said. I *was* too late, I knew. Again I thought of the stone face; the transition had taken place too soon for me to have been able already to banish him from my thoughts. And, quick as lightning, his question continued in my mind in a different form: why had I not shone on to him for longer, why had I allowed myself to be distracted? And particularly as regards the memory of that deathbed of thirteen years ago that popped up again, more threatening than a moment ago, I felt all too clearly how sorely I had failed, now and in the past already, too. For only now did I realise why my father had become more youthful in his death throes. It was to spare me, not to burden my shoulders with what everybody who feels guilty and tortured by remorse when he sees his father die, must bear anyway, even when there has never been any real cause for such things. Through the alteration to his appearance, everything had transpired unnoticeably and more soothingly, through the support of that curiously rejuvenated face, though in reality he was even older than one could ever become in this life. But bridging time, that other, real deathbed for which he had judged me not worthy, had travelled along with me now to reveal itself fiercely all of sudden – fiercely like a reproach, fiercer still than self-reproach and yet akin to self-reproach. For I could have stopped him, the way I had done with the stone face! Even if it had only been five seconds more: I could have let him live – and, who knows, death might have beat a retreat, demoralised, frightened off already by that short-lived resistance. No, no, it was *not* to spare me even so: it had been a chance he had given me which I had not managed to take advantage of! Not for *me* had he rejuvenated himself, but for himself – with my help which he hoped for! Who knows the fluctuations of the heart beat, or the life force of a dying brain? I should have spoken with him, not stand there with a hand on my chin and thoughts of the nuisance of a funeral in my head; I should have pursued that miraculous rejuvenation, laughingly, cheeringly, and bringing all our shared self-confidence to bear, I should have pointed old portraits out to him, memories that are eternal, a childhood that returns, time and again, the tremendous life force that exceeds everything, death included, the . . .

The reality of the staring boy's face made me come to my senses once again. A question forced its way to the forefront, gained power over me: I had to utter it. I made a step closer to him so we were standing eye to eye.

'Is it your father who has died?' I asked softly.

He recoiled, but no reply came from his lips. He now leant sideways, up against the woman who might be a nurse or a mother, and who had kept her arms stretched out as though to receive him. His face fascinated me like a mirror. What was it that strange smile wanted? I no longer expected a reply. Behind them, I

saw the hard, white garden shrink far back, become hazy, die away
. . . It was as though his face came very close to mine, closer still
. . . But how long had this been going on for? . . . Years? . . .

How dark it now was. Dark as though nothing had happened
and nothing would ever happen again. Could I still hear footsteps?
The light had gone out all too suddenly, and the night wind with
its whisperings had taken possession of me again so irresistibly
that I wasn't able to make out whether the young man walked
back to the house along that gravelly drive, or whether he
disappeared a different way. Blinded by that rapid transition from
light to darkness, anaesthetized by emotions without a name, I
only felt capable of making a step forwards after a number of
minutes, the way a sick man does when setting his feet on the
ground for the first time.

I didn't search for the stone face. I knew I could no longer get in
contact with him nor could he with me. Till morning, I roamed
that inhospitable landscape without equal on any map. Poplars
whispered by my side, endless fences fled ahead of me in despair;
they curved and seemed about to return to the same spot again;
constellations I did not recognise gleamed in the sky above. Never
did I see that house again nor have I ever known what might be
true of all this – and whether indeed a father died that night.

Feathered Friends

Jan Wolkers

Herbert stands in front of the steamed-up window of his apartment on the fifth, and top, floor. His hands in his dressing gown pockets, he listens to the rushing in his ears.

I'm in a bit of a state, he thinks, I'm a doomed man, though it may take another ten years. Ten more years with Liesbeth. Horror! I'm perspiring as if I have a fever, yet I haven't one.

He digs his nails into the palms of his clammy hands. The only thing he sees through the foggy window is the Belisha beacon on the opposite side of the road. As if he's standing on a tall mountain and an orange full moon, having just risen above the horizon, is being hidden from view, time and again, by fast moving clouds. Like he has seen in films run at a higher speed. But the flickering, on-off, is too regular and disturbs the illusion. He takes his hand from his pocket and, fingers slightly apart, he draws long, parallel curves down the moist honeycomb, as though he's caressing a woman's long hair. The Belisha ends up on a post of licorice allsorts; the traffic island with its yellow bollards, poisonous aniline blue lights burning within, becomes visible. Of the trees in the park only the trunks can be seen. The tops have been devoured by the mist insects. The houses are wrapped in damp sheets. A neon advertising sign loses its purchasing power and acquires a lofty meaning. A red cross on waves of mist. Herbert puts his hand back in his pocket when the door opens behind him. Liesbeth shuffles into the room. She sighs and pokes the fire.

'You've left the vent open too long,' she says. 'The stove's got red cheeks.'

She's now standing by the stove, bent over, Herbert thinks. I should walk up to her and give her squat bottom a shove. A wee taste of purgatory. But she'd scream the place down. I'm wearing my slippers. Before my shoes were on and I was out through the door, the neighbours would be here already.

'Mind you don't go drawing on the windows, Herbert. Once they've dried, I can barely get them clean again. You might wash them for me.'

'I'm not washing anything. I just want to have enough of a view. Let the moisture evaporate: good for the plants.'

'But it's bad for the furniture; it makes them warp, Herbert. Just bear that in mind, would you? Peter, Peterkin! Come here lad, come!'

That hairy predator approaches to comfort her after the defeat I've inflicted on her, he thinks.

He hears the cat's paws tap the lino. It jumps up at her and climbs up her pinny. She croons over it as over a newborn babe.

Barren womb, yieldless acre, he thinks. Why didn't your womb open itself up to me twenty years ago? Why were you like a pollarded willow that fails to sprout in Spring? I would have had a daughter of twenty by now. The scent of young female flesh in the house. Tunes being hummed, the tripping of high heels, rouge to lend some colour still to my old age. Let's think, now let's think clearly.

Herbert leans his torso forward so his head rests against the cold, damp window.

Ah, that's wonderful! I'm in Rome, sitting on a terrace: a hot summer's afternoon. The tarmac's billowing because of the heat. I order a glass of beer, icy cold. I press the glass to my forehead. The cold makes its way through my brain down to my backbone. What was it again I wanted to think about? Ah, yes: why do men always murder their wives in a rage while the balance of their minds is disturbed? Why not a trip to Austria? A hearty walk, a mountain trek? D'you hear that yodeller in the valley over there, Liesbeth? Look, there he is! If I go and stand on this rocky promontory, I can see him sitting there. Where, Herbert? I don't see or hear him. Bend over a bit more! Look, he's sitting there surrounded by columbine, further down the valley. Then a goodly poke with the walking stick and those two hundred pounds souring my existence tumble out of my life.

He suddenly gives a start because of the shrill squeal of tram brakes. It sounds like the screaming of a hare being jumped by a stoat. He looks down. The tram moves off slowly. Then, all of a sudden, there's a woman lying on the traffic island. The parts of her lower legs dangling beyond the kerb are at an angle of almost ninety degrees to the parts on the traffic island. It is as if her instep reaches a tremendous way up, or her knee joint has slid down. Blood runs along the edge of the traffic island towards the rails. The tram halts, grindingly. A conductor runs to the motionless body, bends over it. He shouts something to the driver, steps on to the pavement and enters a shop.

He's going to ring the paramedics, Herbert thinks. Perfectly pointless. Why not quietly leave her to bleed to death? Why must her husband drag out his twilight years behind a wheelchair?

People abandon cars, bicycles, prams, and hurry to the fateful spot. They surround the victim the way carrion beetles do the cadaver of a mole.

Didn't I hear deathwatch beetles in the bars of the bed this morning? So it was inescapable. Look: the windows are weeping.

Herbert follows the drops that jerkily draw vertical lines among the curves. Then he turns round.

'Can you see, Liesbeth, what's on that piece of paper in the milkman's window? Your eyes are better than mine. Might even be a special offer.'

Liesbeth sets the cat down on the chair and totters over to the window. Herbert walks to the stove and holds his hands above it in the rising warmth.

Wonderful, those hot water springs in Iceland, he thinks. Would the winter be a severe one? The signs are favourable. Would it be suspect to buy a refrigerator at the beginning of Winter? Wouldn't it rouse suspicion? Shucks: there are people who buy a camping tent in January. Didn't I myself once stand beside a girl buying a bathing costume when it was twenty degrees below? But there are indoor swimming pools, of course. And aren't there any houses where the heat's tropical in winter? I can't hear anything by the window yet. Might the mortal ... ehm, might the remaining mother (in-law, grand and great-grand) have been carted off already? That'd be a pity. Haven't heard the siren yet, for that matter. Or are there so many people standing around now that it's as though someone is offering something for sale, just like that, right out in the street?

I must keep a grip on myself, Liesbeth thinks, and with both hands she presses her stomach. There isn't even a piece of paper in the window: he spares me nothing. The blood! She must be draining dry.

She feels the contents of her stomach rise. Quickly, she walks to the door.

'And could you read what was there?' Herbert asks.

He hears the toilet seat being raised with a bang.

A coarse brain but an oversensitive stomach, he thinks.

A siren sounds outside. He walks to the window. A cream coloured car stops at the traffic island. Hurriedly, two men jump out, pull a stretcher from the back of the car and set it down beside the body. Then they pick it up and put it on the stretcher. The left foot, bobbing up and down, perpendicular in its stocking, ends up next to the stretcher. One of the men shoves it back on with his foot.

Liesbeth comes in again.

'It's busy in the street,' Herbert says.

'That's what I saw too, just now. There seems to have been an accident. I couldn't see.'

'Best thing, too,' Herbert replies as he draws a little landscape with a windmill in the top corner of the window. 'You've got enough of a weak stomach as it is. You'd be upset for days. Assuming it was an accident, then it was caused by the tram. Not a pretty sight at all. Those iron wheels shear the lot off, clean. I once . . . Hey, why are you leaving the room in such a hurry?'

Retching, Liesbeth runs to the toilet.

Dinner-for-one this evening, Herbert thinks, rubbing his hands. I'll put the newspaper behind my plate, up against the condiment set. A feast!

When Herbert has reached the top of the stairs, the door to his apartment opens. Liesbeth steps out into the hall.

'Oh, you shouldn't have, Herbert,' she says, ticking him off.

'What shouldn't I have?' Herbert asks, leering with screwed up eyes at the red face.

'Such a big one, far too much space for a small family.'

'Oh, the fridge – has the fridge arrived? I thought it'd take them hours. Hoisting it up and so on.'

'No, they managed it the ordinary way, up the stairs. But such a big one, Herbert; it really is too much.'

'What rot – this is no ordinary birthday: you turned fifty today. Half a century.'

Too many, he adds in his mind, half a century too many.

'Come on, show me,' he says cheerfully.

He follows her to the kitchen.

'It's a whopper indeed,' he says, once he's standing in the kitchen in front of the gleaming white enamel. 'It looked much smaller in the shop.'

What a magnificent sight, he thinks, the polar ice cap seen from a stratospheric aircraft. It gleams and glistens in the polar light. Now for an axe, and we can start on conservation.

'You would have done better to wait till summer, Herbert; it's cold enough here now.'

'That's just why it's so practical *now*. You won't have to turn down the heating in the evening any more 'cause otherwise your food'll go off. And no waiting for hours in the morning until it's warmed up a bit here. Just take a look,' he says cheerfully, pulling the door of the fridge wide open. 'Just you take a look: the space! I bet you could go and sit in it in Summer, when it's hot.'

'Now you really are exaggerating Herbert,' Liesbeth says, estimating its volume by eye.

'Exaggerate? I never exaggerate.'

With a clatter, he removes the horizontal aluminium racks.

'I think you could take the cat in with you too. No, no kidding: you try it, Liesbeth. My lumbago's giving me gip.'

Blood, blood, he thinks, I'll bring it about without spilling blood. The heavens regard me with favour. There'll be no writing on the wall.

'Well, alright then, 'cause it's my birthday,' Liesbeth says, laughing. 'But it's a strange experiment.'

She sets her bottom down on the floor of the fridge, wraps her arms round her drawn-up knees and swivels herself inside.

'Enduring the worst heat of August would be easier than sitting in this position, I think.'

With a powerful sweep, Herbert throws the door shut. Then he puts the plug in the socket.

I can hear her shouting but I can't make out what she's saying, he thinks.

He walks to the living room, switches the radio on and sits down in the tub chair beside it. Circumspectly, he takes a cigar from the cigar case, licks the outer leaf and presses it down. He twiddles the radio until a nice little tune breezes into the room. From the blue banks of cloud that linger in the middle of the room, the temptations of a life of freedom drift towards him. They spin in the surf of his imagination. He gives them girls' names and those of flowers.

There'll be ice flowers on her pupils; she'll be sitting there, hunched up like the tree mummies of Central American Indians. I could have a hole made in the bottom of my car with a broad pipe through it, reaching down to the road. Then, one rainy day, I put her in the back. On the bumpy rural roads, I shove her down the pipe, head first, so that her hair rests on the cobbles. And then I drive about until there's nothing left but the soles of her feet. I won't take her glasses off. But I won't even be able to straighten her out. She'll have wriggled her way into the most impossible angles. She always did. I'll avail myself of other means to get rid of her, as it happens. Now won't I just, you white-shirts you?

Walking over to the window, he addresses the seagulls diving down into the street, after bread being thrown from a window somewhere.

'I'll be spoiling you, lads! For the time being, your hungry beaks won't be eating dry bread any more: they'll be red with all the raw.'

A grand moment, Herbert thinks, eye to eye with the deep freeze princess. A fortnight past already: she'll be feeling the cold.

He pulls open the door of the fridge. With a jump, daylight takes possession of polar night. Liesbeth still sits there exactly the way he last saw her. Her hands rest calmly on her tummy, between the hillocks of her bosom and her thighs. Her glasses are covered in a thin, matt layer of ice as though, with its fragile wings, a butterfly seeks to protect her eyes from the cold. Icicles formed by the condensing water, with pointed fingers probe the hoarfrosted shrubbery of her hair. Her mouth hangs open. The pink tongue of land lies speechless, riveted down in the bitter ice of the inland sea of her oral cavity. An elegantly curved little rod of ice runs from her bottom lip to the remnants of food on her chest, as though her last thoughts had been of the fountains of Italy.

Herbert bends forward and looks intently at the food remnants.

Not such a peaceful death as first it had seemed from the resignedly folded hands on the stomach, he thinks. Perhaps that was a whim of the last death throes. Let's take a peek at the eyes.

Carefully, he grips the frame between the lenses. With his fingertips he stirs the cold marble of her forehead and the bridge of her nose. The cold spreads up to his wrists. He has to apply force for a moment in order to free the spectacles. Then he sees what the butterfly was trying to spare him. Her eyes have bulged out so far that, Herbert suspects, the lenses have prevented them from drooping even further. They hang down over the bottom eyelids like infertile, greenish owl's eggs that have been cast out from the

364

red and yellow veined nest of the eye sockets. In blind suspicion, the pupils stare down sideways into the remnants of food. When Herbert replaces the specs, those pupils stare through them like the eyes of a sea monster through the steamed up pane of an aquarium. He staggers in front of the fridge.

I'm overcome by the cold, he thinks. I must have a drink. I must raise my glass to this memorable fact.

He goes to the living room; he pours himself a glass of genever, warms himself in front of the fire. The liquor warms him all the way down to his digestive tract.

'Now what have we got?' he mutters, taking a sip from the glass at each object he mentions. 'A sharp little cleaver for between the joints, a saw for the bones, a razor sharp knife for flesh and tendons, a chopping board, plastic sheeting, a nutmeg mill. And a glass for the eyes.'

Triumphantly, he raises the glass aloft. Then he goes to the kitchen, spreads a sheet of plastic in front of the refrigerator and fetches the tools from the cabinet. He goes down on his knees in front of the fridge and tries to turn Liesbeth ninety degrees by her ankles, something he only succeeds in after a great deal of effort, for she is frozen to the sides of the fridge in some places. Then he drags her forward so her lower body ends up resting on the plastic.

To be pruned as soon as possible, he thinks, flipping her shoes from her feet with the cleaver. I'll try to get rid of a leg today.

With an old-fashioned razor he draws a furrow in her right leg, exactly along the seam of her stocking which he peals from her leg like bark. Then he cuts her clothes away at the hip, the imprint of them visible on her skin as if she is wrapped in thin tarlatan. The flesh is hard and cuts easily. Not without anatomical insight, he severs the leg from the torso at the hip joint, returns the body in the same position to the fridge and closes the door. Then he lets his knife sink deep into the fluvial landscape of her varicose veins and begins to cut off long strips of flesh. The knife makes a sound like skates on mirror-finish ice. When he has divested the thigh and shin bones of flesh, he strikes the foot off with his cleaver. He then begins to cut the long strips of flesh carefully into little cubes he tosses into a large, shallow tray.

The feet are too complicated to bone for my liking. I can simply put them out by the dustbins tomorrow. Perhaps it would be better, however, if I was first to fit them with the antique lace-up bootees. Let's chop things up as small as possible. They're guzzlers; they'll polish things off as they are, too.

With a swing, he lets the cleaver come down on the bunions. The toes hop forward, away from the foot, like small, pale frogs. Purple splinters rain down on the plastic.

I used to sit in the garden like this, Herbert thinks, wiping the sweat from his forehead. The purple flowers of the lilac dropping around me. In front of me in the loose sand were corks in a long row, wriggling insects pinned to them. I let down a woollen thread into a bottle of petrol and laid that across the caterpillars, beetles and locusts. Then I lit both ends. Once the flames met, the insects would be lying there with burnt off legs and wings. Of some, the body had split open like a roast chestnut. Thick, white goo bulged out. You're worse than Nero, my father said, and he raised blisters on my bottom. You're just like your uncle Louis; he's a bad'un too. Uncle Louis! When there was just a butt left of his cigar, he would walk out into the garden with it. He would stay and wait by the balsam at the back of the garden until a bumble bee came to fetch honey from a flower. Then he'd tap the ash from the butt, suck it so it got a fiery dome at the tip, and put it in the calyx. Can you hear him buzz, little Herbert? he would ask. D'you know what he's saying? He's saying the Lord's Prayer. Soon, when uncle Louis was staying with us, moist brown cigar butts would be sticking up from all the pink calyxes of the balsam, like arses just about to relieve themselves. Uncle Louis, a sensitive man, stimulating his conscience with the annihilation of little insects, Herbert thinks, touched.

'I've become a big game hunter,' he mutters.

He roots with the cleaver in the splintered heel bone. Then he takes up the board and slides the shattered foot on top of the meat in the tray.

That'll do: they'll devour the chaff with the wheat; they'll make no bones about it.

He takes the tray and walks with it to the hall. He sets it down there, takes out a step ladder and puts it underneath the hatch in the ceiling. He mounts the steps carefully, undoes the hooks and pushes the hatch open. Shrieking, seagulls fly up from the edge of the roof when suddenly his head appears above the antediluvian landscape of tar and shingle.

No one can see a thing here, he thinks: there are no taller buildings in the vicinity.

He goes down, takes the tray of meat and, holding it above his head, he climbs back up. Sliding it across the shingle, he shoves the tray a little further away from the hatch, out on to the roof.

If the dead can still feel anything, she must assume she'll share in the Kingdom of Heaven limb by limb. Come on then lads, come on! Just you tuck in. Here lies the manna of twenty years unhappy married life.

Herbert moves down a step, pulls the hatch up over the edge and, through a crack, he watches the seagulls who continue to sit motionless on the edge of the roof in the red light of the setting sun hanging between dark swordfish clouds above the grimy city.

Herbert is sitting on the floor in the kitchen. Round slices of bone are lying around him on the plastic. The electric nutmeg mill whirs beside him.

Liesbeth has no relatives any more, he thinks. Friends and acquaintances have stayed away for years already, driven away by the stale smell she spread. Which leaves the neighbours. When do I actually see the neighbours? Never, surely. Liesbeth hasn't been out in months. Even the shopkeepers no longer ask after her. It'll take years before anyone hits on the idea of asking me how she is. And I will have forgotten it myself by then; my mind'll be a blank. Perhaps, should a seagull be flying over, I'll point up above. And they will say: Oh, she's passed away in peace you mean. Yes, passed away in peace, I'll then reply — in ice-cold peace.

He presses the button on the side of the mill and so silences it. He removes its plastic lid and puts a disc of thigh bone inside. Then he pulls out the drawer at the bottom, throws the bone, ground to powder, in a pan and switches the mill back on. He picks up the pan, fetches a spoon from the drawer and walks to the living room. He puts a chair in front of the stove, sits down on it with the pan clamped between his thighs and he opens the little door of the stove. Slowly, Herbert stirs the bone meal, makes little mounds and draws arabic characters in it. In the flickering fire light, it's just as though there's life in it, as if it's a pan full of little, yellow spiders. Then, a spoonful at a time, he sprinkles the meal on to the fire.

It's a bit damp, he thinks. But I could hardly dry it first, now could I?

It emanates sulphur-like fumes, with poisonous blue flames coursing through. He flings the little door shut. The peaceful scent of a village smithy settles in the room.

Herbert wakes up in the morning with the smell of burnt horn in his nostrils.

Ah yes, the bone, he thinks. I was busy till ever so late, yesterday. But I'm rid of the lot. Air the place first in a minute, and then take a peek what the ash looks like.

He raises his right leg so the cold air streaming in at the footend wakes his body, and he looks at the bedside table.

'Such a liberation,' he says, yawning. 'Only one glass with dentures.'

Then, in a single sweep, he flings the blankets aside and jumps out of bed. He walks over to the window and draws back the curtains. It's snowing. He stands there ill at ease in the marble light, looks up at the snowflakes floating down like grey ash, to be cleansed only in contrast with the houses opposite.

The meat, he suddenly thinks with a shock, the meat has been snowed under.

He walks quickly to the hall and climbs the steps. When his head emerges above the edge of the hatch, the light blinds him. On top of his head, he feels the chill kisses of the snowflakes. In front of him is the tray. Empty. There's a thin layer of snow on the bottom, tinged pale pink by the blood that has stayed behind on the bottom as though it had stood beneath a flowering sweet-brier. It fills him with shame, shame without remorse. When he removes the tray, a reproachful dark square of tar and shingle remains like a freshly dug grave in the snow.

In the kitchen, he puts the tray in the sink and rinses out the snow and blood with hot water. A few toe nails stay behind on the grid above the plughole. The hungry birds have left no more than that.

Let's not get sentimental now, he thinks, picking up the nails and tossing them among the wet tea leaves in the enamel sink tidy. Raskolnikov was a worthless character. Precisely because of his weakness, his conscience. Or perhaps one is allowed to have a conscience but only regarding oneself ... Is a conscience not the most covert of stimulants? The outside world, however, must notice nothing of it.

Rubbing his wrists together, he walks over to the refrigerator and draws it open. He halts, rigid with fright. Liesbeth's sitting just the way he set her down there yesterday, but her glasses no longer cover her eyes: she's holding them in her right hand. In a panic, he runs to the door. It's shut; it's even bolted. Then he walks to the back room and tests the balcony doors.

I must have done it myself, he thinks. I've been sleepwalking. But no, I surely would have known in that case. I always do, don't I, when I've been up in the night and what I did then?

But now he remembers it was Liesbeth who always told him.

She would follow me with a wet floor cloth which she put in front of my feet. But I would always step over it. And she'd be picking it up and laying it down in front of me again. Just like a king being received in state. Where's the cat: where's Peter?

Nervously he goes through the house, searches all the cupboards, but he cannot find the creature anywhere.

Riddles at every turn in this place. Cats disappear, women disappear, I walk the house at night, my arms stretched out in front of me like a blind man. Dangerous, too! Tonight I'll tie myself down to the bed bars. No, I might have an unlucky fall in that case. Then, suddenly, a story from the Old Testament pops into his mind. One of ash sprinkled round the altar in which they found the footprints of the greedy priests next morning. I'll sprinkle a thin layer of flour on the kitchen floor, he thinks. I mustn't go imagining all kinds of things. It's too ridiculous for words. Nobody can get in. And who would benefit by taking off Liesbeth's glasses? Who'd want to open her eyes to what I have inflicted on her?

Reassured, he walks to the refrigerator and places the glasses back in front of the half abandoned eye sockets. Then he drags her round ninety degrees and cuts off her left leg.

It's becoming a routine job now, he thinks. The same actions as yesterday. The two arms tomorrow, the trunk in halves, across, the day after: only leaves the head for Saturday.

Abstracted, he begins to cut into the leg.

Just look what I'm doing, he thinks. Such elegant curves. Yesterday, I began to cut clumsily; as time went by I was cutting splendid, straight strips. Now I'm cutting capricious pieces. Just like in Art. Art, too, is refractory and clumsy at first. Then you get classical harmony, the straight strips of drab-pink flesh. I'm going through the Baroque now. Tomorrow, perhaps, I'll be cutting scrolls and elegant figures and I'll be the Watteau of corpse desecration.

I was at primary school, Herbert thinks, in the fourth form. I must have been ten at the time. I was ten years old when it started. Or much earlier on even: who knows? How is it possible for one to find one's vocation so late? Across from me, at her desk, sat a girl with long, dark hair and spirited, brown eyes. Bent over my work, I turned my head sideways and looked at her profile. Then I looked at her tummy, going up and down like thick, boiling porridge in her tight dress. At night, in bed, I would think of her. I would take her to a lonely house where I tied her hands behind her back. A meat hook hung from an iron bar on the ceiling. I suspended her from it by the roof of her mouth. She sought to speak but I only heard her bottom teeth tap against the hook like a woodpecker hidden in the woods. She wanted to say: you're sweet to me even though you hurt me. I was lying on my belly. With my lower torso I slid back and forth on the sheet. I was covered in a gory membrane in which I threatened to suffocate. Like a child born with a caul. Wasn't I born with a caul? Mother said that at my birth the placenta was stuck to my skull like a Russian fur hat.

When Herbert opens the hatch the sky, mottled drab and yellow, is stretched above the city like the soiled sheet of an incontinent child. An army of mediaeval knights pokes its helmeted, brick face, smoking, above the white hills of the roofs. Swans float like white islets on the dark pond in the park. Great black-backed gulls sit equidistant from each other on the edge of the roof. When Herbert lets the tray of meat down into the soft snow, they approach, hesitantly. Halting a few metres away from the tray, they stare at Herbert, soullessly, with their fierce, yellow, artificial eyes.

'I'll withdraw, lads,' he says, 'so you can dine in peace.'

He pulls the hatch shut over his head and fixes the catches.

Mind I don't forget to lock everything properly and sprinkle flour in the kitchen before I go to bed. I must have an early night: these are tiring times.

Above his head he hears the frightful shrieking and gorging of the hungry birds.

In the depths of night, Herbert wakes from the cold. He is lying on top of the blankets. He sticks his feet up in the air and looks at the soles of his feet.

'Gotcha,' he says loudly. 'I've caught myself out. Just as if I've got perspiring feet and they've been rubbed with talc.'

He brushes them. The flour sticks to his fingers like dough. Startled, he jumps out of bed.

My feet must have been wet before I stepped in the flour, he thinks.

Quickly, he walks to the kitchen. There are his footprints. His eyes crowd with fear against the top of their sockets. Among his prints he sees a damp square, and another, and the floor cloth in front of the fridge. The cat's prints run alongside his. Hurriedly he goes over to the refrigerator. The meat tray's up against the wall, opposite Liesbeth. He looks at the hallway door. He sees by his prints that he has been back and forth through the door. He sees the cat's tracks too, but just one way. He walks over to the hallway door and opens it. Freezing cold envelops his body. Herbert goes to the hatch; the steps are underneath. When he looks up, he sees the stars in the carbon black sky. He clambers up and sticks his head into the East wind. Right in front of his eyes, in the snow, he sees the tracks of the cat.

He's been right behind me, Herbert thinks. He knows everything. He's been spying on me from an untraceable hiding place. But he's up on the roof now. By the tracks I can see he hasn't turned back.

He fills his hands with snow and rubs his face with it.

I must keep a cool head, bring things to a close quickly. But let's tackle the genever bottle first.

He retreats a few steps and closes the hatch.

Warily, Herbert crosses the square, looks up at the windows of his apartment.

It looks uninhabited, he thinks. The lace curtains are yellow with brown rings. Is that something moving there, behind the curtains? He shakes his head and pats his cheeks with his fingers. I mustn't turn into a shying horse. I can see from here the window's ajar. The wind'll be stirring the curtains. How long has it been open? Bad for the plants. I'll shut it before I leave. Liesbeth's head's been standing on the roof for eight hours already. If it's not completely stripped by now I'll leave it there till tomorrow morning; then I'll wrap it in plastic and put it in my suitcase. I'll set it down among the cobbles along the Dordogne.

He feels in his pockets for the key and looks up. The chests of the seagulls protrude over the edge of the roof as though they are part of the building's trimmings.

'You'll miss me,' he mutters. 'Tighten your belts: that's all I can recommend.'

Right by his feet, on the pavement, lies a dirty-white sphere. Herbert bends down and picks it up.

Don't look round, he thinks, I'm just picking something up;

everyone does that from time to time. And I've even read that they peck the eyes out of babies lying unguarded on the beach, and devour them.

He puts his key in the lock and enters the dark stairwell.

It feels like the devil's egg of a stinkhorn, he thinks. I'm still able to walk up the stairs, but I've got to take my time over it.

The front door opens behind him. A neighbour comes in; she halts at the letter box.

'Such a long time I haven't seen your wife,' she says. 'Has she got to stay in again?'

'I took her to the train last week; she wasn't feeling too well; she's gone South.'

'Taken the Sun Express to the deep blue sea?' the woman asks.

'Quite, quite,' Herbert replies. 'To the deep blue sea. I'll be following her tomorrow.'

Carefully, he slips off into the dark stairwell.

That eye was as hard as a billiard ball this morning, he thinks, clenching his fingers. Now it's soft and squishy. There's a thaw on: Spring has sprung.

Notes on the Authors

Arnold Aletrino (1858–1916), doctor and lecturer in criminal anthropology, campaigner on behalf of prostitutes and homosexuals, author of naturalist prose. 'In het Donker' ('In the Dark'), written in 1885, was included in *Novellen* of 1895.

Jan Arends (1925–1974) wrote short stories and poetry, often with a psychologically disturbed slant. In 1974, on the day of publication of his latest collection of poetry, he ended his life by leaping from his apartment window. 'Het Ontbijt' ('Breakfast'), first published in 1969, appeared in the collection *Keefman* of 1972.

Maarten Asscher (*1957) is a lawyer and publisher. 'Het Geheim van Dr Raoul Sarrazin' ('The Secret of Dr Raoul Sarrazin') can be found under the title 'De Brief' in his first published collection, *Dodeneiland* (1992).

Belcampo (H.P. Schönfeld Wichers; 1902–1990) was a doctor and the prolific author of often fantastic tales. 'Uitvaart' ('Funeral Rites') was taken from *Tussen Hemel en Afgrond* (1959).

Huub Beurskens (*1950) is the author of poetry, prose and criticism. 'Hoogste Onderscheiding' ('Highest Honours') appeared in his 1991 collection of short stories *Sensibilimente*.

J.M.A. Biesheuvel (*1939) writes short stories, often autobiographical, at times capricious, imbued with a sense of dark, brooding melancholy, chilling irony and wry humour. 'Brommer op Zee' ('Biker at Sea') has been taken from his first collection *In de Bovenkooi* (1972).

Willem Brakman (*1922), a former company doctor and prize winning author, writes stories and novels often described as 'baroque' with regard to style and content. 'Het Evangelie naar Chabot' ('The Gospel according to Chabot') can be found in *Een Familiedrama* of 1984.

Remco Campert (*1929), is the author of austere and often melancholy poetry, short stories and novels. 'De Verdwijning van Bertje S.' ('The Disappearance of Bertje S.') appeared in 1954 in the collection *Alle Dagen Feest*.

Louis Couperus (1863–1923), one of the great masters of Dutch prose, whose classic novels such as 'Van Oude Menschen, de Dingen die Voorbijgaan' ('Of Old People, the Things that Pass') and the great tetralogy 'De Boeken der Kleine Zielen' ('The Chronicles of Small Souls') have become part of the national heritage. 'Blauwbaards Dochter' ('Bluebeard's Daughter') and 'De Zoon van Don Juan' ('The Son of Don Juan'), first published in the daily paper *Het Vaderland* in Autumn 1915, were collected in *Legende, Mythe en Fantazie* of 1918.

Johan Andreas Dèr Mouw (1862–1919) was a philosopher and poet who, in late middle age, adopted the new identity of *Adwaita*. 'De Heilige Vlinder' ('The Sacred Butterfly'), taken from among his juvenilia, was published for the first time only in 1962, by Ms. A.M. Cram-Magre in her thesis on the author.

Lodewijk van Deyssel (K.J.L. Alberdingk Thijm; 1864–1952) was a critic and author of naturalist and sensitivist prose. 'Zonderlinge Dingen op de Vlakte' ('Curious Things on the Plain') is the first part of a review, taken from *Verzamelde Opstellen. Zevende Bundel* (1904).

Inez van Dullemen (*1925) writes novels, short stories and travel books. 'Na de Orkaan' ('After the Hurricane') appeared in 1983 in a collection going by the same name, but was revised for the anthology of her work *Een Kamer op de Himalaya* (1990).

Jacob Israël de Haan (1881–1924) was a Law scholar and the author of naturalist and decadent novels, journalism and poetry. In circumstances never quite adequately explained, he was murdered in Palestine in 1924 when posted there as correspondent for the daily paper *Het Handelsblad*. 'Over de Ervaringen van Hélénus Marie Golesco' (Concerning the Experiences of Hélénus Marie Golesco'; 1907) is one of the so-called *Nerveuze Vertellingen* which only appeared in book form in 1981.

Fritzi Harmsen van Beek (*1927) published a number of collections of exquisite poetry and short stories tending towards the bizarre and the absurd. Her story 'Het Taxivarken' ('The Taxi Pig') was taken from *Wat Knaagt?* (1968).

Marcus Heeresma (1936–1991) wrote poetry, novels and short stories, some with a touch of the grotesque to them. 'Stortplaats' ('Dumping Ground') appeared in Robert-Henk Zuidinga's anthology of original horror stories *Uit den Boze* of 1984.

A.F.Th. van der Heijden (*1951), published his early work under the pseudonym Patrizio Canaponi. He is currently at work on a huge cycle of novels known by its overall title of *De Tandeloze Tijd*. Like almost all Van der Heijden's work, 'Pompeii Funebri' enjoys kinship with the novel cycle and can be pencilled into its ground plan as sketch material distantly related to the as yet uncompleted volume III of the larger work. 'Pompeii Funebri', too, was first published in the anthology *Uit den Boze* (1984).

Jan Hofker (1864–1945), like Trollope, was employed by the Post Office for most of his working life. He wrote sketches and short stories of which 'Koediefje' ('Rustler'; 1892) has been included here. His stories were collected in *Gedachten en Verbeeldingen* of 1906.

Frans Kellendonk (1951–1990) was one of the most formidable talents among the generation of Dutch writers born in the early 1950s. An English scholar and an exceptional stylist of Dutch, he wrote essays, novels, a novella, criticism and short stories, as well as a number of literary translations from English, the last of which, Emily Brönte's *Wuthering Heights*, which he managed to see through the presses while battling with Aids, must be ranked among the most sensitive and finely crafted renderings of that work ever to be achieved in any language. His 'Dood en Leven van Thomas Chatterton' ('Death and Life of Thomas Chatterton') was taken from *Namen en Gezichten* (1983).

Anton Koolhaas (1912–1992), was a critic and the author of novels, film scenarios and superlative tales of animals which have become classics of Dutch literature. 'Balder D. Quorg, Spin' ('Baldur D. Quorg, Spider') appeared in 1958 in the collection *Er zit geen Spek in de Val*.

Frans Kusters (*1949) is a writer of short stories. 'De Volledige Diagnose' ('The Full Diagnosis') has been taken from *Het Chaplinconcours* of 1980.

Harry Mulisch (*1927) is one of the most exceptional authors of his generation as well as one of the most versatile, with major works in almost all forms of literary creation: fiction, critical and scholarly prose, drama and philosophy. A deeply thoughtful writer of finely honed, incisive yet quite austere prose, his voice is painfully well suited to address the issues surrounding World War II, its essence and nature as well as its consequences, as demonstrated in probably his most widely known novel at home and abroad, 'De Aanslag' ('The Assault') of 1982. 'De Versierde Mens' ('Decorated Man') was taken from a collection of the same name, published in 1957.

Carel van Nievelt (1843–1913) was a civil servant, a journalist and the writer of sketches and tales. 'Dolende Zielen' ('Souls Errant') can be found in the collection *Ahasverus* of 1889.

Hélène Nolthenius (*1920) has been a professor of music history and writes novels and short stories. 'Omzien als Wapen' ('Looking back: the Weapon') has been taken from *De Steeneik* (1984).

Gerard Reve (*1923) describes himself as a Romantic-Decadent writer. A unique voice in Western European literature as a whole, who may prove the greatest stylist the Dutch language has yet seen this century. Several of his novels, such as 'De Avonden' ('The Evenings'; 1947), 'Nader tot U' ('Nearer to Thee'; 1966) and 'De Taal der Liefde' ('The Language of Love'; 1972) have become widely acknowledged classics in his own lifetime, while concepts and sayings from his work have gone into the language as 'Revian', in a manner similar to the way things 'Dickensian' or 'Shavian' have gone into English. Never one to shy from controversy, his work and public pronouncements have probably garnered him as much opprobrium as fame. His latest novel, 'Bezorgde Ouders' (1988), appeared in English under the title 'Parents Worry' in 1990. The novella *Werther Nieland* was first published in 1949.

Arthur van Schendel (1874–1946) was a writer of religious, historical and naturalist fiction. Attracted to symbolism in his early work, in his mature novels he turns to a very personal form of naturalist fiction as exemplified in 'Een Hollands Drama' ('A Dutch Drama'; 1935) and the two related novels that followed, 'De Rijke Man' ('The Rich Man') and 'De Grauwe Vogels' ('The Ashen Birds'): three penetrating, dour studies of the relentless ordinariness of life for ordinary people, their existence ruled and confounded by unanswerable questions of fate, heredity, sin, free will and God's grace. 'De Witte Vrouw' ('The White Woman') was included in the collection *Nachtgedaanten* of 1938.

Willem Schürmann (Willem Fredrik; 1876–1915), Rotterdam-born playwright, son of a wealthy merchant. Author of five plays which enjoyed a degree of success, and of a number of works in prose, among which a two volume, part-autobiographical novel 'De Berkelmans' (1906). 'De Onevenwichtige Koning' ('The Unbalanced King') can be found in the collection *De Beul* of 1910.

Jan Siebelink (*1938) is a writer of novels and stories with at first a decadent and later on a more realist slant. 'Genegenheid' ('Affection') appeared in 1978 in the collection *Weerloos*.

P.F. Thomése (*1958) made his debut in 1990 with the collection of extended short stories called *Zuidland* for which he received the coveted AKO Prize. 'Leviathan' is the first from this collection.

Simon Vestdijk (1898–1971) was a ship's doctor for a short time before embarking on a lifetime of literary endeavour. Prolific author of essays, criticism, poetry, short stories, and novels such as 'De Koperen Tuin' (recently re-issued in English as 'The Garden where the Brass Band Played') and the extended cycle of 'Anton Wachter' novels. 'Het Stenen Gezicht' ('The Stone Face') was taken from *De Dood Betrapt* of 1935.

Jan Wolkers (*1925), as well as being a respected visual artist and sculptor, is a prolific writer of novels such as 'Turks Fruit' ('Turkish Delight') and 'Terug naar Oegstgeest' ('Return to Oegstgeest'), and of short stories. 'Gevederde Vrienden' ('Feathered Friends'; 1958) forms part of the collection *Gesponnen Suiker*.

Dedalus Anthologies

Titles currently available are:

The Dedalus Book of Austrian Fantasy: *the Meyrink Years 1890–1930* – editor Mike Mitchell £8.99
The Dedalus Book of British Fantasy: the 19th century – editor Brian Stableford £8.99
The Dedalus Book of Dutch Fantasy – editor Richard Huijing £9.99
The Dedalus Book of Decadence (Moral Ruins) – editor Brian Stableford £7.99
The Dedalus Book of Femmes Fatales – editor Brian Stableford £7.99
The Second Dedalus Book of Decadence: the Black Feast – editor Brian Stableford £8.99
The Dedalus Book of Surrealism – editor Michael Richardson £8.99
Tales of the Wandering Jew – editor Brian Stableford £8.99

forthcoming titles include:

The Dedalus Book of Belgian Fantasy – editor Richard Huijing
The Dedalus Book of German Fantasy: the Romantics and Beyond – editor Maurice Raraty
The Dedalus Book of French Fantasy – editor Christine Donougher
The Dedalus Book of German Decadence – editor Ray Furness
The Dedalus Book of Polish Fantasy – editor Wiesiek Powaga
The Dedalus Book of Russian Decadence – editor Natalia Rubenstein
The Second Dedalus Book of Surrealism – Michael Richardson

The Dedalus Book of Austrian Fantasy – editor Mike Mitchell

'Subtitled "*The Meyrink Years 1890–1930*", this is a superb collection of the bizarre, the terrifying and the twisted, as interpreted by the decadents and obsessives of *fin de siècle* Vienna. It features big names like Kafka, Rilke and Schnitzler, but more intriguing are the lesser-known writers such as Franz Theodor Csokor with the vampiric "*The Kiss of the Stone Woman*", Karl Hans Strobl, whose "*The Wicked Nun*" begins as a ghost story but twists and turns into insanity and Paul Busson, contributing an uncanny tale of feminine sorcery, "*Folter's Gems!*"'

Time Out

'Divided into five sections (Possessed Souls, Dream and Nightmare, Death, The Macabre, Satire) that tell you all you need to know, the stand out works are those of Gustav Meyrink, Strobl and Schnitzler and Franz Csokor's wonderful, mad chiller "*The Kiss of the Stone Woman*".

   'The best stories faultlessly follow the traditional template of deepening mystery grafted onto time-honoured methods of signalling narrative action. Recommended'

City Limits

£8.99   ISBN 0 946626 93 6 416pp   B Format

The Dedalus Book of British Fantasy – editor Brian Stableford

Beginning in 1804 with Nathan Drake's '*Henry Fitzowen,*' *The Dedalus Book of British Fantasy* traces the development of the genre through the stories and poems of Coleridge, Keats, Dickens, Disraeli, William Morris, Christina Rosetti, Tennyson and Vernon Lee until the end of the century and Richard Garnett's '*Alexander The Ratcatcher*'.

Each text has been chosen to illustrate the development of the various aspects of fantasy in British Literature – the comic, the sentimental, the erotic and the allegorical – and the contribution that these authors made to the emergence of a new genre.

'there are a number of items which very few people will be familiar with that are real gems, John Sterling's "*Chronicle of England*" and Christina Rosetti's *Goblin Market* . . .'

Kaleidoscope, BBC Radio 4

£8.99   ISBN 0 946626 78 2   416pp B Format

The Dedalus Book of Decadence (Moral Ruins) – editor Brian Stableford

Every aspect of *The Dedalus Book of Decadence* (*Moral Ruins*) received praise, from the brown and gold of its cover (Times Higher Educational Supplement), the introduction (The Independent), the choice of stories (City Limits), and the whole book (Time Out). It was a critical and commercial success, which featured in the Alternative Bestsellers List.

A few comments:

'an invaluable sampler of spleen, everything from Baudelaire and Rimbaud to Dowson and Flecker. Let's hear it for *luxe, calme et volupte*'

Anne Billson in Time Out

'*The Dedalus Book of Decadence* looks south to sample the essence of fine French decadent writing. It succeeds in delivering a range of writers either searching vigorously for the thrill of a healthy crime or lamenting their impuissance from a sickly stupor.'

Andrew St George in The Independent

£7.99   ISBN 0 946626 63 4   288pp   B Format

Tales of the Wandering Jew – editor Brian Stableford

'This homage to one of the world's great stories collects the Wandering Jew's many English-language manifestations, a fascinating journey down the tangled roads of European Literature, as infinite as those Ahasuerus is still walking. This collection offers you the chance to hitch a lift on the immortal sufferer's back. It's not the sort of offer anybody should turn down.'

City Limits

'Geoffrey Farrington's *Little St Hugh* is a wonderful 13th century tale of fury and repentance, with a touch of *The Monk*. The historical style is impeccable.

Ian MacDonald's *Fragments of an Analysis of a Case of Hysteria* is brilliantly written, mixing the early analyses of Freud, the Jew, and an evocative and disturbing foreshadowing of the Holocaust. Scott Edelman provides a bit of bizarre allegory with *The Wandering Jukebox*.

The whopper is the editor's own – Stableford's brilliant, appalling *Innocent Blood*. A heroin addict dying from AIDS, is chained up in a cellar by the Jew, and their relationship is a horror show of uncommunicated pain. Some powerful stuff here.'

Locus

£8.99   0 946626 71 5   384p B.Format

The legend of *The Wandering Jew* appears in several other books published by Dedalus: ***The Architect of Ruins*** – Hervert Rosendorfer; **The Green Face** – Gustav Meyrink; and **The Wandering Jew** – Eugene Sue